None So Blind

None So Blind

LJ Maas

YellowRoseBooks
a Division of
RENAISSANCE ALLIANCE PUBLISHING, INC.
Austin, Texas

ISBN 1-930928-13-0

First Printing 2000

9 8 7 6 5 4 3 2 1

Cover design by LJ Maas

Published by:

Renaissance Alliance Publishing, Inc.
PMB 167, 3421 W. William Cannon Dr. # 131
Austin, Texas 78745

Find us on the World Wide Web at
http://www.rapbooks.com

Printed in the United States of America

Copyright permission:

"Back To You" by Mandy Rogers (copyright 2000 by Mandy Rogers)

This book is dedicated to all of the courageous people living in recovery—I applaud you. To those who are searching for the courage to take that first step and for all who think they may never find their soulmate. To these people I say, it is never too late.

Thanks to the many people involved in putting together this novel, especially the folks in recovery who shared their experiences and knowledge with me.

Special thanks to my own warrior. Without her, my words would have no meaning at all.

"There are none so blind, as those who would not see..."

Chapter
1

August 1981: University of Maine, Orono, Maine

"We don't usually room freshman with seniors, but until the new Sorority house is finished, we're kind of tight on space, and well...you are a legacy. Taylor is the only sister with her own room because, well, she, aw hell, never mind. She knows you're a newbie, and she did volunteer to double up." *The brown haired girl talked quickly as she helped Torrey carry her belongings through the busy halls of the Sorority house.*

Samantha Evans was the preceptor for the house's third floor. She wondered if she should tell the young blonde more about her future roommate, but realized what Sam did know about Taylor Kent might scare the hell out of the small blonde. Better leave well enough alone and hope this new girl has a sharp wit and a thick skin, *Samantha mused to herself.*

The two women stopped every once in a while so Samantha could make an introduction. Torrey's mother told her Tau Alpha Zeta was a huge house, even when it was started in the sixties, but the young woman knew she would never be able to remember all of these people she was meeting. She already liked the fact that hers was the last room on the floor, set far back away from the rest of the house. Perfect place to write...I like it already. *Samantha told her it was the largest room in the house. The graduating seniors flipped for it every year and the two winners got the honors for their last year at Benton. Torrey still couldn't get a straight answer as to why she, an entering freshman, should get such an honor.*

They finally arrived at Torrey's new room. Music could be heard from the other side of the door; Torrey was surprised at the listener's taste. Upon opening the door Torrey saw a woman seated on the floor, her long legs stretched across a dirty sheet onto which a dozen mechanical parts were spread. The seated woman didn't bother to look up, her ebony hair fell in loose bangs across her forehead, the rest of her wild mane cascaded freely along broad shoulders and back. She wore a faded Grateful Dead T-shirt tucked into a pair of Levi's that were so worn they probably felt like velvet. She had heavy black biker boots on her feet and her hands were coated in grease the same color as her boots.

Gene Pitney blared through speakers that were nearly as tall as Torrey was. The young woman couldn't believe there was another woman this side of sixty that enjoyed Gene Pitney's music as much as she did. She recognized the strains of "24 Hours From

Tulsa" right before Samantha grabbed the arm of the phonograph and lifted the needle from the LP.

"Shit, Taylor! What did I tell you about bringing that crap in here? Gina is already all over my ass...do you have to give her reasons to put you on kitchen duty?" Samantha shouted.

"Oh, hell, it's just a carburetor," the seated woman growled.

Torrey deposited the two suitcases on the floor and leaned over the seated woman, immediately intrigued by the motorcycle parts. Her shadow fell across the tall woman's hands.

"Get the hell out of my light!"

"Oh, I'm terribly sorry," Torrey said as she quickly backed up, looking at Samantha.

"Taylor, you said you didn't mind if Torrey roomed here this year," Samantha said with exasperation.

"I said she could room here, not get in my way," the dark-haired woman replied in an ominous tone.

"You know it looks like the manifold cover is worn...that's probably what the trouble is. When you shift gears does it sound like the motor is strangling?" Torrey asked in an offhand manner.

Samantha couldn't help the smile that spread across her face. Oh, yea...these two are gonna be just fine.

When Taylor finally looked up at the annoyance, she ran smack into what she would call for years to come, the face of an angel. A young woman all of probably seventeen or eighteen, long blonde hair framing a smiling face and a pair of sparkling sea-green eyes. She wore a Chicago Bear's jersey, tight

Sergio Valente jeans, and a white pair of Nike's. The young girl smiled at Taylor and the seated woman felt her mouth go dry.

"Hey," the dark-haired woman offered.

"Hey." Torrey continued to smile at the older woman.

"Okay, well...Torrey Gray this is Taylor Kent. Taylor...Torrey. I gotta run." Sam set down Torrey's typewriter case and turned to leave the room. "And, Taylor...please, I'm begging you. Find a place inside your bike for all that," the preceptor said before she closed the door.

"She's right, sorry." Taylor grabbed the edges of the sheet. The dark-haired woman stood up, the bundle of parts at her feet.

"Whoa, how's the weather up there, Stretch?" Torrey teased. Taylor looked to be at least six feet tall.

An eyebrow arched over one eye, disappearing under dark bangs. "I'd say that's a bold comment from someone as vertically challenged as you appear to be. Why you're just a little bit of nuthin," Taylor said with a chuckle, crossing her arms in front of her chest.

"I'm five four," Torrey replied, her pride a little wounded.

"With or without a chair to stand on?" Taylor laughed.

"Okay, touché. Uhm, sorry...I was just kidding. Hey, I could help you with your bike," Torrey offered.

"No," Taylor answered, more harshly than she had intended. "It's okay, I can handle it," she added, noticing the slightly wounded look on the young

woman's face. "A Bear's fan, huh?"

"Yea...they're going all the way this year," Torrey said enthusiastically.

"Yea, right," Taylor laughed. "Bet you like the Cubs, too."

"Diehard fan," Torrey replied.

"Figures. You must be from Chicago...good to meet you." Taylor put out her hand.

Torrey took the offered hand in her own, suddenly lost in the blue eyes looking down at her. Regaining her focus, the young woman felt a warm sliminess to the handshake. Before she looked down at her hand, she watched as the cerulean gaze in front of her sparkled, a wide toothy grin playing across the woman's features. When Torrey looked down her hand was covered in black grease.

The young woman just stared at her hand for a moment. "I can't believe you just did that," Torrey said, astounded.

"I can't believe you fell for it." Taylor was barely able to contain her laughter.

"Oh, you." Torrey shoved the taller woman in the stomach.

Taylor looked down at her abdomen where a small, black hand print stood out. She was absolutely amazed that the girl had the nerve to do it. Actually, she was more amazed at the fact that she wasn't throttling the life out of the girl.

Taylor looked up from her shirt and saw the panicked expression on Torrey's face. The dark-haired woman held her own hand up and looked, first at her hand, and then at the smaller woman's jersey, a smile crossing her face.

*"Oh, no Taylor...not my Bear's jersey. I'm
sorry...it was an accident...I lost my head." All the
while Torrey was backing toward the door, the taller
one advancing.*

*Torrey stopped and tried to gauge the distance left
to the door. Taylor saw where the young woman was
headed. The taller woman tossed back her hair with a
shake of her head, looked at the door, then her lips
pulled back in the most feral smile Torrey could have
ever imagined.*

*"Watch it, you're going to step on the carbure-
tor!" Torrey pointed down to Taylor's boots.*

*By the time the dark-haired woman looked down
to move her feet Torrey was out the door and running
through the hall.*

*"Oh, I don't even believe I fell for that," Taylor
said aloud as she raced off after the young woman.*

*Torrey was fast, but Taylor's long legs ate up the
distance between them. Both women were shouting
and laughing as they tore through the three levels of
the old building, one large and one small handprint
left at every turn.*

*Samantha looked up from her desk as a tiny
blonde blur flew past her door, followed by Taylor's
lean, muscular form. "Oh my God, it's only been five
minutes and she's already trying to kill her," Samantha said aloud as she jumped up to intercede.*

*Torrey made it out the backdoor first, but soon
realized she was in an enclosed backyard, most of the
space taken up by a large built-in pool. The young
woman circled completely around only to be confronted by Taylor, advancing slowly, her blue eyes
narrowing and an evil smile tugging at the corners of*

her mouth. "Got ya now, Little Bit."

Torrey backed up as she talked. Most of what she said made no sense, but she didn't want to lose her only jersey so she talked fast.

Abruptly, Taylor's eyes grew wide. "Torrey, look out!" Taylor yelled.

Torrey could feel her body shifting backward into thin air. Her arms windmilled around, but she couldn't get her weight going forward again. In the heartbeat's time this took, Taylor had crossed the distance between the two and grabbed the loose material at the front of the smaller woman's top. Torrey reached out and grabbed the dark-haired woman's arm, her backward momentum carrying both of them into the pool.

The two heads reappeared above the surface at the same time. They swam to the edge of the pool, to the shouts and laughter of half the Sorority House, who were leaning out their windows watching the show. Samantha couldn't help joining in the laughter, watching the usually stoic and reserved Taylor Kent cavorting along with her new roommate. Samantha's laughter died down in a hurry when she saw Gina Rice walk out the back door of the House. Her ever-faithful lackey, Terri Kozla, was behind her carrying two buckets filled with cleaning solvent and rags.

"Well, you must be our new legacy, Torrey Gray," Gina said, leaning down to the edge of the pool where the two women still floated. "I'm Gina Rice, President of Tau Alpha Zeta. Welcome, Miss Gray."

"Thank you, sister." Torrey tried to smile sweetly, knowing this wasn't a social call. She made sure to use the term "sister." All freshmen were to

address upperclass Sorority sisters as such.

"We'd like you to join us for dinner in the dining room tonight. There's just one little catch. You'll be on kitchen duty." The older woman's plastered-on smile changed into a frown. "Along with your new best friend here. Taylor will be happy to show you the ropes...she ends up there quite often." Gina stood and signaled Terri to set the buckets down. "You can start with the handprints you left through the whole damn house." Then she walked back inside.

Taylor was sorry she was the cause of the young girl's bad start, but there was something about her that she immediately liked, and that never happened to Taylor. She couldn't help laughing. "Welcome to the University of Maine, Torrey Gray." She stuck her greasy hand out.

Taking the hand in a strong grip of her own, Torrey smiled right back at the older woman. "Thanks a lot, Taylor Kent," Torrey replied, sending a small splash of water in the dark-haired woman's direction.

Of course, Taylor took this as a direct challenge and soon the two, fully clothed women, were splashing, shouting, and giggling at the top of their lungs, all to more shouting and laughter from the girls in the windows above.

Just like that, they became Torrey and Taylor. It seemed where one was you would soon find the other. Before long people just said T'nT.

December 1999: Chicago, Illinois

"JT? Is that you?" The blonde woman looked up

from her laptop computer to the clock on the bedside table. The clock read two forty-five a.m. and Torrey removed her glasses, pulled from her stroll down memory lane by the sound of a key in the front door.

Torrey stood up to investigate, alerted by the scuffle of boots on the hardwood floor.

"Aw, Jess," Torrey said to her daughter. The young girl was slumped against the door, her blood-shot eyes unfocused and barely able to see. She shook her long dark hair from her eyes and attempted to raise her tall frame from the floor.

"It's okay, Mom...I can do this," the young girl slurred.

Torrey rushed over to help her daughter. Jessica leaned her back heavily against the door, and then placed some of her weight against her mother as Torrey slipped an arm around the girl's waist.

"Come on let's get you to bed," Torrey said, trying not to let her anger show through.

"I swear, Mom, I haven't had a drop to drink tonight." Her daughter smirked. Standing nearly a head taller than her mother, she had to look down to see into the green eyes that frowned in disappointment.

Torrey took a deep breath and walked her daughter to her bedroom. "That's because you're higher than a kite," Torrey replied.

She managed to guide the young girl to her bed where Jessica fell heavily onto the mattress. Torrey pulled at the combat boots and the black leather jacket. "You promised me, Jess. You said there wouldn't be anymore partying," Torrey said.

"Just leave me alone." Jessica rolled onto her

side. Her head was hurting and she knew it was going
to hurt even worse if she had to look into her mother's
eyes. She *had* broken her promise, but she didn't
want to have to think about that now, she didn't want
to see her failure reflected back to her from her
mother's eyes. She *had* failed her, and she probably
would again. *I might as well. I'll never be good
enough for her. I'll never be as perfect as she is.*

Torrey ran a slender hand across her daughter's
cheek, feeling the girl's breathing become deep and
even as she slept. *What did I do wrong with you,
Jess? What* am *I doing wrong? Why is it you act like
you hate me? Why do you only let me touch you when
you're sick or passed out?* Torrey let silent tears fall
from her face as she tried to find answers to all the
questions running through her head.

She gently pushed back the dark locks of hair that
fell across her daughter's face. The long dark hair
framed a face that had proud angular features, relaxed
now in sleep. When her eyes were open, they sparkled with a bright green, which in the right light
appeared blue. When that illusion of light happened,
Torrey was surprised at how much her daughter
reminded her of Taylor. Tonight, while Jessica lay in
the front hall, Torrey would have swore it was her old
friend passed out against the door to the room they
shared at the Sorority House. The black leather jacket
and heavy black boots were a trademark of Taylor's in
her college days.

When she was sure her daughter was sleeping
soundly, she went to her own room. She turned off
the computer; words simply weren't coming to her as
easily anymore. Even though her last novel was

hailed as a sales success, she read a few of the book reviews that said Torrey Gray's talent was slipping. *The New Yorker* did everything but tell her she was washed up. She couldn't get in touch with her own feelings like she used to. Even when performing her morning ritual of Tai Chi, which she'd been doing since she was fifteen, she just couldn't seem to get to that place that held her emotions. Deep down she knew the reviewers were right. If she couldn't feel, she couldn't write. Her mind had been preoccupied with other things for the last few years.

The fixation began when JT started high school. Of course, the tension between mother and daughter always existed. By the time Jessica learned the word, *no*, it seemed as if that was the only phrase she used with her mother. That and *I don't want to*. Once puberty set in it became all out war and neither mother nor daughter understood why. The older Jessica became, the more severe the problems were. She had been expelled from nearly every public and private school in Cook County. Then the drinking started. Torrey made the time to do more with her daughter, she attended every workshop she could, but it only seemed to drive the wedge deeper. After the last program, Jessica promised she would remain on the straight and narrow. True to the young girl's code, she had not had a drop to drink, but Torrey could tell her daughter reeked of marijuana smoke. She could only wonder what else her wild daughter experimented with.

Torrey took a quick shower and checked on her daughter once more. Satisfied the girl would sleep through the night Torrey left her own door ajar just in

case.   Slipping under the cool sheets, she thought
back to the time when she was her daughter's age.
Yes, she smiled to herself in the dark.   She knew
exactly where her daughter's temperament came from.

September 1981

*"You are so lucky I like you, Stretch.   Five more
minutes and I was going to have to start serving sal-
ads without you," Torrey said to her roommate,
quickly tossing her a clean shirt from a backpack on
the kitchen floor.*

*Taylor pulled off her blue T-shirt in one fluid
motion.   Torrey looked away and pretended to busy
herself by putting bowls filled with salad on a large
tray.   The older woman had no inhibitions about her
own body and she rarely wore a bra.   She buttoned up
the clean white shirt while a hint of a smile played
around her mouth at her small friend's embarrassment.   She wondered if it was knowledge of her pref-
erences or just her naked body that embarrassed
Torrey.   Taylor and her roommate never talked about
it, but she was sure Torrey must have heard it from at
least one of the other students at the University.*

*"Thanks, Little Bit, I owe you." Taylor smiled at
her friend.*

*"It just so happens that I know how you can repay
this enormous debt." Torrey smiled back.*

*Taylor groaned.   She knew this was a chat up for
something.*

*Torrey continued as if she hadn't heard the groan,
throwing her roommate a brush and watching her*

tame her ebony locks. "There's going to be a DeBussy concert at Hutchins on Friday night and I really would love to hear it, but I hate going to those things alone. What do you say?" *Torrey pleaded.*

Taylor ran through the list of possible excuses she could use, but was captured by the trusting and loving look in her small friend's eyes. "Alright, consider it done," *she replied.*

"Yes!" *Torrey said triumphantly.* "Okay, you first." *She handed a large metal tray to her friend.*

Both women entered the dining room and served the first course to the already seated women.

"Well, well, if it isn't our favorite serving duo," *Gina Rice began when she saw Torrey.* "Let's see what was it this time...oh yes, pornographic artwork printed in the House newsletter."

Taylor snorted at the narrow-minded description of her work.

* * * * * * * * * *

Actually, it was the first piece of work by the dark-haired artist that Torrey was allowed to see. Taylor was at the University working on a Fine Arts Degree while Torrey struggled to get hers in English Literature. Many nights spent studying in their room or in the campus library, Torrey watched out of the corner of her eye as her roommate filled one sketchbook after another with drawings. When Torrey asked to see some of her work, Taylor would quickly close her drawing pad and mumble something about unfinished work.

One day, when Torrey came back from a day full

of classes, a large portfolio sat on her desk with a note in Taylor's handwriting. "Remember...if ya don't have nuthin' nice ta say, don't say nuthin' at all." Torrey laughed. It was Thumper's line from the Disney film, Bambi. Torrey had to literally drag her friend to the theater to see it, the dark-haired woman hunching low in the seat so no one would recognize her. Torrey wasn't the least bit surprised when she glanced at her friend during the "death" scene of Bambi's mother, and the older woman had tears in her eyes.

The young woman carefully looked at each drawing, some with notes in the margins about how to paint or sculpt a certain area. They were mostly of women, some with lean muscular lines, and others full of soft curves. The last, a line drawing done in black ink, was of two women locked in an embrace.

It was more than just an embrace; it was an erotic pose. Both women had their faces obscured. One by long hair falling across her features, the other had her face turned away. The smaller of the two women had her lips just brushing against the other woman's nipple, the taller of the two seemed to be pulling her closer. The lines were almost compelling in the way you couldn't tell where once woman left off and the other began.

The picture caused an odd feeling within Torrey but she thought it the most beautiful thing she had ever seen. For the first time in her life, she witnessed the difference between art and pornography.

When Taylor finally returned home that night, more than just a little high, she smiled as her roommate helped her find her own bed. The artist felt a *great weight had been removed from her shoulders as sleep overtook her with Torrey's praises in her head.*

****

Gina's face took on a look of distaste. "Did you say something, Taylor?"

Taylor moved over to serve the House President and coughed. "No, I think I may be coming down with something." Then she made a terrible coughing sound and placed the salad in her hand in front of the President.

Gina looked up in disgust and caught the smile on Torrey's face. "Miss Gray, you're becoming a regular at this, I do hope it wasn't a mistake rooming you with Miss Kent." Then the seated woman put on an evil smile. "I do hope Taylor isn't teaching you any bad habits."

A number of the girls giggled at the comment. Torrey thought the words came out like a dirty joke, but she didn't get the jest behind it. She did, however, catch the look Taylor was passing to Gina. An electric blue fire flashed from Taylor's eyes and her jaw took on a tight edge as she stepped toward the seated woman.

Torrey intercepted her friend's move, stepping easily in between the two. "Absolutely not, sister," Torrey said in that subservient manner that Taylor was always amazed the girl could conjure up. She should be an actress.

"You know, if you two weren't both here on a legacy, you'd be sleeping in the dorm by now," Gina said.

"Yes, sister.   I understand, I'll try to do better."
Torrey smiled that sweet appeasing smile she had.

"Miss Gray, how is it possible that you are the
only Sorority Sister here that can make 'yes, sister'
sound like 'fuck you'?" Gina asked.

"I really have no idea what you mean, sister,"
Torrey replied.

Gina didn't like to get beat, but this little kid was
sure doing it to her, at least in her mind.   "Just get
back to work...both of you!" Gina snapped.

"Yes, sister," the roommates said in unison as
they left the dining room.

Chapter
2

"Are you gonna say anything or just look at me?"
Jessica spat at her mother.

The young girl had a headache the likes of which
she'd never experienced before and a hot shower did
nothing to ease the pain. When she woke up she had
every intention of apologizing to her mother, but now,
seeing the older woman's sad gaze, her good inten-
tions went flying out the door. She wished she could
control her temper but it always seemed to get away
from her. Especially when dealing with her mother.

"What else should I say, JT? What haven't we
said to one another before?" Torrey asked quietly, sipping on her tea. "Tell me, Jess. Tell me what I can
do...what haven't I done? You tell me and I'll do it,"
Torrey said, her voice rising as her body did from the
chair. It was then that Torrey noticed the bruises on
her daughter's neck.

"Please tell me you're at least practicing safe

sex," Torrey said in exasperation.

JT stared at her mother. *Should I tell her? Nah, it'd curl her hair. Just one more reason I'm not the perfect daughter.* "Practicing safe sex, Mom? What the hell for?" Jessica asked, turning away to pour herself a cup of tea.

"So I don't have to go to your funeral before your eighteenth birthday." Torrey roughly grabbed the young girl's arm.

JT's eyes narrowed, her voice dropping lower. "No, Mom, I don't practice safe sex. Maybe I'm looking forward to getting AIDS and dying. That way you wouldn't have to be burdened with this poor excuse for a daughter."

Torrey then did something that she never thought herself capable of. Something she hadn't done in her daughter's entire life, the one thing that she feared more than anything else. The slap was so unexpected it rocked JT's head to the side. Both women could only stare at one another.

"Jess, I—" Torrey started.

The young girl shrank back from her mother's touch. She grabbed her jacket from the chair and ran out the door.

Torrey couldn't believe what she'd done. She ran trembling fingers through her shoulder length blonde hair, propelling herself into motion, but beyond feeling. Each one of their fights left her a little more drained than the last. This time she hit her own daughter. Even though it was a daily battle she felt she was losing. She was terrified that she had finally become the kind of mother Evelyn was. *Jessica acted like she wanted to die! Have I made her feel that*

*way? Should I have told her about Stevie...would she
even understand about the uncle that she never got to
meet? Would she understand about me?*

Torrey went into her bedroom and pulled off the
robe she wore. She put on a black tank top and a pair
of drawstring pants and walked into the exercise room
in her bare feet. It had been a dance studio at one
time long ago, designed by a previous owner of the
loft. The walls on three sides were mirrors; the fourth
wall comprised of windows that looked out onto Lake
Michigan. Torrey did her morning Tai Chi ritual here
as the sun rose over the Lake.

She lit a small bit of incense dropping it in the
shallow clay container. She mixed a bowl full of a
variety of scents so she never knew what she was
selecting for the day. She knelt in front of the window and sat back on her heels, breathing in the aroma
of Patchouli. The tendrils of smoke rose in the air
and all Torrey had to do was close her eyes to picture
Taylor's face. *God her beautiful face.* She remembered it was Taylor that first bought Patchouli for her
and Taylor who finally told her the truth about what
her brother's death meant.

December 1981

*"Hey, Judy, how about coming to the frat kegger
with me Friday?"*

"Eric, I'm going out with your best friend," Alicia said impatiently.

"Oh, yea, right." The young man turned his chair
toward Torrey. *"How 'bout you beautiful?"*

A throaty growl was heard from behind Torrey. The young woman knew immediately who her savior was and smiled. The young man looked up, swallowed once, and quickly vacated the chair.

"Hey, Stretch," Torrey said, not bothering to turn around.

"Hey," Taylor said as she turned the chair around and straddled the seat, resting her hands on the back. "Hey, Ally."

"Hi, Taylor," the young woman replied, surprised the older woman even knew her.

"Are you on your bike with only this on? Taylor, you're going to catch your death," Torrey chided, pulling at the sleeve of the leather jacket.

"Yea, and I froze my ass off too, it's starting to snow again," Taylor replied, blowing a warm breath onto her hands.

"Well, here, at least take my scarf." Torrey leaned over and wrapped her Bears scarf around the taller woman's neck.

"Thanks, Mom." Taylor grinned. "Hey, I got something for you," she said, pulling down the zipper of her jacket and producing a book that was tucked against her chest.

"Oh, Stretch, this is too excellent, in the original Greek, too. Wait a minute. The University library couldn't even get a copy of this. How did you do it?" Torrey asked.

"I happen to be very proficient at a great many things," the dark-haired woman answered with a Mona Lisa like smile and her trademark eyebrow arch.

"You're too wonderful, thanks," Torrey said, cov-

ering Taylor's hand with her own.

"No problem, Little Bit." Taylor smiled at her friend.

"Hi, Taylor," an attractive blonde called out to the seated woman.

Taylor looked up and winked at the girl. "Gotta go." She rose from her chair. "We're still on for tonight? You're going to help me study for that Spanish test, right?" Taylor asked her roommate.

"Yep, our place at seven, I'll be there," Torrey answered.

"Great, adios. Hey, I've got it down already, I'll pass with flying colors." She laughed.

"Yea, right," Torrey replied sarcastically.

Torrey returned to her French fries, as her friend, Ally, shook her head. "You know, Tor, this is the eighties...you really should try to keep a tighter rein."

"Huh?" Torrey questioned.

"Free love went out a ways back. I mean, if my lover just winked at someone else—"

"Ally," Torrey pushed her food aside, "what in the hell are you talking about?"

"I'm saying that if you expect to keep Taylor—"

"Keep her doing what? I think we're on two different pages here. What are you talking about?"

"You and Taylor."

"Me and Taylor what?" Torrey was losing her patience.

"You and Taylor as a couple."

"Couple of what?"

"Lovers," Ally finally said.

"What? Have you lost your mind?" Torrey sat back, dumbstruck.

*"I'm sorry Tor, I just assumed...I mean, most peo-
ple do. Didn't Taylor ever tell you?" Ally asked.*

*"Tell me what?" Torrey asked, suddenly very
afraid of her friend's answer.*

*"Torrey, you live with her, couldn't you tell? I
mean you're her best friend. Hasn't Taylor ever told
you that she's gay?"*

*For a moment, Torrey thought she could pretend
that she hadn't heard what her friend said. She felt
the tears that threatened to break through at any
minute, and she didn't want to be around anyone when
they did. The young woman jumped up from the table
and rushed from the cafeteria.*

"Torrey!" Ally called out to her friend.

* * * * * * * * * *

*Taylor paced the floor of their room. Torrey was
an hour late. She was never late for anything and
Taylor was becoming worried. Just as she was throwing on her leather jacket, she heard a knock on the
door.*

*Alicia took a step back as Taylor flung open the
door. The dark-haired woman saw Torrey's coat and
leather backpack in the young woman's hands and
took them from her. "Where is she?" Taylor
demanded.*

"Taylor, I'm sorry...I mean, I thought she knew."

Taylor stopped and looked at Alicia.

*"You know, knew about you," the young woman
finished.*

*"Did you tell her?" Taylor asked flatly. They
didn't have to say it aloud. Taylor knew exactly what*

the young woman meant.

Alicia nodded.

"What happened...where is she?" Taylor asked.

"She just got up and ran. I looked for her, but I couldn't find her anywhere," Alicia said tearfully.

"How long ago?" Taylor questioned.

"A couple of hours."

"You mean she's been outside without her coat for a couple of hours? For God's sake, it's snowing out!" Taylor sped past the young woman and out the front door of the Sorority House.

A half-hour later, Taylor still couldn't track the young woman down. She gave herself fifteen more minutes, and then she would call the campus police. There would be a hell of a stink, and if the reason why Torrey ran away ever came out, Taylor was sure her scholarship would be kissed away, but none of that mattered to her now. The only thing she was concerned with was finding her friend. Taylor searched everywhere the two ever hid out on the campus, or so she thought until she looked up.

As soon as the dark-haired woman pulled herself up the last rung of the ladder, she could see Torrey, huddled in a dark corner of the bell tower. The young woman was shivering so much her teeth chattered loudly.

"Oh, Torrey...what the hell are you doing?" Taylor came up next to the woman. She grabbed the young woman and put her ski jacket on her small, freezing frame. "You want to hate me, fine you go ahead and hate me," Taylor hissed rubbing the woman's arms to get a little warmth into them, "but don't try to kill yourself over it."

"Are you really gay?" Torrey asked, still shivering.

"Yes," Taylor answered impassively.

Torrey started sobbing uncontrollably.

"Hey, I said you could hate me, not cry. Please, Torrey, don't cry," Taylor pleaded.

"I don't want to lose you," The young woman cried.

"You're not losing me, I'm right here." Taylor wrapped strong arms around the smaller woman and pulled her closer. "Talk to me, Little Bit. Tell me what this is all about."

"My brother, Stevie, was gay. He got sick and he died last year." Torrey sobbed as she told the rest. "My mother wouldn't let me go see him anymore. She said that if you were gay, God made this disease to kill you. So, if you're gay, then you'll get it, too. I don't want you to die, Taylor, I love you too much. You're the best friend I've ever had."

"Oh, honey, no, no." Taylor pulled the young woman into her lap and held her tightly. "Was it AIDS? Is that what your brother died of?"

Torrey nodded before burying her head in the older woman's shoulder.

"Honey, it was a disease your brother died from, but gay people aren't the only ones that get it, and it most certainly is not some kind of judgment from God. I don't believe in a God that would do something like that, do you?"

Torrey shook her head, but couldn't stop crying. The older woman held her until all her tears were spent.

"Come on, Little Bit. We've got to get you

inside," Taylor said. *The taller woman helped Torrey down the ladder and onto her bike. By the time they were inside their own room, Torrey admitted she felt like a Popsicle. Taylor made the young woman soak in a hot tub until Torrey complained she was turning into a prune.*

"First you're a Popsicle, then you're a prune. Everything really does revolve around food for you, doesn't it?" Taylor teased.

She wrapped the smaller woman up in her robe and an extra blanket, and built a fire in the brick fireplace, which was one of the perks to the large room. Sitting alongside one another, drinking instant hot chocolate, Torrey started out the conversation.

"I guess you think I'm pretty stupid, huh? I mean, to believe everything my mother tells me like that."

"No, Little Bit, I don't. How are you supposed to learn things if the people you trust won't even tell you the truth? I guess the sad part is that to them, that is the truth. I have some papers and stuff about AIDS if you want to learn more."

"I'd like that, thanks," Torrey said. Both women silently drank their cocoa, still too shy to bring up the inevitable. "That's why I'm sharing this room, isn't it?" Torrey asked, breaking the silence.

"Nobody else wanted to share a room with a queer," Taylor replied flippantly.

"Why didn't you ever tell me yourself, Taylor?"

Taylor was waiting for that question. She didn't really know the answer herself for sure, but decided to be as honest as she could. "I've never had anyone offer me the kind of unconditional friendship and love that you do, Tor. At first I didn't care if you knew, then later I figured you knew and didn't care. Once I realized you didn't know anything about it, I guess by that time I was too afraid of losing your friendship."

Taylor looked up from her lap and into Torrey's sea green eyes. Tears slowly slid across the dark-haired woman's cheeks. "What we have is very special to me. I've never had fun with anyone like I do with you. I never...never cared about anyone else but myself. It feels so good to have a friend like you, and I like the kind of person I become when I'm around you."

Torrey reached out and brushed the tears from her friend's face. "I'll always be your friend, Stretch." The young woman smiled, leaning into the body that wrapped a protective arm around her.

"And I'll always be there for you, Little Bit. All you have to do is call and the answer will always be yes."

The older woman didn't realize, until that very moment, that she gave her heart away to the young woman in her arms.

Chapter
3

The muscles in Torrey's lean body flexed and extended as she went through the motions that were as natural as breathing to her. When her mind focused once again on her present day surroundings she could still feel Taylor's arms around her, the memory of the warmth of the fire still felt hot against her damp skin. The dark shadow and taller presence she felt behind her reminded her of a day when that body would glide with her through each movement. They were two entities moving together, one light and one dark, the perfect symbols of balance and harmony.

This time the dark shadow behind her waited impatiently with a loud, exasperated sigh. Jessica crossed many lines, but she hadn't yet interrupted her mother's daily Tai Chi. She leaned restlessly against the mirrored wall, her balance wavering slightly.

Once Torrey finished her moves, she knelt on the

floor with her eyes closed for a few moments more. Leaning back and resting on her heels, she watched as her daughter's reflection in the window bobbed from side to side.

"God," she ran her fingers through her hair, "I don't think I could even find a place to buy drugs, let alone get wasted in just two hours, Jess."

"Then you don't know where to look *and* you're not takin' the right drugs," JT replied, moving up behind the older woman, a wise-ass grin plastered on her face.

Torrey moved so fast, Jessica barely had enough time for the smirk on her face to disappear. The young girl stood six inches taller than her mother and outweighed her by a good bit, but Torrey had the advantage of surprise and twenty years of martial arts training behind her. The older woman was still in control of her actions. If she hadn't been, Torrey mused to herself later; she would have flung her daughter across the room. She didn't want to hurt her daughter, but she was getting closer and closer to her breaking point. Torrey backed the young girl against the wall with a cross-shoulder hold designed to restrain Jessica, not injure her.

"This is not a goddamn game, Jessica Taylor!" Torrey seethed.

Torrey's only mistake was trusting in the fact that her daughter hadn't yet become physical with her. The young girl's eyes took on a panicked expression as she struggled against the hold. Torrey jerked the girl loose, but wasn't prepared for her daughter's reaction. As the older woman took a step back, Jessica realized her arms were free and lashed out with a powerful backhand to her mother's cheek. The blow rocked Torrey hard enough that she dropped to one knee, her hand going up to her eye.

Jessica stood there, frozen in place. She never thought herself capable of striking her mother, even though she felt she was angry with the woman most of the time. Now she could only look down at the fallen woman, her gaze returning to her own hand. Finally, the hand closed into a fist and Jessica turned and slammed it into the mirrored wall behind her. "Why did you make me do that?" She cried, running from the loft.

February 1982

"Are you kidding? You're still a virgin?" Taylor looked in amazement at Torrey.

The two women sat on the rug in the center of their third floor room, books piled around Torrey, sketch pads around Taylor. Gene Pitney resounded from the stereo as usual. All it took, for Torrey, was to hear "Town Without Pity" and she was spilling her sexual woes to her friend.

"Could you say it a little louder? I don't think they heard you on the first floor," Torrey answered sharply.

"Well, I can't believe it. You're what? Eighteen?" Taylor laughed out loud.

The dark-haired woman caught the wounded expression on her friend's face, the young woman turning away with tears in her eyes. "Oh, Little Bit, I'm sorry." Taylor's expression naturally turned into a frown whenever she ignorantly hurt her young friend's feelings. "I didn't know it was such a big deal."

"Well, it is to me." Torrey couldn't stop the tears that spilled from her eyes.

"Hey, don't do that." Taylor moved next to the young woman and put an arm around her small frame. "What's up with this, Little Bit?"

Torrey explained her feelings regarding her innocence and started talking about the boy she'd been dating for the past two weeks. Taylor's shoulder muscles tensed at the sound of Stephen's name. Tall, jet-black hair, and sky blue eyes, even Taylor had to admit that Torrey did well for herself with this one. He drove a bike that Taylor rolled her eyes at, a Honda Shadow...a wannabe compared to her Harley, but he appeared to treat Torrey with respect, and that was something that Taylor would insist on from any man that hoped to date her young friend.

Of course, no one would ever be good enough for Torrey in the older woman's mind. Ever since the night that she was forcibly outed to her friend, the dark-haired woman fought the knowledge that she was hopelessly in love with the young woman. She wanted to take Torrey in her arms and show her how deeply her emotions ran, but Taylor had a feeling if she did that; it would be Torrey doing the running. So the artist swallowed her feelings up and became the best friend she knew how. Naturally, hearing about Stephen was the hardest part.

"Stephen wants me to sleep with him." Torrey brushed her tears aside.

"Yea, well that's no surprise," Taylor answered

dryly. Okay, she doesn't need sarcasm, Kent. You're just mad because it's not you she wants.

"*Are you saying I shouldn't?*" *Torrey asked.*

Damn right, that's what I'm saying! "*Well, I guess that's not up to me, Tor. I guess it's kind of a personal thing,*" *Taylor answered.*

"*So I should?*" *Torrey continued.*

Only if it's with me.

"*It's just that I'm confused, Stretch. I mean, part of me wants to, but part of me doesn't see what all the fuss is about. Stephen said he doesn't know how long he can stay with a girl who doesn't trust him enough to sleep with him,*" *Torrey continued on tearfully.*

That bastard! I should break his scrawny neck.

Taylor was fighting an internal battle as well, in this situation. Her love for the young woman was obviously clouding her judgment, but the dark-haired artist quickly realized the way she wanted Torrey in her life would never come to be. She looked into her small friend's eyes, wanting Torrey to see what was in her heart, to realize the depth of her love. For a moment, Torrey's eyes grew bright, then her brow furrowed in puzzlement.

Taylor looked away, suddenly afraid that her friend would see the hunger in her blue eyes. Unable to stand the confused expression and the tear filled eyes of her friend, the dark-haired woman moved around to face her. Sitting cross-legged, Taylor took Torrey's slender hands within her own.

"*Little Bit, I can't tell you whether you should or shouldn't do this. I lost my virginity when I was fourteen to a guy that was old enough to be my father.*"

Seeing the wide-eyed expression on Torrey's face,

Taylor grinned at her friend. "Yea, I know how both
sides live. The point is I thought I was special and
loved, turned out all I was to this guy was a fourteen-
year-old piece of ass." Taylor felt her own eyes grow
misty with the memory of her first time.

"Torrey, honey, your first time should be with
someone you love, someone special to you, but most of
all someone that you know feels the same way about
you." Taylor brushed a stray lock of hair back from
the girl's face and used her thumb to brush away a
tear from her cheek. "Just remember that it's a gift
you can only give away once."

Torrey couldn't shake the feeling that the person
she wanted to bestow this gift on was the woman sitting in front of her. Shaking her head to dispel the
disturbing notion, she smiled up at her friend and
squeezed the hands that tenderly held her own.

****

Torrey walked into the darkened bar and had to
squint and stop moving for a moment until her eyes
adjusted to the dark interior. It was two o'clock in
the afternoon and the bar was relatively empty, all
except the back room where the pool table was. Torrey could hear the sounds of the balls as they were hit
against each other and fell into the pockets.

"Hi, Jack. Is she here?" Torrey asked, not even
bothering to show the bartender her ID as she
reached for the wine cooler the man pushed toward
her. Torrey was a regular and Jack smiled down at
the petite young woman.

Jack was the owner of the small bar. Part biker

hangout, it was also where all the college students bought their liquor and drugs. Of course, that made it Taylor's favorite hangout.

"Yea, you better give her an excuse to leave. She's winnin' again and you know Billy don't like that a whole lot," Jack answered.

"Will do, thanks," Torrey replied.

She liked Jack, no matter what a lot of people in the community thought. He was a giant of a man, who wore an old Hell's Angels vest that Torrey suspected was authentic. He looked like Jerry Garcia would have looked if the Grateful Dead star had been a line-backer with the Chicago Bears.

Torrey made her way to the back of the bar. She pulled up as she saw Taylor stand up from her chair and stretch her arms over her head. The dark-haired woman had on a black muscle tee with her usual worn denim jeans. Her lean, muscular frame caught the young woman's eyes immediately. Oh God, I made a huge mistake last night.

Before Torrey could examine her thoughts any further, Taylor looked up and smiled at her. The look on the smaller woman's face caused the muscles in Taylor's belly to clench. For an unguarded second, Torrey had a positively carnal look in her eye as she watched the artist. The young woman's face returned to its casual appearance as soon as Taylor smiled.

Torrey walked over and placed her wine cooler bottle by the chair where Taylor's leather jacket was draped.

"Want another?" Torrey held up Taylor's empty beer bottle. "I got my allowance today," she whispered.

"Well then, I'm not proud." Taylor winked as Torrey made her way to the bar again.

"Wish I had an old lady who took as good a care of me!" Billy yelled over at the tall woman.

"Eat yer heart out!" Taylor tossed back, watching Torrey's backside as the young woman walked away. Taylor kind of enjoyed the bikers thinking someone like Torrey could belong to someone like her.

"Okay, yer up, Taylor," one of the men called out.

Torrey had a cold bottle of beer in hand as she returned, but Taylor caught the odd expression, almost sadness, on the young woman's face. *"Hey, you okay?"* Taylor asked, touching Torrey's cheek.

"Yea, I'm fine," Torrey lied.

Taylor stood close to Torrey and let her hand rest on her shoulder. Torrey looked up into the cerulean gaze of her concerned friend, taking in the bloodshot eyes and the smell of pot on the woman's clothes. She knew Taylor hadn't returned home last night because she was there all night, most of it spent with someone other than her roommate.

The impatient pool player walked over and stood beside the two women. *"I said yer up. Kiss her, fuck her, or play pool...either way I'll watch, but make up yer mind!"*

So fast Torrey hardly knew what was happening, Taylor reached out with her left hand and grabbed the man around his throat. The muscles in the tall woman's arm tightened and stood out as she cut off the man's flow of air. *"I don't like it when you use that kind of language in front of her,"* Taylor hissed to the man who was well on his way to being on his knees. *"Apologize."*

"*Taylor, please. Let him go,*" *Torrey pleaded with her friend.*

"*Apologize!*" *Taylor applied more pressure to the man who could only grab at the iron grip of the woman who towered over him.*

"*Apologize to the pretty lady, Dennis...now,*" *Billy commanded of the kneeling man.*

Dennis gasped an apology and Taylor immediately released the man. He slumped to the floor, desperately pulling much needed air into his lungs, glaring at the dark-haired woman.

"*So, Taylor, introduce me to the lovely lady,*" *Billy said.*

Taylor scowled at the amiable biker, attempting to discern if he was trying to jerk her around or not. Noticing the relaxed grin on the blonde haired man's face, she introduced her roommate.

"*Okay, now for that game of pool,*" *Billy said, slapping his hands together.*

"*No can do, I gotta go,*" *Taylor replied, turning back to Torrey.*

"*Come on, one last game for a hundred bucks,*" *Billy said good-naturedly.*

"*Where the fuck am I going to get a hundred bucks?*" *Taylor asked with a smile.*

"*Hey, I thought you said you didn't talk that way around her,*" *Dennis rasped.*

"*Nooo.*" *Taylor smiled wickedly at the man.* "*I said I didn't like it when you talked that way around her. Like I said, Billy, where am I going to get that kind of cash at?*" *Taylor asked, grabbing her jacket.*

"*From me.*" *Torrey stepped forward.*

"*There ya go...your old lady will bankroll ya.*"

Billy laughed.

Taylor grabbed Torrey's elbow and pulled her away from the laughing bikers. "Torrey, put your money away," Taylor said under her breath.

"But, you can beat him, I've seen you play before," Torrey replied.

"What if I lose? You're out your allowance for the rest of the month."

"I believe in you," Torrey answered the older woman.

It was a simple answer, but it implied so much to Taylor. In later years when her confidence would run low, she would always look back on this day and remember that Torrey was the only person, other than her mother, to ever utter those words to her. Taylor rewarded the young woman with one of her sparkling smiles and then turned back to the bikers.

"Rack 'em," she said, removing her jacket.

* * * * * * * * * *

Torrey and Taylor were lying on the rug in front of fireplace. The Sorority House was its usual chaotic self on a Friday night, but set back from the rest of the floor, such as they were, the noise was almost completely muffled. Taylor's stereo was tuned in low to a local jazz station and the two women were relaxing after the pizza that they had devoured.

Torrey tried to give the money won from the pool game to Taylor, but the older woman refused. She said she would be happy with a pizza and a six-pack as her share. Taylor pulled a joint from her leather jacket, searching her pockets for a lighter.

"*You got any matches, Little Bit?*" *Taylor rolled over onto her stomach, waving the joint in front of Torrey.* "*I'll share,*" *she offered.*

Torrey shook her head at her friend, in answer as well as in exasperation. In the last month, Taylor always seemed stoned. She smoked pot to calm down and took speeders to keep going. The last couple of months seemed especially bad, and Torrey was worried about her friend's drug habit.

"*Aha!*" *Taylor found her lighter in her jacket pocket and sat back down on the floor. Just as she was cupping her hands to light the hand-rolled item, Torrey reached over and placed her hand over the dark-haired woman's fingers.*

"*Not tonight, huh, Stretch?*" *Torrey asked.*

Taylor looked over at the young woman and lost her heart all over again. How could she tell her that became such a habit because she used it to forget, to feel, and to accept? Forget that Torrey didn't belong to her, that the woman she was in love with didn't love her back. To feel something when another woman was touching her and all she could picture was Torrey caressing her body, most of all, to accept that Torrey would never be with her that way; could never love her that way.

The older woman had trouble refusing this girl anything so Taylor simply smiled and tucked the joint away for another time. Torrey smiled back at her friend in thanks and the look of sadness from earlier crossed her face again.

"*Little Bit, what's wrong?*" *Taylor questioned.* "*And don't tell me nothing this time because I'm not buying it.*"

Torrey gave a half-hearted grin to her friend and told her the truth. "I slept with Stephen last night," Torrey said, without looking up into her friend's eyes.

"I figured as much," Taylor replied softly.

Actually, Taylor knew what happened in their room last night. They had a system to avoid embarrassment. If one or the other was home entertaining someone, they left a Do Not Disturb sign that Taylor lifted from a local motel, on the door. When Taylor arrived home from her date, which was more of a quickie in a car in the Library parking lot, the artist was amazed to see the sign on the door. Torrey never put the sign out. She never had a reason to. Taylor listened at the door and the unmistakable sounds coming from their room cut through to her heart. Of course, she didn't hear Torrey, but she heard male grunts and could only assume Stephen finally got his wish.

Taylor couldn't get out of there fast enough. She never thought about all the nights Torrey came up to their door and heard the same type of sounds. The young woman never said a word, she would just find a warm spot to crash and spend the rest of the night there. Taylor never thought about that, especially not now when her heart was breaking. Up to that point she kept hoping that something would happen and Torrey would see all the love the older woman had in her heart for her small friend, but hoping never made it so.

Taylor rushed out and managed to get as drunk as humanly possible while still being able to remain upright, landing in Orono's one and only lesbian bar. The inebriated woman was so out of it, she let herself be coaxed into the bathroom by a pretty blonde who, somewhere in Taylor's intoxicated mind, reminded her of Torrey. The woman went down on her in the bathroom stall and Taylor simply allowed it to happen. As the dark-haired woman climaxed, she groaned out Torrey's name, which earned her a slap in the face from the pretty blonde.

Now, Taylor looked into the sad eyes of her friend and felt her heart break for her. It was hell to lose your virginity, and wake up the next day, not certain it was to the right person.

Torrey looked back into the frank gaze of her roommate and realized with a sudden clarity that she gave away her precious gift to the wrong person. Her mind finally accepted the truth. She was in love with Taylor Kent. Oh, Taylor, it should have been you.

Taylor was shocked at first by the open look on Torrey's face. The young woman's eyes looked at her with such a loving expression, Taylor would not have been at all surprised if Torrey leaned over and kissed her at that very moment.

"It was kind of—" Torrey searched for the words to explain her experience, but found she couldn't come up with any, "disappointing," she whispered at last.

Taylor moved behind her seated friend and wrapped her arms around her. The dark-haired woman couldn't speak her heart. If she did, she knew her secret would slip out, too. Instead, she offered a strong shoulder and a warm pair of arms.

"I'm sorry, Little Bit," Taylor murmured against Torrey's ear.

"It just seemed so...I don't know, not really rough,

but not gentle," Torrey remarked as tears filled her eyes.

"Did he hurt you?" Taylor tensed, pulling back in alarm.

"Yes, I mean no, not the way you mean. I guess it was just the usual 'first time' pain," Torrey answered.

Tears slipped from Torrey's eyes as she allowed herself to be held by the woman that she now realized she was in love with. She cried for the loss of the gift she gave away for such a foolish reason. More so, she cried, as she understood that the woman she loved would never return that love. Taylor gets laid, she doesn't make love, *she thought to herself,* and she certainly doesn't fall in love.

"I know I'm not the first woman in the world to lose my virginity," Torrey sobbed into her friend's shoulder, *"but right now, I feel like it."*

Taylor held tightly to the weeping young woman. She remembered the regret and the heartbreak she herself felt, the morning after she lost her innocence. She wished for someone, anyone, to simply hold her just like this. Someone to caress her and tell her things would be all right again.

So, Taylor pulled the small woman close against her and did exactly that.

****

At midnight, Torrey heard the key turn in the lock. Her stomach burned and she realized this minute that she hadn't eaten a thing today. The stress was taking its toll on her body and she reached over to her bedside table and popped another antacid tablet into her mouth.

Jessica appeared at her door. It was slightly ajar, but she tapped lightly anyway.

"Come on in, honey," Torrey answered the knock.

When her daughter stepped into the light Torrey could see her eyes were red and swollen from crying. She realized that her own eyes probably looked the same.

Jessica looked at the large bruise that already formed on her mother's right cheekbone and her eyes filled once again with tears, the green orbs darting back and forth in nervousness and humiliation. "I'm sorry, Mom," she said so low that it was barely a whisper.

"Oh, honey, it's okay. You didn't hurt me; it looks worse than it is. Come here." Torrey patted the bed.

If either woman stopped to think about it, they might have experienced an attack of nerves, but the young girl nearly fell, sobbing, into her mother's arms. It had been so long since the last time her daughter allowed this kind of contact that it felt almost strange to hold Jessica in her arms again. The young girl sobbed and hours later, after Torrey knew Jessica had no tears left to cry, the older woman simply held her daughter in a tight embrace.

"I'll do better, Mom, I'll really try this time," she promised.

"I know you will, love, and I know you believe that right this minute, but we've said these things so many times already." Torrey stroked her daughter's hair, kissing the top of her head.

"I want to be different, to be good, but then I get

around my friends it's so hard to say no. When I drink or smoke it makes me feel like stuff is going to be better." Jessica tried to explain feelings that she didn't even understand herself. She couldn't even verbalize what the *stuff* was, that always seemed wrong, why she always felt there was something missing in her life.

"I do understand that, Jess, I really do. I don't expect you to be perfect, but I feel like we're losing ground here. I have an idea, though, if you'll go along with it. It's going to be hard, sweetheart." Torrey bent down and whispered to her daughter. "It's going to be hard on both of us, but you have to promise me you will at least try, Jess," Torrey finished. "I need your solemn promise."

Jessica looked up at her mother, the older woman wiping the tears from her face. "I promise, Mom, no matter what it takes."

"I'm afraid you might forget that promise by morning, Jess," Torrey said softly.

Jessica looked at the angry purple bruise on her mother's face. "Will you still have this in the morning?" she asked.

"Yes." Torrey nodded.

"Then I won't forget," Jessica added with grim determination.

April 1982

Taylor walked into the Sorority House realizing this would be one of the last times she would be crossing this threshold as a student. She had already began the countdown to being alone in the world without Torrey. The two women tried not to talk about it much, but this was Taylor's last semester, with only a month before graduation and she already had a scholarship opportunity all lined up to get her Masters at Berkley.

It was hard for the artist to find any excitement in going back to California. She knew that without Torrey in her life, she would revert back to her solitary ways. Always keeping to herself, never allowing anyone to touch the real person, the one she kept hidden away. She tried to tell herself it was all happening the way it was supposed to.

That's what Torrey believed anyway. The young woman said everything in life happens for a reason. The young writer was always trying to explain to her friend about balance and harmony, light and dark, the yin and the yang. After two months of watching Torrey practice her Tai Chi every morning, Taylor finally worked up the nerve to ask the smaller woman to teach her the moves. The dark-haired woman admitted to her friend, and herself, that there was something to the relaxing movements, which seemed to add a certain focus to her life. Torrey used them as a way of losing herself to her thoughts and emotions, a way of letting her feelings rise to the surface, so she could examine and then release them.

Taylor repeated the words to herself on a daily basis, everything happens for a reason. *She had to make a hard decision, and her answer was due by the end of this week. She could stay in Maine and take the job offer from Diamond & Allen, a cutting edge design firm that offered Taylor the moon to become their new Art Director. The position was full of incentives and prestige, and quite unheard of for a new graduate to be offered. They immediately saw the young artist's talent and liked her drive and no-non-sense personality. The job would afford Taylor the kind of living she only dreamed of previously. Most of all, it would allow her to stay by Torrey. Taylor even thought about coaxing the young woman out of the Sorority House and into an apartment they could share.*

Then there was option number two. A paid educa-tion was nothing to be sneered at, especially the chance to go back to California to do it. She would have three years to work on her Masters in Art, plus the opportunity to work with some incredible artists, all paid for by the State of California. The only catch was that she would end up on the other side of the country from where Torrey was. Taylor had thought about little else in the last month.

Torrey wasn't seeing much of Stephen lately and Taylor worried that maybe it was because she monop-olized so much of the young woman's life. It was almost as if the small blonde were resigned to a rela-tionship with the good-looking young man, though. There wasn't any excitement when Torrey talked about him. Of course, the last couple of weeks you couldn't say anything to Torrey without the girl flying off the handle or simply breaking down crying.

Taylor knew that even though her small friend loved her dearly, a real, committed relationship with the artist was something Torrey could never handle. So, Taylor made the heartbreaking decision that she would have to move on and let her friend get on with her own life as well. Maybe without Taylor in the picture, Torrey would work on a future with Stephen. On Friday, she would notify Diamond & Allen of her decision.

Taylor started up the steps to the third floor, nearly running into Torrey's friend, Alicia. The young girl had obviously been crying.

"Hey, kid, you okay?" Taylor asked sincerely.

"Taylor, have you seen Torrey? I don't know if she's heard yet," Ally asked tearfully.

"Heard what?"

"Stephen...Stephen Townley is dead. He was killed last night outside of Bangor on Interstate 95. I guess he got hit by a truck while he was on his motorcycle."

Taylor dropped the jacket she had slung over her shoulder and headed for the door. She had no way of knowing if Torrey knew about the accident, but she didn't want her friend to find out from anyone else.

The dark-haired woman at least knew where to look first. On these warm spring days, Torrey spent a great deal of time studying on a bench that was behind the Sciences Building. The classes used a small lagoon as a simulated ecosystem and it rivaled a nature park, even though very few people knew about it.

When she came around the corner of the building and walked through a small copse of trees, she immediately heard Torrey's sobs. Taylor's heart could do no more than ache for her friend. When she stood over the young woman, Torrey looked up at Taylor. Once she recognized her roommate's face, she sobbed uncontrollably. Taylor scooped the smaller woman into her arms and held her, whispering soft words of tenderness.

Half an hour passed, but Taylor still couldn't get Torrey to talk to her. When the young woman tried, she got frustrated and cried all the more.

"I'm sorry, Tor. I didn't know what Stephen meant to you. I guess I didn't realize you were in love with him," Taylor said.

Torrey pulled a clean piece of tissue from her pocket and tried to settle herself enough to talk. She blew her nose and wiped eyes that immediately refilled with tears. "I'm so sorry this happened to him, but I wasn't in with love him. Oh, Taylor...I'm pregnant." Torrey softly cried again.

Taylor was frozen. For her friend's sake, she prayed she heard wrong.

"You're probably disgusted with me too, aren't you?" Torrey sobbed at her friend's silence.

Taylor quickly knelt in front of the young woman, taking both the of the girl's small hands in her own. "Torrey that could never be true. Honey, you know I love you...I could never think anything like that about you." The dark-haired woman reached up a hand and tenderly caressed Torrey's cheek as salty tears wet the palm of her hand. "Honey, are you sure. Did Stephen know?" Taylor asked.

Torrey shook her head. "I just went to the doctor this morning. Taylor, what am I going to do?" she asked, the crying starting anew.

Taylor jumped up and moved next to the seated young woman, the older woman's arms wrapping easily around the familiar form. "What do you want to do, Tor?" Taylor asked, stroking the woman's hair, gently rubbing her back in small circular motions.

"I don't know where to go...if I'm pregnant, I lose my scholarship...I called my mother and she said I—I have to come home, but she said I have to get an abortion first! I can't do that, Taylor...I just can't, and I don't have any where to go..."

Torrey was unable to go on and Taylor didn't want her to. The dark-haired woman thanked the powers that be that Torrey's mother wasn't in front of her now. Taylor would have laid the woman out. The older woman held and rocked the young woman.

"Shhh, It'll be all right, Little Bit." Taylor tried to relax the young woman. She tenderly kissed her forehead, her wet cheek, and finally the artist leaned down and softly brushed her lips against her friend's. There was nothing erotic about the kisses. Taylor simply tried the only way she knew to convey the power of her love and friendship to her frightened friend.

It worked, and Torrey eventually let her head fall into the crook of Taylor's shoulder. Torrey was heart-sick and her body ached all over from the tension of the day. She could barely think anymore and Taylor's touch felt so reassuring, she gave in to the older woman's caresses and the tears subsided.

"You know, I already have the perfect solution to all your problems. I just haven't been able to get a word in here," Taylor teased.

Torrey blew her nose again and looked up at her friend.

"I already decided I was going to take the job at Diamond & Allen, so I'll be staying in Maine. Just when you thought you'd be rid of me too." She wig-

gled her eyebrows. "It'll work out perfect. We can get a place not too far from here and you can go to school. After the baby's born, you can take afternoon and evening classes, and I can watch the kid." Taylor smiled proudly at the plan.

"Stretch, if I stay here and have the baby, I'll lose my scholarship. I don't think I can get a job that will pay enough to afford to raise my baby and go to school," Torrey replied.

"Job? No, you're not getting it, Tor. I work and earn the dough and you get to spend it."

"Taylor, I can't allow you to do that," Torrey said softly, speechless at the gift her friend was offering. "It wouldn't be right."

"Oh, but it would be right for me to move clear across the country when my best friend doesn't have a dime to her name, is pregnant, and soon to be homeless...that would be right?" Taylor asked gently. "Tor, these people are paying a hugely obscene amount of money for a twenty-three year old right out of college. I think we should take advantage of it. After all, how much money can I actually blow on drink, drugs, and women?" Taylor intercepted her friend's look. "I'm just teasing," she added. "Please let me do this for you, Little Bit. I like having you in my life. I'm not quite ready to give that up yet," Taylor admitted.

There was a long silence before Torrey responded. "How are you at changing diapers?" she finally asked with a smile.

"I'm highly trainable," Taylor answered with a grin of her own.

"Thank you, Stretch...I love you," Torrey said as

she wrapped her arms around the taller woman's neck.

When they separated, Taylor kissed the top of Torrey's head. "I love you too, Little Bit. Remember, whatever you need, whenever you need it, all you have to do is ask and the answer will always be yes," Taylor replied.

* * * * * * * * * *

Torrey pulled her address book a little closer, slipping on her glasses to read her own small handwriting. *God, I can only hope she isn't home and I can leave a message for her to call me. I can't believe my palms are sweating.* The writer picked up the cordless phone and leaned back against the bed's headboard.

Fourteen years had gone by since she'd heard her voice. They faithfully sent gifts for Christmas and birthdays, cards would be interspersed throughout the year and, with the advent of computers, e-mails were exchanged at least once a month. They never saw one another and they never called. Both of them understood the danger in that, even though each woman had her own reasons.

Now Torrey had to swallow her pride and put her emotions in a place where they couldn't hurt her. Just as her friend was willing to do anything for Torrey so long ago, so she was willing to do anything now; suffer any heartbreak or humiliation for her daughter. *God, I know I always wanted her to be happy, but I hope she's not with anybody. That would definitely be too much.*

Torrey punched in the long distance number and held her breath as the phone rang.

Chapter
4

Taylor was covered in the dust the electric buffer threw around. Her long raven hair was pulled back into a braid while she worked, a filtered air mask covering most of her face. Between the sound of the equipment and the muffled air within the mask, she almost missed the phone. It was an odd sensation. Similar to the feeling you get when you turn off the vacuum because you swear the phone is ringing, but you don't hear a sound once everything is shut off.

She growled and ripped the mask off, reaching for the phone that was resting on a stool in one corner of the studio. She was sure it was Samantha. The gallery owner always got into a panic before a big show.

"Yea," she barked into the receiver.

"It's nice to hear that your phone manner is as pleasant as ever, Stretch."

Taylor stood in the middle of her studio, letting the mask quietly fall from her grasp. *The sound on the other end must not have been real. Then again, only one woman ever called me that name.*

"Taylor, are you there?" Torrey asked.

Oh, yes, the voice was definitely real. No one in the world said the artist's name quite like her old friend did. "Torrey?" A feeling like the blood was draining from her body spread across her flesh. Her stomach became queasy and she started to sweat. Taylor sank heavily onto the stool. "Are you okay? Is Jess—" The artist started, suddenly alarmed.

"No, we're okay...in a manner of speaking," Torrey answered, not knowing where to begin. Taylor knew Torrey was having an occasional problem with Jessica, but she would never have guessed the extent.

"Stretch, I need..." Torrey raised her eyes to the ceiling, willing the tears not to fall. They rarely obeyed her, even though she was making a valiant effort.

"What is it, honey?" Taylor asked, fourteen years disappearing into nothing as she felt she was seated on the floor of their room once again.

The sound of her friend's voice combined with the term of endearment opened the way as Torrey's tears fell. "I need to ask you a huge favor," Torrey said.

"The answer is yes," Taylor answered.

"You don't even know what the favor is yet." Torrey laughed and cried at the same time.

Taylor grinned into the receiver. "You know that doesn't matter. What? You need to pay off a gambling debt? The answer is yes. You need a kidney? The answer is yes. You need—"

"I need you to raise my daughter for six months," Torrey interjected.

"You sure you wouldn't rather have the kidney?" Taylor shot back.

Again, Torrey couldn't help but laugh at her friend. *God, it's been so long since anyone could make me laugh like this.*

"Talk to me, Little Bit. What's going on there?" Taylor asked with concern.

It was the nickname that not one other soul ever called her, which broke her resolve to be strong. Torrey found herself pouring out the experiences of the past few years, the anger, and the pain, along with the frustration over her inability to repair the damage that had already been done, without making it worse.

Three hours later, they still talked. Taylor was now seated in the high back leather chair behind the desk in her office. She ran a slender finger along the wooden base of a model jet that sat on one corner, listening and crying along with her old friend. Taylor knew the situation was much worse than Torrey was making it sound. Torrey never would have called if she weren't at the end of her rope.

It was like some bizarre, unwritten agreement they had. Taylor's love for the woman hadn't diminished with time. If anything, Torrey became an unshakable obsession to the artist. When they parted, Taylor knew the only way to let Torrey get on with her life was to never speak to her or even see her in person. Once they separated, her need for the young woman became so overwhelming at times the artist would spend hours with the phone in her hand, poised to dial Torrey's number, just so she could hear her voice. If she were ever to see her again, Taylor's secret, at some point would make its presence known.

So she distanced herself from what she so passionately desired, but would never be allowed to have.
She assumed Torrey was simply acquiescing to her
wishes all these years.

It would also have to be a desperate situation for
Torrey to ask for help, from anybody. In Taylor's
mind there was only one woman that suffered from
being as proud and headstrong as she was, and that
was the woman on the other end of the phone line.

Finally, Torrey told Taylor about the previous
day's battles. The writer was reduced to tears again
as she told her friend how she slapped Jessica in the
face. Taylor's brows came together in a frown, her
hands clenched and unclenched. How she wished she
could reach out, pull the younger woman into her
arms, and make everything all right, just as she tried
to so many years back. Torrey secretly wished for the
very same thing.

Lastly, Torrey related what happened when Jessica hit her.

"She did what?" Taylor's voice dropped low with
an icy edge to it.

"It's okay. It just looks worse than it is," Torrey
assured her, repeating the words she used for Jessica's
benefit.

Taylor was already flipping open her Rolodex.
"I'm going to catch the next flight to Chicago."

"No, Taylor, I don't think that will help the situation much. It's the friends that Jess has here that are
half the problem. She can't seem to stay away from
them and when she's around them, she can't seem to
say no to them."

"So, what's the other half of the problem?" Taylor

asked.

"I think it might be me," Torrey answered sadly.

"Tor, don't say that. You're a great mother, you always have been," Taylor said adamantly.

"You haven't seen me lately." Torrey started to cry again. "I hit her, for God's sake!"

"Yea, well," Taylor sneered, "sounds like she needed to have her ass kicked." She leaned back in her chair and ran her hand across her face, realizing how that sounded. "You know what I mean. Look, hon, I don't know if I'll do any better. She may push me too far and you know me well enough to know that I'm not about to let her hit *me*. I know she's got a lot of valid problems we need to address, but it sounds like she's got a lot of good old fashioned attitude going, too."

"I know," Torrey said in defeat. "God, Stretch, I don't know if what I'm doing is right or not and you know how much I hate asking anyone for help. I only know I've run out of options. JT knows what she can get away with here...with me. I surprised her by what I did the other day, but I think she and I both know that I can't control her. I was hoping in a different environment, with someone other than me...I just think you could be good for her. I don't think I did the right thing by letting Jess grow up not knowing you, Stretch."

Torrey couldn't stop the tears after that. Taylor let her stay that way for a few minutes, running through her own gauntlet of emotions. She always thought of JT as *her* daughter too. Saying goodbye to the two-year-old was one of the hardest things Taylor ever had to do. It wasn't Torrey's fault alone. Taylor realized that she never made the effort to stay in Jessica's life because of her own pain. Now she was going to have to put her money where her mouth was.

"Don't cry, honey. We'll get through this," Taylor said into the phone, and to both women, it was as if they were back on that bench on that warm day in April. Taylor's arms were wrapped protectively around the smaller woman, promising that she would make everything better.

August 1982

Taylor faced the window and wondered why doctor's offices were always so cold. It was ninety degrees outside and felt to be slightly above the freezing mark inside. She watched as the cars sped by outside while listening to the conversation behind her. Torrey hated going to the doctor alone, especially once she started showing.

The young girl always seemed to have a run in with the same old crony of a nurse. The much older woman noticed Torrey didn't wear a wedding band and that she signed everything "Miss." Last month when Taylor came home from work, Torrey was in tears over the situation. The dark haired artist promised that from then on she would leave the office early and join her friend for her obstetrics appointment.

Actually, it was starting to get to Torrey. She felt that everywhere she went, people looked down at her hand, then at the missing wedding ring, and instantly she felt inferior. It was hard for Taylor to convince her to blow off people like that. Her young friend was sensitive at the best of times, but being six months pregnant and a walking hormone factory did nothing for the woman's self image. Of course, it didn't help when Taylor had to go to San Francisco for a client meeting and Torrey couldn't go along because of classes.

Taylor made up for it though. While wandering around down on the Pier, a wedding band set caught her eye in one of the small jewelry shops. Platinum settings were circled completely with small stones of pale green jade and blue sapphires. The color combi- nation of their eyes prompted the dark haired woman to purchase the set. She had one sized for her while she waited, and the other sized down to Torrey's ring finger. The look on the young woman's face made the expensive purchase worth it all.

"I mean, I don't think people will...I mean you don't have to tell them you and I are...well, I got it mostly so people wouldn't think..." Taylor stammered incessantly when she arrived home. She was feeling rather tongue tied as she tried to give Torrey the duplicate ring to the one the young woman immedi- ately noticed on the older woman's hand.

Torrey slipped the band on the ring finger of her left hand and threw her arms around the taller woman's neck, but not before placing a kiss on Tay- lor's cheek. "You're wonderful, you know that, Stretch?" The young woman beamed.

Taylor didn't think her young friend would be hav- ing any more problems here in the doctor's office after today. The tall woman smiled to herself as she looked out the window. Taylor was running late and got a hold of Torrey between classes to let her know

*she would meet her at the office. As Taylor walked
through the waiting room door, Torrey sat, about to be
brow beaten by the frowning nurse. Every head in the
room turned to look at the striking woman as she
walked in.*

*Taylor's foray into the professional world gave
Torrey reasons to go clothes shopping and one thing
Taylor could say was, the girl had good taste. The
dark-haired woman came directly from the office and
so still wore her dress clothes, black slacks, a purple
silk blouse, and a black jacket. With the high heel
pumps, that Taylor hated, but tolerated for the office,
she stood well over six feet tall.*

*She immediately noticed the nurse that Torrey
described to her and was in no mood for her. She had
a hellish day and if the old bat wasn't careful she was
going to become the next in a long line of victims the
artist had to crucify today. Torrey watched as her
friend got that look in her eye. It reminded the young
woman of a cat who just cornered a mouse, knowing
mealtime was a sure thing and within easy reach.*

*Taylor walked up to Torrey and leaned over, plac-
ing a small kiss on the top of the girl's head. "Hey,
Little Bit, you look like you've already had a long
day," Taylor said, noticing how tired the young
woman looked, brushing her fingers against her
cheek.*

"Excuse me," the nurse interrupted.

*That's when Taylor gave the woman the look. Tor-
rey witnessed it plenty of times. Taylor recently per-
fected it, finding it most beneficial to instill the fear
of God into her employees. Of course, it deflated the
dark-haired woman's ego a bit when she used it on her*

roommate and Torrey merely laughed at her. She realized then, that it helped if the person didn't know you had no intention of wringing their neck.

The ebony-haired artist pulled herself up to her full height, arms crossed upon her chest. She shook back loose strands of hair that framed impossibly high cheekbones, an eyebrow arching up and disappearing beneath dark bangs. "Yesss," she purred.

"Can I help you?" The nurse asked.

Torrey had to reach her hand up over her mouth to cover her smile. Oh, someone should have warned this old gal.

"Nooo, I've done my part," Taylor whispered quietly, winking at the nurse as she looked from Torrey's swollen belly to the old woman.

Torrey was biting her lip to hold back her laughter by this time. Taylor had a look on her face that was as serious as surgery as the nurse sputtered and coughed. "Do you belong here?" the flustered woman asked.

"I belong to her," Taylor replied, her fingers drumming against her crossed upper arm, the band on her finger gleaming as the light caught it.

The nurse looked at the ring and then at the ring on Torrey's hand, opening her mouth to say something, but thought better about it as Taylor's smile turned into a withering "back off" glare. The old woman turned on her heel and disappeared into the back office.

* * * * * * * * * *

"Taylor, do you want to listen?" Joanna Weller, Torrey's doctor asked. She offered the stethoscope *portion of the Doppler to the tall woman.*

"Yea, why not? I bet he's singing Gene Pitney or Tony Bennett." She winked at her young friend, lying on the examining table.

Torrey giggled at the remark and watched as her friend's eyes widened slightly, the corners of her mouth curling upward, then breaking into a toothy grin.

"That is totally cool!" She pulled off the earpieces and grinned at her friend. "That's some good work you're doing, Little Bit."

Dr. Weller wrote in Torrey's chart. She watched the two women and couldn't think of a better pair to raise a child. It seemed obvious they adored one another. "Well, everything looks great. I've got all the information you'll need for your Lamaze classes here, Torrey," she said, laying a few papers on the table beside the young woman as Torrey buttoned her blouse. "I do have a small group that will be meeting on Monday nights that's comprised of female partners. We have five couples so far, if the two of you would be more comfortable in that class," Joanna offered.

"Uhm," Taylor started, feeling she was going to have to explain.

"That would be great," Torrey answered, without hearing Taylor's voice or seeing the look of stunned amazement on the taller woman's face.

Once they were outside of the office Torrey turned to her friend. "I guess I should have asked you first. I mean, you may not even want to go to Lamaze with me."

"Hey, we're in this together, right?" Torrey

smiled down affectionately at her.

* * * * * * * * * *

Taylor stumbled into the darkened kitchen to get a drink of water. The muffled sound of crying woke her from her drowsy half-sleep state. She quietly peeked into the living room and saw Torrey huddled on one end of the couch.

"Torrey, are you okay?" the older woman asked in alarm.

Taylor surprised the young woman. She wiped her cheeks with the sleeve of her robe. "I'm all right," Torrey answered.

Taylor sat next to the blonde, stretching her arm along the back of the couch, her chest pressed softly against the smaller woman's back. Taylor ran her hand up the woman's arm reassuringly. "Honey, what's wrong?"

"I'm going to be a terrible mother," Torrey blurted out.

Taylor smiled and chuckled out loud. "Torrey, you're going to be a great mother." Taylor comforted her.

"Yea, well I bet Evelyn thought that, too. Look what happened there." Torrey's tears reasserted themselves.

Torrey recently started calling her mother by her first name. The fight the two engaged in was almost enough to melt the phone wires when the young woman told her mother of her plans to keep her baby. When Torrey told her that she would be living with Taylor and the artist would be providing for she and her baby, Evelyn exploded. The things she said to her daughter that evening, the names she called her, caused an incendiary reaction from Taylor, who was listening in on the extension per Torrey's request.

The dark-haired woman slammed the phone down in her hand and quickly walked into the other room. She pulled the receiver from Torrey's hand. "Torrey, go take a walk," Taylor hissed.

Taylor's eyes turned dark with anger and she was trying to control herself in front of her small friend. Torrey, sobbing hysterically by now, ran outside, but as soon as she heard the door close behind ner, she heard the first few words Taylor had to say to the woman on the phone.

"You goddamn bitch..."

They never talked about what happened after. Torrey never asked her friend what words were exchanged and Taylor didn't volunteer the information. Now, sitting in the dark with Torrey in her arms, Taylor felt something inside her that said Torrey would be a wonderful mother. She felt this young woman's child would be blessed with a love beyond anything Torrey could now imagine.

"Whoa, wanna feel something neat?" Torrey took hold of Taylor's hand and placed the woman's palm on her abdomen.

"Wow," Taylor exclaimed as she felt the baby's kick for herself. "Does that hurt?"

"No, it just feels kind of...I don't know, weird," Torrey answered.

Torrey relaxed back against her friend, Taylor resting her chin on the smaller woman's shoulder. "Hey, Tor, after the baby's born, why don't we take a *little vacation?" Taylor asked.*

"Did you have somewhere in mind?"

"Ever been to California?" Taylor asked, already knowing the answer.

"No. Are you thinking of taking me?" Torrey laughed.

"I thought it might be kind of cool. I could show you where us beach bums grew up and you could meet my mom. I may be a little on the wild side now, but I guarantee you, my mom knew all the tricks. I'm sure she can give us some pointers."

Torrey smiled at the way Taylor said, "give us" some pointers. She enjoyed the feeling that they were a family, even if it was only temporary.

"You will be a great mom," Taylor whispered in the young woman's ear.

"How do you know?" Torrey asked.

"Because, like you're so fond of telling me, every- thing happens for a reason. You're having this baby for a reason. You have so much love to give, Tor. I just can't picture you being a bad mother. I don't think you have it in you. I think you'd do any- thing...make any sacrifice to see that your baby grew up healthy and happy," Taylor responded.

****

"Hi, I picked up Chinese. I hope that's okay?" Jessica said as she walked into the loft loaded down with her treasures.

"That sounds good; smells good too," Torrey said with a smile. "I'm more than ready for a break."

Jessica watched her mother's face when the older

woman wasn't looking. The young girl noticed that the purplish bruise seemed even larger than it did last night. The fact that her mother's eyes told her she spent the afternoon crying didn't escape her attention either.

They sat on the living room floor, a number of food cartons still spread out on top of the coffee table. They didn't converse much, but mother and daughter enjoyed the time simply because they weren't fighting. These kinds of interludes were rare for them lately.

They both leaned back against the couch, but eventually Torrey moved up to sit on the piece of furniture. "God, I'm getting too old for hardwood floors," she laughed.

After a few moments, Jessica turned and leaned her elbow on the seat of the sofa by her mother's legs. "So, are you gonna send me to one of those drug rehab places in Malaysia, where they treat you like POW's?" Jessica asked quietly.

"Where in the world would you get an idea like that?" Torrey asked, sitting up a little straighter.

"I saw something on *60 Minutes*. These parents were all happy, even though it looked like their kids were all brainwashed zombies when they got out," Jessica replied. Deep down, she didn't think her mother would really set her up in a place like that, but she'd crossed the line this time and there was no telling what that might prompt her usually loving mother to do.

"I have no intention of sending you anyplace like that."

"But, you are sending me somewhere, aren't

you?" Jessica questioned.

Okay, here goes. "I thought it might be a little fun for you. You've never been to California. Well, actually you have, but I don't think you would remember, considering the fact you were only five months old at the time," Torrey answered.

"Is it like Betty Ford or something?" Jessica asked nervously.

"Jess, I'd like you to go live with Taylor for six months," Torrey said seriously.

"I don't even know her, Mom. I mean, I know you two are like friends forever and she's the most incredible woman in the world, according to you, but she's a stranger to me," Jessica explained. "Couldn't I just go to school or live in an apartment out there?"

"Honey, first of all, I'm not sending you out there to get rid of you or so that you can live it up." Torrey reached down and stroked her daughter's hair. Jessica rarely accepted affection from her anymore and she could tell that, even though her daughter was trying, the young girl still tensed at first. "Second of all, do you really think you've earned the right to go out there unsupervised?" Torrey asked.

"I guess not," Jessica answered.

The young woman closed her eyes and enjoyed her mother's touch. It bothered her a little at first, but suddenly she was craving the tender caresses. A feeling like fear ran through her. She would not only be living with a stranger, but for the first time in seventeen years, without her mother. Jessica lay her head on her mother's knee and let the woman's soothing voice comfort her for the first time in a long time.

"I already asked Taylor and she's looking forward

to it."

"Mom," Jessica smirked up at her mother, "either you're lying or you didn't tell her what I've been up to lately."

Torrey returned the comment with a grin. *God, she looks so much like Taylor when she does that.* "Touché. Let's just say she's looking forward to seeing *you* again," Torrey replied.

"At least it sounds a little more honest. I barely remember her, though," Jessica said. Her remark tinged with worry.

"You used to cry if she wasn't home to tuck you in. She loved you very much," Torrey finished quietly.

Her mother told stories of her as a young child and her interaction with Taylor, but she couldn't remember much of it. She was only two-years-old when the two women went their separate ways, but sometimes when Jessica watched her mother doing simple ordinary tasks, she would get the feeling that she witnessed the same scene once before, but her mother was not alone in her memory. There was always a dark figure that stood silently alongside her mother, but Jessica couldn't put a face to the apparition.

After so many years it was almost as if the silent stranger wasn't real, only a part of Jessica's dreams. Sometimes in the middle of the night, when the nightmares of a child felt like reality, there was always a memory of someone in her dreams that protected her. Her dream guardian was as dark as her mother was light, filled with a power and grace that haunted the young girl's senses for many years.

"If she loved me so much and you two got along so well, then why didn't you stay together?"

"It's...complicated," Torrey answered, and Jessica knew by the look her mother was giving her, there would be no more explanation than that. "It's funny. I met Taylor for the first time when I was your age," Torrey mused aloud. "You promised me, Jess. Will you keep that promise?" Torrey asked, pulling her daughter's chin up until their eyes met.

Jessica tried to give her mother a casual smile. "I promise, Mom. I won't let you down this time," she responded.

"I know how hard what I'm asking you to do is, Jess. When you have one of those overwhelming days just remember, I believe in you, honey," Torrey replied, leaning down to kiss her daughter's head.

Both women held tight to the spoken promise and the reassurance, wondering if the promise would actually be kept.

November 1982

"Torrey," Taylor shouted with her hand over the receiver of the phone. "It's Joanna. She wants to know how you're feeling."

Dr. Weller called once a day to check on Torrey's condition since she'd hit the ninth month. It wasn't usual for women having their first baby to be overdue, but it wasn't rare either. The doctor tried to explain to Torrey that the young woman's calculations as to the date of conception may have been off a little. The small blonde had to indignantly explain to the good doctor that she'd only had sex with a man once in her entire life to get this way, and that date was not one she would easily forget.

"Tor, are you awake?" Taylor called again. She lifted her hand off the receiver and talked to Joanna.

Torrey's head popped out of her bedroom door. "Tell her it's been nine months, I want it out!" Torrey shouted back.

"Did you hear that?" Taylor asked the doctor. "Oh no, she's in a lovely mood," the dark-haired woman answered sarcastically. Taylor laughed at something else the doctor said, and then looked up as Torrey came into the room.

"Don't hang up," Torrey said in a serious voice. "My water just broke."

"Hey, doc," Taylor grinned into the phone, "I think it's show time!"

* * * * * * * * * *

"You're up to six," the older nurse said a little too cheerily for the two women.

"Six...that's good, right?" Torrey said between pants as her contraction ended.

"Well, it's better than three and that's what you were at this morning when you came in. Torrey, what I'm putting on now is a fetal heart monitor," the nurse said.

"Is that necessary?" Taylor asked with a worried expression.

"It's okay." The nurse patted the dark-haired woman's shoulder as she worked around her. "We always put it on for women opting for natural child *birth and no drugs. It will let the doctor know if the baby is in any distress. It's all right, see, your baby's got a nice strong heartbeat."* She pointed to the small monitor by the bed.

Another contraction hit Torrey and she squeezed Taylor's hand, a grimace of pain crossing her face until the muscle action subsided.

The nurse gently pushed Torrey's damp bangs from her forehead and gave her a few ice chips. She smiled down at the young woman before she turned to leave. "You know, if you two wanted a baby, you should have let her have it." The nurse jerked a thumb at Taylor. "With her hips she would have had a much easier time." She winked at Torrey and walked from the room.

Torrey laughed at the expression on her friend's normally reserved face. "Oh, don't look that way," Torrey chuckled.

"For God's sake, Tor, that woman just said I had big hips!"

Torrey winced as another contraction tightened her abdomen.

Taylor was looking down into her own lap. "Do you think I have big hips?" she asked.

"Taylor! Do you think we could focus on why we're here?" Torrey hissed.

"Oh, I'm sorry," Taylor apologized, moving over to help her friend with the breathing techniques they learned in Lamaze class.

For the next hours, Taylor knew how fathers felt in the delivery room. She felt utterly useless and entirely helpless to take away any of her friend's pain. All she could do was fetch, carry, coach, massage, anything to try to ease the young woman's suffering. Although, throughout the entire ordeal, Torrey caught occasional glimpses of her tall friend looking down at her hips and frowning. To Torrey, that made it worth it all.

Chapter
5

Taylor shifted her feet nervously as she stood at
the arrival gate at John Wayne Airport. She milled
about with a number of people who also appeared to
be waiting for incoming flights. Finally, she leaned
her tall frame against the back wall. The flight was
supposed to be on time, five more minutes until she
made a total ass out of herself in front of a seventeen-
year-old girl.

The dark-haired woman drew a few double takes
from passersby, but in Southern California that was to
be expected. They probably thought the tall beauty
was an actress, knowing they'd seen her face, but not
remembering from where. She stood, clothed in her
best black leather blazer, white starched shirt, and
frayed denim jeans. Her leather boots were worn and
comfortable. If one could remember last month's
issue of *Architectural Digest*, they would have recognized her from the cover. She wore the same outfit,

except the leather blazer was a leather vest, and she stood posed in front of her latest sculptures, inside of the studio in her home.

Taylor's cellular phone trilled and she reached into her jacket pocket to answer the call. "Yea," she growled impatiently.

"Geez, you must not have had your coffee yet this morning," the voice said to her.

Taylor's frown turned into a smile and anyone watching would have been amazed at the transformation. "Honey, her plane hasn't even landed yet," Taylor chuckled. She was still surprised that the old term of endearment rolled off her tongue so easily.

"I guess I'm nervous..." Torrey trailed off.

"You're nervous?" Taylor responded.

"Are you sure about this, Stretch?" Torrey asked.

"I find this an extremely interesting time to ask me that."

The writer laughed and Taylor imagined she was running her fingers through her blonde hair, which in truth, she was. "Torrey..." the artist slowly drawled.

Torrey felt a distinct shiver run up her spine when Taylor drew out her name that way. She swallowed hard, wondering what the woman was up to. "Yes?" she asked.

"Are you going to call me everyday for the next six months? Not that I'm complaining considering this is the most we've talked in fourteen years, but I just wondered if I should call and up my allotment of minutes on the cell phone or not," Taylor teased.

"Oh, very funny, Stretch," Torrey shot back. She could hear Taylor's lilting laughter and it pulled at her heart.

Taylor knew this would happen. All the years apart melted away into nothing as soon as she heard Torrey's voice last week, this was why she distanced the two of them, physically. She teased the younger woman, but they *had* spoken for at least a few minutes everyday since Torrey's first call. Of course, it was about Jessica and the arrangements to be made, but Taylor craved the sound of her friend's voice. The dark-haired woman understood plenty about addictions and she just fell into the classic trap; once you go back, it's harder to give it up than it was the first time.

"Will I be able to talk to you at all?" Taylor heard Torrey's voice ask.

The artist tried to focus on the reason she and her friend were even talking in the first place. She always tried to be honest with Torrey, about everything, aside from her own heart, and she wasn't going to stop now.

"You know I have to admit, Little Bit, that hearing your voice has got me feeling better than I have in a long time. I enjoy it and I don't think I'm going to like giving it up again, but I want Jess to feel like she can trust me. I don't want her to think I'm reporting back to her mother everyday. This whole thing is going to be rough enough on her without that added pressure. Even if things go great and she gets her act together, she'll have setbacks and bad days. I want her to feel like she's living in the kind of environment where it's okay for that to happen," Taylor finished.

"You're right, I agree. So, six months then," Torrey said softly.

"Six months," Taylor repeated. "I'll still e-mail

and let you know how I'm doing, just like before, and
you know I'll call right away if anything goes
wrong...which it won't," she quickly interjected.

"I know you're right, Stretch. I can do this, can't
I?" Torrey asked.

"Yea, honey, I know you can. Hey, plane's in,
guess I better go meet the kid."

"Good luck, Stretch," Torrey said not wanting to
hang up the phone. "You'll make a great mom," she
finished as the line went dead in Taylor's hand.

November 1982

*"Looks like you're ready." Doctor Weller smiled
at the young woman.*

*"Joanna," Torrey panted, "remember when Tay-
lor said she'd do this for me if there was a way? You
heard her say that, right?"*

*"I believe I did." The doctor watched the con-
fused artist's face with amusement.*

*"I think I'd like to go with that option right now,
if you don't mind," Torrey said casting a grimace in
her tall friend's direction.*

*Joanna laughed at the young woman and the look
on Taylor's face. "Don't worry Taylor. Most of the
husbands that come through here get told the same
thing."*

****

*"Okay, Torrey, I want one more big push from
you," Doctor Weller said from behind her mask.*

The doctor was worried about the small woman. Another couple of strong pushes and the baby's shoulder would be through. The only problem was that Torrey had such a long and painful pre-labor; the young woman was near exhaustion.

Taylor sat behind her friend, supporting her back and giving her a hand to hold onto. "Come on, honey, one more push," Taylor encouraged.

"I can do this. Right, Stretch?" Torrey breathed hard through her mouth, squeezing her friend's hand.

"You betch ya can...come on, Little Bit," Taylor replied.

"Okay, Torrey, breath in and out a few times, then bear down...ready?" Joanna instructed.

Torrey breathed in and out.

"Okay, now push...come on, that's it," Joanna said loudly over Torrey's cries.

Suddenly Torrey screamed as a stabbing pain pierced through her abdomen, stealing her breath away.

"Tor, are you okay?" Taylor asked, her face filled with fear and concern.

"Torrey, stop...stop pushing!" Joanna yelled. "Taylor get out of there and lay her down. Jill, get an IV going, call over to surgery and tell them we're coming in. NOW!"

"Taylor?" Torrey called weakly as her mouth and nose were covered with an oxygen mask.

Taylor was physically pushed aside as the fetal heart monitor blared out its warning sound. Nurses moved in all directions.

"What the hell is wrong?" Taylor shouted over the sudden confusion.

"Not now, Taylor," Joanna Weller shouted back, moving through the double doors that exited into the Labor and Delivery surgical area.

"Torrey!" Taylor yelled as the double doors slammed shut and the dark-haired woman was unceremoniously deposited into a small waiting room.

****

Taylor bent her knees to sit simply because she felt they wouldn't hold her weight any longer. She never felt so frightened or helpless in her entire life. It all happened so fast. One minute she was seated behind Torrey, the next minute they were wheeling the exhausted woman into surgery. In the chaos, no one even had time to tell Taylor what was going on.

I can't lose her, not now...please, I can't lose her.

Taylor closed her eyes tightly, her folded hands pressed close against her lips, the knuckles white with tension. She silently prayed to a Higher Power that she wasn't even sure existed. Rocking herself forward and back, her lips moving in silent prayer, she begged for the life of the woman she loved and their baby. It was at this moment of understanding that she thought of Torrey's child as her child also. She could have sat like that for five minutes or five hours; she was completely lost in her entreaty. So caught up in her meditation she didn't feel the hand on her shoulder.

"I'm so sorry, Taylor." Joanna Weller was at her side.

Taylor looked up at the doctor as tears spilled from her eyes.

"I'm sorry I couldn't take the time to let you know

what was going on, I needed to work quickly," the doctor apologized.

"Torrey? The baby?" Taylor was almost afraid to ask.

"Mom and the baby are doing just great." Joanna smiled down at the seated woman.

Taylor lowered her head and continued to cry. She didn't really know why, but she felt like an emotional wreck. *"Can I see them?"* She wiped her eyes with the sleeve of the scrub top she wore.

"Torrey's not awake, but she's in the Recovery Room. You can take a quick peek at her, okay?" She motioned for Taylor to follow her.

"What the hell happened in there?" Taylor asked.

"The umbilical cord ended up around the baby's neck, it all happened pretty fast. I had to go in and do a c-section, but Taylor..." Joanna stopped the taller woman before they entered the Recovery Room. *"Torrey had more of a problem than that. She was bleeding a great deal, from what's known as a uterine torsion. She had a big baby and, well, she's a tiny gal. Her uterus kind of went through what you might do when you twirl a wet towel. It twisted and,"* Joanna paused, lowering her eyes, then returning her gaze to the tall woman before her, *"I had to perform a hysterectomy to get the bleeding under control. I'm sorry, I hated like hell to do that when she's so young, but I didn't have much of a choice."*

A wave of pain visibly washed across Taylor's face and she understood how this would impact her small friend. Taylor hoped that someday Torrey would be able to have the love and the family the young woman deserved, but this would be the only *child for her young friend.*

"I'll tell her...later on, when she wakes up," Taylor said softly.

Walking in to the Recovery Room and up to the gurney that held the tiny blonde, Taylor took in the pale features. Moving carefully around the IV's and blood tubing, Taylor wrapped a hand around Torrey's cold fingers. Not caring who might be watching, she bent down and brushed her lips lightly against the soft lips of the sleeping woman.

"So, do you want to meet your daughter?" Joanna asked.

Taylor grinned. A girl. "Uhm, maybe I should wait for Torrey."

"Come on." Joanna pulled her out of the Recovery Room. The doctor saw the look in Taylor's eye and knew she'd never make it until Torrey woke up.

The two women put on masks and fresh lab coats and Dr. Weller led her into the Nursery. "The Gray baby," the doctor told the nurse.

A young nurse walked up with a small, screaming bundle in her arms. Taylor looked up at the two women with a sudden panic in her eyes. "I—I've never held a baby before. I can't break her or anything, can I?"

The nurse was helpful and patient, asking Taylor to sit in the wooden rocking chair behind her. Then, she demonstrated to the tall woman how to support the baby's head and neck. When the pint-size body lay in Taylor's arms, she pulled back the blanket to reveal the tiniest creature she'd ever seen.

"Oh, God, she's beautiful. She's so tiny." Taylor grinned up at the nurse and the doctor. "I mean, she's

perfect, just like a regular person, but her nose and ears and everything...I mean she's just like a tiny little person," Taylor babbled.

The dark-haired woman knew she was grinning like an idiot behind the mask, but she couldn't stop herself. Then she couldn't stop the tears that fell at the sight of this perfect, beautiful creature.

Oh, yea, *Joanna Weller thought to herself.* This one is going to make a great mom.

****

Taylor pulled back as the passengers streamed through the arrival gate of Flight 119. She wanted to see Jessica before the young woman saw her. She couldn't explain it, but she wanted the chance to prepare herself, and she wondered if the young girl was as terrified as she was. The dark-haired woman self-consciously wiped her sweaty palms along muscled thighs.

Taylor didn't even have a recent picture to go on. Torrey told her that Jessica absolutely refused to be photographed the last few years. When the older woman asked how she would recognize her friend's daughter, Torrey laughed.

"She looks and acts just like you did when I first met you, Stretch," Torrey said.

Taylor's groan could be heard through the telephone line. "Little Bit, are you sure you wouldn't rather have that kidney?"

The young girl walked among a number of other passengers, looking around, trying to catch sight of a familiar face. Taylor smiled. Torrey was right on the money. It was odd how Jess looked so much like the woman standing in the background. Of course, if anyone knew Torrey's face half as well as Taylor did they would say the young girl looked exactly like her mother, green eyes that sparkled with mischief, nose slightly upturned, and the subtle air that this girl had the potential to be a total wise ass.

Jessica saw the woman as she pushed herself off the back wall and sliced through the crowd to make her way to where the young girl stopped. An odd feeling of déjà vu passed through the young girl and she could see why her mother always described Taylor as incredibly beautiful. She was, and then some.

Jessica was caught up in the woman's strength. Up until this moment, if asked, Jessica would have said her mother was the strongest woman she ever knew, but her mom's power was deceptive. She knew her mother could have broken her like a twig if she had wanted, but Torrey's size gave her a subtle advantage; she was able to camouflage her strength. The woman walking toward Jessica simply exuded power and energy. She not only had a commanding aura about her, but her physical appearance was overwhelming. Jessica watched the play of corded muscles in the top of the woman's hand as she grabbed one of the girl's bags.

Jessica was nervous about the whole deal and, unfortunately, when she was nervous or scared her best self didn't shine through. When it came right down to it, Jessica lashed out when she was frightened and became a smart-ass bitch. It was very unfortunate for her that she was about to meet the master of attitude.

Taylor knew the first few minutes, or even hours, had to be played carefully; or else she would lose control as Torrey had. The delicate chess game was about to begin. *Taylor moved her white pawn first.*

"Hello, Jess. Welcome to California," Taylor said with a slightly reserved smile.

"From the famous author," Jessica said as she moved past the taller woman, thrusting an envelope at her as she passed.

The envelope was torn open. That's when Jessica made the mistake of smirking up at the older woman. *Black pawn moves forward.*

Taylor's eyes didn't reflect half of the anger she felt at this moment, and she cursed herself for letting the girl push her buttons this fast. *Black takes white pawn.* "I see your mother's having that old trouble of not being able to seal her packages properly," Taylor returned dryly.

The envelope held a letter from Torrey that Taylor quickly scanned. It didn't say much; Torrey must have realized that her daughter would open the small package. Inside the letter was a ten thousand-dollar check. "For Jessica's expenses," the letter stated. Taylor shook her head. She would put the money in the same place she put all the checks Torrey sent her over the years.

When Torrey moved up into the ranks of successful authors she started sending Taylor checks as repayment for the time they lived together, raising Jessica. Taylor was never offended; she knew that was just the way Torrey was. The young writer was proud, never wanting to owe anyone a thing.

At first, the artist refused to cash the checks, then

she came up with a solution that made her happy and caused Torrey to think her friend accepted the money. Taylor opened a trust account for Jessica with Torrey as executrix years ago in Maine. After Stephen was killed, Torrey's nightmares prompted Taylor to sell her beloved Harley. She deposited the money into an account and forgot all about it. She'd been depositing the checks in that same account over the years. By now, the account held enough to pay for Jessica's college education twice over, if the girl could keep her life in order long enough to go.

"One thing you have to say about Mom. She's not cheap," Jessica said flippantly.

Taylor felt a response rise to her lips and made a conscious decision to go ahead with it. Torrey may have decided to be long suffering with her daughter's attitude, but Taylor was going to make it clear that she wasn't about to put up with it. "You ought to be surprised she thought you were worth that much." Taylor sneered as she walked past the girl toward the luggage carousel.

Jessica stopped short at the taller woman's response. She hadn't expected that. *White knight takes black bishop...queen's in trouble. Check.*

Silence ruled as Taylor led their way to the black Ford Explorer. She thought earlier about impressing the girl with the red Mercedes, but knew the luggage would be a problem. Since the young girl was being a total pain in the ass, she was glad she hadn't bothered.

Unlocking the back hatch, she lifted the lid and quickly stowed the young girl's luggage. *Jesus, she's got more shit than her mother did when we went to school for four years.*

Taylor pulled out into the fast moving traffic smoothly, years of driving California's highways under her belt. It's funny how silence can unnerve some people more than anything. Taylor was comfortable with the quiet. It drove Jessica nuts. The young girl was accustomed to her mother's endless chatter and never realized before what a comfort sound her mother's voice was to her.

She watched the artist out of the corner of her eye. Taylor seemed lost in her own thoughts, listening to her favorite Gene Pitney CD on the car stereo, her blue eyes unseen behind dark Ray Bans. Jessica was going out of her mind. She was getting desperate for a little conversation.

"Is it always this warm in the winter?" she asked, hoping to get the ball rolling. At home, all she had to do was ask one question to get her mom going.

"Pretty much," Taylor answered.

Taylor watched as the young girl fidgeted and tapped her fingers on her legs. The tall woman never let on that she knew, but she had a feeling any daughter of Torrey's would be used to a lot more verbal stimulation than would be forthcoming from Taylor.

Jessica couldn't stand it any longer. She reached her hand out to adjust the controls of the stereo and listen to some music *she* liked.

It was so fast that Jessica didn't see it coming until the hand was around her wrist. Instinctively she tried to pull back, but the older woman held her hand in an iron grip, never turning toward the girl, her eyes fastened on the traffic ahead of them. "Do not touch things that don't belong to you without permission," Taylor hissed.

Once released, Jessica rubbed her wrist and stared over at Taylor like the older woman was some kind of psychopath. "I only wanted to see what was on the radio," the young girl whined.

"But, it's *my* radio," Taylor shot back.

Five more minutes of silence went by and Taylor could see the war the young girl was waging on the inside by the expressions on her face. "May I please change the radio station?" Jessica asked, hating herself for giving in.

Taylor didn't grin or laugh, even though she wanted to do both. "Yes, you may," she said, hitting a button to stop the CD and switching it over to the radio.

Black queen outmaneuvered. Checkmate.

Chapter
6

They drove for about an hour; Taylor only
answering questions when Jessica asked. There
would be plenty of time for talk in the next six
months, but right now, the dark-haired artist was trying to establish a sort of pack dominance. She wanted
the young girl to be clear on the fact that Taylor was
the alpha female in this house.

Jessica would have had an even better time had
she not been sulking so much. Being a big city girl,
she never knew this part of the country could be so
beautiful. Taylor knew the drive down to Dana Point
on the Pacific Coast Highway would impress the
young girl.

"Are those really seals down there?" Jessica
asked in amazement, peering down at the rocks in the
water.

"Yep. Bet you don't have those in Chicago, huh?"
Taylor responded.

"That's for sure." Jessica grinned and for a moment forgot to be angry with the tall stranger.

They pulled off the highway and went by the harbor, headed up toward the cliffs. They stopped at a locked gate and Taylor punched in a series of numbers on a keypad inside the car.

"Looks like the outside of a prison." Jessica referred to the gate.

"I'll give you the codes. It's not as if you're a prisoner here, Jess," Taylor explained as the black gate swung opened and automatically closed behind them. "I have a lot of expensive work up there and it has to be protected."

"Whoa," Jessica exclaimed as they pulled into the garage. The young girl was quick to get out and examine the red convertible Mercedes. "Nice ride," she remarked.

"Thanks," Taylor replied proudly.

* * * * * * * * * *

Jessica was desperately trying not to walk around the place with her mouth open. All she kept thinking was that her mom would love this place. Skylights and stained glass were in practically every room. It was obvious an artist lived there. The rooms were decorated with a practiced eye and impeccable taste.

They walked around a huge kitchen that looked like it was rarely used. "We can go grocery shopping tomorrow. I've got the bare necessities, but my hours and my eating habits aren't too regular. I promised your mom I would feed you right, so I'll try to limit our trips to the Pizza Outlet to twice a week. Oh, wait a minute, can you cook?" Taylor hurriedly added.

"You're kidding, right?" Jessica looked at the woman in surprise.

"Well, who cooks for you back home?" Taylor asked.

"Mom. Who cooked when you two lived together?" JT returned.

"Your mom." Taylor looked a little sheepish. "Okay, tomorrow we go shopping for groceries *and* a cookbook."

"This is your room," Taylor said opening the door to a large room with its own balcony and a bath. "You can change anything you want, I wasn't too sure about your tastes. If you're anything like your mom, you'll love going shopping to fix it up." She smirked.

"I take it shopping isn't your favorite thing?" Jessica asked.

"Not in a million years will I understand the concept of a bargain. If I need it, I buy it. If I don't, then I leave it be," Taylor replied.

"Well, you must have been loads of fun to live with," Jessica said dryly.

"You're about to find out, darlin'," Taylor chuckled. "Do you want the rest of the tour?"

"Sure, just let me get some bread crumbs so I can find my way back again," Jessica said.

"Oh," Taylor said bringing her brows together and pursing her lips, "that's very funny."

Taylor's home was larger than the woman would ever need, but she was proud of what she put into it. She led Jessica through the small gymnasium and spa on the floor beneath the young girl's bedroom, then led her through a series of rooms designed as game and entertainment rooms before heading back up the stairs. On the other end of the house was the library, and Taylor' private office, which was connected to her bedroom.

When Jessica tried, unsuccessfully, to turn the knob she realized the door was locked. She turned a questioning head in the tall woman's direction.

"Those are my private rooms, my bedroom and office. I would appreciate if you didn't go in there," Taylor replied to the unasked question. "I like to have someplace to myself."

Jessica shrugged and turned the corner toward the very back of the house. "Wow, that's incredible," the young girl said of the stained glass set in the double doors. "My mom has a necklace just like that."

Taylor smiled at the mention of the familiar object that Torrey always wore around her neck. Her brother gave it to her before he died. The small blonde confided that it was her brother who first introduced her to the Tai Chi and it's philosophies. The symbol came to mean a great deal to the dark-haired artist, since her friend acquainted her with its meaning. So much so, that she commissioned a glass artist to create the symbol in stained glass for the entrance to her studio.

Jessica ran her fingers along the glass, the yin/ yang symbol was split in two halves at the top of the door, but the bottom portion of the doors displayed the halves set into a whole, one complete symbol on each door. The round circles within the black and white halves were made of molded glass, one black, and one white sun and moon face.

Taylor pushed open the doors. There was more of

a mess than usual, and more completed pieces sat around the perimeter of the studio than was customary, due to the upcoming show. A feeling of trepidation passed through the artist at the young girl's reaction to her work. Taylor molded herself into a hard woman on the outside, but she was far from being secure on the inside. She stood there waiting for the girl's first biting comment.

"This is so very cool! You get to work here all day?" Before waiting for an answer, Jessica inspected some large sculptures that were well over seven feet tall. "Excellent," the young girl said as her hands ran across the smooth lines of the wood, investigating the highly erotic piece of female imagery.

All of Taylor's work symbolized the female form. She was able to cut from wood or stone, slices of life that symbolized the strength of women. Not just in character, but the strength of a mother lifting her child high over her head, or of two women making love. The sculpture that Jessica was viewing was such a work. A little more risqué than most of Taylor's pieces, but Samantha insisted it still go into the show.

The sculpture was carved from Mahogany and pictured two women in the act of making love. The manifestation of a woman's strength was never illustrated any more powerfully than this. Both women displayed arms and back muscles bunched, necks straining in their passion, thigh muscles flexed taut. The part that Taylor wasn't sure people could handle was displayed when you walked around the sculpture and viewed it from the opposite side. One of the women had entered the other with her fingers, and the look of rapture on the other woman's face was apparent, but the shoulders and back of the woman on top was a lesson in anatomy as striated muscles disclosed an inordinate amount of power and passion. The viewer was automatically drawn to that woman's arm, not so much for where her hand ended up, but from the power and energy exhibited in the tightly corded tendons that wrapped around the arm, as the woman thrust her hand into her lover.

Jessica was caught up in the whole studio and she stopped at nearly every piece to examine it.

"This is an incredible place to work," Jessica said with enthusiasm, looking out the glass windows that ran the length of one wall. The ocean and the harbor displayed below were breathtaking.

"Your mom tells me you draw," Taylor said trying to shift the focus off her a little.

"Yea, well, I do, but nothing like this." She indicated everything around her.

"Well, if you like we can get some stuff and set you up over there, I don't use that end much. You know, table and such. Who knows, you might find the view more inspirational than Lake Michigan."

Suddenly Jessica felt herself smiling and that made her bad temper flare. She didn't like the fact that she was letting this woman's talent and easy manner seduce her into being the perfect little girl. *Doesn't she know I'll just blow it? Doesn't she get it? Well, she'll find out soon enough.*

"Whatever," the girl said as she walked from the studio, leaving Taylor to wonder at the young woman's rapid change in behavior.

The two spent the rest of the day getting used to

what it would be like to have a stranger by their side for the next six months. Jessica roamed outside and considered that it would be nice to be somewhere for the winter that didn't get down to forty below zero in January. Taylor left the girl to her own devices, not wanting to hover over her, and also encouraging Jessica to become familiar with her new home.

"Hey, what do you say to pizza, you hungry?" Taylor found Jessica outside with the headphones to her CD player on and a sketchbook in her lap.

"I could eat. Wait a minute. You're not one of those California people that put stuff like pineapple and artichokes on their pizza, are you?" Jessica asked.

"I've always found pepperoni and mushrooms to be enough for me," the dark-haired woman replied.

"Sounds good to me," Jessica responded.

By the time the Pizza Outlet delivered their dinner, Taylor already gave the young woman the tour of the kitchen.

"Can I ask you a question?" Jessica asked.

"Shoot."

"Do you ever use anything in here? I mean, everything looks brand new," she said.

Taylor's eyes swept across the large kitchen. How could she tell the young girl that she didn't have the house built for her alone? *How do I tell her that everything here, the kitchen, the stained glass, the Japanese garden; were all built with Torrey in mind?*

"Well, like I said I don't really keep many regular hours, and my eating habits are none too standard. I guess I always figured that someday I'd get around to learning how to cook," Taylor finished as she pulled a wineglass from the cabinet. Absently weighing the glass in her hand, Taylor seemed momentarily lost in thought.

"My mom does that when I'm around too," Jessica said noticing Taylor's actions.

"What?" the older woman asked.

"She doesn't drink in front of me."

"Drink?" Taylor appeared confused.

"Actually, it bugs me more to know people are giving up something because of me. Look, if you want to have a drink, just go ahead, I'm not gonna freak out or anything."

Taylor looked at the glass in her hand, realization setting in. "Oh," the artist chuckled, and then she filled the glass with ice cubes and grabbed a can of soda from the refrigerator.

Jessica was a little surprised and her face displayed that fact. She wasn't used to someone listening to her like that. She never expected the dark-haired woman to forgo a glass of wine simply out of courtesy. That didn't seem her style.

Taylor saw the play of emotions on the girl's face. She thought that the sooner Jessica recognized the fact that a woman of integrity lives by her word, the better off the young woman would be. "This is the strongest stuff I drink nowadays," Taylor explained, sitting down at the table.

"You don't drink alcohol at all...you mean that?"

"I don't say things unless I really mean them," Taylor said to the girl's slightly shocked demeanor, as she took a sip of the soda. "I had some problems with drugs when I was younger," the artist added in explanation.

"So, what's that have to do with alcohol?" Jessica

asked in confusion.

Taylor gave her a little half smile. It's the first question most people asked and she was used to it. "Alcohol *is* a drug, Jess. When you start thinking of it as being different from other drugs, that it's not the same or it doesn't count, that's when you can get in real trouble."

By the time dinner was over, Taylor was mildly amused by the fact that Jessica was able to bring the artist out of her shell and actually volunteer information instead of playing twenty questions. Jessica told Taylor about the last school she went to before being thrown out. The one saving grace of the institution, in Jessica's mind, was their art department. She told the older woman seated across from her of the young teacher who did everything in her power to keep Jess out of trouble and in school, but when it came right down to it, Jessica was on an unstoppable path of destruction.

Taylor smiled inwardly at the young girl across the table from her. The dark-haired woman leaned her elbow on the table and held her head in the palm of her hand. She listened intently to Jessica as she rambled on about the beautiful teacher who tried to make a difference in the young girl's life, and how Jessica felt she was just another in a long line of people she had disappointed.

Two things caused Taylor's mirth. First there was the incessant chatter the young girl let loose with. As Taylor listened, she could picture so much of Torrey in the girl before her. Second was the way Jessica described her teacher. The adoration was easily evident in the girl's voice and Taylor wondered if it was the usual schoolgirl crush at that age or if Jessica's feelings ran deeper. She remembered how taken Jess was with the artist's work, how she was mesmerized by the wooden sculpture of two women together. *Oh, God...we could be in trouble here. Please, don't let me be the one who has to handle that "Mom, I'm a lesbian" chat.*

Finally, Jessica confided that she'd gotten into a fight and destroyed half a classroom before being summarily expelled.

"How did your mom react to that?" Taylor asked curiously as she stood to rinse out her glass. She knew how violence affected her old friend.

Jessica stuffed the pizza container into the garbage. "She paid the bill and gave me that tight ass look she has."

Taylor smiled, her back facing the young girl. "Somehow I don't remember your mother having a look like that in her repertoire."

"You haven't seen her lately. In my opinion she'd be a lot better if she'd just loosen up and get laid or something," Jess responded.

Taylor's motion at the sink stopped. "Don't talk about your mother like that," she said slowly in a low voice.

"Well, it's true," Jessica replied, sulkily walking past Taylor. "Maybe she'd be easier to deal with if she just paid somebody to give her a good fuck—"

Taylor turned and grabbed the young woman by her shirt collar, slamming her up against the nearest wall. Jessica scarcely recognized the eyes that burned into her own. The young woman's feet barely touched the ground as Taylor showed the physical strength she was capable of. "You will learn what the first rule of this house is, Jessica Taylor Gray," Taylor hissed, her arms shaking in anger. "When you speak of your mother you will do so with respect. Do you understand me?"

Jessica gave a slight nod of her head. She had never been as afraid of anyone as she was at this moment, Taylor's face appearing to turn into another creature completely.

"Then, tell me you understand," Taylor demanded.

"I understand," she replied weakly.

Taylor released the young woman, pressing her into the wall again as she did. The dark-haired artist turned her back and stood at the sink, waiting for her rage to dissipate. She listened to the sound of JT moving out of the kitchen, hearing a door slam down the hall. *Shit! Well, Taylor, one day down, 179 to go. This is gonna be fun.*

****

Taylor slipped between the silk sheets of her bed, raising her eyes to the wall across from the bed. *Oh, Tor, I have no idea what I'm doing here. One day and I already fucked it up royal.*

Taylor thought about what the petite blonde would say to her. Yes, she admitted now that she lost her temper big time. It was so sudden; it even shocked Taylor with its voracity. Just when she felt she and Jessica were forming some type of an alliance, too. Now, she could only wonder what the young girl would be thinking about her and the coming months.

What would Torrey's advice be?

Oh, damn, I'm gonna have to go apologize to my lovely little brat.

It was late but Taylor pulled her body from the bed and wrapped a blue silk robe around her naked form. When she reached Jessica's bedroom door, she listened for a moment and then lightly rapped on the heavy wood. Receiving no response, she knocked louder and called out Jessica's name. Slowly turning the knob and peering inside, Taylor saw the young girl's bed showed no signs of being slept in.

Taylor walked through the house calling Jessica's name. The artist even walked outside, but couldn't find a sign of the young girl. Getting a little panicky by this time, Taylor came back into the house and headed for the girl's bedroom again. Looking into the closet and drawers, she saw that all Jessica's belongings remained.

Suddenly, the dark-haired woman got a feeling of dread, deep in her gut. *Oh, no,* was all she could think as she rushed to the garage and flung open the side door. She was met with the sight of a large empty space where her Mercedes was usually parked.

"Eat me!" she cursed vehemently and moved quickly toward her bedroom.

Grabbing a fresh shirt and pulling on her worn jeans, Taylor dialed a familiar number as she dressed.

"Detective Hobarth, Vice," the voice said on the other end.

"Billy, Taylor Kent...I need your help like yesterday!"

Chapter
7

"So you mean to tell me you gave some girl you're shackin' up with all your security codes and the keys to your Mercedes?" Billy asked his old friend. He and Taylor were a long way from their days at the biker bar in Maine, but the man that sat behind the unmarked squad car's steering wheel looked with disbelief at his friend.

"She's not a stranger...and she's not sleeping with me, for Christ's sake, she's Torrey's girl, she's practically my daughter too," Taylor replied. The artist was seething and barely able to carry on a civil conversation with her friend.

"Are you kidding? This girl that stole your car is Torrey's kid?" Billy was stunned. He remembered the cute blonde every time he was in a bookstore and saw her green eyes smiling out from her picture on a book jacket. The memory of losing a hundred bucks to her would always make him smile.

"Dana Point's pretty quiet, but if you want something bad enough you'll find it," the detective explained. "We'll start there. You know that if she heads for L.A. it could be a situation. A cocky seventeen year old alone and driving a Mercedes is gonna be an easy mark."

"Thanks for cheering me up. She may be cocky, but she's insecure as hell. I don't think she'll try driving to the city, maybe Laguna, but I can't picture her having the jewels for anyplace else. Geez, Billy, we've got to find her. What the hell will I tell Torrey?"

The police detective looked over at his friend's tired face. Her hair was a little rumpled and she didn't have any makeup on, but she was still one of the most beautiful women he'd ever laid eyes on. Her blue eyes narrowed in concern and he could see through her like glass. She tried to hide it for years, but her heart was and always would be, completely owned by a petite blonde, two thousand miles away.

"I really do appreciate what you're doing, Bill. Thanks. I didn't want to come down here in the Explorer. I figured if she recognized the car that she might do something stupid like try to run. Plus, it's been so long that I wouldn't know where to go to buy any grass nowadays anyway."

"Well, we can breeze by a couple of spots. Mostly young kids, mostly pot. Let's hope she's there."

She was.

At the first place they looked; at the corner of a small convenience store, a group of teenagers milled about. A couple of them rode on bicycles, while some bounced around on skateboards. They didn't even hide what they were doing, and there was Jessica, lighting up a joint inside of cupped hands. She wore her black leather jacket, worn jeans, and combat boots, and when she shook her hair from her face, Taylor thought it was like looking into a mirror. Poor Torrey must have been forced to relive it all again. All those bad times with Taylor, reflected in her own daughter's behavior. Taylor made a mental note to send her small friend two-dozen roses first thing in the morning.

The unmarked car had its windows tinted almost completely black. Even if Jessica did turn in their direction, she wouldn't have been able to see inside the vehicle to recognize Taylor. Billy parked the car like a store customer, went in, and bought a pack of gum. By the time he got back out Taylor eased the door open and walked silently up behind Jessica. Billy decided to hang back and leaned against the car, watching his old friend at work.

Jessica took another hit from the joint and finally felt that subtle click in her head that told her everything would be cool. She saw a dark shadow come up behind her, a very tall shadow. Like her mother before her, she recognized the growl without looking. "Oh, fuck." She turned around, the joint dangling from her lips.

Taylor thought she'd lost it in the house, but that was nothing compared to the anger that was filling her now. She ripped the smoke from the girl's mouth and crushed it in her hand. With the same move she used earlier, Taylor pinned the girl against the wall of the building.

"Hey, dyke," one of the boys on a skateboard, said, moving toward the two.

Billy decided to join in the fun. He pulled his badge and put on his serious voice. "LAPD, don't you kiddies have curfews?" he asked slowly.

They all scattered at that, leaving their new friend to her own fate.

"What the hell is wrong with you? Don't you realize what could have happened to you?" Taylor hissed.

"What the hell do you care? My mom doesn't give a damn about me, why should you?" Jessica spat back at the older woman.

Taylor kept hold of the neck of the girl's shirt in one hand, drawing back her free hand to slap her across the mouth. Jessica tried not to look hurt, but the truth was her skin stung painfully where the woman's hand had hit her.

"First my mom, now you. Anyone else want a shot at me?" the drugged girl shouted.

"I heard you gave as good as you got back home," Taylor returned hotly.

Jessica pupils bounced nervously back and forth, her bloodshot eyes filling with tears at the memory of her mother's face and the bruise she put there. She had no idea her mother told Taylor about that. "You bitch," Jessica answered feebly, lowering her head.

"Okay, Taylor, take it easy." Billy placed a calming hand on his friend's shoulder. "Why don't you take the Mercedes and I'll bring the kid back up with me, okay?"

Taylor felt the strong hand on her shoulder and pushed the girl away from her roughly. "Keys," was the only word she allowed herself to say. The dark-haired woman turned and got into the convertible, kicking up dirt and gravel as she sped the Mercedes toward the cliff road.

"Well, that could have gone better," Billy said, to no one in particular. "Get in." He motioned toward the car. "So, you're Torrey's daughter?" Billy asked, thinking the girl looked like an uncanny combination of Torrey and Taylor.

"Oh, let me guess...you went to college with her too?" Jessica asked sarcastically.

"Hell, no. You couldn't have paid me enough to go to that snobby school those gals went to. Nope, you're mom used to hang out with Taylor down at the biker bar I did business at. It was kind of like my office, if you get my meaning," Billy answered. The detective thought it felt like a lifetime ago when his livelihood existed on the other side of this badge.

"My mom, in a biker bar? You must have the wrong woman," Jessica reacted in amazement.

"Don't believe everything you read on the cover of a book, kid. Sounds to me like you don't know anything about your mother."

"She never tells me anything about stuff from those days," Jessica replied honestly.

"Maybe you're just asking the wrong questions...or maybe the wrong people."

"What's that supposed to mean?" She questioned.

"You are thick, aren't you? You're living with the one person in the world who knows more about your mom than her own mother." Billy finished his statement as he pulled up to the open security gate. Driving up to the front door, he motioned for the girl to get out. "Guess it's time to face the music, kid."

Jessica sat there for a few moments longer, suddenly afraid to get out of the car. The woman that threw her against the wall tonight scared the hell out of her.

"You want a word of advice, kid?" Billy asked.

"If I listen to it, will you stop calling me kid?" she snapped. Her nervousness was showing through.

"Touché. Taylor may scare the snot out of you, but she's a fair woman. Okay, so she's got a sore spot where your mother's honor is concerned, but you'll never find a woman with more integrity than Taylor. Just be honest with her. No wise-ass attitude. You play it straight and she'll be there for you."

Jessica nodded silently at the detective before she left the car and entered the house.

* * * * * * * * * *

"What are you doing?" Jessica asked in a weak tone. Taylor was throwing Jessica's clothes and personal items into pieces of luggage that had been emptied only this afternoon.

"What does it look like? You're going back, tonight. I'll let *you* tell your mother what you did," Taylor said in a low even tone.

At the mention of her mother's name, Jessica's eyes filled with tears. "Please, Taylor."

"Don't even try that shit now because it's way past the time for tears," Taylor responded.

Jessica backed herself against the wall and sobbed, watching Taylor jam her clothes unceremoniously into her bags. "Please, Taylor, I can't go back...I promised. Please." The young girl sobbed hysterically.

Taylor never stopped, even as the sound of Jessica crying ripped at her heart. *I'm sorry, Tor, but this girl is just too far-gone to help.*

"I can't go back now, Taylor. She believes in me!" Jessica finally cried out.

That was the one comment that was able to bring the dark-haired artist up short. She remembered the words as if it were yesterday. *"I believe in you, Taylor."* The tall woman stood there for a few minutes, unable to look at the young girl.

Jessica sat down on the floor and wrapped her own arms around herself and continued to cry, tears rolling down her cheeks. Taylor sunk heavily to the floor beside her and opened her arms for the young girl. Jessica fell into the older woman's embrace and it felt vaguely familiar.

"Jess, you've got a drug problem, you know that don't you?" Taylor asked.

"It's just that I can't...I can't feel good without it. Some days I can't feel anything," Jessica answered. "I don't know how to stop. I'm so tired of not being able to feel anything."

Taylor stroked the girl's hair and kissed the top of her head, wiping tears from her cheeks. "This doesn't look like someone who doesn't feel anything. Maybe you just don't know how to handle the feelings that you do have. I know a way to help, Jess, but you have to work with me here. You've got to help yourself a little too, okay? It's not just going to get better and go away without a little work."

Jessica nodded and wiped her eyes.

"Okay, get a good night's sleep, what's left of it anyway, and we'll talk in the morning, all right? You like omelets? Those I can make," Taylor asked.

Jessica nodded again and the two women rose to their feet.

"One other thing, Jess," Taylor said before she turned to leave. "Clean up all this crap will ya? It's a mess," Taylor finished with a wink.

Jessica smiled and sniffed, wiping more tears from her eyes. Taylor reached over and with a tenderness in complete contrast to her earlier actions, she lightly kissed Jessica's forehead. "Go to bed," the woman said as she closed the door behind her.

Again, Taylor stared at the wall in front of her once she was comfortably settled in her bed. With just a few spoken words, Taylor now understood how Torrey felt those years with her, how helpless and powerless the young woman must have felt watching the artist party her life away. It's so hard to watch someone you love screw up their whole life. Taylor was thankful Torrey never gave up on her.

January 1983

"Oh, yea. That's it, baby, right there," Taylor moaned, moving in closer to capture the woman's nipple in her teeth.

A young blonde straddled the artist's hips. Her skirt was around her hips, her panties having been discarded before they even made it to the bed. It seemed Taylor preferred petite blondes these days. It helped when it came to imagining it was Torrey's body that was bringing her such enjoyment.

Taylor groaned again in pleasure. She learned her lesson from her drunken encounter in the bar and trained her body not to call out Torrey's name while in the arms of passion, even though it always took the image of the young writer's face to send Taylor over the edge.

The dark-haired woman's shirt was unbuttoned, still clinging to her broad shoulders. The buttons of her jeans were undone, and the young woman's hand disappeared within the dark curls between the artist's legs. The fingers that stroked her knew what they were doing and Taylor lay back on the bed, letting the sensations catch up with the visions in her mind's eye.

A couple smokes. A few pills, and she had a nice buzz going, one that allowed her to believe that it really was Torrey lying on top of her. The artist's hips rocked urgently against the fingers that slipped inside her.

"Taylor?" Torrey's voice came from the other side of the bedroom door.

Torrey walked into the house, carrying her very grumpy, but finally sleeping baby. Jessica was teething and the baby seemed to feel that if she couldn't sleep through the night, nobody should. Jessica was such a handful tonight that Torrey left her writer's group meeting earlier than usual. She settled the youngster in her crib, returning to the living room. She noticed Taylor's car in the garage, and wondered if the dark-haired woman was in her bedroom. Walking down the hall she called out the artist's name.

Taylor's eyes snapped open at the sound of Torrey's voice and she practically threw the woman on top of her to the floor. "Shit!" Taylor said, quickly buttoning her shirt and pulling up her jeans. "I'll be out in a minute, Tor."

"Who is that?" the young woman asked, trying to smooth her skirt and her dignity.

"My roommate," Taylor answered gruffly.

The blonde looked down at the band on Taylor's ring finger, then back up at the artist. "Are you with somebody?"

"What's it matter?" Taylor smirked. She decided against telling her that Torrey wasn't her wife.

Just then, Jessica woke and started to cry again.

"And you've got a baby? You are such a snake!"

By now, Taylor was just grinning at the angry woman. If her night of pleasure was ruined it kind of made her happy she could return the favor. Taylor followed behind the blonde as she made her way out the front door.

She passed by Torrey on her way to the baby's room. "I am so sorry," she said to Torrey. The young writer just stared open mouthed at the girl. "I didn't know, I mean, I don't fool around with married women," the woman continued to Taylor's amusement and Torrey's bewilderment. The woman reached out and slapped the amused look off of Taylor's face, then walked out the front door.

Torrey could only shake her head and walk past her tall friend toward Jessica's room. The smaller woman undid the top few buttons of her blouse, Taylor following her into the baby's room. Torrey lifted the crying baby up easily into her arms and eased herself into the large rocker Taylor gave her as a gift once Torrey returned home from the hospital. She settled the hungry child against her breast and tenderly stroked her baby's face.

There was never any question of Torrey being uncomfortable with Taylor watching her breast-feed Jessica. This simply became one more moment the two friends shared. Taylor couldn't have looked away even if she wanted to. The combination of the strength in her small friend's arms to lift the large baby with such ease along with the gentle act of cradling the child in her arms to feed became a vision that she would, in later years, turn into a work of art.

Now the dark-haired artist could only watch as mother and child experienced a bonding that could not be undone by time or circumstance. To the artist, the sight always caused feelings of comfort, jealousy, and arousal all at the same time. She was in awe that the woman seated by her could look so maternal, yet so sensual at the same time.

"You should have explained to her," Torrey's voice broke the silence.

Taylor merely shrugged.

"Did you even know her name?" Torrey asked sadly, trying to cover the break in her voice by clearing her throat. It shattered her heart to understand that the woman she loved so much didn't find her attractive in that way.

Taylor's earlier high was gradually wearing off and she felt like an ass, screwing another woman in the same house where Torrey and their baby lived. "I'm sorry, Tor. I didn't think you'd be back...I—I won't do that again," Taylor apologized.

Torrey became angry with herself for denying her friend her own life. She had no claim on Taylor's heart and no right to force the artist to give up the pleasure of another's company. "You can do whatever you want here, Taylor. It's your house," Torrey said, but it came out more harshly than she intended.

Taylor looked up with wounded eyes. "Don't say that, Little Bit. This house belongs to you and Jessica, too. We're a family remember?"

"I'm sorry. I didn't mean that the way it came out. I just want you to know you don't have to give up your whole life for the two of us." Torrey's eyes misted over with tears.

Taylor stumbled slightly as she knelt beside the seated woman; her bloodshot eyes resting on the now sleeping baby nestled against the small blonde's breast. She reached slender fingers out to gently stroke the thick patch of dark hair on Jessica's head. "But, the two of you, you are my whole life," Taylor admitted softly.

Torrey smiled sadly at the honest admission from her friend. The young woman wished they could be a real family, but Taylor's apparent lack of interest in her as a potential lover wasn't the only thing that stood in their way. Torrey tried to hold Jessica in one arm while refastening her bra.

"Here I'll take her," Taylor said standing up and weaving slightly.

"No, I've got her." Torrey moved past the taller woman and placed the sleeping baby in the crib.

"Now I'm not even allowed to hold her? I thought you accepted my apology," Taylor said with an edge to her voice.

"You're stoned aren't you?" Torrey turned to face her friend.

"*Not much anymore,*" *Taylor replied with a lopsided grin.*

Torrey stood there and stared up into her friend's clouded blue eyes.

"*Yea,*" *Taylor acknowledged, lowering her eyes in shame. Only Torrey seemed able to provoke this feeling of guilt within her.*

"*I don't want you holding Jessica when you're high like this,*" *Torrey said.*

"*I would never do anything to hurt her,*" *Taylor said immediately, her voice rising slightly.*

"*I know that, Stretch. I also know you get unsteady on your feet, like you are right now. If anything happened while you were with Jess, you'd never forgive yourself and I would be just as at fault because I would have been able to prevent it,*" *Torrey responded.*

Taylor's eyes burned into the smaller woman's with a blue fire. She abruptly turned from the room and left.

The dark-haired woman's high was crashing down on her and she wasn't enjoying the feeling. She paced the floor of her bedroom, cursing her inability to feel anything but anger without drugs. She flung open her top drawer and pulled the carved wooden box from beneath the clothing. She never, ever used anything in the house, but if Torrey thought she was an addict, then she might as well fit the picture.

The smell hit Torrey immediately and she followed the scent to the open door of her friend's bedroom. Seated on the floor, leaning against the bed, Taylor had her eyes closed as she drew in a long, slow breath from the pipe in one hand, as her other hand held a small lighter to the bowl of the pipe.

"So do you still want to share?" Torrey asked, stepping into the room.

"Wha-?" Taylor asked, a very perplexed look on her face.

"Well, if it's so good I figure that I must be missing something," Torrey replied, reaching for the pipe.

Taylor pulled the pipe from the young woman's reach. "No," she said, shock still registering on her face.

"Why fight it anymore?" Torrey asked, trying to reach her friend's hand.

"I said no, don't do this!" Taylor hissed.

"At least let me give it a try. I mean, if it's good enough for you"

"It's not good enough for me!" Taylor shouted, slamming the pipe down into the ashtray next to her and shoving it away. "I just don't know how to stop," she said in a small voice, tears rolling down her cheeks.

Torrey wrapped her arms around her friend's broad shoulders and pulled the strong woman within her embrace. "Oh, Stretch, why didn't you ever ask me to help?" Torrey felt her own tears start.

"That's not how it's supposed to work. I don't ask for help. I take care of you and Jess. That's the way it's supposed to be," Taylor answered, trying to hold on to her emotions.

"Oh, honey, that is not the way it's supposed to be. We're friends, remember? This is a fifty-fifty deal here."

The small term of endearment that Taylor usually reserved for her friend broke down the walls around the artist's heart, and she cried in earnest. Within seconds, Taylor was weeping in Torrey's arms, afraid to let go of the young woman who held her tightly.

"I know some people that can help, but you have to be willing to work at it, Stretch. It won't be easy and you can't give up. You'll have days when you slip, but you can't beat yourself up over it. I'll be there with you every step of the way. Jess and I will always be there to catch you if you should fall," Torrey murmured to the woman who finally spent all the tears she had in her.

"Little Bit?" Taylor asked quietly.

"Yes?"

Taylor thought better of the request she was going to make. It would be too much to ask and her pride wouldn't allow her to. "Never mind."

"Would you like me to stay in here with you tonight?" Torrey knew what her friend wanted.

Taylor simply nodded her head, afraid the sound of her own voice asking for her friend's loving arms around her would start her crying again.

By the time they changed and readied themselves for bed, Torrey needed to check on Jessica one last time. The baby fussed and kicked as Torrey walked the floor of the room trying to calm her. Taylor walked in and leaned against the doorframe, watching the young mother.

"Here," Torrey said, placing the baby in Taylor's arms, "maybe she'll be better for you."

Taylor held the child in strong arms, whispering, then humming into her ear. Finally, the child's movements stilled and she allowed the dark-haired woman to lay her down once again.

"Thanks."   Taylor looked down into green eyes that smiled back up at her.

"Come on, let's go to bed," Torrey said.

It was awkward for both women at first, sharing the same bed for the first time.   Torrey eventually broke the ice and beckoned her tall friend into her deceptively strong embrace.   Taylor's worried brow eventually eased as Torrey ran her fingers through the ebony locks.   Both women relaxed surprisingly fast into the tender touches.   Taylor closed her eyes as she felt herself drift off.   She knew this wasn't a night for lovers, but rather a night for best friends.

"I'm kind of afraid I'll let you down, Tor," Taylor admitted before sleep claimed her.

Leaning down, Torrey whispered into her friend's ear.   "It's okay, I know you won't."

"How do you know that?" was Taylor's sleepy response.

"Because I believe in you, Taylor."

****

"Wake up sleepyhead," Taylor called as she opened the door to Jessica's room.

"Oh, it can't be morning yet. I think I just went to bed," the young girl moaned from under the covers.

"Come on...I'm getting ready to make cheese omelets," Taylor said enticingly.

More groans from under the covers.

Exactly like her mother, Taylor smiled to herself.

She was in a surprisingly good mood this morning and she wasn't really sure why. The artist was pretty sure it had something to do with the revisited memory. She rarely allowed herself the luxury of day-dreaming about those days, but remembering the way her friend helped her turn her life around that day had her feeling better than she had in a long time. Torrey was the sole reason that Taylor was where she was today.

Taylor reached into the front pocket of her jeans and pulled out a small, flat object the size of a poker chip. She looked intently at the number fifteen stamped onto one side. If it hadn't been for her young friend's belief in the dark-haired artist, Taylor would never have been able to stay clean all these years. Now it was time to pay up on that debt. She would do everything in her power to instill that same feeling of unconditional love and support in Torrey's daughter.

"Come on, JT." Taylor pulled back the covers. "After breakfast we're going shopping," Taylor said, as if she were dangling a carrot for enticement.

"Shopping?" Jessica opened her eyes.

Yep, the apple doesn't fall far from the tree, Taylor chuckled to herself.

Showered and clean, but still a little sleepy after only a few hours of sleep, both women sat down to toast, juice, and omelets.

"So, what are we going shopping for, besides food?" Jessica asked.

"Anything you need, want, or desire," Taylor said, popping the last bite of toast into her mouth.

"Oh, well, I don't really need anything..." Jessica responded letting her voice trail off.

"Well, then you're the first seventeen year old girl in the world that can say that," Taylor said with a grin. "There's got to be something?" Taylor phrased the question, looking expectantly at Jessica.

"Well, yea, but I figured after last night, I mean...well, I guess I figured I'd be grounded till I was about twenty or so," Jessica said uncertainly.

"Trust me, I thought about it," Taylor replied pouring herself another cup of coffee. "But, I also have to admit that I was just as much to blame over what happened yesterday as you were. Coming to a strange place with a woman you don't even remember. I didn't make your first day very easy, did I? Hey, do you drink coffee?" The artist indicated the glass carafe in her hand. "Oh, shit. I bet you drink tea don't you?" she asked without waiting for an answer to the previous question.

"Yea, how'd you know that?" JT asked.

"Your mom. She always tried to tell me I'd live longer on green tea, but I could never seem to give up my one hundred percent Colombian. The whole time we lived together, we always had two automatic cof-feepots, one for coffee, one for tea. Here," Taylor said throwing Jessica a notepad and pen. "Start a list of stuff we'll need to pick up."

"So, what did I do right to deserve all this?" Jessica suddenly asked, a little mistrustful.

"Oh, there's a price to pay all right," Taylor answered. "You've got to do two things for me."

"Here it comes," Jessica replied.

"Oh, don't get panicky on me, it's not that bad. First, I have somewhere I have to be tonight; kind of a meeting, and I want you to come with me. Second, I want to take a look at those drawings in all those sketchbooks you packed."

Jessica swallowed and lowered her eyes at the last

request. "They're not much. I mean, I'm nowhere as good as you," Jessica said nervously.

"I should hope not. I've been doing it a lot longer and I get paid a hell of a lot more," Taylor responded with a wink.

Looking into Jessica's green eyes, Taylor softened her voice. "Jess, I won't laugh at anything you show me. I won't even say whether I think they're good or bad if you don't want to hear my opinion. I just want to know how much of my studio to give up to you," Taylor said with a smile. "I mean, you seemed serious about wanting to work on your art while you were here. I think I can tell how serious you take your work by looking at your drawings, okay?"

Jessica nodded her assent. "And, what kind of meeting are we going to?"

"Narcotics Anonymous," Taylor answered without hesitation.

"Am I that hopeless?"

"It has nothing to do with you or being hopeless. I've gone to a meeting every Tuesday for the last fifteen years, before that I went every damn day. Jess, has your mom ever talked about any of this with you? Told you anything about me?" *Like I'm gay, I'm a drug addict, you know, little things like that.*

"Mom doesn't talk about anything much that happened while she was in college. Sometimes I ask, but her answer is always that 'it's complicated.'"

"Jess, does it bother you when I bring up your mom?" Taylor asked. She noticed that an expression something like pain crossed the young girl's face whenever Taylor mentioned Torrey's name.

"No, of course not. I just don't think I'll ever be

in my mom's league. I manage to screw up everything I lay my hands on and Mom...well, she's perfect."

Taylor chuckled slightly. "I can think of a lot of
things to say about your mom and most of them are
highly complimentary, but I think even she would be
the first one to tell you she's far from perfect."

"Well, yea she says that, but the way everyone
talks about her. I mean, it's like she gave up the
world just so I could be brought into the cradle of
humanity," Jessica replied with exasperation.

"Yea, your mom has sacrificed a lot for you, Jess,
and she'd do anything for you, but that's called loving
your child, nothing more. Your mom is just a little
better at the self-sacrifice thing than most," Taylor
explained.

"She believes in me and all I ever do is let her
down. I keep on screwing up and she keeps on forgiving me. How many times will she do that?" Tears
formed in the corners of the young girl's eyes. "I'm
afraid some day she'll stop forgiving me."

"I'm living proof that she'll do it a long time,
Jess," Taylor said quietly and related the story of how
Torrey's actions finally prompted the artist to admit
she had a problem and get some help.

Taylor pulled the ever-present marker from the
pocket of her jeans and placed the black chip number
side up, on the table between them. "This shows that
I've been clean for fifteen years. You think you've
got a past, that you've done some pretty rotten things?
Your stories can't hold a candle to mine, kid, and your
mom knows all of my past. Even though she knows,
she still cares about me...she never gave up on me,"

Taylor said, tears forming in her own eyes. "And, I owe this to your mom. I would never have even had the strength to try if she hadn't told me those very words that she believed in me. I want you to know, Jess, I believe in you too and I'll do everything I can to help you get a handle on this problem."

"I'm just not good like Mom. I'll never be as good as her," Jessica admitted dejectedly.

"Jess, the last place your mom would want you to live is in her shadow," Taylor responded, wondering where in the world the teenager received these impressions of her mother. It didn't seem like Torrey, not to be honest. "Talk to me, Jess, I feel like you're holding something back. What is it that's really bothering you about opening up to me?" Taylor asked finally.

"I'm a little...I don't know, I guess I'm a little nervous about telling you stuff. Are you gonna turn around and tell Mom everything I say, even the things I say about her?" Jessica asked.

"I wouldn't do that to you, JT. I'll tell you what, let's make a little pact. Everything we say within these walls has to be the truth and goes no further than between us. That way we've got a safe place where it's okay to talk and be ourselves. What do you say?"

"That means you too, right? If I ask you a question, you promise to tell the truth?" Jessica asked.

Taylor took quick seconds to think about what she was doing. She hadn't opened up to anyone in a long time, especially about certain things. *God, what if she asks me about how I feel about Torrey?* The artist decided it would be a risk she would have to take, to make the young girl feel comfortable with the situation. "Absolutely, I promise to tell the truth," Taylor said.

"Can I start and ask you stuff now?" Jessica asked hopefully.

Taylor nodded with a wry smile.

"Why do you think my mom won't tell me anything about when you guys were in college?"

Taylor was sure she didn't know how to answer this one. "JT, all I can give you is my opinion there. I was never aware that Torrey didn't tell you anything." Taylor ran long fingers through her hair and pushed her cold coffee aside. "Your mom was determined to be a much better mom than hers ever was. She was always so afraid that she wouldn't do right by you. I can only guess, when I say that she wasn't proud of some of the things that happened in her younger life. She ran with me and I tended to get her in more trouble than was good for either of us. I think, maybe she was just afraid you wouldn't love or respect her if you knew. You know she loves you more than her own life, Jess, but I know she always felt guilty that she only knew your father casually before she slept with him. Man, we did some wild things back then."

"Like what kind of wild things?" Jessica asked.

Taylor smiled. "Oh, like the time I let her get drunk and we got tattooed when we were here in California, or all the stunts we pulled in the Sorority House and ended up pulling kitchen detail...which was about every night," Taylor added quickly.

"Wait a minute. My mom has a tattoo?" Jessica asked in disbelief. "Of what?"

Taylor unbuttoned the top two buttons of her cotton shirt. Pulling open the shirt to expose her left shoulder, she pushed aside her bra strap. There on the uppermost swell of her breast was a tiny cartoon image of the Tazmanian Devil. Jessica laughed at the sight of the cartoon character.

"Hey, we were young and we were Sorority sisters. Tau Alpha Zeta...we were Taz's, so that's what we got. It helped that Torrey was heavily inebriated at the time," Taylor added.

Suddenly Jessica frowned and looked lost in thought.

"Hey, what's wrong?" Taylor asked, afraid she'd gone too far.

"That detective friend of yours, he was right." The young girl leaned back and sighed. "I don't know my mom at all."

Taylor watched the young girl she thought of as her own daughter. Jessica was staring down at the table, concentrating on some thought so hard, Taylor thought she might burn a hole in the table.

"My mom thinks she's part of my problem, doesn't she, Taylor?" The girl asked.

"Yea, she does," the older woman answered honestly.

"She's not, ya know. I think it's me; what I'm doing."

"What *are* you doing, Jess?" Taylor asked.

"I think...I kind of put my mom on a pedestal, ya know? It's like I'm the one who made her perfect. I was setting myself up with a built in excuse to be a shit. Like, if I set my mom up as perfect, then I can screw up all I want, because no matter how hard I try,

I can never be as good as her, so after a while you just don't bother trying anymore. Know what I mean?"

"Yea. I know exactly what you mean, Jess. Your mother was and always will be an incredible woman in my eyes, but she's far from perfect. She has her faults, and buttons that can be pushed just like the rest of us mere mortals." Taylor stood and rinsed her coffee mug out at the sink.

Turning to the picture window in front of the kitchen table, she continued to speak with her back to Jessica. "You've made a good start Jess. Hell, you're a lot more mature than I was at your age. You need to work at getting your mom off that pedestal and a little bit closer to the ground, though. You see the trouble with putting people we love way up on those pedestals is that sooner or later they fall off. The truly unfortunate part is that it's a given...they will fall, and we're usually standing under them when they do." Taylor turned to Jessica. "Hey, at this rate we're never going to get out of here. You ready to hit the road?"

"Sure. Hey, Taylor?"

"Hhmm?" the artist responded.

"Does my mom really have a tattoo?" Jessica laughed.

"Oh, man," Taylor groaned aloud. "Torrey is gonna kill me." She placed her arm over the younger woman's shoulder and pulled her toward the door.

Chapter 8

The two women finally compromised on a radio station they could both live with, which made driving into Laguna Beach considerably easier. Grocery shopping went smoothly, Taylor and Jessica both finding out that cooking was going to be a little bit more challenging than they previously thought. They stopped for lunch at Simon's Deli. Taylor was less than enthused when Jessica bought fresh lox, cream cheese, and bagels for breakfast the next day.

"You get that from your mother, that's for sure," she said to Jessica's grin. "I'll just have the bagels." Taylor got even by ordering a Simon Special for lunch.

Jessica just watched as the older woman devoured a huge sandwich comprised of rye bread, chopped liver, and egg salad. "I can't imagine Mom even liking a concoction like that," Jessica said.

"Don't be so sure. The first time Torrey came

here, she ate two of them," Taylor responded between bites.

Driving to the Art Supply store, Taylor became caught up in her own thoughts as she listened to the radio and Jessica did a little sightseeing. All this talking about Torrey caused the artist to reach back into her memories, reliving the time they spent here in California together. It was the one and only true vacation they went on together and it was nothing short of magical. If the dark-haired woman had any thoughts before about the level of her commitment to Torrey and her child, they were dispelled after their two weeks together out west. Torrey loved everything about San Diego; she especially loved Taylor's mom. The two hit it off instantly and Jean Kent knew that she found a daughter of the heart in the petite, caring young woman.

A song came on the radio and Jessica brought Taylor from her dreaming. "Do you mind if I turn it up?" the girl asked.

Taylor shook her head. "Who is it?" she asked. She loved music, but could rarely remember who sang what.

"I don't know the chick's name, but it's called 'Back To You', a real heartbreaker," Jessica answered.

Taylor found herself caught up in the lyrics and the haunting melody.

> *Time slips past and I lose my way*
> *The years go by so slow*
> *And the only love I wasted then*
> *Was all that I couldn't show*

And there were none so blind, as I
When I thought you could never be mine

I just wanted to hold your hand
I swear I'll never run again
You followed my step
But you led my heart
Too many days and nights
Lead into years we spent apart
And there were none so blind
As those who would not see
And there were none so blind as me
All to find the road inside that leads
Back to you

Taylor couldn't be sure she even heard anymore of the song. After hearing the words of the chorus, she became lost in the memory of a smiling face and sea-green eyes.

April 1983

"*You get one choice in this house Torrey Gray. You can call me mom or you can go stay in a hotel,*" the older woman said just before she gave the young girl a hug.

"*I give up, Mom it is,*" Torrey said as she returned the older woman's warm welcome.

"*And, this must be Jessica,*" Jean Kent said as she gently took the baby from her daughter's arms.

"*I think we owe her one.*" Torrey indicated the smiling baby. "*She was an angel through the whole*

flight. I couldn't even keep this one from fidgeting
every five minutes. " The blonde nodded in Taylor's
direction.

"Hey, if you had adult size legs, you would have
been fidgeting, too, " Taylor said in mock indignation.

"Oh, you poor baby...would you like me to fix you
a bottle too? Would that make you feel better?" Tor-
rey teased the dark-haired woman.

"How do you put up with these two?" Jean spoke
to Jessica, the baby giggling at the two women before
her.

Taylor laughed and gave her mother a warm hug
and a kiss on the cheek.   "I missed you," Taylor
admitted to her mother.

Jean Kent knew her daughter.   Better than the
young woman thought she did. The older woman saw
it on her daughter's face the moment she walked
through the door and introduced her roommate.

Jean already liked Torrey. She had spoken to the
girl on several occasions, and when Taylor wasn't
around, the young blonde and her roommate's mother
would chat for hours about anything and everything.
Jean felt from the beginning that the relationship that
existed between the two young women was something
special.   When Taylor told her that she planned on
staying in Maine and taking the lucrative position
with Diamond & Allen, then revealed the reason why,
Jean had to question her daughter's judgment. Once
she spoke with Torrey, however, the older woman real-
ized what a special girl she was and the genuine
affection the girl held for Taylor.

Now, with both of them standing before her, the
look in their eyes was unmistakable.   Taylor seemed

*more at ease with herself and her surroundings than
her mother ever remembered. The young girl who left
home nearly five years before had been withdrawn,
sullen and angry most of the time. The grown woman
that appeared on her doorstep was confident and
open. The dark-haired beauty threw a pair of sapphire eyes at her roommate and smiled. That was
when Jean saw the whole picture. Her daughter's
sparkling eyes held nothing but love as she looked
down at Torrey. The look that the small blonde cast
up at Taylor was one of complete adoration. The
older woman wondered why two people so much in
love couldn't see it for themselves.*

*Torrey had more fun with Taylor's mom, hearing
stories about the young artist and looking through
photo albums, than anything else. Of course, Taylor
just groaned and played with Jessica. The dark-
haired woman felt her humiliation was complete once
the naked baby pictures were discovered.*

*It was a nice relaxing getaway for both the young
women. Taylor's mother adored Jessica and encouraged the young women to go out and see the sights
while she played grandmother. At first, Torrey
refused. She didn't want to impose on the older
woman's hospitality. When Taylor cornered her, the
real reason for the blonde's reticence made itself
known.*

*"Stretch, I've never left Jess alone with anyone
but you. What if something happens?" Torrey questioned tearfully.*

*"Honey, remember who your leaving her with.
Hey, my mom didn't do such a bad job with me, did
she?" Taylor asked.*

"No," Torrey chuckled as her friend wiped an errant tear from her cheek.

"Tell you what. Why don't we start out by going for a quick lunch today? I know this Deli you'll absolutely flip over, the sandwiches are this big." Taylor indicated the size of a plate with both hands. "That way you can take it a little bit at a time and you won't be so nervous leaving Jess with someone other than me."

Taylor wasn't sure if it was her company, the southern California sunshine, or the food, but after a few days the two women spent the whole day at the beach and Torrey had the time of her life. When the young blonde admitted to Jean Kent that she felt a little guilty, the older woman waved her off and told her this was as close as she would ever get to being a grandma and she was loving every minute of it. It turned out that Jessica was the hit of the Tuesday afternoon bridge club and Jean was the envy of every woman there.

****

"Oh, Little Bit, this is definitely the shirt for you." Taylor laughed as she held a T-shirt in front of her chest. It was a picture of the universe with a large arrow saying, "You Are Here."

"Oh, very funny," Torrey said with a smile and a slap to the taller woman's arm. "If I was blind you wouldn't make fun of me, but because I'm directionally challenged it's another story, well, you just go ahead and laugh," Torrey said pretending to ignore her roommate.

Taylor was constantly amazed at Torrey's inability to tell north from south unless the sun was in clear view. The artist teased the small woman by telling her she could get lost in her own home.

"Taylor Kent," a female voice called.

Taylor and Torrey both turned toward the sound. A tall woman with extremely short blonde hair smiled at Taylor. She had soft brown eyes that smiled even when her lips didn't.

"Robin?" Taylor said with uncertainty. "Damn!" she exclaimed, grasping the stranger's hand in a firm handshake.

"I told Cin it was you. I can't believe it. What in the world, are you doing back here? I heard you lived back east somewhere." Robin finished by taking in Torrey and smiling down at her.

"Oh, I'm sorry. Tor this is Robin Manyon, an old high school troublemaker like myself. Robin, Torrey Gray," Taylor said introducing the pair.

"This is so wild, you know Kelly and Barb are in town too. They live in San Francisco now. Hey, we're getting together at Chancey's tonight, why don't you two come, it'll be a blast," Robin said excitedly.

"Oh, ya know I'm not sure about a baby-sitter, and—" Taylor paused weakly.

"Geez, you've got kids too? Things have changed! Hey, hold on to that thought, let me grab Cindy," Robin said without taking a breath. The old friend walked away toward a small brunette who was talking to a shopkeeper across the street.

"Taylor, why don't you go, you deserve a little fun," Torrey said.

"Tor, you know I wouldn't go out without you.

This is our *vacation, remember?" Taylor responded.*

"Then take me with. I deserve some fun too."
The small blonde smiled.

"Little Bit, Chancey's is a lesbian bar," Taylor
said quietly.

"Oh...does that mean they don't have fun there?"
Torrey asked mischievously.

"Yes, they have fun." The dark-haired woman
laughed out loud.

"Well, then," Torrey said.

"Are you sure?" Taylor questioned her friend.

"Well, I mean, you're not going to pick some
woman up and dump me in the middle of nowhere, are
you?" Torrey asked, a little fearful.

"Of course not. I'd never do anything like that,"
Taylor said softly. "Tonight you'll be my date." She
finished just as her friend returned with the brunette
in tow.

"Cindy, you look great," Taylor said to the
smaller woman, and then introduced Torrey.

It was evident the two smaller women were des-
tined for friendship. It seemed as if they had known
one another for years as they chatted easily for the
next half-hour.

"Well, we better get going, it's getting late. We'll
meet you up at Chancey's at eight, right?" Taylor
said.

"You got it," Robin responded, nearly pulling
Cindy by the arm to get her going.

"Oh, no, now I do have to shop before we go
home. I don't have anything to wear tonight," Torrey
exclaimed.

"Honey, you brought two suitcases full of clothes

with you," Taylor said, dreading the idea of shopping for clothes.

"But those are all clothes I've been seen in before," Torrey said.

"These people have never seen you in them." Taylor tried to reason with her.

"But, you have," Torrey responded; hands on her hips, her jaw set firmly.

"I know there's a kernel of sanity in that statement somewhere, but damn if I know where it is," Taylor said more to herself than anyone listening. *"Here,"* she said, pressing her credit card into the small blonde's hand. *"Get whatever you think you'll need. I'll be waiting on that bench over there."* Taylor indicated an empty bench in the sand, across the street on the beach side.

Torrey reached up and kissed the taller woman on the cheek. "I won't be long," she added.

Taylor knew that would be a lie.

* * * * * * * * * *

"Taylor, are you alive?" Torrey asked, standing above her.

The dark-haired woman lay sprawled across the bench as if passed out. "No, I died waiting here," she answered dryly. *"Is it still Friday?"*

"Har, har," Torrey answered.

Taylor stood and grabbed a couple of the young woman's packages. "Gee, you sure you got everything?" the tall woman asked sarcastically.

"Well, I got an outfit, then naturally I had to get some shoes to match," Torrey began.

"Oh, naturally," Taylor said with mock enthusiasm.

"Oh, you," Torrey said with a nudge to her friend's shoulder.

"You know, you push me around a lot." Taylor smiled as they walked along the beach side of the street.

"You love it!" Torrey laughed back.

Yea, you're right. I do, Taylor thought to herself.

****

Taylor brushed a few pieces of lint from her jeans. She'd decided to go the extra few steps and dress like she knew how. Leather boots and black jeans started the outfit, and a tailored black leather blazer topped off a silk lavender shirt.

"Tor, are you ready yet?" She asked as she knocked on Torrey's bedroom door.

"I'll just be a few more minutes," Torrey called out.

"I'll be downstairs then," Taylor said as she moved toward the staircase.

When Torrey walked down the stairs of the home that Taylor grew up in, the dark-haired woman knew she'd never fantasized as a teenager about anything that looked like this. Torrey had on a white leather mini skirt and a sleeveless pale green, silk blouse. She held a matching white leather jacket in her hand.

Taylor stood, realizing too late that it probably wasn't a wise move considering the fact that her knees suddenly felt weak and her mouth felt like it was stuffed with cotton. Oh my God. I can't take her to

Chancey's looking like that. There'll be a riot!
"Wow," was Taylor's only response.

*"Do I look okay?" Torrey asked, enjoying her
friend's reaction.*

*"You look...stunning," Taylor said after a short
pause.*

*"You look pretty nice yourself," Torrey returned
the compliment.*

*"Oh, these are for you." Taylor reached for the
table behind her and held out a bouquet of fresh
roses.*

*"Oh, Stretch, that's so nice. They're beautiful,
but what did I do to deserve this?" Torrey questioned,
breathing in the scent of the flowers.*

*"Well, I figured if this is a date, you ought to get
the works." Taylor smiled back at her friend.*

*"Torrey you look absolutely beautiful...you both
do," Jean said, holding Jessica in her arms.*

*"Jean, are you sure you don't mind watching Jess,
because if you do—" Torrey began.*

*"Nonsense. You two go out and have a good time.
Just remember no driving if you're drinking."*

*"It's all right, Mom, I already called a cab. Just
a little planning ahead." Taylor winked at her roommate.*

*As if on cue the cab pulled up outside and honked
his horn. Unable to keep her eyes off Torrey's legs as
they slid into the cab, Taylor knew she was a goner.*
Oh man, something tells me I'm gonna get into a lot
of fights tonight.

****

"You sure you feel comfortable with this?" Taylor asked her friend as they found the large table in the back of the bar that Robin reserved for the evening.

"Sure," Torrey said with a bright smile in her roommate's direction.

Taylor wasn't at all sure if she could handle it. She was used to men doing double takes at the attractive blonde by her side, but it was a tad unnerving to see other women looking at Torrey with that same gleam in their eyes. For her part, Torrey was enjoying the evening so far. She imagined that she and Taylor were actually out on a real date and that the beautiful woman who stayed protectively by her side really was interested in her. She didn't know what to expect from a gay bar, but it looked pretty much like every other bar she'd ever been in.

"Feel like something to drink?" Taylor asked.

"A wine cooler would be nice," Torrey said, and then watched her friend rise and move away to the bar.

"Would you mind if I told you that you have the most beautiful eyes I've ever seen," the stranger said to Torrey with a smile.

Torrey laughed as a woman even younger than she was, knelt down by the table and proceeded to extol the blonde's physical virtues. *"Actually, I'm here with someone,"* Torrey interrupted politely.

The young woman had a charming smile that only deepened with Torrey's rebuff. *"Someone should tell your date that she is a very lucky woman,"* the stranger said softly.

"She already knows," Taylor's low voice responded from behind the kneeling woman.

"*I bet that's your date now,*" *the stranger looked up and said to Torrey with a knowing grin.*

"*Uh huh.*" *Torrey nodded, smiling back.*

The young woman looked up at Taylor towering over. "*Whoa,*" *she said, still looking up even though she straightened herself to her full height.* "*I'll just be moving on now.*" *She walked off with an embarrassed grin. The stranger knew she didn't have enough going on to compete with this woman.*

Taylor simply stood there with two bottles in her hand. When she first turned away from the bar and saw another woman hitting on her young friend, her first thought was to run over and throttle the kneeling woman. Then she heard Torrey's laugh. No one had a laugh that sounded like Torrey's, at least to Taylor's ears. It was so genuine and easy. No other sound ever stirred the artist's senses like that one did.

Taylor watched as the kneeling woman continued to chat up her friend. More amazing was the gracious manner in which Torrey accepted the flirtation. For a brief moment, the dark-haired woman at the bar thought her roommate was actually enjoying the attentions of another woman. Then Taylor realized that Torrey was always open and friendly, she was just being herself.

"*I can't leave you alone for a minute, can I?*" *Taylor said just loud enough for the surrounding patrons to hear her, a sly smile on her face.*

Torrey lowered her head as the blush in her face deepened. Taylor thought that she'd never seen anything more attractive. "*Well, she was awfully nice and I didn't want to hurt her feelings,*" *Torrey explained.*

"Oh, well, I can get her back if you want me to,"
Taylor said, feigning an attempt at rising from her
seat.

The wide-eyed expression Torrey rewarded the
artist with caused Taylor to laugh out loud at the
young woman. Putting her arm around her shoulder
and placing two fingers under the blonde's chin, Tay-
lor tilted the face up until their eyes met. A large grin
lit up the dark-haired woman's face. "Don't ever
change, Tor. I like you just the way you are," Taylor
said softly, leaning over to kiss the young woman's
cheek.

There weren't many women in the bar that seemed
willing to risk life and limb by defying the dark-
haired woman, and asking the young blonde to dance.
The ones that thought they were brave enough were
quickly turned aside by the sight of the two women
huddled close at the table.

Taylor had just brushed her lips against the soft-
ness of Torrey's cheek when they were interrupted.

"Well, it's good to know married life hasn't taken
all the romance away." Robin grinned as she and
Cindy sat down at the large table.

"Very funny, you know—" Taylor started but was
stopped by Torrey's hand placed over her own.

"It doesn't matter," Torrey said with a smile that
melted Taylor's heart.

For a split second, Taylor thought she saw an odd
look in Torrey's deep green eyes. A look that said she
welcomed the idea. The dark-haired woman realized
the young blonde was just being herself. She probably thinks it would be a huge blow to my ego to have
to tell them I'm not sleeping with her. *Her friend was*

always looking out for Taylor's feelings.

The night was one of the best Torrey and Taylor ever spent together. They laughed and joked all evening. Torrey and Cindy already bonded as friends when they met, and Barb and Kelly couldn't stop talking about the change in Taylor, giving Torrey full credit for the transformation. Torrey heard stories that left her reeling about what Taylor and her friends did as teenagers. It seemed that no one in San Diego was safe from their wild antics.

"Yea, and look at us all now, respectable professionals," Kelly said with a wicked grin on her face.

"Well, at least you're professional, I wouldn't push it any further than that," Torrey teased.

The table broke into a raucous laughter at the petite blonde's assessment of them.

"Oh, I definitely like her. No flies on her at all." Robin laughed.

"I love this song," Barb piped up, as she and her partner left the table and made their way to the dance floor.

"Come on, babe, dance with me?" Robin pleaded with the small brunette that sat next to her.

"And have everybody laugh at the way I dance, unh uh," Cindy replied.

"What do you say Torrey, wanna dance?" Robin looked across the table at the blonde.

"I, uh..." Torrey stammered. She never danced with a woman before and somehow thought it might be different.

"Not this time, kiddo," Taylor responded, rescuing her friend from embarrassment. Taylor stood and held out her hand. "She promised this one to me."

Torrey looked at Taylor's outstretched hand for a few seconds before she made her decision. If she was going to make a fool of herself, then she couldn't think of a nicer place to do it than in Taylor's arms. She placed her hand in the larger one of her friend and let the dark-haired beauty lead her onto the dance floor.

"I'm sorry, it's just that I'm not that hot of a dancer in the first place and, well—" Torrey apologized as Taylor laid a gentle hand against the small of the woman's back.

"It's okay, I understand. We could always duck outside for a little bit," Taylor offered.

"No. I mean, now that we're here..." Torrey's voice trailed off.

Torrey stepped on her partner's feet a couple of times until she got frustrated. Taylor could feel the tension growing in the young woman's body.

"Hey," Taylor said softly to get her friend's attention. Torrey's eyes locked into the intense blue of Taylor's gaze. "You'll be all right if you look into your partner's eyes and not at their feet. When you're dancing with someone, one of you has to give up a little control. Just lead where my body takes you and don't think so much about where you're going." Taylor's voice was as melodic as the music and she felt the calming effect her words were having on her friend. "Just look into my eyes. You should be able to see everything your partner thinks and feels in their eyes."

The artist gazed into the depths of Torrey's eyes as if to impart the deeply hidden secrets of her soul. She lost herself in the green color that reminded her of the ocean under the early morning sun. A deep, sea green, tinged with a ring of gold that circled the pupil. A stab of nervousness pierced through to her belly, desperately afraid Torrey would see all the love that Taylor held for her, all the while, desperately afraid she wouldn't.

"See, not that much different than dancing with a guy, is it?" Taylor asked quietly.

Torrey could only smile and wonder how her friend knew what she'd been thinking. God, how do I tell her it's a lot different? No guy ever made me feel this way before.

Torrey was caught up in the sensations of being held close to Taylor, their bodies slightly touching. Torrey allowed Taylor to take control and the young woman felt their bodies meld together and move as one. Aside from the gift of her child, Torrey would have to say that dancing on this evening with Taylor was one of the most delightful experiences of her life.

"Much better," Taylor whispered in her ear as the music stopped.

Torrey wasn't quite ready for the spell to be broken just yet. As the music started into another slow song, the young woman tugged on the artist's sleeve. "Can we do it again?" She looked up hopefully into Taylor's face.

The dark-haired woman gave Torrey a lopsided grin. "That would be my pleasure," she said, taking her friend in her arms once more.

Taylor never could remember what song the band played during those two dances with the woman who held her heart. She did remember the feeling, though. It felt like she always loved this young woman with the giving nature and open heart. She knew that no matter how many years passed them by, this would be the woman that she would always try to find her way back to.

* * * * * * * * * *

"Uh, Taylor? Isn't the name of the art supply place, Danny's?" Jessica roused the artist from her memories.

"Yea, I know." Taylor sneered, suddenly realizing where she was. "I passed it."

"Where in the world were you?"

"Just dazed out for a minute, I guess," Taylor replied.

Taylor wasn't about to admit to the young girl that she had her head in the clouds and she especially was not going to admit that she was dreaming of Torrey. *Geez, what's with me lately? I haven't sat around daydreaming about these things in years.*

She turned the car around and pulled into Danny's parking lot, finding a spot right in front of the large glass doors to park the Explorer. Walking into the huge store that supplied artists from all over southern California, Taylor motioned to Jessica. "The art tables and easels are in the back, let's take a look at those first," the artist said.

Jessica followed the taller woman to the back of the shop and was nearly run down by a wiry fellow only about as tall as she was. "Sorry, dear heart...comin' through," he apologized. Then his face broke into a smile. "Taylor! I thought you wouldn't step out of your castle till the big show. What's up?"

"Hey, Danny." Taylor looked up from a drafting chair she was inspecting. "I've got a friend's daughter visiting and she needs the works, table, chair, lights, then all the miscellaneous supplies she'll need. Jessica this is Danny Paries, this is his fine establishment you're standing in."

Jessica shook hands with the man. "You know, I think my mom has pottery with that name on, any relation?" Jessica asked.

"Probably me. It's what I do, dear heart, when I'm not supplying my customers with paper, pencils, and the latest gossip. Who's your mom?"

"Uh, Torrey Gray, only she lives in Chicago—"

"Oh, my God...not *the* Torrey Gray that writes the books?" Danny looked from the young girl to Taylor, both of them nodding their heads. "Oh, my God," the young man repeated.

Jessica grinned at the small man's reaction. Something inside her told her she was headed in the right direction with her life. A week ago she would never have admitted Torrey Gray was her mother, now she actually felt proud to be able to show off a famous mom.

Taylor sat back in one of the drafting chairs and waited for her friend to calm down. She knew if Danny ever found out Torrey was her best friend; there would be no dealing with it. Torrey's first book, *Stevie*, was about her older brother and his battle with AIDS. It not only spent an eternity on the NY Times' bestseller list, but it endeared the young author to a community who applauded her open and honest look at gays and the often hostile world they had to tolerate. Danny and Alec, his lover of the last twelve years, were two of the few people Taylor became close to over the years.

"Well, you've come to the right place my dear, and Taylor, I expect that money will not be an issue?" Danny took Jessica's arm and led the young woman away before turning back to Taylor.

"The sky's the limit." Taylor smiled.

"All right, ladies and gentleman...we have a celebrity in our midst. Now, Jessica...what kind of art are you interested in?" Danny asked as the young woman was pulled away to another part of the store. Taylor decided to find Alec in the back office and hide out with a cup of coffee.

* * * * * * * * *

"Do you think you could use acrylic paint on this kind of paper, or would you have to use canvas?" A pretty blonde turned to Jessica as she was looking through stacks of sketch pads.

Jessica looked up at the voice from her kneeling position on the floor and felt the power of speech leave her. The young woman was a couple inches shorter than herself and her short blonde hair lay in casual curls all over her head. Her large brown eyes looked expectantly at the dark-haired girl on the floor.

"Huh?" Jessica asked, trying to buy some time for her limbs to take orders from her brain so she could stand.

The blonde noticed her confusion and suddenly realized her error. "You don't work here, do you? I'm sorry. You just looked like you did. I'm really sorry."

"Oh, it's no big deal." Jessica finally found her voice. "I have a friend who paints. She might be able to answer your question. I can get her if you want to wait just a sec."

"Sure." The girl smiled sweetly, her smile growing as she watched the retreating backside in tight jeans walk off in a hurry to the back room.

"Taylor!" Jessica hissed, nearly causing the artist to dump her coffee cup on the floor. "I need your help. There's a girl who's asking a paint type question. Can you help?"

"Oh, I'll take care of her," Danny jumped up.

"No!" Jessica said, her voice struggling to stay low. "I need Taylor to...it's just that...oh, Taylor come on, I can't explain right now."

Taylor chuckled at the girl's attitude, but rose from her seat to see what the problem was.

"And, try not to let me look like an idiot, okay?" Jessica begged as she dragged Taylor through the door into the store.

By the time the artist explained the answer to the young woman, it became apparent that Jessica was completely enamored of the girl. It was also evident that the young blonde felt the same way about Jessica. The girl flirted as if Taylor wasn't even standing there.

"Well, if you don't have any other questions..." Taylor nearly waved her hand in front of the girl's face.

"Oh, uh, no. You've been more than helpful, thank you so much."

Taylor returned to the back office as Alec and Danny moved away from the door. "Oh, subtle guys.

What if they turned around and saw you?" Taylor chided.

"Are you kidding?" Alec's deep baritone voice laughed. "They've only got eyes for each other. Score!" the man whispered as he turned back into the office where Taylor and Danny stood. "Your daughter got the blonde's phone number. Gee, chip off the old block, Taylor."

"She's not Taylor's daughter," Danny explained who Jessica's mother was.

"Torrey Gray, huh? Cool, think she'll write a book about it?" Alec asked Taylor seriously.

"She might...*if* she knew," Taylor said, with a keep your mouth shut look.

"Did you know she was gay?" Danny asked.

"I suspected as much."

"Do you think she knows yet?" Danny shot back.

"Oh, God I hope so. If she doesn't I may have to call my mother for pointers," Taylor replied in exasperation.

Taylor and Jessica actually spent a pleasant day together. By the time they got home and had something to eat, they still had a couple of hours until they were to leave for Laguna Beach. Taylor noticed that Jessica was getting a little nervous and fidgety. The older woman knew the feeling well. She used to exhibit the same pacing behavior and learned to recognize it as a sign that her body or her mind, or both, were craving the peace that drugs could offer.

Taylor pulled the girl by the arm into the studio. Jessica's furnishings wouldn't arrive for another day or two so the artist sat the young girl in front of her own drafting table. "Here, draw," Taylor said succinctly.

"Draw what?" Jessica looked up confused.

"This is the time when you just start drawing whatever comes into your head. Don't worry about what it looks like, just get your mind and your hands busy."

Taylor looked up from her own sketchpad about twenty minutes later to see Jessica's head bent to the paper, completely lost in her work. The dark-haired artist smiled to herself, knowing she couldn't take credit for the trick. Torrey came up with the plan of substituting one addiction for another, one harmless addiction for a destructive one.

It was going to be touch and go with the young girl and Taylor knew she would have to keep one eye open all the time. You don't just grow integrity overnight, even though Jessica was doing well now; Taylor figured she would be playing nursemaid and babysitter for quite a while yet. It would definitely become a test of her patience with her own artwork due to be displayed in another six months. *Give me strength*, the artist pleaded to whomever took care of such requests.

Chapter
9

"So, did you get the name of the girl you met at Danny's today?" Taylor asked. She decided to break a little of the tension in the car. Jessica was more quiet than usual, from nerves or withdrawal, Taylor couldn't tell. She remembered how literally terrified she was, going to her first NA meeting.

"Val, Valerie Kane," Jessica replied. "Taylor?"

"Hmmm?"

"I don't know if you know it, but I'm gay," Jessica said nervously.

"I'm always honored when someone trusts me enough to share that information," Taylor replied. "Jess?"

"Yea?" Jessica responded.

"So am I," Taylor announced with as little fanfare as possible.

"What?" Jessica nearly shouted, but as soon as her brain had a half-second to think about it, it made sense. Suddenly, somewhere in the back of her mind, a lot of things made sense about the older woman, but Jessica couldn't quite get a grasp on what she was thinking, it was only a bunch of feelings. "Does my mom know?" was all the girl could think of to say.

"Yes," Taylor chuckled. "Your mother knew when we were in school together."

"She never told me," Jessica responded.

"Well, she probably thought that unless I told you, my personal life wasn't anyone else's business," the artist replied.

"Wow." Jessica sat shaking her head. "I thought my mom would freak if I told her about me. You and she weren't...you know?"

"Not that it's any of your business, but no," Taylor answered. "Your mom has always been my best friend and our relationship drew the line there."

"Did you ever think about it?" Jessica asked as they pulled into a parking lot in front of a small single level building.

"This is the place," Taylor said, quickly opening her door to avoid answering the question. "Why don't you save up your questions for later and just listen for a while, okay?" Taylor finished, ushering the young woman through the front door.

Taylor knew that she narrowly avoided certain disaster with that one. She could only wonder if the young girl walking along side of her would forget the line of questioning by the time they got home tonight or if, like her mother, she had a little bit of pit bull in her and would hold on until she received her answer.

Taylor showed Jessica to a couple of seats by the back aisle. She had a feeling the girl might be a little panicky about the whole scenario and she wanted to give them clear access in case Jessica decided to bolt in the middle of the meeting. If that turned out to be the case, then so be it. They would come back tomorrow night and try again.

There was about twenty minutes before the start of the meeting. "You okay?" Taylor asked the young girl.

"I guess," Jessica answered uncertainly.

Taylor reached over and squeezed the girl's hand. "Don't worry, Jess. You don't have to do anything and you don't have to say anything, just listen. Nobody will embarrass you in any way, so relax, okay?" Taylor said softly.

Jessica nodded her head and gave a weak smile.

"Taylor, how are you tonight?" A woman nearly as tall as the artist leaned down to kneel on one knee next to Taylor's chair. The two women shook hands and smiled. Jessica noticed the woman had the most beautiful brown skin she'd ever seen.

"Natalie, I'd like you to meet someone. Jess, this is Natalie." Taylor looked at the young girl. "This is Jessica. Jess is staying with me for a while," was the only explanation Taylor offered.

"Very nice to meet you Jessica. Don't let us scare you too bad," she said affectionately, with a small wink. "Taylor, I need a favor," she continued, turning to the artist. "Jenny had to go home, she's not feeling too hot. I desperately need someone to speak. You always do a good job. Would you mind?"

Oh great! What timing. "Uh, I don't know," Taylor answered, turning to look over at Jessica.

"It's okay," Jessica responded to the unanswered

question. "I'll be okay."

That wasn't exactly the answer Taylor was hoping for. She spoke at numerous meetings and counseling groups, but it was always easy when you talked about your past in front of strangers. Now, with Jessica sitting here she wondered what she would say. "Sure," Taylor answered with a *'you caught me'* look.

"Great, you're a lifesaver. I owe you," Natalie said, rising from the floor.

"That's what you always say. I'm waiting to see some of this payback," Taylor responded with a smile.

"You'll get your reward in heaven, my child." Natalie gave her a wicked little smile.

Taylor snorted. "Yea, and what happens when they don't let me in?"

Natalie laughed and winked at the dark-haired woman. "Welcome, everyone. My name is Natalie."

The meeting started like it always did. Whenever they asked Taylor to speak, she always came up with something different, a little on the inspirational side. She overcame a lot to get where she was right now and that gave others a reason to hope too. Now, she sat there a little nervously, waiting for Natalie to call her up to the podium.

There were about two dozen people of all ages, races, and backgrounds scattered throughout the room, but the one that scared the hell out of Taylor was the one sitting next to her. She had no idea how Jessica would take it, hearing about her past misdeeds. The artist worried she would end up showing the girl what not to do, as opposed to what she should do. *Hell, I just want to be a good example for her.*

That little thought tweaked her brain a bit. *Isn't*

that what we've all been doing with Jess? It's damn sure that's what Torrey did. Thinking that she could protect the girl from all the rotten stuff out there by simply pretending it didn't exist. Poor Torrey didn't know that by trying to protect her daughter, she was driving her right into the things she hid her from.

God, it's true, we do become our mothers. Didn't Evelyn try to do the same thing with Torrey and her brother? The woman went through her life thinking if she just never said the words out loud, if she never admitted her son was gay, then that made it true. I will not become that...not with Jessica, and I won't let Torrey go there either.

Taylor broke from her reverie just in time to hear her introduction. Giving a confident wink to the silent girl sitting next to her, she took her place behind the microphone. The static hum of the mic would give anyone stage fright, the artist thought to herself. Taylor had the kind of speaking voice that didn't need very much amplification in the first place. She stepped to one side of the podium and asked if everyone could still hear her all right. She liked a more casual approach. When everyone nodded, she told them a little about herself.

Some in the audience already knew the usually reserved artist. She showed up every Tuesday night for over fourteen years. Most people shied away from the beautiful woman, but some came up to her to comment on what an inspiration her story or her life was for them. To those brave individuals that crossed her path, she always reserved one of her sparkling smiles and a few moments of encouragement and conversation.

As Taylor spoke, the back of her mind filled with memories of a room just like this one. Although that room was in the basement of an old church in Maine and in August it was sweltering. That's when she first showed up at a NA meeting. It was right after She and Torrey returned from their vacation in California.

Taylor was sticking to her word; she hadn't touched so much as an aspirin since the night she admitted she had a drug problem. Some days were definitely easier than others were, but she never gave in to the temptation. Torrey was always there with a hug and practically held Taylor's hand on the bad days, but while the young blonde listened and tried to be supportive, she couldn't completely empathize with her friend's predicament.

Torrey had never been addicted to anything. She could practice moderation in anything and often had a hard time trying to put herself in Taylor's place. That's when Torrey found out about Narcotics Anonymous. It was a place where Taylor could talk to people that were in the same boat and even talk to some who made it to shore. That day in August changed Taylor's life, but she never admitted, even to Torrey how truly terrified she was.

August 1983

"I can do this, right?" Taylor asked Torrey as she released Jessica from the car seat in the back of the vehicle.

"You betchya." Torrey smiled confidently up at her friend.

Oh God, Torrey, what that smile does to me, only for you, Little Bit, only for you. Taylor took the nine-month-old baby from her mother's arms.

Jessica was growing at quite a pace. At the rate she was going, it seemed as if she actually was Taylor's child. The dark-haired artist would lie on the floor with Jessica and roll a tiny plastic basketball in front of her, teasing her mother, saying that by the time they let women in the NBA this one would be ready to play for the Lakers. Torrey would always stop what she was doing, walk into the room, and say it would be the Chicago Bulls or no one.

The two women walked through the church doors and down the stairs, Torrey leading the way. When they reached the basement there were a number of people sitting in folding chairs, some were milling about, visiting before the meeting got underway.

A woman perhaps Taylor's age sat at a small folding table and motioned them over. "Hi, I'm Eva, how are you folks tonight?" *Eva said with a crooked smile.*

"Just fine, Sister," *Torrey answered holding out her hand to shake Eva's.* "I'm Torrey, I talked with you on the phone this morning."

"Right, Torrey, and this one must be the angel responsible for the screaming I heard in the background," *Eva replied indicating Jessica.* "You must be Taylor. Nice to meet you."

"You too, Sister," *Taylor responded nervously. After all, one doesn't give up twelve years of Catholic schooling overnight.*

"Oh, please, just call me Eva. Nobody calls me Sister. Well, maybe my mom, but she only does it to impress the ladies at bingo." *Eva laughed.* "So, Tay-

lor, you're gonna give us a try, huh?"

"Well, try is the operative word," Taylor responded. *"I really don't know anything about this twelve step stuff, but I'm game."*

"Excellent! That's just what I like to hear. It all starts with a will to want to change, you know. Torrey, why don't you take the baby from Taylor so she and I can go in the back for an informal chat. Is that okay with you, Taylor?"

"Uhm, I guess so," Taylor replied. *Her knees were doing everything but shaking together.*

Once Eva turned and walked away, assuming Taylor would follow, the artist turned to her roommate. "Tor, I don't know if I can talk to a nun."

"It's okay. She's not exactly your run of the mill nun. Go ahead, Stretch. Jess and I will be sitting out here waiting for you," Torrey said to her friend, *watching as Taylor's tall figure retreated into the back offices.*

"It's okay, Taylor, loosen up. You don't have to do anything you don't want to here," Eva said with a pat on the dark-haired woman's shoulders.*

Taylor relaxed then, her shoulders losing a little bit of the tension they held. Eva offered her a cup of coffee and once the woman across from her started asking questions, the artist found herself opening up more than she thought she'd be able to. By the time they were through, Taylor found that she revealed things even Torrey didn't know about her.

Eva smiled to herself as she watched the tall dark-haired woman slip into a seat next to the small blonde. She'd seen a lot worse since she started working with this program, but it would be hard to

*come across a woman who wanted to kick the habit
more than this one did. Eva liked it when they had
someone to come in with them, someone who cared
enough to help them become whole again. She could
tell the tall woman was nearly ready to bolt, though.
She looked like a scared rabbit, even though she was
putting up a good front. This one was strong. She
knew that if Taylor ran tonight, she'd never be back.*

*"Hey," Taylor said, slipping into the empty seat
next to Torrey.*

"Hey, yourself. How did it go?" Torrey asked.

*"She's pretty nice," Taylor replied, wiping sweaty
palms along her thighs.*

*Torrey knew that Taylor was scared. Her friend
tried to hide it, but the taller woman always came
down with sweaty palms when she was extremely nervous. Part of her could understand why the artist was
fearful. Taylor believed in keeping everything locked
up inside, only showing people what she wanted them
to see. She was different with Torrey, but even still
there was that smallest part of her that wouldn't give
up control.*

*The meeting was half way through and Torrey
already learned a great deal about addiction, especially drug addiction. For casual, mild drug users it
was almost the psychological addiction that was
worse than the physical. She was also amazed to
learn that even if you didn't have a problem with alcohol, the Narcotics Anonymous program demanded
complete abstinence, from liquor as well as drugs.
They stressed the fact that alcohol was a drug and
that thinking it was different from other drugs was
what caused many addicts to relapse. It was also*

expected that newcomers attend at least one meeting every day for the first few months.

Out of the corner of her eye, Torrey could see her friend trying to listen, but when some people stood to give personal testimonies, Taylor rose and whispered that she needed some air. She walked out of the building and Torrey was at a loss as to what she should do. Should she follow her? Would Taylor leave without her?

Ten minutes went by and Torrey reached down to grab Jessica's bag. Just as she was rising, Sister Eva came over and sat in Taylor's vacated seat. "She'll be back," she whispered, placing a gentle hand on Torrey's arm.

"She's pretty scared about all of this. She's trying very hard, but I don't know what to do anymore. If I turn my head I'm afraid I'm just enabling her to continue taking the drugs," Torrey admitted.

"You've already done more than a lot of people might have. Now it's time to do the hardest thing. You have to let her decide if she wants to be free of her habit or not. You won't be around every time she starts to feel this way. Taylor needs to find something, in her own heart and mind that's worth giving it all up for. When she does that, then she'll be able to fight it even when you're not around. If you go out to her now, she'll talk you into leaving and if she does that I have my doubts as to whether she'll ever be back. Just relax for a little while longer, Torrey. I'm betting that if you don't go looking for her, she'll come back in for you." Eva gave the small blonde a reassuring smile and moved to the back of the room.

Torrey tried to relax and let Eva's words sink in.

The hardest choice in her young life was deciding to stay inside and wait for her friend to return. She hoped Taylor would realize that she would always be there for her, would always love her no matter what, but that the artist would have to take that scariest of all steps, that first one, on her own.

Another twenty minutes went by until Torrey felt the familiar presence next to her. She looked up into Taylor's contrite face that tried to mask her fear. "Sorry, Little Bit, guess I kinda freaked out," she whispered.

"Don't worry about it, Stretch. I listened in case they give us a test at the end." She winked.

Taylor let out a chuckle and a sigh at the same time, afraid that she let her friend down. "Thanks," she whispered into the young woman's ear.

"Yea, yea," Torrey said in mock exasperation. "Hey, take your turn with this girl. Your daughter is gaining a lot of weight," Torrey teased the older woman.

"Oh, that hurts," Taylor responded, trying to keep her voice down.

"You still never forgave that nurse for the comment about your hips, did you?" Torrey whispered back as she handed Jessica to the woman next to her.

The two women only had to look at one another and suddenly they were trying to stifle their laughter. A raised eyebrow and a knowing smile from Sister Eva hushed the two. Yes, twelve years of Catholic schooling is a very hard notion to dispel.

Torrey watched as Taylor held and rocked Jessica against her. She purposely handed the baby to her friend knowing that Jessica seemed to have an almost calming effect on the artist. Besides, Taylor always felt she was being rewarded with something special when Torrey entrusted the baby into her care.

Jessica snuggled into the tall woman's embrace and promptly fell asleep. Taylor stroked the tiny baby's face while she listened to a woman on the stage speak. The woman said she grew up as a typical child of the sixties and by the time she was twenty, was a hopeless addict. What turned the woman's life around was when she found out she was pregnant. She realized that she no longer lived her life for just herself. She had someone she was responsible for and who would love her unconditionally, no matter what. The woman was celebrating ten years in recovery and soon her child's ninth birthday.

Taylor looked down at the sleeping baby in her arms and realized that she too had the unconditional love of people who cared for her when nearly everyone else gave up on her. Wasn't she responsible for them? If something happened to her, Torrey might never finish school; worse, she would have to go groveling to her mother. A small tear escaped out of a sky blue eye.

Torrey was quick to notice the change in her friend's demeanor, and when Taylor bent her head down to Jessica's and placed a light kiss on her forehead, it nearly broke Torrey's heart. She didn't care what it would look like. She placed her arm along the back of Taylor's chair and rubbed the woman's back in a light circular motion. Leaning toward the taller woman, she rested her chin on Taylor's shoulder.

The instant Torrey offered up her comforting touch, Taylor knew she found her reasons. If there were ever days when the artist found herself unworthy, all she would have to do is remember that she was staying clean for these two also. She didn't want Torrey to be ashamed of her and she wanted Jess to grow up thinking the girl could always count on her. She said to herself right then that she wanted to be the woman who was standing on that stage. She wanted to look back after all those years and know that she did something good with her life. Most of all, Taylor wanted to know that she did it all for the love and welfare of these two incredible women, one, the woman who would always own her heart, the other, the girl who would always be the child of her heart.

* * * * * * * * * *

Taylor stopped talking, noticing it had grown very quiet. She stood in front of everyone and dug her hands into her pockets. "I want all of you to do something," she began. "Take a look around you. Look at the people sitting next to you, in front and behind you." Everyone looked around at one another.

"All of you have something in common," Taylor said. "And, no, I don't mean that." She chuckled as the members of the audience laughed. "You're all scared, scared senseless," she said flatly.

Jessica looked up to watch the older woman. She held the audience with rapt attention; her natural alto voice had the ability to command you to listen. When she said those last words, Jessica wondered how the woman could know what she was thinking.

"Most of you are so scared being in this room that you want to run, the other half of you are just too ter-

rified to run. However, you're not alone here; we're
all scared just like you. We're afraid that we won't be
able to stop or we're afraid because we did stop.
There are tons of things to be afraid of, trust me I
have enough of them to know," Taylor said with a wry
smile. Again, most of the people laughed, but not one
person got up to leave.

"I'll let you in on a secret. I know the trick to
making that fear disappear." Taylor's voice lowered
to nearly a whisper, some of the audience literally
holding their breath for the older woman's words of
wisdom.

"It's having people around you to care about you,
to love you, just to be your friend. Those are the reasons you want to stay clean. A lot of us won't do it
for ourselves. Frankly, we just don't believe we're
worth it, but we can't let anybody else do it for us.
We can accept their help, though. Because, rest
assured, there are going to be days when you need a
friend, and I promise you, someone to hold your hand
through a rough time can be priceless." Taylor
walked off the stage and stepped down onto the floor.

"I can tell by looking out at you that a lot of you
have someone with you that can already be that reason
you decide to care. If you don't have a lover, or family member, or even a coworker to bring with you,
don't think you're without friends. We've got a lot of
people that work here that are just dying to make
friends," Taylor said with a smile.

"Natalie," Taylor called to the back of the room.
"Couldn't you use another friend?"

"Absolutely," the counselor shouted back up to
the front of the room.

"So, there's no reason to leave here today with your fear. Let somebody help you help yourself, but you have to take the first step. And, if you don't believe it can happen—" Taylor reached into her pocket and pulled out the black chip. She held the marker up to the light so everyone could see it. "I'm living proof that you can find reasons to stay clean. I have been for fifteen years."

The audience clapped their hands and Taylor returned their thanks with a warm smile before taking her seat next to Jessica.

"Wow," Jessica said under her breath.

"Is that a good wow or a bad wow?" Taylor asked.

"That's a wow, you should have your own infomercial," Jessica replied with a grin.

Taylor laughed out loud. The young girl's statement and the sound of her own laughter eased the tension she was feeling. Now if she could just get Jess to find her own reasons.

Jessica leaned against a back wall and watched as her mother's friend kneeling in front of a young girl. The youngster didn't seem to be much older than twelve or thirteen, with her baggy jeans, an oversized T-shirt, and a long sleeved flannel top she looked like she was trying to play dress up. The two spoke in low tones, a woman who appeared to be the girl's mother sat alongside and ran her fingers lovingly through the girl's long brown hair. Jessica thought of her own mother and wondered what she was doing now and if she should call her.

The girl started crying and Taylor wiped away the tears from her cheeks with a gentle touch. The artist stood and put her arm around the girl, directing her to the table where Natalie sat.

"Nat, how about giving me a white chip?" Taylor asked.

Natalie searched in a box of chips and handed one over to the taller woman. Taylor flipped the piece in her fingers. "Corey, here, has been clean for over eight hours," Taylor said.

"Excellent job, Corey, we're proud of you," Natalie responded encouragingly.

Corey sniffed and wiped her nose with the sleeve of her shirt, smiling she mumbled a thank you. Taylor continued to twirl the chip through her fingers like a casino dealer. Corey's eyes lit up. Taylor held the chip out to the girl.

"You practice just like that," Taylor said, pulling a business card from her wallet and turning it over to write her cell phone number on the other side. "And, and if it starts to get too rough, you call me and we'll talk, okay?"

The girl nodded, still seeming a little in awe of the tall woman. Then the dark-haired woman stood, bent down and said something quietly to the young girl, then gave Corey a very heartfelt hug. While Jessica watched this interaction between the young girl and the artist, she realized that she missed her mother. As she continued to watch, she wished, for entirely selfish reasons, that Taylor and her mother had stayed together longer.

****

This time the silence in the car unnerved Taylor. Jessica hadn't said much since they left the meeting.

The older woman wondered if hearing her speak so honestly about her past upset the girl. She cleared her throat and it echoed oddly within the darkened vehicle.

"Taylor?" Jessica asked with her face turned toward the window of the car.

"Hhmm?" Taylor responded.

"You think it would be all right if I called my mom tomorrow?" Jessica questioned.

Taylor was just happy that the darkness inside the car hid her smile. "Yea, I think she'd like hearing from you," the artist answered.

There wasn't much conversation after that. They arrived home and each woman headed straight for a hot shower and bed. Jessica looked around for a few minutes and finally found the artist wrapped in her robe sipping a mug of tea on the patio overlooking the cliffs. Her head rested against the back of the chaise lounge she sat in, her eyes slightly closed.

"Hey, I'm turning in," Jessica said from the door.

Taylor opened one eye and smiled at the girl. Jessica wasn't quite sure what to say. She wanted to say so much, but none of the words seemed to come to her. Finally, she turned to go back inside and stopped in the open doorway. "Taylor, what were your reasons? The things that made the fear go away," She asked without turning around.

Taylor placed her mug on the small table beside the chair and leaned her head back, closing her eyes once again. "I thought you knew that already. It was you and your mom," she said barely above a whisper.

Jessica nodded as if the answer made perfect sense to her. Then the young girl said goodnight and was gone inside the house.

Taylor waited a few minutes until she was sure Jessica was in her room before she allowed the silent tears to spill down her cheeks. It still hurt so much, even after fifteen years the pain was as fresh as if it happened moments ago. Her arms ached with a pain that was as real as the desire that still burned hot within her. Her heart grieved for a love that would always be unrequited.

Chapter
10

Jessica woke up the next day feeling pretty good. She didn't know why, but she didn't want to question it. The first thought on her mind was that she wanted to talk to her mother today. Watching Taylor interact with Corey last night started her thinking about her relationship with her mother.

Jessica spent so many of her growing up years being angry and resentful of her mother, and for the life of her, she couldn't figure out why. It wasn't like Torrey was hurtful, selfish, or mean. On the contrary, the small blonde was a completely loving, caring, and nurturing mother. The woman went out of her way, made so many self-sacrificing gestures for her daughter that Jessica lost count. All the lengths her mother went to. Did she really deserve such love?

Jessica was scrubbing her face in the shower by the time the answer came to her. Why hadn't she taken the time before to think like this? She rinsed her face and knew it was a lot easier to think clearly when you weren't drunk or stoned. There were a lot of times when she got high, that things seemed clearer to her and she assumed it was an effect of the grass she was smoking. That kind of clarity never lasted, though. It never seemed to make sense. Now as she stood under the warm water of the shower, she realized that persistence of vision was relative to where you were at the time.

Now the answers to all her anger toward her mother seemed to open itself up to her like the petals of a flower. Her mother was a wonderful person, just as wonderful as Taylor described her. She loved Jessica more than the young girl thought she could ever understand, but Jessica never thought she deserved that kind of love. The idea had started at a young age. She never thought she was deserving of that kind of love. She certainly wasn't worth all the trouble that Torrey went to. Didn't her mother understand that?

It dawned on the young woman that her mother was a pretty smart lady. Would she keep wasting her time on her daughter if she knew Jessica to be a lost cause? Look at Evelyn. Torrey never spoke to her mother, saying it was a falling out of sorts, even though they both lived within minutes of each other now. Torrey gave up her mother and wrote her off as forgotten. Why didn't Torrey want to do that to Jessica? So, maybe the answer was that Jess wasn't the loser she always thought she was.

She rinsed her mouth over the sink and still held the toothbrush in one hand as she examined her reflection in the mirror. She tried to think of things that made her worth something in another's eyes.

"Well, I'm pretty good looking and I've got cool

eyes." She pointed to her image in the mirror with the end of the toothbrush. "I can draw pretty well, uhm...do a cartwheel, make pancakes and macaroni and cheese, use a computer..." She listed her qualifications aloud.

Jessica frowned at herself in the mirror. *All these years, all the hell I put my mom through. Pissing my own life away, and why? All because I actually resented my mom for loving me. Like I held it against her because I thought she should see that I wasn't worthy of her love. Geez, Jess, you really fucked this part of your life up.*

In moments, Jessica's frown turned into a crooked smile. She would call her mom right now and tell her what a great mom she's really been. Deciding on a course of action, the young woman quickly dressed and made her way into the kitchen. She found the new two-pot coffee maker they purchased yesterday and set it up, filling the filter on one side with green tea leaves. She ran back to the hall to see what time it was, since the maker wouldn't brew until the time was set. The Grandfather clock near the living room said 5:15. Jessica was amazed. She couldn't remember ever getting up this early without an alarm. *Guess what mom said was true. If you get to bed at a decent hour, you can get up. Geez, I'm gonna hate it if she's always gonna be right now.*

Once she had the tea brewing, she knew she couldn't call her mother. There was at least an hour's time difference between California and Illinois, maybe two because of daylight savings time, she wasn't sure, but 7:15 was still way too early to wake the famous author. Jessica had no idea what to do at five o'clock in the morning; she rarely even saw that hour unless she was coming home. She was kind of hungry, though. She got an idea and she hoped Taylor would be all right with it.

****

Taylor awoke to a smell that reminded her even more of the woman she'd spent most of the night dreaming about. It smelled like someone was actually cooking, and unless her mother was here for a visit, Jess must have gotten inventive. She was afraid of what she would see so she gave up the idea of heading for the bathroom first and sauntered out to the kitchen.

"Morning," Jess said with a smile.

"Morning yourself, what have you got going there?" Taylor asked.

"Bacon is frying now and I'm going to start the pancakes in a few minutes. Do you like pancakes?"

"I don't know," Taylor responded with a chuckle. "I haven't had them in years. It all smells pretty good, though." She poured herself a cup of the hot tea. "Do I have time for a shower?"

"Sure, go for it," Jessica replied.

Taylor made her way back to her bathroom and turned the shower stall's faucet on to warm up the water. She took another sip of tea and placed the mug on the vanity. She smiled to herself, thinking how easy it was to become domesticated again.

"So is today a holiday or what?" Taylor asked, sitting down to the table and shaking wet hair from her eyes. Jessica made enough pancakes for a small army, bacon, and orange juice.

"I would have made coffee too, but I didn't have a clue how much to use. Does there have to be a reason? I mean, can't it just be thanks for everything you're doing for me?" Jessica answered sincerely.

Taylor continued to stare at the girl, one eyebrow rising up to disappear beneath her ebony bangs.

Jessica knew when she was beat. "Okay, you win," the young woman said and related the story of how she, not realizing how early it was, rose before the sun. She also threw in the fact that her mother was right about how getting enough sleep let you wake up earlier. "Don't you hate it when your mom's right all the time?"

"We're in absolute agreement there, but the longer you live the more you will find that statement to be true. Trust me, it can be unnerving at times," Taylor agreed.

Once they each finished eating, both women were more than full. Taylor was amazed at the amount of food the young girl could put away.

"Jess, this was great, thanks. I haven't had anyone cook for me, aside from my mother, in a long time, and, if you don't mind me saying it, you have an appetite like your mother's. If I ate the way you two did I'd be as big as a house."

Jessica grinned. "Yea, the Chinese place loves to get our carry out business. Don't get too used to it, though. I only know how to cook two things, pancakes and macaroni and cheese. I sure wish I knew how to make that pot roast my mom always fixed in the winter time."

"Yea," Taylor agreed. "With all the vegetables

cut up with it."

"Yea," Jessica added, wistfully. "I think we should have gotten that cookbook yesterday."

Taylor laughed. "I think you're right. You can call your mom now if you want. She should be up by now," Taylor said, consulting the sports watch on her wrist. "I'll get out of your hair, on one condition."

Jessica looked suspiciously at the older woman.

"Let me look at your sketch books," Taylor whispered.

Jessica smiled and walked off in the direction of her bedroom. She came back with about a half dozen small sketch pads and laid them on the table in front of the artist.

"Just don't expect too much, okay?" Jessica asked nervously.

"Don't worry, I have no expectations." Taylor poured one more cup of tea and moved to the patio doors. "I'll be outside if you need anything. Tell your mom I said hi," Taylor said as she closed the door behind her.

Jessica grabbed the cordless phone from its cradle on the wall and paused. She wondered if she ought to plan out what she wanted to say. She finally decided that playing it by ear would work better. She quickly punched in the numbers that she knew by heart. Her mother's voice answered on the second ring.

"Hey, Mom," Jessica said nervously.

"JT? Honey, are you okay?" Torrey asked in alarm.

"No, Mom, it's okay. I'm doing fine. I just wanted to call you and, you know, let you know I got here okay and say hi."

"I'm so glad you did, Jess. You've been on my mind a lot," Torrey replied realizing that Taylor probably made the girl call. "Is everything going all right so far?"

"Oh, yea. Taylor's pretty cool. I mean I've managed to piss her off a couple times, but she's fair, ya know? You should see this house, Mom."

With that, Jessica did a descriptive narrative about the house and Dana Point. She told her mother about everything from buying an art table at Danny's to eating at a deli called Simon's.

Torrey smiled at the memory. "I could kill for a Simon Special," Torrey said.

"Oh, Mom, those are so disgusting. Taylor ate one and said you ate *two* of them when you were here when I was a baby."

Torrey laughed at her daughter's comment. "So, tell me more."

Jessica just kept going. She couldn't remember a time when she'd chattered away with her mom like this. Actually, Torrey couldn't either and the writer's greatest fear was realized. Her daughter's problems were because of her. Suddenly Torrey became silent and Jessica had to ask a couple of times if she was still there.

"How are you getting along with Taylor?" Torrey asked, but to Jessica, her mother's voice sounded strange.

Jessica looked outside onto the patio love seat. Taylor was looking at the young girl's drawings, occasionally sipping from her mug; her bare feet tucked up under her legs. At first, Jessica sang the artist's praises, but she stopped short, as she understood why her mother's voice sounded strained.

"You know, Taylor is really great, I mean, I know why you were such good friends and she makes a pretty good second mom, but...well, she's not you, Mom." Jessica could tell her mother was crying and it pulled painfully at her heart. "Mom...I went to an NA meeting with Taylor last night, do you know what that is? I think it's really going to help me," JT admitted.

"Yes, sweetheart, I know about NA. I'm so proud of you, Jess," Torrey said softly. "That takes a lot of courage. I know you'll do well."

"Well, I wanted to call you today because...well, I wanted you to know what a great mom I think you are."

Torrey couldn't stop the tears that took over. Relief at her daughter's words flooded through her.

"Please Mom, don't cry," Jessica pleaded help-lessly.

"Oh, honey, it's okay. I'm crying because I'm so happy." Torrey tried to reassure her daughter.

"If you say so," Jessica responded. "Not sure I get why you would cry if you're happy, though."

"JT, my greatest wish for you is that someday something happens to make you so happy that you cry. It's the only way you'll know how I'm feeling right now."

Jessica continued to share some of the things she discovered in the last two days. The young woman never thought she would ever hear pride in her mother's voice over her. She thought it was the great-est sound in the world. She had her reasons now. If she ever thought giving up her addictions for herself wasn't a good enough reason to keep going, she now had two other reasons: her two moms.

"I miss you, Mom," Jessica whispered into the phone.

"Honey, I miss you too, more than you'll ever know," Torrey responded in a loving voice.

"Hey, Taylor says hi. Do you want to talk to her?"

"Uhm, yea that would be great." Torrey meant to say no, but the thought of hearing the low alto of Taylor's voice took control of her decision. "Hey, Jess, before you go I want you to know I love you," Torrey said.

"I love you too, Mom," Jessica said. The young woman thought it was probably the first time she'd said those words to her mother in a very long time.

Jessica opened the door to the outside patio just as Taylor looked up. "Mom wants to talk to you," Jessica said as she handed the artist the phone.

"How did it go?" Taylor asked as she held her hand over the receiver.

Jessica gave her a thumbs-up sign and a smile. Just as she turned to go back inside, she thought of something else she wanted to ask her mother. "I forgot, let me talk to her again when you're done okay?" Jessica asked.

Taylor nodded her head and watched Jessica walk back inside to clean the kitchen of their breakfast dishes. "Hey, Little Bit," Taylor said into the phone.

"Hey, Stretch," Torrey answered. "I only have one question for you."

Taylor's eyes narrowed as she wondered what Jessica told her mother. "Yesss?" she drawled.

"Who was that girl I just talked to and what have you done with my daughter?" Torrey asked in amazement.

Taylor leaned back her head and laughed. The sound was a balm to the soul for two women whose hearts were hurting for much the same reasons.

Nearly an hour later Taylor walked back into the kitchen. "Here you wanted to talk to your mom again?" Taylor asked, holding the phone out.

"Yea," Jessica replied reaching for the telephone. "Hey, Mom? How do you make that pot roast of yours?"

****

"You and Mom talked for quite a while. Did I come up at all?" Jessica fished for information later that morning.

"Believe it or not, squirt, your mom and I were having conversations long before you were even around, but no we didn't talk about you. I promised, remember?" Taylor responded. "Oh, wait she did ask me one thing about you."

"Yea?" Jessica asked.

"She wanted to know if I'd placed some kind of pod under your bed and you'd changed into an alien," Taylor said with a straight face.

"She did not!" Jessica finally said as she watched the large toothy grin break across the artist's face.

Taylor laughed as she went outside to retrieve the young girl's sketchbooks. "Jess, I'm very impressed, and I think you know me well enough by now to know that I don't impress easily. These are very, very good."

"Really?" Jessica sounded stunned.

"Would you stop drawing if I said I was just being nice?" Taylor asked.

"No, probably not," Jessica responded honestly.

"Good, because I'm not. You've got a great deal of talent Jess, but talent won't always be enough. There are a lot of talented artists out there. You have to work damned hard, every single day to achieve your goal if you want to be doing this for a living," Taylor lectured. "Have you ever thought about doing something with your art for a living...ever think of going to college?" Taylor asked as she stood next to the girl.

Jessica looked up into the taller woman's cerulean gaze and gave a wry smile. "Frankly, Taylor, the only thing on my mind so far is how to get through the whole day without screwing something up," Jessica replied.

Taylor laughed at the girl's response and the serious look on her face. She put her arm around Jessica's shoulders and pulled her toward the art studio. "Well, let's just see if we can help you with your dilemma," the artist said with a smile.

****

Torrey was back in Chicago feeling alone most days, but clung to the hope that it would all become right in the end. That belief carried her through some of the roughest periods in her life and it was never more important for her to believe than right now. Her writing still wasn't coming around, but that too she gave up to the fates to decide.

She toyed with the idea of teaching again. There was a time when she was an Assistant Professor in English Literature at the University, downtown, when she and Jessica first moved to Chicago. Now, she had had three offers for faculty work. The University here wanted her to head up their English Literature Department, as well as her alma mater offering her the same position. The one that tempted her the most was the University of California. It would definitely be a life altering decision and she wasn't in any frame of mind to make it yet, until she knew what would happen with Jessica. Then there would be the fact that she would live within driving distance from Taylor. Yes, the woman that still held her heart so completely was single *now*, but what if she should finally meet someone and settle down? Could Torrey's heart take that?

A lot of pain and loneliness was dispelled for the writer when she answered her door on Valentine's Day. The local florist delivered two-dozen white roses, her favorite. Each dozen were arranged in a separate vase with a card attached. When she opened the two cards, she immediately recognized the hurried scrawl of her daughter and the precise, angular characters of Taylor's handwriting. She fingered the jade heart around her neck, remembering this same holiday many years ago. Each card in her hand bore the same message.

How in the world did you ever live
with this woman?!?
Happy Valentine's Day

The laughter those cards caused carried her through until the next time she heard their voices on the telephone, and just like walking, she put one foot in front of the other and with grim determination, kept going each and every day.

Chapter 11

Days quickly turned into weeks. Taylor and Jessica both had good and bad days. Taylor would sometimes get silent and brooding as she worried about a new project or a sculpture that she was currently trying to finish for the show. Jessica had days when she never thought about drugs at all, and then there were the days when it would all come crashing in on her. When that happened, Taylor would drop everything to spend additional time with the girl.

In the meantime, Jessica earned hero status in the eyes of Corey, the young girl from their NA group. Taylor had Corey's mom bring her by the studio and they would all go down to the beach or out for a sandwich, sometimes a movie. Even Jessica had to admit that she found a friend in the youngster and soon overlooked the case of hero worship Corey suffered from. Each of the girls were doing well in their first ninety days of recovery. Natalie turned into the perfect sponsor for Jessica, giving her a trusted friend, besides Taylor, to confide in. In turn, Taylor volunteered as Corey's sponsor, attending meetings on a daily basis with her new charge.

On one occasion, Corey's mother dropped the girl off and Taylor took the two younger girls to Anaheim for the day. It was the first time either of them had been to Disneyland and they had the time of their young lives. Jessica even tried to get Taylor to go on one of the newer daredevil rides with her and Corey.

"Come on, Taylor. Look. See? It's not that bad," Jessica pleaded.

Taylor looked up and up as a car filled with strapped in passengers climbed higher into the sky, then the artist watched as the car plunged straight toward the earth at a dizzying speed. Twenty years ago, she would have been the first one in line, but now the only thing the dark-haired woman could do was groan. "I'd like my lunch to stay in my stomach where I put it, thanks. I'll just have a nice cold drink and wait for you two over there." She indicated a shaded park area.

As she watched the two girls walk off to wait in line, she did indeed feel a little old. She was only forty and felt wonderful, physically. She felt old, however, when she realized sixteen years had passed since she and Torrey visited this park. Jessica was a little over a year old on that trip to San Diego. The dark-haired artist looked back with regret because it was the last time she and Torrey ever went anywhere together. It was only a long weekend, but since Taylor was representing her company at a convention in Los Angeles on Friday, they thought the perfect way to spend the rest of the weekend would be to visit Jean Kent.

February 1984

"What an incredible place, Stretch. It makes you feel like a little kid again. Oh, wouldn't it be great to come back when Jess is old enough to enjoy it?" Tor- rey chattered on about Disneyland as Taylor drove her mother's borrowed LeBaron back to San Diego.

Taylor smiled and her blue eyes sparkled behind her Ray Bans, the artist loved seeing her young friend enjoy herself. Torrey worked so hard between jug- gling a full class schedule and being a mother, she deserved to let loose every now and then. Taylor especially liked the way Torrey planned things in the future that included her. It was as if they were a real family, even if Taylor knew that someday it would come to a stop. Right now, she didn't want to think about that. She only wanted to enjoy the beautiful blonde by her side.

Jean told "her girls," as she liked to say, that this was their weekend to have fun and if they came home before midnight they were in serious trouble. They took the older woman at her word and had dinner at a small seafood restaurant overlooking the harbor in Dana Point. Between the ocean and the cliffs, the view was breathtaking and they lingered over dinner, sharing their thoughts and dreams. Torrey had a cou- ple more glasses of wine while Taylor ordered another Perrier.

Taylor asked Torrey if she would ever consider

living somewhere like California. The small blonde wanted to say that anywhere Taylor lived would be her home also, but Taylor didn't belong to her that way and it was foolish of her heart to pretend that it was so. She simply said that yes, from what she had seen of it, she could imagine herself living there someday. Taylor smiled inwardly as she admitted to her friend that here, in Dana Point, is where she had always dreamed of building a cliff side home.

They walked along the beach as Torrey spoke of her writing and how frustrated she was at how inane everything she wrote sounded. She had the words, but somehow she couldn't make them say what she wanted to.

"That's because you're trying to write with words, that's just not you, Little Bit. What you need to do is write in a feeling*, that's you. Tor, you have the ability to make people experience, to sense what you're telling them about. Remember those short stores you gave me to read? I couldn't put them down. There are very few people that can invoke those kinds of emotions in me, but you did," Taylor explained.*

Such a short and simple conversation, but Torrey would always remember those words from her friend. It was that honest assessment of her ability and style that created the author that Torrey eventually became. Three months after they returned home, the young woman finished her first manuscript entitled, Stevie.

The sea breeze cooled off the warm city streets and the two women strolled around looking into shop windows. Finally, Taylor realized what day it was. She couldn't believe she forgot, but it was never like she had anyone to outwardly celebrate it with anyway.

Something caught her eye and she asked Torrey to wait for her at the end of the pier.

Returning to her friend who was absently staring at stars overhead, Taylor whispered in her ear. "Tilt your head forward."

Torrey did as she was instructed and felt Taylor's arms come around her neck. She felt something smooth and cool lay against the skin just above the valley between her breasts. Looking down she saw the long gold chain that held a jade pendant. It was a soft green to match her eyes and it was cut in the shape of a heart.

"Happy Valentine's Day, Little Bit," Taylor said softly.

Torrey held the beautiful pendant up to the light. "Stretch, it's so beautiful, thank you. But, I don't have a gift for you," Torrey replied, turning to face the artist.

Taylor looked down into the face that she would be able to draw from memory for many years to come. "Torrey, you're my best friend. Nothing you ever give me will possibly compare to that."

The artist knew that wasn't completely true. There was something else, but Taylor understood that Torrey's heart would never be given to her. There was a bittersweet taste to the realization, that all she could ever desire in life stood inches away from her, but in reality, a chasm as big as eternity separated her from it.

They stopped for one more drink, Taylor casually ordering black coffee, while her friend had two Irish Coffees. She smiled; knowing Torrey would feel it in the morning. Taylor simply sipped her coffee and lis-

tened to the lovely young woman across from her.

It was evening by the time they cruised along Mesa Boulevard. San Diego was alive on a Saturday evening and the two women enjoyed having the car's top down, taking in the people and the sights.

"Oh, Taylor there, stop there," Torrey said excitedly.

"Torrey, that's a tattoo parlor," her friend pointed out in amazement.

"I know. Let's get a tattoo," she replied with enthusiasm.

"Are you insane? You would kill me in the morning. Hell, my mother would kill me for letting you." Taylor was usually game for anything, but the dark-haired artist felt that Torrey's preoccupation with obtaining a tattoo had more to do with the amount of alcohol the small blonde consumed than anything else.

"I really want to. I want us both to. Come on, it'll be fun."

"Are you serious, Little Bit?" Taylor asked.

"Absolutely! Will you?" Torrey looked at Taylor with those green eyes so sincere and appealing that there was little else the captured heart could do but to agree.

"Okay, but we're not stopping here. If you're really serious, I know somebody whose work i trust." With that, Taylor turned off Mesa Boulevard and headed toward the University.

"Kenny." Taylor smiled as she and her friend walked into the shop.

"Taylor, holy shit! What are ya doin' slummin' with the little people? Heard you had a choice spot

with D&A."

"*My friend and I are on vacation and when we thought tattoos, I obviously thought of you.*" *Taylor turned to Torrey.* "*Torrey, this is Kenny, another one of those beach bum artist types I spent my wayward youth with.*"

It was a madhouse on a Friday night, but Kenny motioned for the two women to follow him and they walked down a narrow hall into what appeared to be private quarters. The tattoo artist let Torrey look through some books as he readied his work area.

"*I found it,*" *Torrey exclaimed.*

She pointed to it as Taylor leaned over her shoulder. "*Are you sure? I mean, we have to live with this for the rest of our lives.*"

"*I'm sure,*" *Torrey answered confidently.*

"*Both you gettin' this?*" *he asked Taylor, a little surprised.*

An indulgent grin lit up Taylor's face as she nodded then explained. "*We're Sorority sisters, Tau Alpha Zeta.*"

"*Ahh, TAZ,*" *Kenny said as the light finally went on.* "*Okay, two Tazmanian Devils it is. Where do you want it?*" *he asked as Torrey settled into the comfortable lounger.*

"*Right here,*" *the small blonde said, opening buttons and pulling her sleeveless blouse away to expose the uppermost swell of her left breast.*

"*Okay. You'll have to take your top off, do you want a tow—*" *Kenny stopped abruptly.*

Torrey pulled her blouse off in one fluid motion, both artists staring open-mouthed.

"*Torrey, honey,*" *Taylor quickly came to her*

senses as a fire rose up between her legs, "you're going to give poor Kenny a heart attack," Taylor said as she adjusted the young woman's blouse across her naked chest.

Torrey didn't mind the minimal amount of pain. As a matter of fact, she actually fell asleep at one point.   Taylor's was finished just as quickly, and Kenny gave them instructions as to how to care for their skin until the slight redness and swelling went away. Taylor slipped a large tip to her old friend in thanks and she gently guided Torrey out into the late night air. Weaving slightly, Torrey suggested they stop for a drink.

"How about we just head for home and you can put your head on my shoulder and watch the stars," Taylor suggested.

"Mmm, yea, that could work too," the slightly inebriated woman replied.

The ride home was as perfect as any the artist could ever wish for. Taylor's small companion fell asleep in the dark-haired woman's embrace.   Once they arrived and put the car in the garage, she was reluctant to release her hold on the young woman. Torrey was passed out cold, so Taylor swept the slight figure into her arms and carried her upstairs and gently placed her in bed.

After removing her sneakers, Taylor pulled a small comforter over the still blonde. She meant to simply place a light kiss on Torrey's forehead, but the proximity of her friend's sensuous lips caused the artist to throw caution to the wind.

Leaning over, the dark-haired artist pressed her lips fully to those of the prone woman. Taylor caught *a moan before it escaped her own throat as Torrey's breath quickened and the young woman's lips responded unconsciously to the kiss. Quickly pulling away, Taylor swallowed hard and tried to bury the passion that rose to the surface so abruptly.*

"Oh, Torrey, what you do to me," Taylor whispered, looking back into the bedroom before silently closing the door.

****

"Morning, Little Bit," Taylor sang out a little louder than usual to the young woman who just entered the kitchen. Jean Kent slapped her daughter on the arm for her behavior, knowing what kind of shape Torrey came home in.

"What are you so damn cheerful about?" Torrey asked, unable to open her eyes beyond a squint, her normally sunny disposition having all but disappeared. She held her hand up to shade off what seemed like an extraordinary amount of light coming through the window.

Taylor laughed at her small friend and the young woman's first hangover. She jumped up and returned with a cup of tea, placing it on the table in front of the aching young woman.

"Did we really do what I think we did last night?" Torrey asked, her voice barely above a whisper.

"Uhm," Taylor said, tapping a slender finger against the rise of flesh above her own left breast.

Torrey pulled open her robe slightly to reveal the small tattoo on her chest. "You too?" She asked.

Taylor smirked across the table as she pulled her

shirt aside to reveal the twin image.

"I guess I feel a little better, then." The young woman chuckled. *"Oh, geez, my head even hurts when I laugh."*

She pushed the tea aside and rose to go upstairs, Taylor following. Taylor walked into the bedroom with her friend and they leaned over the crib to check on the still sleeping youngster.

"I'm going to take a quick shower," Torrey said.

"Take a long hot bath instead, it'll make you feel better. I'll keep an ear out for Jess," Taylor whispered back.

Taylor sat in her father's study, glancing through some trade magazines she brought along. The room was directly across from Torrey's and she left the door open, listening for any sound from Jessica. She watched as Torrey walked out of the room, her freshly washed hair still damp, dressed in faded jeans and an oversized T-shirt.

"Hey," Taylor called softly.

Torrey still looked a little out of it and rubbed her aching temples.

"Come here," Taylor said pulling her friend over to the large leather couch that the artist remembered with fondness from her childhood.

This was her favorite spot to snuggle up with her father. Oblivious to the young woman's protests, she settled Torrey on the couch and wrapped a soft warm blanket around the prone woman.

"You get the rest of the day off, in celebration of your first hangover. After this though, you're on your own," Taylor said softly, her eyes smiling down at the blonde.

"What about Jess?" Torrey began.

"I'll play mom today. Go on, honey, close your eyes and relax. I can attest to the fact that this is the softest, quietest, most relaxing spot in the whole house," Taylor replied.

Taylor stayed seated on the couch by her friend for a few minutes more until she was satisfied that Torrey would stay there.

"Taylor, would it bother you if I asked how your father died?" Torrey asked softly.

"No, it's okay, Little Bit, I'm surprised you never asked me that before," Taylor responded, running the back of her fingers against the young woman's cheek.

"Ironically enough it was during the Vietnam War, but he died over here, over the Pacific Ocean. He was a jet pilot, which is why we lived in San Diego in the first place. It was 1968. He had a cushy job all waiting for him, according to Mom, to teach over at Miramar. They wanted him to make just one more run in a new jet they were testing. He was no test pilot, but he was a Navy man, so he agreed. I'll always remember the name of that jet. They called it a Striker. They finally figured out that the damn thing blew apart at a certain speed and the Navy eventually scrapped it. I heard there were some models of it available, but I never could find one."

Taylor's eyes once again focused on the green ones of the woman lying below her and she gave a sort of sad half-smile. *"I still miss him a lot. He was the kind of parent you are, you know? Loving me just seemed to come so natural to him."*

Torrey smiled up at her friend and brushed the tears from her tanned cheeks. *"Maybe that's because *you're so easy to love,"* Torrey said softly.

Taylor grinned. *"Yea, right. Wanna know what his call sign was?"*

The artist got up, opened the folding door into the room's closet and pulled an object from the top shelf. It was a pilot's helmet. Above the visor was stenciled Captain Robert Kent's call sign, REBEL.

Torrey was grinning now, too. "The apple sure didn't fall far from the tree there, did it?" Torrey yawned and her eyes closed as she snuggled into the thick cushions of the sofa. Taylor moved to go, but was drawn for one more look at the beautiful young woman.

Torrey opened her eyes to the intense blue gaze of her friend. "Taylor?" She asked.

"Hhmm?" Taylor responded.

"Did I take my clothes off in front of someone last night?" the young woman asked, her brow furrowed in concentration.

Taylor chuckled. "Yea, but it was only your blouse and I'm sure it was the highlight of my friend's young life."

Taylor smiled at her friend's groan as the artist walked from the room to check on the baby.

* * * * * * * * * *

Sunday morning dawned and Torrey felt like a new woman. She had a little trouble wondering why anyone would put themselves through that agony on a regular basis, vowing to stick to moderation in all things. The sun just rose above the eastern mountains and hit the surface of the ocean. Torrey loved this effect while doing her Tai Chi routine. She never understood what it was about light on the water, but it seemed to portend something good in her life. Something that hadn't happened yet, but when it did, it would be the culmination of something extraordinary.

She wore a pair of shorts and a tank top, placing Jessica, who was already awake, in the large playpen in the middle of the dining room floor. Torrey tended to lose herself in her routine. She always wanted to make sure that Jessica was out of harm's way since the toddler had learned to walk and did so at an amazing speed.

Sliding open the screen door to the outside patio, Torrey knelt in the green grass, sitting back on her heels for a few moments of silent meditation before beginning. She felt the presence before she heard anything, the corners of her lips curling upward slightly. When she opened her eyes and rose from the ground she saw the tall figure of her friend a few feet away and slightly behind her. Their movements were unhurried and relaxed, Torrey's motion a little more graceful as opposed to the artist, who had only been practicing the ritual for a little over a year.

There was no speech during this time, no verbal communication, but occasionally the young blonde felt as if she were a part of the artist's thoughts until, just as quickly, the door to those emotions was closed. The goal was to become as relaxed as possible, to concentrate on each move without the physical act of concentration, like trying to balance on a precarious ledge without trying to balance at all. The moves were to come as naturally as standing.

As the two women moved in perfect harmony, Jes-

sica sat mesmerized by the actions. The baby was at her quietest when watching the ebb and flow of the small blonde and the tall dark-haired woman.

****

As Jessica sat at the kitchen table sipping her tea, she watched the artist on the outside patio. Donning black silk drawstring pants and a black muscle tee, the artist was as oblivious to the outside world as Jessica always thought her mother to be when she worked her Tai Chi routine. The tall woman moved without a sound, her eyes heavy lidded as she acted without really thinking about the motions.

The young girl thought it strange that she should have the same sensation watching Taylor run through her morning ritual as she did when watching her mother. It was an odd feeling of incompleteness. Like she was only seeing part of a picture, waiting for something more to be revealed. She didn't understand it, but shook it off like so many of the memories floating in her subconscious from days long ago.

Since she moved here to live with the quiet, reserved artist she felt a number of odd sensations like that. Taylor tried to explain that they were probably just memories that a child's brain stores up. She went on to tell Jessica that it shouldn't feel all that strange if her touch or her smile seemed familiar to the young girl, considering that Taylor lived with her for the first two years of her life. It was good to finally be able to put a face to the dark stranger who played protector through Jessica's childhood nightmares. She was glad the memory turned out to be real and that it turned out to be Taylor.

Jessica had a great deal of difficulty remembering things that happened when Taylor lived with them. When her mother related an incident from that time, Jessica would get a feeling that she existed in a world where love abounded, and although she didn't recall particulars, the feelings were enough to get her by.

Jessica was pulled from her musings by the patio door opening as Taylor stepped inside and tousled her hair as she walked by. The young girl never lived with anyone whose emotion ran the gamut like Taylor's did. Open and passionate, she could also be sullen and brooding. There were days when they would take a walk and Taylor would place her arm around her shoulder just as her mother would sometimes slip an arm around her waist. Then still other days when they barely exchanged a word. Taylor would apologize and explain that the deadline of her show was drawing near and she was feeling the tension of it. Jessica thought it was good that she was learning to live with someone else other than her mother, deal with conflicts and personality clashes, while still remaining clean.

Today, Jessica was in her own thoughts working on a special drawing. It was almost finished, but she still needed to have it framed. It was a pen and ink sketch of her mother and Jessica as a baby, taken from a photograph that Jessica always kept with her. She worked hard on it in order to finish it in time to be a Mother's Day present. She was cutting it close, but there was a place in Dana Point that would matte and frame it for her in only two days time.

After Taylor showered and worked at her drawing

table for a couple of hours she reentered the kitchen for a glass of iced tea. "Tell me again why we spent so much money on an art table for you," Taylor said in amusement.

Jessica was sprawled across the kitchen table; paper and lead pencils of varying widths lay scattered across the table, too. The young girl smiled sheepishly up at the dark-haired woman and shrugged her shoulders slightly.

"That's what I thought." Taylor answered with a smile.

Jessica moved off to the studio and Taylor walked outside, making her way toward the back of the house and the large Japanese garden. This was her quiet place. The cool shade of the bamboo trees and the sound of the water cascading down the natural rock waterfall served to relax her more than any other form of meditation. She sipped on her cool drink and wondered to herself what Torrey would think of the garden.

Taylor smiled. The blonde would probably want to bring out her laptop and write, sitting here on the cushioned loveseat. Then again, Torrey always had the ability to write anywhere. Perhaps that's why the writer and the artist fit so well together. They were both cut from the same creative bolt of cloth. *What had Torrey said one time? Yes. Two sides of the same coin.*

Whenever Taylor was to meet her small friend for dinner or drinks, she would inevitably get hung up in her office. The artist would walk into the bar or restaurant to find Torrey furiously scribbling away on napkins. If she had a thought, she just had to get it down on paper, lest she lose the flavor or meaning of the words. In the same circumstance, when Taylor got something in her mind that would make a good drawing or a sculpture, she would start sketching the idea out on whatever was handy at the time. One of her most expensive works to date had been born in the local grocery store on the side of a paper bag. Neither woman ever took offense at the other's preoccupation. It was a given that the creative flow came first in their household.

Taylor laid the length of her body down on the loveseat, clasping her hands behind her head. She and Jess had a late night of talking the previous evening and her eyes were so tired she couldn't quite focus on her work. Jessica seemed to be having no problem, however. *Oh to be seventeen again*, Taylor thought to herself as her eyes drooped a little, the sound of running water lulling her into a sleepy state.

She was so proud of Jessica. The young girl and their friend Corey received their red ninety-day chips a few weeks ago during their NA meeting. Taylor wanted to do something special for Jessica. The day after, Taylor surprised the girl by taking her to the computer store and letting her pick out the system that she'd been dropping hints about for the last few weeks. The young girl admitted to having a fascination with animation. With a computer and a scanner, she wanted to try her hand and see if she was any good at it.

Last night Taylor saw the fruits of the girl's labors. Jessica created a character based on herself. She said if she was ever able to do anything with it, the cartoon character might be able to help other young people. The animation she created only lasted about two minutes, but she put hundreds of drawings into it. Of course, Jessica's faithful sidekick, Corey came over to help. Jess gave the younger girl the task of handing her the right picture to scan and keeping all the drawings in the right number order.

Taylor was extremely impressed with the end result. It showed her that Jessica definitely had a talent in this area. That's why the late night. The two had talked about what Jessica wanted to do with her future and the girl's wish was to try to get into a decent art school. That kind of thinking thrilled Taylor, and she and Jessica stayed up half the night discussing school, and the pros and cons of the ones that Taylor was familiar with. The early morning conversation ended with Taylor promising the young girl that she would get in touch with an old friend who was now working at a major animation studio. The artist explained that her friend would probably know what direction Jessica should start off in.

So, Jessica was clean for ninety days and when the young girl stood up to thank the people of the group for their friendship and support, the dark-haired artist looked on with pride in her heart. Taylor's eyes were fully closed now, but her brain was working overtime as she remembered the summer of her first anniversary of living drug free. It was the summer that Torrey graduated from the University.

June 1984

"Torrey Joan Gray." The sound system boomed

out the young blonde's name as she and a few hundred other students waded through the line to shake the Dean's hand and pick up their diploma.

"See, there's Mommy," Taylor said to the young girl bouncing all over her lap. She lifted Jessica until the girl was standing on the artist's thighs.

"Ma—Ma." Jessica tried to jump in the air, even as the artist's strong grip kept a hold of her.

Once the ceremony was over, they met Torrey and her friend Alicia over by the Hudson Museum. The campus was crazy with students, parents, and friends all over. Torrey waved as soon as she caught sight of the tall woman with the laughing nineteen-month-old in her arms. Torrey stopped her conversation simply to watch the beautiful woman who held her child. She enjoyed watching the two of them together. Taylor was as breathtaking as Torrey always thought any actress was; the artist's taste in clothing reflecting the salary she was paid.

"I knew you could do it, Little Bit," Taylor whispered in her ear, embracing her with one arm while the other contained a squirming child.

"Mama," Jessica giggled.

It was disheartening to Torrey that her daughter learned that word first and then proceeded to call everything and everyone by that name. She loved when she used it on Taylor, the artist's face would turn red, and she didn't know whether to be flattered or embarrassed. Torrey swept her daughter into her strong arms and hugged her tightly. Once Jessica found the tassel on Torrey's hat, it was pulled swiftly from the young woman's head. Torrey said her good-byes to Alicia, whose parents flew in for the occasion, and she and Taylor walked around the campus once more before leaving.

They spent the rest of the day together, just the three of them. Jessica was the perfect little girl in the restaurant Taylor chose for the occasion. The youngster seemed to understand in some way that this was a special day for her mother.

When Taylor turned the car onto their street she looked over at the blonde next to her. "Torrey, close your eyes," the artist requested.

"Close my eyes. For what?" Torrey looked up at her friend with a curious expression.

"So I can give you your graduation present. Just do as I say for once in your life, okay?"

"Okay, okay," the young woman laughed, closing her eyes.

"Good, now keep them closed until I tell you to open them, and no peeking," Taylor responded.

They pulled into their driveway and Taylor got out to open up the passenger side door. "Okay. Come on out, but don't open your eyes yet," Taylor said, leading the woman into the driveway. Taylor checked to see that Jessica was sleeping soundly in her car seat and ran to flip on the outside lights.

"Can I open my eyes yet?" Torrey asked impatiently.

"Good things come to those who wait, my friend," Taylor whispered from behind Torrey. The young woman jumped at the warm breath on her ear and the feel of Taylor's hands on her hips was definitely doing some outrageous things to her brain. She breathed in the scent of the artist's cologne and found herself not wanting to open her eyes just yet.

"Okay, Tor, open your eyes."

The young woman did open her eyes. Then she blinked hard once or twice. In the middle of the driveway sat a deep green Jeep Cherokee with a huge ribbon and bow tied around it.

"Oh, Stretch...I can't, I mean, it's too big," Torrey stammered.

"What do you mean, too big? I though you wanted something this size," Taylor said, her face taking on a puzzled frown.

"I mean it's too big a gift. Taylor, this must have cost a fortune," Torrey replied.

Taylor chuckled and slipped her arms around her small friend's waist, until Torrey was leaned back against the artist's chest. "Just a small fortune, not a really big one," Taylor responded. "Besides, you deserve it." She turned Torrey's face to look into her eyes. "There aren't a lot of women who could have pulled off raising a child and getting a degree, Tor. In addition to what I've put you through. I just wanted you to know how proud I am of you."

Torrey turned completely and nearly tackled the taller woman as she jumped into her embrace. She kissed the artist's cheek, and then whispered back to her, "Not many women have you, Stretch." Torrey pulled back slightly to gaze into the sparkling blue eyes of her friend. "Let's get Jess and go for a ride right now."

"I was hoping you'd say that." Taylor grinned. "I already put a car seat in the back."

* * * * * * * * * *

"Nervous?" Torrey asked, looking over at the dark-haired artist in the passenger seat. Torrey volunteered to drive everywhere in the two months since she received the new car as her graduation present. It was like a new toy for the young blonde and Taylor was just as happy to play passenger for a change.

Taylor nodded her head at her friend's question. "I get up and speak at work, in business meetings, at conventions all the time, I don't know why I'm so nervous about getting up in front of thirty people in a church basement."

"Mama." Jessica pounded on the tray in the front of her car seat.

Taylor reached around and handed the child her stuffed bear that had fallen to the floor.

"Mama!" the youngster repeated.

Torrey glanced at her daughter in the rear view mirror. "She wants her juice cup," Torrey said to Taylor.

The artist looked up in disbelief at her young friend; the blonde's eyes still fixed on the road. She reached into the back seat and placed a red plastic cup with a snap on lid on the tray in front of Jessica. The girl quickly picked up the cup and drank.

"Okay, I give up. How do you tell the juice cup mama from the stuffed bear mama, or the I'm sleepy mama?" Taylor asked.

Torrey just shrugged her shoulders and smiled at her friend.

"Guess it's a mom thing," Taylor turned and whispered to the youngster. "You know, we've got to teach this kid some new words," she added with a wry smile.

They walked into the basement of the church and talked with Sister Eva along with a number of people, both new and old, to the group. Torrey, with her usual cheerful demeanor introduced people to Taylor. Then the artist smiled down at them and their discomfort disappeared. She was an imposing figure and although she was more reserved than her small friend was, she wasn't an unfriendly woman. Taylor just hung back on the fringes a little more, taking everything in, whereas Torrey was like a happy puppy, looking for friendship and acceptance. People tended to talk to the tall artist a little more when her companion was around. It was as if Taylor's wild ways became tame when in the company of the small woman with the open, caring heart.

"I'd like to introduce you to someone very special to all of us here." Sister Eva stood on the stage to begin the evening. "A lot of you already know her, but for some of you new folks, I'd like to introduce Taylor. She will not only be sharing a few words with us tonight, but we also have something pretty special we'd like to give her. Taylor?" Sister Eva indicated that Taylor should come up to the makeshift stage. "Taylor, you've become quite a regular figure around here," Eva continued as she held up a glow-in-the-dark plastic chip. "Taylor has been clean for one year today. She'll be the first one to tell you that it hasn't been easy. On second thought, just ask Torrey how easy it's been, she's had to live with her."

A number of people laughed, as did Taylor. Torrey's face flushed slightly as she was temporarily thrust into the spotlight. Jessica, upon hearing the laughter, giggled and clapped her own hands.

"Even though it took a lot of hard work, Taylor will also be the first one to tell you that it was worth it. So, if you new folks want to shoot for something, listen to what this gal has to say. Taylor, we want you to know how very proud we all are of you," Eva said as she pressed the round piece of plastic into the artist's palm.

The volunteers in the back of the room applauded and soon the whole room showed the woman on the stage their appreciation and support. Taylor watched as Torrey clapped along with Jessica bouncing around on her lap. Raising her head, she unconsciously tossed her head back and forth to shake ebony locks from her eyes.

It was that abstract gesture that captured Torrey's attention and her heart. In that one heartbeat, that one fraction of a second, Torrey felt a hunger she'd never experienced before. She remembered telling her friend that she couldn't understand what the big attraction was to sex. She'd done it and it certainly wasn't anything to write home about. Taylor simply smiled at her young friend in the oddest way. The artist told Torrey that she could only hope that someday the young woman would meet someone that caused an absolute hunger within her soul. Then she would know what all the fuss was about.

Torrey wasn't that naive eighteen-year-old anymore. Yes, she still had a certain amount of innocence about any number of things, but she knew what women did together and now, in the middle of a crowded room, she understood what Taylor meant. What she felt at that moment went far beyond a romantic profession of love for the dark-haired artist.

She wanted her, in every imaginable way.   When she looked up at Taylor she literally hungered for her, deep in her soul.

Taylor waited for the applause to stop before she spoke. "Okay, stop. Geez, you'd think I was running for office." The artist smiled nervously.

She leaned against the podium and flipped the chip through her fingers. It was a trick her father taught her when she was a little girl. He told her once that he learned it from a blackjack dealer in Vegas.

"I guess a lot of people wouldn't think this little piece of plastic is anything special. There will be a lot of folks that you run into that won't get what it represents. Actually there a lot of you who don't yet understand its full impact," Taylor started.

The artist looked down at Torrey and gave her a little lopsided grin. The smile that lit up the face of her blonde-haired friend clutched hard at Taylor's heart, her stomach actually doing a little flip at the absolute love and devotion that smile spoke of. Tears threatened her eyes and she lowered her head for a moment.

"I'm sure this little chip could mean a lot of different things to a lot of people. When it comes right down to it, though, the feelings that this small piece of plastic invokes in us are all pretty much the same. Let me tell you what it means to me." Taylor paused. When she continued, it was as if she were only talking to Torrey.

"It means that when I walk down the street with my friend, I know she's not ashamed of me. It means that I know when I meet one of her friends, they can't

smell grass on my clothes or see bloodshot eyes. It means that when she asks me for a favor, I know it's because she knows she can trust me. And, when I'm two hours late for dinner and I haven't called, she knows I'm not lying in a ditch somewhere. Well, okay, she's still convinced I'm lying in a ditch somewhere, only now she doesn't think it's my fault," Taylor said with a smirk as the audience laughed knowingly.

"It means that when the baby cries in the middle of the night, she doesn't have to be the only one who jumps out of bed because this little chip tells her that she can count on me to help. Most of all it means that the two pairs of viridian eyes that are watching me right now can be assured that they can depend on me to always be there, no matter what," Taylor finished softly as she looked into Torrey's face; tears falling down her friend's cheeks.

* * * * * * * * * *

Taylor stood talking to Sister Eva and a few others when Torrey walked over with Jessica in her arms. The child squirmed and twisted, reaching her arms out in Taylor's direction. "Tay...Tay!" the child yelled.

Taylor turned an incredulous look, first at Jessica, then at Torrey. The young blonde relinquished the youngster to Taylor's arms as Jessica still called out the artist's name. "I swear I had nothing to do with it," Torrey admitted, throwing her hands up in the air.

"Tay!" Jessica said again, locking her arms around the artist's neck.

Taylor hugged the child back and held her even as they left the building, the youngster seemingly satisfied within the tall woman's strong embrace.

Opening the door of the Jeep to place Jessica in her car seat, a young man passed, walking his dog.

"Tay! Tay!" Jessica said pointing to the dog that two hours ago was called "mama."

"Oh, no!" Taylor and Torrey said in unison, looking at one another from opposite sides of the car. Both women laughed at the young child's limited vocabulary.

* * * * * * * * * *

"What you said tonight," Torrey began, "it was beautiful."

Taylor smiled down at her friend. They were seated on the loveseat outside on the patio, watching the stars. "I just wanted you to know..." Taylor paused and found herself lost in Torrey's gaze. "I know I haven't always been the best kind of friend."

"Oh, Stretch, please don't ever think that," Torrey said, placing her hand over the larger one of her friend. "You've had your problems, sure, but I've never once doubted the depth of your love to myself or Jess. Do you want something to drink?" Torrey asked, rising from her seat.

"Sure, I'll have a beer," Taylor answered with a grin. The artist watched as her friend's eyes grew wide. "I'm just kidding. I'll take a soda." She laughed.

When Torrey returned she juggled the two glasses of soda in one hand and a wrapped box in the other.

"Well, this is sure no car, but I hope you like it just the same. I'm so proud of you, Taylor, and I thought I'd give you a little gift to celebrate the night," Torrey said as she sat down next to the artist.

"Honey, you didn't have to get me anything, but then again, I never say no to presents." Taylor grinned as she tore open the wrapping.

The artist lifted the glass case from the box and looked at it in silence. Torrey immediately thought she'd made a huge mistake until Taylor spoke.

"Oh, Torrey...I can't...I don't even know what to say." Tears slipped from her eyes.

"Do you like it or do you hate it?" Torrey asked in a worried voice.

Taylor gazed at the woman next to her and bent her head, placing a gentle kiss on the young woman's lips. She hadn't planned the move, but it was the only way she could think of to show her friend how very much she loved this gift. Torrey, in the meantime, was desperately trying to bring her erratically pounding heart within normal limits.

Taylor sat the box on the ground, cradling the dark mahogany base across her knees. Within the glass case was an exact replica of a Striker Deuce, the experimental jet Taylor's father flew on his last mission.

"I love it, Little Bit. No one's ever given me anything as special before. I—I don't know what to say," Taylor repeated.

Torrey let out a small breath in relief. She brushed Taylor's long bangs from her eyes and rested her hand on her friend's shoulder. "It's all right, you don't have to say anything at all. I was a little afraid it would be inappropriate. I wanted you to know that I think your father would be so proud of you, Taylor. I know I am."

They carried the precious gift inside and set it on the mantel. Then the two women spent the rest of the night talking quietly as they watched the stars appear and then slowly fade from the sky.

Chapter
12

"Hey, Taylor, do you have any large size paper? This is all I have left," Jessica asked.

"Sure. Take a look in one of the drawers in the large wooden organizer against the back wall of the studio," the artist replied absently as she chewed on the end of her pencil. She and Jess were trying to work on their tans and sketch at the same time on the front patio. Taylor was preoccupied lately with one last piece she had in mind for her show, but she just couldn't get it right.

Quite a bit of time went by and Jessica hadn't yet returned. Taylor looked through the patio window into the kitchen, but didn't see any sign of the young girl. Suddenly the artist remembered what the young girl asked her for. Taylor's eyes took on a slightly wide-eyed, panicky look. Jumping up from her chair, the sketchbook in her lap fell noisily toward the ground. She never saw the book hit, loose papers fluttering across the tiled patio, as she stepped quickly over it and rushed into the house, headed for the studio.

The stained glass doors stood open, Taylor could make out Jessica's form leaning against the wooden organizer, loose pieces of paper scattered across it's top. Half a dozen of the drawers were partially pulled open, their contents clearly visible. Jessica turned to the sound Taylor made as she walked into the room.

The artist stopped when she saw the look on Jessica's face. When their eyes met, Taylor knew her secret was no longer her own. The dark-haired woman slowly walked to the young girl and stood beside her. With deliberate slowness, she took the drawings from Jessica's hand and replaced them into the drawers.

Jessica continued to stare at the images on the paper, hundreds, thousands of drawings. Some were quick and sketchy, while others were well thought out, their lines dark and permanent. All the images that looked back up at Jessica were those of her mother. The sheaves of paper on top of the organizer, now loose, were nudes, some in very erotic poses. Taylor silently collected those too and placed them in a drawer. The tall artist opened the bottom drawer of the organizer and pulled some blank sheets of paper out. After placing them in front of the speechless girl, Taylor turned and left the room.

Jessica wasn't certain what was going on, but she was sure of one thing, there was a lot more to Taylor and her mother's relationship than either one of them ever told her. The young girl wasn't exactly sure what she was going to say, but she left the studio in search of Taylor.

The dark-haired woman sat in the corner of the Japanese garden on the familiar loveseat. She knew that if and when Jessica wanted answers she would find her. When the door to the garden clicked open, Taylor never looked up. She felt Jessica's weight as the young girl seated herself beside the older woman.

"I'm sorry, Jess," she said in nearly a whisper. "I never meant for you to find out, especially not that way."

"I thought you said you and Mom were never lovers?" Jessica asked. It wasn't an accusation, just curiosity.

"We weren't," Taylor said flatly, tears glistening in her eyes.

Jessica may not have been the sharpest tool in the shed, but this one seemed obvious. "You wanted to be, though, didn't you?" she questioned.

Taylor thought of the many ways she could answer this one, the word games she could attempt in order to try to get out of this situation. She couldn't lie, though, not to Jess and not about this. If she lied right now then Jessica had every right to believe she lied about other things. There was only one thing she could do to keep their relationship from unraveling. She had to tell the truth. Taylor looked into the young girl's eyes, giving her a sad half-smile, and, as a tear slid from her own eye, she answered. "Yes, I did. As a matter of fact, I still *do*."

"Wow," Jessica sighed. "I, uhm, I don't know what to make of this. You mean to tell me that Mom never knew?"

"No, and I don't want her to either, Jess. Please

promise me you won't interfere, that you won't say anything to your mother about this," Taylor pleaded.

"You should tell her, Taylor. I mean, maybe she feels the same—"

Taylor interrupted the young girl. "Jessica, your mom is straight and I'm gay. I fell in love with her and she left the life we shared to be with someone else, a man. It doesn't get any plainer than that."

"Who was this guy?" Jessica asked.

"I don't know. I never met him. I think you can kind of understand now, why I never wanted to. Torrey and I went our separate ways in January of eighty-five and she took a job in Chicago to be with him. I guess I just assumed it never worked out. She never volunteered any information and I never asked," Taylor explained.

"You must have that part mixed up. I can't ever remember Mom having a thing with any guy. Hell, she always used to go out with Rick, her agent, to parties and stuff because she said she didn't want to have the hassle of a date," Jessica replied.

"You were only two, Jess. Hell, you barely remember me," Taylor responded.

"Yea, I don't remember a lot, but the thing is I *do* remember you and I was a lot younger when you were with us," Jessica shot back.

"One of us is mixed up, Jess," Taylor said as a thoughtful frown graced her features. "What reason could your mother possibly have had to lie to me about it?"

"I don't know, Taylor, but I know one thing. In the last fourteen or fifteen years since you two split, I don't think I've ever seen my mom go out with a single person, period," Jessica said softly. "Taylor?"

"Yea?"

"Can you tell me why you don't want Mom to know?" Jessica asked.

Taylor didn't look over at Jess; she just ran her slender fingers through the raven mane and leaned against the chair's armrest. "I don't want to ever think that I pressured Torrey into something she didn't really want. You know how your mom can be. She always used to be so concerned with my feelings, not even thinking about herself half the time. I guess I was always afraid that if she felt like I wanted her that way, she might sleep with me out of obligation and not love. If that happened, it would kill me, Jess. I'd rather go on just dreaming of her loving me than to ever have that happen."

Jessica nodded her head in sympathy and understanding. In a strange way, she could comprehend the artist's fears, but she had the oddest sensation that she wasn't seeing the whole picture. Like one of those three-dimensional pictures, you had to practically look cross-eyed at to see the full picture. She tried once to describe to her mother the focusing technique necessary to view the picture. The only way she could think of to explain the process was to say that you had to act like you were trying to look through the picture. That's the way this whole scenario felt to the young girl, like they were missing the forest for the trees.

"Is that why you stayed with Mom? You know, supported us, and helped raise me? Is that why I'm here now?" Jessica asked unexpectedly.

"Know this, Jess. The things I did for your

mother, I did because I loved her, not because I was *in* love with her. Torrey was my best friend long before *I* wanted more from our relationship. She was, and is, an incredibly giving and caring woman who cares more for other people than she ever has for herself. Tell me, how do you not love that?" Taylor asked the young girl honestly.

Jessica smiled and nodded her head at the older woman. "Taylor, do you have any of Mom's books here?" Jessica asked.

"Sure, in the library, I have all of them," Taylor answered with a quizzical stare. "Have you ever read them?"

Jessica looked embarrassed, as she shook her head no.

"Help yourself," Taylor responded. "I've told you the stories, Jess, but you'll never learn more about what's in her heart or the way that woman thinks, than by reading her books." Changing the subject, Taylor asked, "Hey, you hungry? How about we take an early break and have lunch at the Szechwan place?"

"Excellent suggestion." Jessica smiled, the two women rising at once. "Don't worry, Taylor," Jessica said, slipping her arm around the older woman's waist. "Mom will never hear it from me."

"Thanks, squirt," Taylor replied, leaning down to lightly kiss the young girl's forehead.

January 1985

Torrey quietly folded the letter closed and slipped it back into its envelope. She gazed pensively from the bay window out onto the white landscape. It was a good thing she made Taylor drive her Cherokee to work today. One thing you could count on in Maine was a white Christmas. They had that and then some this year. The snow continued to fall heavily as Torrey pondered the letter she received.

She read it through a dozen times now, but couldn't make her heart be glad about it. It was the opportunity of a lifetime, her head told her. Her heart simply ached at the choice she would have to make. She realized at that moment that it didn't matter how wonderful the offer was, she simply couldn't leave Taylor. The truth was that she wouldn't leave. She wouldn't give up the relationship they had. They weren't lovers, but they did love one another and as for the rest, Torrey tried to pretend that it didn't matter. Taylor seemed content with things the way they were, although there were times when Torrey caught the artist in an unguarded moment and the sadness that her face expressed nearly broke Torrey's heart.

The University of Chicago would have to do without her. Once more, she read the letter. Professor John Armistead, the Head of the English Literature Department was requesting that she take the open position as his assistant. A good job, a nice paycheck, and the opportunity to work on her Master's did have its appeal, but only if Taylor was there to share it all with her. She remembered how much fun it was showing Taylor the sights of Chicago and taking in some of the haunts that Torrey grew up around.

It started out as simply a way to earn a little money and take a trip to Chicago. The proctor for Torrey's weekly writers group had a project that was right up the young blonde's alley. A friend of his was doing research for a new textbook he was writing in English Literature and he was looking for someone who could devote a few weekends through the fall to assist him. Torrey jumped at the opportunity and she and Taylor went together the first time. After that, Taylor said it made more sense for her to stay home with Jessica so Torrey could concentrate on doing a good job. It must have worked, as the letter in her hands was the proof.

The cordless phone rang and she jumped at the sound. Quickly flipping the switch so Jessica wouldn't wake up, she answered it on the first ring.

"Hey, Little Bit, Happy New Year. It's not fit for man nor beast out here, I'm calling it a day. Need me to bring anything home?" Taylor's voice came through the static filled line.

"Just yourself." Torrey smiled, recognizing the sound of Taylor's car phone. "How far away are you?"

"As a matter of fact," Taylor drawled.

The sound of the garage door opening prompted Torrey to look out the window and she watched as the familiar sight of the Jeep Cherokee pulled into the driveway and on into the garage.

"You're a sneak." Torrey laughed and hung up the phone as Taylor laughed out loud.

Taylor pulled off her gloves and scarf, hanging her long leather jacket in the hall closet before entering the living room. "I don't think my California blood will ever get used to this kind of weather," The artist said, walking over to her friend and giving her a quick kiss on the top of her head.

"Wimp," Torrey responded with a grin.

"Oh, yea...see how wimpy this feels," Taylor said as she leaned in, placing her ice-cold hands on the young woman's neck.

"Oh, Taylor!" Torrey squealed, jumping up from her seat and backing away from her attacker.

"What's the matter? I thought you just said I was being a wimp." Taylor advanced, wiggling her fingers at her friend.

"Very funny. Back...back," Torrey yelped as Taylor lunged at her again.

"Tay...Tay!"

"See what you did?" Both women laughed in unison as Jessica's impatient voice came from the downstairs bedroom.

"Tay, Tay, Tay!" Jessica said as she bounced up and down in her crib.

Once the dark-haired woman was close enough, the young girl practically threw herself over the crib's rail, Taylor catching the giggling girl in her arms.

"Hello, princess. Have you been a good girl today?"

Torrey stood back and watched as her daughter and Taylor carried on a conversation together. The artist didn't have a clue as to what the youngster was saying, but she interjected all her comments in the right spots.

"Look, Jess, it's snowing." Taylor pointed out the window.

"Ooooh," Jessica responded appropriately.

Torrey pulled some fresh clothes from the large dresser against the wall as Taylor removed Jessica's T-shirt and changed her diaper.

"I can do that, Stretch," Torrey said.

"Nah, I don't mind," Taylor replied with a wink in her friend's direction.

The truth was that Taylor really didn't mind. The young blonde smiled as she watched the artist inter-act with the child. Taylor never did mind taking care of Jessica. It was the highlight of her day, walking in the front door and having the small bundle of energy jump into her arms. Tucking the girl into bed at night was another of the dark-haired woman's favorite times. Jessica would snuggle into Taylor's lap as she sat in the wooden rocking chair, reading a story to the sleepy child.

Taylor's voice interrupted Torrey's musings. "I'm afraid we're going to have to cancel our reservation tonight, Tor. Besides, I don't think Mrs. Green is going to be able to get out in this weather to stay with Jess," Taylor said apologetically.

"It's okay, Stretch. I'm way ahead of you. I already called Mrs. Green and told her not to even think about trying to get out here. I made a pan of my famous lasagna and put it in the oven just before you got here, and if you're very nice to me tonight I'll share your favorite dessert with you." Torrey smiled.

Taylor looked up in surprise. She had assumed Torrey would be more upset about having to cancel their New Year's Eve plans. "You made Tiramisu?" the artist asked in amazement.

"I guess you'll just have to wait and see, won't you?" Torrey replied with a sly grin.

* * * * * * * * *

"Once again you have outdone yourself, Tor. I just keep wondering what I'm going to say to my mom the next time she asks me who the best cook I know is. You're spoiling me, you know," Taylor said with a wink as she took their dessert dishes into the kitchen.

Torrey poured both of them another cup of coffee and enjoyed the view in the kitchen, watching the tall woman place the final pieces of china into the dishwasher. The artist reached into a cabinet and brought out two fluted champagne glasses. She then opened the refrigerator for the bottle of sparkling cider she brought home.

Torrey watched as her friend carefully removed the foil at the top of the bottle and then untwisted the wire that wrapped around the top. The beginning of another year and yet she was still living in the arms of unrequited love for the woman that now busied herself in the kitchen.

It would be nearly five years since she and Taylor first met, not much less since the young blonde fell in love with her best friend. She wondered sometimes why Taylor couldn't see what she felt. She hadn't been on a date once in all that time, with the exception of when she dated Stephen. Torrey had to think twice about that one. When was the last time Taylor went out with anyone?

Torrey's face turned into a frown that she couldn't shake off. Would Taylor stay single just because she thought that Torrey couldn't be left alone? The knowledge hit Torrey hard and caused a sinking feeling in the pit of her stomach. Am I keeping her from finding someone? Am I just being selfish?

Taylor walked into the dining room with the open

bottle and glasses. "Put on your coat, I have an idea." The artist grinned.

The two women bundled up and walked out onto the covered patio. The snow still fell and there was nothing but silence all around them.

"It's beautiful isn't it, Stretch? I feel like I need to whisper," Torrey said softly.

Taylor watched the young woman as Torrey's attention was drawn to the flakes of snow falling from the sky. Taylor noticed that the blonde's cheeks and nose were quickly turning red, her green eyes sparkling. Once again, Taylor felt her body go weak at the sight.

"Here," Taylor said, handing Torrey a glass of the bubbling liquid. "To another year..." Taylor trailed off as she touched her glass to the one in Torrey's hand.

"How will we know when?" Torrey asked, realizing she didn't have her watch on.

"We'll know, a few more minutes," Taylor said cryptically.

"Stretch, why were you going to go out with me tonight?"

"Huh?" Taylor asked in confusion.

"I mean, there must have been some girl you know, maybe someone from your office that you could be out with tonight," Torrey continued.

"Yes, but nobody that can make Tiramisu," Taylor joked.

Torrey smiled, but she needed to know why. Was it her company or did Taylor feel she had an obligation to her? "I thought that maybe you might want to, you know, go out on a date once in a while," Torrey finally said.

Taylor gazed down into quiet green eyes and answered as honestly as she could. "I don't need a date...I have you," Taylor said softly gently taping the tip of Torrey's nose.

The artist thought she'd said the wrong thing when a look like pain crossed the young woman's face. Before Taylor could say anything else, a bottle rocket went off into the air, and then another and soon the whole neighborhood became filled with firecrackers and rockets, their sounds muffled by the falling snow.

"See," Taylor said with a grin. "I told you we'd know."

Torrey laughed and looked up at the impromptu display, the words on her tongue forgotten for the moment. Taylor watched and knew there was little else in this world that could rival what she had in her life right now.

"Happy New Year, Little Bit," The artist whispered.

Torrey turned to look at her friend, her eyes taking in the incredible blue hue of Taylor's eyes. "Happy New Year, Stretch," Torrey whispered back.

Taylor paused to lightly brush the backs of her fingers along the smaller woman's cheek. Reaching down, she gently covered Torrey's lips with her own. She kissed Torrey that way before and, in the past, it was simply a display of emotion, something that occurred when Taylor was too overcome to speak. This time, with each woman wishing in her heart for something more, the kiss lasted perhaps a single heartbeat longer than good sense dictated.

Taylor found herself pulling away seconds before she would have moaned in pleasure at the contact. Torrey felt like her heart was going to pound out of her chest. They embraced, neither woman wanting to look into the other's eyes, not now.

If the balance of all things could have been pulled out of alignment from the wanting of something so badly, yet not acting upon the thought, then the world was surely driven askew on this night.

* * * * * * * * *

Taylor lay in bed staring up at the ceiling, her hands clasped behind her head, her foot nervously rocking back and forth. She couldn't believe what almost happened tonight. That one kiss nearly had a profession of love tumbling from her mouth. She couldn't put her finger on it, but it seemed as if Torrey responded to her touch. Taylor realized it was probably wishful thinking on her part. She had to know. More importantly, should she let Torrey know how she felt about her?

Taylor smiled a slight lopsided grin as she reached her fingers up to her own lips. She casually brushed her lips against Torrey's before, but it was never like this. Actually, Taylor knew in her heart that kissing Torrey would feel that way. Her lips still tingled at the sensation. She had to say something, at least feel Torrey out. She would never jeopardize their friendship, but she would at least see where she stood. If there were one chance, a single billion to one chance that Torrey could love her like that, wouldn't it be worth the risk?

The snow finally stopped and Torrey sat up in her bed, one ear always on the baby monitor to Jessica's room. The moon peaked from behind the clouds and bathed the room in a surreal blue glow. The light caught the tears that rolled silently down Torrey's face.

Tonight she felt her world collide in heartbreak and ecstasy. One moment her heart ached to know that she was being so selfish, to keep a hold on the woman that she loved, denying Taylor the opportunity to find someone the artist could truly love. The next moment, Taylor was kissing her and even now, the young woman felt the sweetness and taste of the dark-haired woman's mouth still lingered within her own.

Torrey pulled her knees up to her chest, wrapping her arms around her legs. She buried her head to muffle the sobs that shook her small frame. Taylor would always stay with Torrey, denying her own plea-sure, her own happiness, just to take care of Torrey. That thought became too much for the young woman to deal with. How could she have been so selfish, to want to refuse Taylor her chance at love and a future of happiness?

Torrey cried now for the decision she would have to make and the one she would have to live with for the rest of her life. She cried for her daughter who would grow up without the love of both the women she had become accustomed to, but most of all Torrey let her tears loose for the love that she realized life would never hold for her. It lay two doors down, but she would have to release it from her grasp. It would be an unbearable torment, but she would always say she did it for love.

****

Torrey was sitting at the kitchen table sipping on a cup of tea when Taylor made her way to the coffee-pot. As usual, the young blonde fixed Taylor's coffee as well as her own tea. The same brief thought passed through her consciousness that did every morning; she wondered what she would do without the young woman. Turning to the table, she mumbled a greeting and was stopped short by the look on Torrey's face. You couldn't live with a woman as long as Taylor had with Torrey without knowing when she spent the night crying.

"Honey, what's wrong?" Taylor asked with concern.

"I—" Torrey started, but stopped abruptly and held out a piece of paper for Taylor.

Taylor looked at the seated woman and then quickly read the letter from the University of Chicago. She didn't expect this. Of course, Chicago winters couldn't be any worse than Maine winters, right? As long as they were together, they could be a family anywhere.

"This is good, right? I mean, the guy you worked with was the best according to you, Tor. Well, hell, I can do what I do anywhere, if we—"

That's when Taylor looked in Torrey's eyes. The young woman pulled away from her gaze and Taylor finally figured it out. There was to be no "we" in this move. Her knees felt weak and she sat heavily in a chair at the table, across from Torrey. "Oh," was all Taylor's brain could formulate.

The older woman looked at the paper in her hand

again. Her fingers slid through her tousled hair in an attempt to give herself time to understand what was happening. The only thing she could feel was the blood pounding furiously in her head. Then she remembered the questions Torrey was asking her last night. Would Torrey want to leave if she thought she was in the way?

"Torrey, if this is about what you were asking me last night, about me not dating—" Taylor started, but was cut off abruptly.

"I met someone," Torrey said flatly.

Taylor felt like she was just punched in the stomach. She took slow, deep breaths to fight the feelings of nausea. "What?" *Taylor asked in disbelief.*

"In Chicago, at the University," Torrey explained, unable to meet Taylor's eyes.

Torrey didn't mean to lie, but it quickly became apparent that Taylor knew her all too well. The artist figured it out and Torrey knew that she wouldn't be able to stand up against Taylor's persuasive arguments. Torrey did the only thing she knew how to do. She made Taylor feel as if she would be standing in the way of her happiness. Torrey realized that Taylor wouldn't care about finding someone for herself, but she would care about denying Torrey. So, the young woman made up an imaginary lover as her trump card.

Taylor felt like she was dying. Her mother's words came back to her and they were true. She never revealed the truth of her heart to Torrey and if she ever had a chance before now, it was gone. Torrey's heart finally found someone else.

She looked over at the young woman across from

her. Torrey's head was bowed and tears escaped from her already swollen eyes. As always, those tears touched Taylor's heart like nothing ever had, or ever would. Taylor silently cursed herself. Torrey was upset, wondering how Taylor would take the news. Probably thinking about how Taylor would get along without her. God, did this woman ever think about herself?

Taylor decided right then and there that she would not cry; not one single tear, not in front of Torrey anyhow. She would be strong and make this as easy as possible on the young woman. She would support her and make Torrey think this was the greatest thing in the world. The young blonde was taking a chance on love and it was more than Taylor could say that she'd done. She would be strong for Torrey, and then she would fall apart when it was all over.

"Torrey, honey," Taylor said, as she moved next to the woman and pulled her up into her arms. "Don't be sad, you should be happy. This job is what you've worked so hard for all this time; you deserve it. You also deserve all the love and happiness in the world. This guy, does he make you happy?"

Torrey cried even harder, but murmured a yes.

"Then that makes me happy," Taylor lied, lifting the young woman's chin until their eyes met.

Taylor lightly brushed her lips against Torrey's forehead, guiding the young woman along with her into the living room. Torrey never said a word as Taylor sat down, practically lying on the couch, then pulled Torrey down beside her. The small woman rested her head on the broad shoulder of her friend, strong arms holding her tightly. Taylor took the opportunity to calm the young woman by running her fingers through her blonde hair, letting her innocent caress fall on skin that would soon be gone from her life.

Torrey closed her eyes tight, but still the tears slipped through. She tried to concentrate on the way her body felt against Taylor, the way the artist's fingertips felt as they slid across her skin. She created a memory that she could lock up within her heart and carry with her. She wasn't sure what hurt more. The fact that she would be leaving and that someday Taylor would be caressing another woman this way, or that the woman she loved with all of her being was simply going to let her go.

"When do you plan on going?" Taylor's hoarse whisper broke the silence.

"They want me to start the first week of February," Torrey answered solemnly.

Taylor took deep breaths to calm herself when all she wanted to do was let go, scream and cry in Torrey's arms, plead with the woman, and promise her a lifetime of love if only she would stay. Five years of their life together and it would be over in a matter of weeks. It was unraveling so fast.

"It will all be wonderful for you, Little Bit, just wait and see. I can tell that someday all your dreams are going to come true," Taylor whispered.

Torrey cried again. The young woman knew one dream that would never come true.

* * * * * * * * * *

The University took care of everything on their

*end. They found a nice apartment in a good neigh-
borhood that fit an Assistant Professor's salary, they
arranged for movers, and even encouraged Torrey to
come and visit the city again at their expense, just to
be sure she would like it there. Torrey declined the
latter. She didn't want to spend one minute apart from
Taylor and she knew if they went to Chicago together,
Taylor would insist on meeting her imaginary lover.*

*Taylor took an emergency sabbatical from Dia-
mond & Allen for the next month. For her part, she
wasn't about to miss one last moment of time with
Torrey or Jessica. That was the hardest part. The
youngster was too young to explain Taylor's eventual
disappearance to, so Taylor just tried to spend as
much time as possible with the child.*

*The artist's tears did fall when she was away from
Torrey, especially as she played on the floor with Jessica. She thought about all the things that she would
miss in the young girl's life, the girl that felt as much
of a daughter to her as if she gave birth herself.*

*Hearing the low murmur of a voice, Torrey paused
at the doorway to Jessica's room. She often did this
simply to enjoy the sound of Taylor's voice as she
read a bedtime story to her daughter and Jessica's
small voice filled with questions.*

*"Tay, was dis?" Jessica's tiny voice asked as she
pointed to a picture in the book.*

*Torrey peeked in to see Taylor's back to her; Jes-
sica snuggled into the artist's lap as they sat in the
large wooden rocking chair.*

*Taylor would read, and then Jessica would inter-
rupt with a question. Taylor would answer the child,
tickle her until she giggled, then they would start the*

whole process over again. Torrey finally heard Taylor pause, and the deep sigh that accompanied that silence was heartbreaking. Finally, Torrey heard Taylor's voice.

"You need to take care of your mom for me now, Jess. She's strong and she can be stubborn as all get out sometimes, but she always means well. She's going to be too far away for me to watch over her anymore, you're gonna have to help me, squirt," Taylor said as tears rolled down her cheeks.

"'Kay," Jessica replied. Taylor chuckled knowing the youngster had no idea what she was talking about, but she responded with the appropriate word in the correct place anyway.

"I love you, Jess. Please, sweetheart, don't ever forget about me, all right...okay?" Taylor asked.

"'Kay," Jessica responded once again. "Wuv you." The child stood in Taylor's lap and threw her arms around the woman's neck.

"I love you too, baby. I'll miss you so much, Jess. You be good for Mommy, okay?"

Jessica nodded and once again settled herself into the artist's lap. Torrey was leaning heavily against the wall, just outside of the room. She walked back to her own bedroom, unable to halt the tears that were becoming a part of her daily routine.

Inevitably the day came, and it was all too soon for the two women. The moving van was already there for a few hours in the morning. Torrey was adamant about not taking furniture, but Taylor won the argument. She explained that Torrey would just be starting out and she shouldn't make her life harder than she had to. There were some items that she absolutely should have. The car was Torrey's to keep or sell, Taylor told her, and as Torrey readied herself, the artist pressed a passbook into Torrey's small hand. Taylor explained to her that she absolutely refused to take it back, and for Torrey to be sensible.

Taylor carried Jessica's bundled form out to the car. Torrey purposefully following behind a little slower to give Taylor the time she needed with the child. Torrey knew of no other way to make all of this turn out all right, and she silently cursed herself at the pain this would cause her daughter, growing up, not knowing the love of the other woman that was as much a mother as Torrey herself. The small blonde could only hope that someday, both of these women of her heart would forgive her for what she felt was the only thing to do. The artist hugged Jessica tightly, whispering into her ear. The tall woman started the girl giggling and then placed the child in her car seat in the back of the Cherokee.

The weather was warmer than it had been for quite some time and since the last two weeks had also been clear, driving shouldn't be too bad, Taylor explained. The two women walked around the car, Torrey with her arm around Taylor's waist, the taller woman had her arm draped over Torrey's shoulder. Torrey agreed to call from the motel every evening and would call as soon as they got into Chicago.

Tears glistened in Torrey's eyes as she finally stopped and looked up into Taylor's azure gaze. The artist's brow was furrowed as she struggled to keep a grip on her own precarious emotions. "I'm so scared," Torrey admitted, as tears fell.

Torrey pulled the young woman into a fierce

embrace. *For the last time, the artist wrapped strong, protective arms around the smaller form and tried to infuse a strength that she didn't really feel, into the woman in her arms. "It's a scary thing," Taylor agreed. "I'm scared too," she whispered in a broken voice.*

"Promise me, Stretch. Promise me that you'll take care of yourself, and that you won't..." Torrey trailed off. They both knew what the young woman was asking. Torrey's greatest fear was that Taylor would go back to using drugs without her around, before she even had a chance to meet someone she could fall in love with.

"I promise, Little Bit. I won't go and undo all the hard work you've put into me." Taylor smiled gently.

"You did it all yourself, Taylor. You should always be proud of yourself for that."

"You just keep believing that," Taylor whispered, placing a kiss on top of the golden hair.

Pulling back from the small figure, Taylor wanted to kiss those lips one last time. She leaned down and brushed her lips across Torrey's so delicately, they barely registered the contact. Then, without caring who might be watching, they kissed once more. This time the kiss was stronger and Taylor cupped Torrey's jaw in her hand and held it there. "I love you, Little Bit," Taylor said softly.

"Oh, Stretch, I love you," Torrey responded, encircling the taller woman's neck with her arms and squeezing tightly.

Taylor didn't really remember much after that. She did feel that she would always remember the sight of Torrey's car as the young woman and her child drove out of her life.

Some of the neighbors that knew the young women already understood what was happening. Those that didn't really didn't have to look far for explanations. Whether straight or gay, they knew what a breakup looked like. Most everyone liked the young couple that seemed to compliment each other so well and who cared for their child with a love and selflessness that was unequaled. Some watched with sad eyes as the tall artist simply stood on the curb for the longest time. When she did move away from the street at last, she acted as if going into the empty house would be too much for her. She sat on the front step, pulling her knees up to her chest and wrapping her arms around her own legs. It was dark before she found the courage to enter the house again. That's when she told herself that it was okay to fall apart now.

Chapter 13

Torrey hung the picture and stepped back to make sure it was straight. She moved forward and made one more adjustment before stepping back again to enjoy the drawing. It was certainly not her daughter's first piece of art, but the first that Torrey ever received as a gift and the first one with such meaning. Her daughter drew the picture from a photograph that Torrey and Jessica both carried in their wallets.

She was never sure what it was about the picture that made both mother and daughter gravitate toward it. Taylor took the photo just after Jess learned to walk. She just ran up to her mother and touched the tip of her index finger to Torrey's nose, both mother and daughter giggled as Taylor snapped the picture. It said more than words, to know Jessica drew this image, which spoke of happier times in their life, for her Mother's Day present.

She thought back to a Mother's Day a long while

back. The young writer was feeling lonely and unloved, and then she remembered Taylor's birthday, which spiraled her into an even deeper depression.

September 1991

Torrey leaned against the wall and smiled at one more nameless person her agent introduced her to.

"You're starting to look bored," Rick said in his singsong falsetto. "Remember all these people are here for you."

"Well, find the prettiest one and I'll leave with her," Torrey shot back.

"Oh, you are in rare form aren't you? What's gotten into you?" Rick asked, waving to someone from across the room.

"My daughter hates me, her nanny just quit, and I haven't had sex in two years, tell me, do I need any other reasons?" Torrey quipped.

She wasn't being mean. She and Rick were old friends and they bantered back and forth like this all the time. Once she found out her friend was gay, she hauled him with her to every party she was invited to, so she wouldn't be propositioned and groped by every man in the room. Soon the rumors were that the author, Torrey Gray, and her agent were a long-standing item.

Rick walked off to the bar and returned with a glass of Glenlivet, handing it to his friend. Torrey thanked him and took a sip from the glass. When she raised her eyes again, she was staring into a pair of cool blue eyes that were hauntingly familiar. The

*woman across the room shook dark hair from her face
and smiled seductively at the writer.*

*Torrey felt a warmth permeate her body with that
smile. Someone must have addressed the woman
because the brunette turned her head back toward the
conversation. It was an amazing coincidence that she
should meet a woman that reminded her so much of
Taylor, especially since she and her friend were separated for nearly seven years now. Even more so on a
weekend when Torrey was missing Taylor more than
ever.*

*The woman standing across the room wasn't
nearly as tall as her old friend, perhaps five foot nine,
or so. Nor was the young woman as breathtaking.
This woman was beautiful to be sure, but she didn't
have Taylor's stunning beauty. Torrey found her eyes
roaming the woman's body and ran right into the
indigo orbs, watching her once again. This time the
woman smiled and winked, telling Torrey that she
caught her. The writer merely shrugged at being
caught in the act. Once again, the brunette turned
back to the people talking next to her.*

*"You may want to be forewarned about that one,"
Rick whispered in her ear. "She's a pro."*

*"Are you kidding?" Torrey was surprised. Of
course, she had no idea what a prostitute looked like
other than the ones that hung around down on Fifty-
eighth Street in Chicago.*

*"She's very expensive, but from what I hear, very
good at what she does," Rick said under his breath.*

"How expensive?" Torrey asked.

*Rick looked over at the young woman and smiled.
He hadn't thought of Torrey as a woman who would*

ever have to pay for sex, but she didn't like the com-
plications of dating and two years could be a long
time. "Would you like me to make inquiries on your
behalf?" Rick asked with a knowing smile.

Torrey watched as the young woman across the
room looked in her direction with a smirk that seemed
to want to know what she was waiting for.

"Oh, yes," Torrey stated, finishing off the last of
her scotch.

* * * * * * * * * *

Torrey ran the key card through the lock and
pushed the door open. The suite at the Plaza was the
same one she stayed in every year when she came to
New York. The staff was courteous and attentive to
the writer's needs. The young man at the desk never
even blinked when he saw the small blonde walk in
with the tall brunette. Whatever people well off
enough to afford a suite at the Plaza did in their
rooms was none of his business.

Taking off her jacket Torrey headed straight for
the bar. "Would you like a drink, Kat?" she asked the
taller woman.

"Sure, whatever you're having is fine," the
woman answered.

Torrey handed Kat her drink and taking a large
swallow of her own, she moved toward the bathroom.
"I need to take a shower. Give me a few minutes,
won't you?" Torrey turned away and wandered into
the bathroom before the call girl could answer.

Kat sipped on her scotch and a smile played
across her lips. She slowly removed her own clothes.

She had to wonder at the beautiful blonde. Usually the only women who sought her out were older dykes with lots of money who had long ago lost their ability to attract younger women. The only reason an attractive, wealthy man or woman paid her for sex was because they wanted no strings and wanted it on their terms. She recognized Torrey Gray right off, but by the woman's innocent smile and the way she wrote, Kat would never had thought that this woman was one of those no strings clients, yet here she was.

Kat opened the door to the bathroom and leaned her naked body against the doorjamb. She watched as a partially robed Torrey prepared to enter the shower stall. "Would you like some help?" Kat asked.

"I wouldn't say no to a little company," Torrey replied without turning her head.

The brunette made her way behind the smaller woman, reaching her hand around the front of the blonde's body and releasing the loose knot that held the robe together. Pulling the collar down from each shoulder, Kat let the robe fall to the floor. She knew the blonde was good looking, but she wasn't prepared for this body. Firm muscles rippled under the smooth tanned skin. Kat brushed the blonde hair to one side of Torrey's neck and placed a series of feather light kisses across the woman's neck and shoulders. Kat reached forward and opened the shower door, allowing Torrey to enter first.

The act of sliding soapy hands across one another's bodies was simply a pretense for what was actually going on. Once they were thoroughly rinsed, Torrey pressed her body firmly against the taller woman's torso, effectively pinning her against the

*warm ceramic tile. She kissed and licked all the way
down Kat's neck, running a wet tongue the length of
the woman's collarbone. Moving her head further
down, Torrey allowed her tongue to reach out and
flick a taut nipple.*

*Kat moaned loud and long at the sensation. Tor-
rey glanced up at the woman and smiled. "Easy. I'm
good, but I'm not that good," Torrey responded.*

*Kat chuckled out loud. This woman was no idiot.
She knew what a whore's gambit was. Usually for a
client to feel like they were getting their money's
worth you had to moan like it was the best fuck of
your life. Obviously, this small dynamo was on to
that and didn't want any part of it.*

*Torrey once again ran her tongue over the hard
nub of flesh, quickly clamping down on it with her
front teeth. That one surprised the call girl and the
sharp intake of breath, and the breathless moan that
came from her own throat surprised her.*

"That's better," Torrey murmured into her breast.

*Kat leaned her head back against the wall and
enjoyed the sensations the woman was creating in her
body. It had been a long time since a beautiful
woman worked her over and she certainly wasn't
averse to giving a customer what they wanted, so she
let the blonde slide down her body and settle herself
on her knees between Kat's legs.*

*Kat didn't want to assume what Torrey wanted to
do; the writer seemed to want to lead this dance, so
the call girl simply looked down waiting for some
kind of instruction. Torrey finally reached up and
parted the brunette's thighs, placing Kat's left foot on
the ceramic seat in the corner. With her leg bent, Kat*

spread her legs as wide as possible, watching in delight as the blonde slid her tongue beyond dark curls and used firm strokes of her tongue on the hooded bundle of nerves.

"Jesus," Kat moaned, thrusting her hips forward shamelessly for more of the woman's delicious touches.

Kat could only writhe and moan as Torrey brought her body up to the precipice again and again only to pull back at the last moment. The blonde would pull Kat's clitoris into her mouth and suck hard, then just when the brunette's thighs trembled, her body expecting release, Torrey pulled back to nibble on her nether lips.

"Good God, woman." Kat looked down at the blonde who smiled back up at her. "Are you trying to ruin me?"

Torrey just smiled with a Cheshire Cat like grin before losing herself within the taller woman's sex. The writer used the flat of her tongue to stroke Kat's now swollen center. "What else do you want?" Torrey paused to ask with a knowing look.

"Fuck me, dammit!" Kat replied emphatically. She wasn't used to being on the begging end and money or no money, if this gal didn't finish her off there was going to be hell to pay.

Torrey's eyes narrowed as she pressed three fingers inside the woman, wrapping her lips around the neglected nub of flesh that pulsed with need. It only took moments before Kat came with a loud groan, her inside walls contracting and releasing against the fingers inside her. The call girl was breathing hard as she pulled Torrey up to kiss her. It had been a very

long time indeed since she'd kissed a beautiful woman
who had her taste on their lips.

Torrey ran her face under the still running water
as Kat spoke to her. "I don't want you to take this the
wrong way, because it's definitely meant as a compliment, but..." the call girl paused to control her
breathing, "you ought to be a whore."

Torrey leaned her head back and laughed. Amazing, this woman thought she was good simply because
she knew enough to take what she wanted. She
reached down, turned off the water and exited the
shower. Grabbing up two towels she kept one for herself and handed the other to Kat.

Once she was dry, Torrey moved to enter the bedroom, but stopped in the middle of the doorway, staring at the bed that was turned down earlier by a maid.

Kat watched the woman in front of her and felt a
certain confidence leave the woman's body. She came
up and pressed her own body against Torrey's back.
"Would you like me to lead now?" she asked.

Torrey only nodded her head in assent.

Running gentle fingertips along the sides of the
smaller woman's well-defined arms and up the muscled abdomen, Kat leaned down and sucked at the
flesh where Torrey's neck met her shoulder. "You are
beautiful," Kat whispered.

Torrey snorted. "Not everyone thinks that," she
snapped bitterly.

So that's it, Kat thought to herself. As desirable
as this woman in front of her was, the writer pined for
someone that didn't want her back. That's why she
paid for sex. She obviously didn't want it any other
way.

"*Then she's a fool,*" *Kat responded, kissing her way up Torrey's neck.*

"*She's very beautiful,*" *Torrey replied almost mournfully.*

Kat stroked the length of the woman's ear with her tongue, leaning in closer to suck on her earlobe. She enjoyed the shiver that she felt run through the woman's frame. Her hot breath blew against Torrey's ear. "Then she's a beautiful fool," Kat simply stated.

Kat pulled the smaller woman into bed on top of her, making sure to caress every inch of the woman's back and shoulders, before reaching the firm backside and massaging the flesh there. She rolled over; Torrey underneath her now, as Kat slipped her thigh between the woman's legs, pressing her leg into the wet flesh at Torrey's center. She firmly kissed a trail up the writer's neck to her jaw, lowering her mouth to taste the woman's lips. Kat tenderly ran the tip of her tongue across Torrey's bottom lip before nibbling and kissing the writer's mouth.

Torrey reached up and slipped her fingers into Kat's damp hair, pulling the brunette down and into a harder kiss. She moaned into the woman's mouth. Meanwhile Kat let her hands sensually explore the woman's body.

The call girl let her lips trail downwards until they wrapped themselves around a hard nipple, Torrey's hands grasping the woman's hair even tighter.

"*Yesss,*" *Torrey sighed, arching her back into the sensations of the woman's tongue swirling around the hard nub of flesh.*

Kat made an attempt to slide down Torrey's body further, but the writer stopped her. "No," she said gently, *"that's not what I want."*

Kat moved up and kissed the soft lips once again. *"Then show me what you want, baby,"* Kat whispered in her ear.

Torrey boldly placed the palm of the woman's hand against her wet center, spreading her thighs further apart. The call girl swirled her fingers in Torrey's wetness, gently stroking the slick folds, spreading the moisture across her center. Torrey shivered at the touch and rocked her hips against the woman's hand.

Kat reached down to kiss the blonde again, resting her fingers against each side of Torrey's clit. *"God, you're wet,"* Kat moaned, as her fingers slid in an alternating up and down motion.

"Oh, God, yesss...just like that...oh, right there," Torrey dictated to the woman on top of her. She wrapped her legs around the taller woman as Kat urged two long fingers deep inside with a gentle thrust.

"What's her name?" Kat whispered, licking the sides of Torrey's neck. *"This woman who doesn't want you?"*

"T-Taylor," Torrey breathed heavily, her hips lifting off the bed as the tempo of Kat's thrusts increased.

"Go ahead and call out her name, baby," Kat moaned against Torrey neck. *"You know you want to."*

"Oh, God...Taylor, yesss," Torrey responded to the call girls prodding.

A new flood of wetness covered Kat's hand, indicating the small woman's impending orgasm. She moved her thumb in a circular motion against the *swollen bundle of nerves, pressing slowly and deep into the woman below her. Within seconds Torrey's fingernails dug into the muscles of Kat's shoulders, as the small blonde released with a cry of Taylor's name.*

Torrey never cried out Taylor's name that way before and she felt tears at the loneliness the action caused.

"Ssh, it's okay," Kat whispered, moving off Torrey's body and lying on her side next to the small woman. She pulled Torrey against her chest and continued to lightly kiss her shoulders, running her fingers through the blonde hair. "Would you like me to stay with you for a while longer?" Kat asked softly.

Torrey silently nodded her head and enjoyed the feeling as the tall woman wrapped her arms around the smaller figure.

Two hours later, Torrey awoke to a light kiss on her neck. "I have to go, baby," Kat's voice said.

"Mmmm, okay," Torrey murmured, raising herself up on one elbow and reaching into the bedside table for her wallet. She counted out five one hundred-dollar bills and put them on the table.

Kat placed a card on the bedside table next to Torrey as she scooped the bills into her hand. "Take this, the next time you're in town give me a call," the call girl said.

Torrey took Kat up on her offer. The writer made it to New York at least once a year and she always made a point to call Kat ahead of time and arrange a night together. It wasn't anything more than what it was; paid sex. She never even learned Kat's last name, but the knowing call girl listened to Torrey's ramblings about Taylor, and when they were in bed, sometimes Torrey could almost believe it was Taylor making love to her.

* * * * * * * * * *

The ringing of the phone finally wrenched Taylor from sleep, her hand moving up, and knocking the phone from its base. "Yea," Taylor's sleepy voice answered.

"Taylor?" the voice asked.

"Who is this?" the artist questioned, slow to wake up fully.

"Emily, Emily Matthews...Corey's mother?"

"Emily, what time is it?" Taylor asked.

"It's two a.m. I'm so sorry to call this late. But—" The woman's voice broke and there was a moment's silence.

"Emily, what happened?" Taylor asked, knowing that at two in the morning it would not be good.

"I thought you should know. I...well, since you were her sponsor and your Jessica and Corey were friends I thought maybe you could tell her," Corey's mother rambled on.

"Tell who what?" Taylor was confused.

"Tell Jessica. I'm sorry to tell you like this, Taylor, but my daughter died last night," Emily Matthews replied tearfully.

"What? How?" Taylor thought she was still sleeping and this was just a bad dream.

"She—She went out yesterday afternoon with some old friends and she never came home." Taylor listened as the woman sobbed quietly. "They brought her in as a DOA from a drug overdose."

Taylor listened with incomprehension as Corey's mother explained the rest to her. Emily was a nurse, but her skilled detachment couldn't conceal the depth of her anguish from the artist. "Emily, can we do anything for you, anything at all?" Taylor asked.

"If you and Jess would be at her funeral, day after tomorrow at Westberry. Taylor, please don't let Jessica go off because of this, please make her understand what Corey would have wanted," Emily pleaded.

"We'll be there. Don't worry, I'll take care of Jess," Taylor replied. "Emily, don't be afraid to call if you need something, or even just somebody to talk to, okay?"

Taylor held the phone in her hand until the loud blaring of the line called her attention to it. Replacing the phone in its cradle, she rolled onto her back and let hot tears slide from her eyes. Placing a pillow over her head, she pounded her fists into the bed, letting the cushion over her face muffle her screams of frustration over another life that she couldn't save.

****

"Jess, honey, wake up." Torrey gently shook the sleeping girl's shoulder.

"Aw, go 'way, Tay. It's too early," Jess moaned from underneath the covers.

Taylor smiled gently at the young woman's abbreviated use of her name. Fifteen years later and to Taylor's ears, it still sounded like the voice of that two-year-old.

"Jess, something's happened. You need to wake

up so we can talk."

The artist debated over whether to wake the young woman or let her sleep and tell her in the morning. She tried to think back to when she was seventeen. What would she have wanted her mother to do under similar circumstances?

Jessica jerked awake. Looking up at Taylor's face, she noticed the woman's red, swollen eyes. She quickly tried to think of what would cause tears in the stoic artist. "Mom? Is Mom okay?" Jessica asked in alarm.

"Your mom is fine, hon, it's not about her. Come on and get up and wash your face off so I know you're awake, then meet me in the living room, okay?" Taylor requested.

"Okay," Jessica replied, getting out of bed as Taylor pulled the door closed behind her.

Taylor was seated in the pit area of the living room in front of the fireplace, clothed in an old MU sweatshirt and worn jeans. The artist had the fireplace going and the clean wood smell was a sort of comfort scent to Jessica. A fire on a cold evening was the way her mom used to relax at the end of her workday.

"I made a cup of Earl Grey for you," Taylor said quietly, indicating the mug on the end table.

"Taylor could you just tell me, 'cause this is kind of freaking me out," Jessica said suddenly.

Taylor looked up at the girl with understanding, but she wasn't certain she knew how to begin. "I got a call a couple of hours ago from Corey's mom, Jess."

That's all it took for the light of fear to burn in the young girl's eyes. *Calling in the middle of the night,* she thought. *Corey must have fallen off the wagon.* That's when Taylor's expression changed and the older woman couldn't keep the tears from her own eyes. Jessica's fear grew as the solemnity of Taylor's face changed.

"Jess, I'm sorry, but...Corey, she...she died last night, hon."

"But, she was just here. I mean, this weekend, we just worked together..." The young girl's voice trailed off. People always seem to say that when you tell them someone has died. They always seem to comment on the fact that they just saw them.

Jessica didn't know why but she immediately thought it was a car accident. Frankly, she'd seen Emily Matthews drive through Southern California's twisting mountain roads and she was none too confident in the woman's ability.

"What happened?" Jessica asked in a very small voice.

"Emily said that she went out with some friends yesterday afternoon and she never came home. She was brought into the hospital last night. She was already dead...an overdose," Taylor replied in a broken voice that she was trying very hard to keep together for Jessica's sake.

"No, that's impossible!" Jessica responded.

Taylor sat her mug down as she watched the girl pace back and forth above her, her eyes nervously darting back and forth.

"She was just here, she would have told me if she was having trouble...she trusted me!"

"Jess, we don't always tell our friends everything we're going through, especially as addicts. You should know better than a lot of people that we hide shit better than anybody." Taylor rose from her seat as she spoke and leaned against the arm of the sofa.

"I should have done something. I should have been able to see what she was going through. I should have helped...I should have been there for her...she should have told me."

That's when Jessica made the move that Taylor was waiting for, the young girl bolted toward the front door. The artist knew this would come and steeled herself for it. *It's what we always try to do in times of extreme panic...fight or flight.*

The older woman jumped up with a speed that would have surprised many, and was behind the girl in no time. She reached out a tentative arm and was slapped away hard by Jessica. That's when Taylor wondered if she was still strong enough to physically restrain a seventeen year old nearly as strong as her. She didn't expected Jessica to go full out with her, but the girl wasn't exactly herself at the moment.

Taylor reached out an arm around the girl's waist and pulled back hard, stopping the girl and nearly lifting her off her feet at the same time. "Let go of me!" Jessica screamed. At the same time, she jabbed an elbow in the taller woman's midsection.

Taylor gave a grunt as the blow was taken in her stomach, but still kept her grip on the girl who was screaming and crying by this time. The artist may not have been as strong as she was twenty years ago, but she knew the tricks and had the experience. She easily ducked the next jab that came toward her head, and then slipped an arm through the girls flailing arms until she was in a tight restraining hold.

"It's not fair!" the girl cried. "She was doing so good, it's not fair that it should happen to her. Why would she let someone do that to her?"

"JT," Taylor shouted to be heard. "Jessica! She did it to herself, honey."

"Why, Tay...why would she do that to herself?" Jessica slumped in Taylor's hold. The girl sobbed as the dark-haired artist turned her around and held her in arms that still shook from the strain of keeping the girl from running.

"Her mom said the doctors told her it was probably an accident. She hadn't done anything in a while and the coke she took was too much for her. They said her heart couldn't take it," Taylor explained, not revealing that the doctors said the young girl's heart had literally exploded in her chest. She was dead instantly.

"I don't get it," Jessica said through her tears. "Why did she go out partying in the first place? Why didn't she call us? We would have been able to stop her."

Taylor stroked the young girl's face and guided her back into the living room. They both sat down in the oversized loveseat, Taylor wrapping her arms around the girl much as she always had for Jessica's mother.

"This is the one lesson that I hoped would be a way off for you yet, Jess. It comes with the territory when you make friends with other addicts. And, I'm not saying you shouldn't, I'm just saying you have to be aware that things like this can happen, and there are some important rules to remember when these kinds of things do happen to our friends. Wanna hear what I have to say?" Taylor asked, stroking the girl's hair.

Jessica just nodded her head.

"First thing is, that it's not up to you to save someone. It's near impossible to keep them from themselves. If any of us, you, me or Corey wanted to go back and start using, and if we really wanted to do it, there's no way our friends could stop us. They could threaten and try, but you can't be with someone else twenty-four hours a day."

"You could try," Jessica responded.

"Yea, honey, you could, but if you did that then you'd be running their life. It wouldn't be their choice. The only way to beat an addiction is on your own, Jess. I am always here for you and so is your mom, but ultimately it is all you and the choices *you* make. That's why staying clean is such an accomplishment for us. I mean, sure we have people we're doing it for, but they don't go through all the hell, do they? It's something that we do. Although, that doesn't mean I wouldn't beat the crap out of you if I found out you started using again, fear can be very motivating at times," the older woman said with a little grin as she lifted Jessica's face up until their eyes met.

Jessica gave a small laugh, sniffing and wiping her tears away. Taylor reached over to the coffee table and handed the girl some tissues. The young girl blew her nose, but the tears didn't stop and Taylor didn't encourage them to. The older woman knew this was the best way for the young girl to begin her grieving process. She reached over and brushed damp bangs from the girl's face.

"Just remember, Jess. The way you feel right now about losing your friend is only a drop in the ocean compared to the way your mother and I would ever feel if we lost you." Tears glistened in the artist's eyes as the thought came to her brain. "It won't always keep you from doing what you want to do, but I think it's important for you to hear it and believe it, okay?"

"'Kay," Jessica replied, resting her head in the crook of the older woman's shoulder.

Taylor's broad smile unconsciously spread across her face as she remembered one of the last times she held the young girl in her arms like this and the exact same response that came from the girl's lips. Taylor squeezed Jessica in a strong hug. "I love you, Jess. I'll always think of you as my daughter, too, I want you to know that," Taylor said.

"I love you too, Tay. You make a good mom," Jessica replied, returning the hug and relaxing in the older woman's arms.

"Thanks, hon." Taylor kissed the top of Jessica's head and rested her chin there.

Taylor felt they narrowly avoided a real disaster tonight, and she knew it wasn't over yet. One more day and they would find their nerves and their emotions tested again when they found themselves at Corey's funeral. She wouldn't push it now, but tomorrow she would probably have to take Jess shopping for some appropriate clothes. *God, this is going to be a really long weekend.*

* * * * * * * * * *

The funeral was hard on everyone, the least of which were Corey's friends from the NA group. It always hit addicts the worst. It was like losing one of your own, and for a reason that you were only a step away from yourself. Natalie stayed with Corey's mom and helped her get through the day.

Taylor couldn't have been more proud of Jessica. She and Taylor went shopping the day before and each of them purchased new clothes suitable for the solemn occasion. Early that morning Jessica asked Taylor if she knew of a place the girl could get her hair cut. Taylor called and was able to get an appointment for them both later that day.

Once they made it to Adrian's for their hair appointment, Jessica pretty much decided to get her long hair trimmed down to shoulder length. The final results looked good on the girl and in her new clothes she looked more of a woman than Taylor was prepared to admit to. Taylor had her bangs and split ends trimmed up, refusing Adrian's good-natured attempt to get her to cut off any more than that.

"Taylor, come on. With that height and those muscles, wouldn't you like to look a little more butch? Let's take it real short, it'll look great, the women will love it," the hairdresser said.

"I cry too much to be butch," the artist dead-panned, raising an eyebrow filled with intimidation at the young woman.

Adrian took the hint and both women left the shop looking and feeling a little better. "You're daughter's turning into a beautiful young woman," Adrian said to Taylor before they left.

Taylor didn't explain; she simply smiled and

agreed.

The drive home after the funeral was as long as any Taylor ever made. She worried that Jess wasn't talking. Like her mother, the girl was a veritable chatterbox and when she was silent that usually meant something was wrong.

"Taylor?"

"Yea?"

"I think I'd like to see Mom. Would you mind?" Jessica asked.

"No, Jess, of course not. You know it's almost time to go back. Your mom only wanted you to stay out here for six months." Taylor approached the subject she'd been dreading.

"Do you want me to go?" Jessica asked quickly.

"No, Jess, I love you and I love having you in my life again. You can live with me whenever you'd like for as long as you like. I just meant that you'll have to talk to your mom about whatever you decide you want to do," Taylor answered.

"I feel bad, guilty, you know? I don't think Mom's gonna like what I want to do. Besides, part of me feels like I'm being unfair to her. I mean, she lives with all my shit for so many years and now that I know how to act like a respectable human being, I'm going to take off on her," Jessica replied solemnly.

Taylor chuckled at the young woman's assessment. "Yea, I can see where you'd be a little torn, but your mom can be a very understanding woman, Jess. She knows that this is your life to live, not hers. I'm sure she'll feel the same way I do about it. If we know that you're healthy and happy, then that will make us happy. I guess the only advice I can give you is to make the time you do have with your mom, pleasant. Show her that you've grown up and that you don't act like a complete ass anymore," Taylor finished with a smile at the girl.

"Thanks, Tay." Jessica grinned at the artist. "I can always count on you to make sure my ego doesn't get out of hand."

"That's what I'm here for, squirt." Taylor returned the sly grin. "So what *have* you decided to do with your life?"

"I want to go to school. I have the credits just not the grades. If I can talk Mom into paying for college then I won't have to depend on miserable SAT's to get a scholarship. I could always get a job too, that might help," Jessica explained.

"Sounds like a good plan," Taylor replied proudly. "Why don't you hold off on the money end, and let me talk to your mom first, okay?" Taylor said, realizing that now she was going to have to talk her extremely proud friend into taking the money she had been depositing in Jessica's college fund. "So where's it gonna be?"

"I've narrowed it to Cal Arts or U of C in Irvine. Your friend Kenny seemed to think they would be the best," Jessica answered.

Taylor nodded remembering the day they visited Kenny at the studio where he now worked. She never thought the young man responsible for the one tattoo she sported, would now be an animator for a major studio in California. "When do you want me to make a reservation for you to go back and for how long?" Taylor asked.

"Uhm, I was kind of thinking it would be kinda

cool if Mom could come out here. That is if it wouldn't whack you out or anything," Jessica said cautiously.

Taylor took a deep sigh. *Could she handle it? Hell, she couldn't expect Jessica to stay out here and never have her mother visit. God, she wouldn't bring a date with her, would she?* "You sure your mom isn't seeing anyone, Jess?" Taylor asked nervously.

"Tay, I told you, Mom never dates. Look, I won't ask her if it will make you uncomfortable at all. I just thought that if she came out here and saw everything, the way you and I get along, and then maybe we could visit the University while she's here, and, well, that maybe she'd feel more at ease with the whole thing. You know she loves California. She's always talking about coming back here some day. Hey, wouldn't that be cool, if we all lived here?" Jessica said enthusiastically.

Taylor looked over at the young woman. "I never knew she felt that way. I know she liked it when we came out, but I didn't know it was someplace she'd actually live. I wouldn't let your hopes soar too high on that last part though, Jess. It's kind of hard on me sometimes, just being in the same room with your mom knowing that someday she'll find someone she loves."

"I know, Tay, I'm sorry. I don't want to see you or Mom unhappy. You sure you can handle this?"

"Hey, sometimes it's hard, but most of the time I love being around your mom. She's the best friend I have, aside from you, and I love her dearly. As a matter of fact I can't wait to see your mom again." Taylor smiled and she surprised herself by actually believing those words.

"Great!" Jessica smiled broadly. "I'll call her as soon as we get home."

Chapter
14

"But, Mom, it'll be so much fun. You said you'd love to come back out here for a vacation sometime," Jessica pleaded.

"I know I did, honey, but this sounds like it could be a bad time. Your friend is gone and I'm sure it's not an upbeat kind of time. Taylor's show is coming up and she probably doesn't want me underfoot while she's trying to work." Torrey desperately racked her own brain to come up with plausible excuses as to why coming to California would be a bad idea, but try as she might, the best she could come up with were a pathetic few.

"Mom, it's not like that. Tay was the one who said she can't wait to see you." Jessica tried attacking from a different point.

Torrey chuckled when she heard that name from Jessica's own voice.

"What are you laughing about?" Jessica asked,

slightly confused.

"You used to call Taylor that when you were little. I'm surprised you remembered," Torrey replied.

"Actually, I didn't remember, it just sort of felt right, you know? I wonder why she didn't say anything about it?" Jessica pondered.

"She probably didn't want to embarrass you, honey," Torrey responded.

"So, Mom...what about it? I really want you to come out here, you'll love Tay's place, I just know it."

The truth was that Torrey did indeed want to see her daughter and Taylor in the environment that Jess had obviously grown fond of. She ached to hold her daughter in her arms and a different kind of ache pulled at her at the thought of seeing Taylor again. She really couldn't fight it because she simply didn't want to.

"Okay, babydoll...just tell me where and when," Torrey said as she swore she could feel Jessica's grin across the phone line. "And, honey, you tell Taylor that if she leaves me waiting at the airport like she did in Maine, I'll have her hide."

Torrey hung up the phone and began making mental lists of what she would need to pack. Jess wanted her to stay for a couple of weeks, so that meant at least two suitcases and at least one carryon. She swept into her bedroom and perused the items in her walk in closet. They were suitable for everyday wear in Chicago and the occasional party, very East Coast, but she realized that she was about to see the woman she still loved after an absence of fifteen years. This definitely called for a shopping trip.

Torrey walked into the bathroom, turning on the shower faucets. She paused in front of the mirror over the sink and her hand went up to her short blonde locks.

"Oh, my God! Why did I get my haircut now?" she yelled at her image. It was a good cut and practical now that she worked out and swam everyday at the health club, but what would Taylor think? *Good Lord, Torrey, you're acting like you've got a chance with the woman. You look great and you know it, you're just going out there to see your daughter and your best friend. You can do this. Now straighten up and don't worry so much.*

* * * * * * * * * *

Torrey leaned back in the reclining chair, her eyes closing slightly as she sipped on a mug of warm tea. After flying first class only once, ten years ago, the writer swore she would never travel any other way. After so many years of jetting to different parts of the country, you would have thought a fear of flying would no longer be in her repertoire, though. It didn't put her in a panic, but she never quite gave up the thought that this could be the one, her time.

"Excuse me," a voice across the aisle said softly.

Torrey raised green eyes to a woman with blonde hair and smiling eyes.

"I know you probably get this a lot, but are you Torrey Gray?"

Torrey displayed a sunny smile that was, in a way, her trademark. Truth be known, it was the only way she knew how to smile. Yes, she'd heard the line for years, but secretly, she never tired of it. "Yes, I am," she replied softly.

Two hours later, the women were side by side, discussing everything from daughters to Maine. When the flight attendant announced they would be landing in a few minutes, the stranger was tempted to give the writer her card. She enjoyed the woman's laughter and cheerful personality. She had heard all the rumors, but always wondered if they could be true. Was Torrey Gray really gay? The blonde smiled back over at the writer and decided she'd wait until they landed and see if she could entice the woman out for lunch, and later, possibly more.

Taylor pushed herself from against the wall and paced impatiently in front of the monitors that flashed incoming flight information. She consulted her watch then walked back to resume her vigil by the wall. When she looked down, Jessica's green eyes were smiling up at her.

"Geez, Tay, are you gonna be okay?" Jessica asked with a snort.

"Why?" Taylor growled.

"Well, you look like you're having a mini-break-down for one thing." Jessica laughed.

"Don't laugh at me, squirt. It's a long walk home," Taylor said, arching an eyebrow for effect.

Jessica laughed again. Like her mother before her, the artist's intimidating stare had little effect on the young woman. "Don't worry, Tay. After all, it's just Mom," Jessica said, with a hint of understanding.

"I know." Taylor gave a little half smile. Taylor seemed unable to make Jess understand that it being Torrey *was* the problem.

The passengers on the flight from Chicago were disembarking. Jessica made a motion to go forward, but Taylor stayed back, not moving. "Why don't you go and, you know, and I'll just hang back here," Taylor uncharacteristically stammered.

Jessica smiled slightly, not even guessing herself at how much this first meeting after fifteen years meant to the tall artist. She spotted her mother right away, even with the new haircut. Taylor hung back and watched as mother and daughter met in a tearful, yet delighted reunion.

"Oh God, JT, you look wonderful," Torrey said with tears in her eyes. She hugged her daughter close and kissed her cheek. "Your hair, it looks great on you," she said, running her fingers through the girl's hair.

Torrey looked up at her daughter and saw a light in the girl's eyes that hadn't been there six months ago. Her green eyes sparkled brightly and she shared a hug with her mother that Torrey thought she would never feel again.

"You look beautiful, Mom," Jessica whispered proudly.

Torrey simply gazed at her daughter for a few silent moments. The writer never thought the day would arrive when her rebellious young girl would look at her with anything but contempt. Now, Torrey heard the pride in her child's voice and saw the love in her eyes. She promised herself she would spend the rest of her life repaying Taylor for this gift.

With that thought, the writer felt her stomach do a slight flip in anticipation of seeing her old friend again. "Jess, where's Taylor? Is she with you?" Torrey asked.

Jessica nodded and motioned with her eyes to the figure walking toward them.

Taylor didn't realize she was holding her breath until the air was knocked from her lungs by the sight of the small blonde. Torrey looked absolutely perfect. Dressed in white slacks and a pale peach blouse under a white linen jacket that had the sleeves casually pushed up to her elbows. Taylor was more surprised at the new hairstyle. She finally did what she threatened to do for years. The casual cut, soft wisps of blonde hair falling loosely over her ears and nearly into her eyes caused the petite writer to look sexier than ever in Taylor's eyes.

Fifteen years of wanting made itself known, as every nerve ending in the artist's body felt like it was just shocked with an electric jolt of fire. She melted at the sight, as she watched Torrey laugh and smile at her daughter and when she saw the woman raise her eyes to where she stood, she couldn't stop the goofy grin that she was sure appeared on her face.

Torrey looked over to where her daughter indicated and fell into sparkling pools of cobalt light. Taylor was already giving her that lopsided grin she seemed to reserve only for Torrey, as she walked toward the two women.

Jessica took a step back as Taylor approached. Torrey let loose of her daughter's waist and stood before the taller woman. Without hesitation Torrey slipped her arms around the artist's waist, reaching up on her tiptoes, she kissed the dark-haired woman's lips. They kissed like this before, but Taylor was always the one to initiate it. The artist was shaken when Torrey established the intimate contact. Torrey felt the warmth of Taylor's strong embrace, then pulled back to look into the taller woman's incredible eyes. "You look great, Stretch." Torrey smiled.

Taylor reached down and gave another squeeze to the smaller woman's shoulders. "As beautiful as ever," Taylor whispered in her ear.

It was then that the blonde, Torrey had chatted with on the plane, disembarked. If the woman ever thought she had a chance with the petite author with the sexy, jade green eyes, all those thoughts were squashed as she looked over at the small woman being greeted by two other women. It was the taller of the two dark-haired women that caught the stranger's eye. The way they looked into one another's eyes, punctuated by the kiss they shared in the middle of the airport, had the blonde turning away with a sigh of regret. *Well, at least I know the rumors were true*, she said to herself as she walked away.

"I can't believe that neither one of you has said one thing about my haircut," Torrey stated as they moved to the luggage area.

"It's nice, Mom," Jessica said.

"Oh, yeah," Taylor added. The artist didn't dare tell her how gorgeous she really looked.

"Well, judging by that thoroughly under whelming response, I think I'll let it grow out." Torrey laughed.

"Oh, no Mom, really, you look great," Jessica said with more conviction.

"Uhm, yeah, beautiful, Tor." Taylor tried not to stare.

"Actually, *really* stunning," Jess said, stopping to

admire her mother.

"Absolutely breathtaking," Taylor added, taking her cue from Jessica.

Torrey looked between Taylor and her daughter as the two exchanged knowing grins. "Oh, I can see I'm going to be outnumbered with you two together," Torrey responded.

They couldn't help but laugh at the smaller woman. Torrey placed an arm easily around her daughter's waist and slipped her own hand within the artist's callused one. They walked along looking for the entire world, like a family. Taylor held on to the small hand within her own and relished the sweet contact. Torrey made no move to pull away and the artist knew she wasn't going to be the one to extinguish the familiar touch. They picked up Torrey's luggage and in moments Taylor returned with the Explorer, pulling in front of the airport to pick up her friend.

Taylor jumped out of the car to store the luggage in the back, opening the passenger side door for Torrey to get in. Jessica watched with a hidden smile at the way the two women treated one another. In her heart, the young girl knew that Taylor would be attentive and charming with her mother. They moved like two people who had long grown used to the other's moves. When Taylor opened the door for Jessica's mother, Torrey slipped in without saying a word, as if this were a courtesy extended to her by someone everyday.

"So, where are you two taking me for lunch, I'm starving," Torrey said to break the silence.

"You...starving? What a surprise," Taylor said in a voice dripping with sarcasm.

Before the artist knew it, Torrey slapped her thigh. "Five minutes I've been here and you're already abusing me," Torrey said with a mock air of disdain.

"That's because you make it so easy, Little Bit," Taylor replied with a laugh, which earned the artist another smack.

"How about Simon's? Unless you're in the mood for something fancier?" Taylor asked.

"Oh, a Simon Special, yes!" Torrey leaned her head back, enjoying the idea.

"Gross," Jessica said from the back seat. "I'm gonna have to watch both of you eat those disgusting sandwiches, aren't I?" she groaned. Secretly the girl was already ecstatic at the way the two women were getting along.

****

"This place is wonderful, Taylor, I absolutely love it," Torrey said to the woman seated on the couch next to her. "You've done very well for yourself, I'm proud of you."

The two women sat talking late into the night in front of the fireplace. Even though it was now officially summer this evening was cool, giving them the perfect excuse to light a fire. Jessica had long ago gone to bed. The young woman wasn't quite as tired as she pretended to be, but she knew it would be good for the two older women to be able to spend some time together.

Taylor enjoyed the closeness of Torrey, the way she smiled and teased, the way she touched the artist's arm to make a point. Taylor was realizing, with each passing moment that this was no longer the young girl she cared for and protected for so many years. That eighteen-year-old was gone and a grown woman existed in her place. The artist never grasped that from her writings. Even while reading Torrey's letters, Taylor still pictured the college girl that broke into tears at the slightest provocation. Now Torrey spoke with an air of confidence, the look in her eye, the way she held her body all combined to attract Taylor to her in a way the artist never felt before.

Torrey, in the meantime, felt her breath catch in her throat each time that she looked up to take in the woman who sat beside her. Taylor's beauty certainly hadn't diminished at all in fifteen years. If anything, Torrey wondered how she could have desired the twenty-two year old girl, when this sexy forty-year-old woman was coaxing her stomach into some major acrobatics. The lines around the artist's mouth and eyes were set a little deeper, but the sapphire orbs still sparkled when she spoke, filling with an electric blue fire when she talked of her art, clouding over to a steel gray when she was hurt or worried, just as they did now.

Taylor found herself talking to Torrey as if no time at all had gone by. Her fears and her dreams were all revealed to the green-eyed woman who was always so good at slipping under the artist's defenses and seeing the vulnerable woman that Taylor hid from the rest of the world.

Taylor found herself talking about Corey, watching Torrey's eyes grow misty at the thought of the young girl and her troubled life. Tears became an

actuality for the young author as she envisioned a
mother trying to cope with the death of her only
daughter, to an addiction that the mother couldn't
defeat.

Jessica wasn't able to fall asleep and she wandered out into the kitchen, pouring herself a glass of
ice water. She heard the low murmur of voices from
the living room and was pleasantly surprised that her
mother and Taylor were still up talking. She passed
by the hall that led down into the living room and sat
on the stairs that led to the lower level of the house.
She told herself that she would leave immediately if
she heard anything at all about herself, that way she
wouldn't feel like she was eavesdropping. Actually,
the only thing the young woman wanted was to hear
the voices of the two women she loved most. She
smiled to herself, being able to distinguish the low
alto of Taylor's voice as compared to the soft melodic
tones of her mother's. Finally, Jessica listened as
Taylor opened up to Torrey about Corey and the
responsibility the artist felt she had to the youngster,
letting her slip through her fingers. She was her
sponsor and she felt like she let everyone down.

"Stretch," Torrey whispered, gently wiping the
tears from Taylor's cheeks. "You can't be responsible
for everyone. Remember what Sister Eva used to say?
When you're standing out in the snow, you can only
catch as many snowflakes as *want* to fall on your
tongue. She was such a young girl and it breaks my
heart too, but you can't make all the teenagers in the
world your personal responsibility. That's too much
for anyone."

Jessica listened as she heard Taylor's fears and

insecurities for the first time. Taylor said a lot of the same things that Jessica herself felt, Torrey responding with many of the things Taylor already said to Jessica.

"I guess it hit me kind of hard, having Jess here now," Taylor explained to Torrey. The artist ran her fingers through her hair, leaning her elbow on the back of the couch, near Torrey's head. "I didn't know how attached I would grow to Jess in such a short time. I didn't realize how much I love her, Tor, and what I would ever do if the same thing happened to her." Taylor's voice broke and Torrey realized how much the artist was holding in since the young girl's death. Taylor was being strong for Jess, but she had no one to comfort her and the artist's pain was so close to the surface Torrey knew it wouldn't take much to bring it out.

She leaned closer to the dark-haired woman, catching the familiar scent of Opium cologne on her skin. Torrey wrapped strong arms around the artist's shoulders and gently kissed Taylor's forehead. She felt Taylor's body war with itself, tensing before realizing that she was safe in arms that would never let her fall. "It's okay, honey. You can let go now," Torrey whispered.

The ragged sob that came from Taylor's chest caused an ache in Jessica's own heart. She never realized the stoic woman was hurting so much. She heard Taylor's weeping and the murmurs of her mother's voice and realized what her mother didn't. That Taylor hurt for a lot of reasons her mother didn't know about.

Jessica swallowed the last of her drink and made

her way back to her bedroom. She felt like she was intruding on something very private between these women, something that had nothing to do with want or desire, but had everything to do with love and friendship.

* * * * * * * * * *

"Torrey, honey, wake up. It's after three, do you want to go to bed?" Taylor asked the sleeping woman lying mostly on top of her. Sometime in the night, the two women fell asleep on the couch, the fire burning down to glowing embers. Now, Taylor's body was mostly being used as a pillow by her old friend, the small blonde's leg draped over her thighs.

"Uh unh...too comfortable here," Torrey murmured sleepily, tightening her hold around Taylor's waist and burrowing her face into the soft flesh of Taylor's neck.

The artist could have moaned in pleasure at the feel of the body lying half on her own. If Torrey didn't want to move then Taylor was the last person on earth who was going to talk her into it. The artist brushed her lips against the blonde's forehead, pulling the down comforter from the back of the couch over the two of them. Torrey snuggled deeper and Taylor whispered, "Good night, Little Bit."

"Night," Torrey mumbled.

Taylor relaxed and enjoyed the weight of the woman's body on her own and the way her arms felt, holding Torrey close to her. She had a feeling Jess might freak if she found them in the morning, but right now, it was the farthest thing from her mind.

Chapter 15

Taylor groaned and rolled over. She had to remember not to fall asleep on this couch again; her back was killing her. The artist opened sleepy eyes and found she was alone, but the distinct aroma of food told her where her couch mate was. She smiled. *God, it was so easy to fall into an old habit.*

She walked into the kitchen and nearly ran into Torrey walking in at the same time. The petite blonde wore a tank top and drawstring pants, her hair still damp from the shower.

"Morning," Taylor mumbled. "I thought that was you cooking."

"Hey, I'm on vacation," Torrey said with a smile, slipping an arm around the artist's waist and walking into the kitchen with her.

"It's about time, I thought you two were never getting up," Jessica said as she poured more batter into the waffle maker. The young woman found the machine a couple of months back, tucked into a cabinet in Taylor's kitchen and realized it was pretty much like making pancakes. "I was going to wake you up, but you were snoring so loud I figured you were dead to the world," Jessica said to Taylor.

"I do not snore," Taylor replied, defensively.

"Oh, yea you do." Jessica laughed.

"Tor, tell her I don't snore." Taylor looked at her friend for support.

"Uhm, well, the truth is...you do," Torrey said apologetically.

"What? Since when?" Taylor asked, dumbstruck.

"Well, I never noticed it before, but I did when we were sleeping together last night," Torrey answered.

Now it was Jessica's turn to become speechless. "When you did what last night?"

"What?" Torrey asked her daughter.

"You said the two of you slept together," Jessica questioned.

"I can't believe I snore and nobody even said anything to me," Taylor chimed in with her own obsession.

"Honey, it's not that big a deal," Torrey answered.

"You slept together and you don't think it's a big deal?" Jessica answered.

"Okay, hold it both of you." Torrey raised her voice to be heard above the two other women. "God, do you two always have this much stimulation before breakfast?" Torrey rubbed her temples. "You," she said pointing to Taylor. "I'm sorry honey, but yes, somewhere in the last fifteen years you've started to, well, it's really more of a relaxed, heavy breathing."

"Snoring," Jessica muttered under her breath.

"You, hush," Torrey scolded. "It's not annoying, Stretch. It's actually kind of cute," Torrey finished with a grin. "And you." She pointed to Jessica. "We fell asleep on the couch last night while we were talking. We slept there."

Torrey walked over and smiled approvingly at the two side-by-side coffee makers, one with tea, and the other with coffee in the glass carafes. "She's taught you well, my child," she teased her daughter, pouring a mug of tea for herself and handing Taylor her coffee.

"See I told you I didn't snore." Taylor bumped Jessica's shoulder and growled as she went by.

"Hah, she was just being nice," Jessica replied.

"Watch it, squirt, you're not so big I can't toss you from these cliffs," Taylor shot back.

"Oooh, you're so butch. You and what army?" Jessica retorted.

Taylor and Jess smiled at one another, suddenly turning to face Torrey. Taylor moved to sit at the table and looked up at her old friend with a sheepish grin. "I have no idea where she gets that," the artist said innocently.

"I can't imagine," Torrey said, shaking her head.

****

"I can do that, Mom," Jessica said, rising from the breakfast table and taking the empty dishes from her mother's hand.

"Well, since you've got a handle on cleanup, squirt, I am off to a hot bath. That couch played hell with my back last night," Taylor said. "Tor, what would you like to do today?" she asked, pouring a cup of coffee to take with her.

"Sleep, mostly."   The petite blonde grinned. "Actually, I wouldn't mind sitting by the pool for a while."

"Whatever you want just yell, Jess knows where we hide everything. I don't want to ignore you, but I've got some calls to make to get some things ready for the show. Jess will make sure you don't get too lonely." Taylor smiled at the blonde, as she looked up at the artist a little sleepily.

* * * * * * * * *

"Come in," Taylor responded to the knock on her office door.

"Tay," Jessica started.

"Not on your life," Taylor said without looking up. The artist pushed aside her Rolodex and leaned back in her chair. "Jess, your mother is the most open and nonjudgmental woman I know.   Just tell her you're gay, it won't be that bad."

"She's gonna freak, I just know it. Or she won't even want to meet Val," Jessica replied fearfully.

Valerie Kane, the young woman from the art store called Jessica at least three times a week until Jess invited her to the house for dinner. Once it was apparent the two young women seemed to be serious about one another Taylor had to put her foot down. She told Jess that she wouldn't be able to date, aside from having Valerie over to the house, until her six months were over.   After that, she could ask her mother what the rules would be.   Taylor also reminded her that NA encouraged newcomers to be clean for at least a year before starting any new relationships. It wasn't a hard and fast rule, but many NA members called it the *13th step.*

Taylor was proud of the fact that Jess decided to be honest and up front with Valerie from the beginning. She told Val everything about why she was here in California. Surprisingly enough, the young woman said she could wait until Jessica's six months were up and whatever came after that. She reassured Jess that anywhere they spent time together would be all right with her. Taylor thought Jess had a winner for her first serious relationship.

"Jess," Taylor chuckled. "Where do you get these perceptions of your mother? You know her better than that. Look I have to go into L.A. to the gallery real quick, that will leave you and your mom here for the afternoon to have a little heart to heart. Just be honest with her and I bet she won't disappoint you. Okay?"

"'Kay," Jessica said dejectedly.

****

Torrey closed her eyes, a slight smile playing on her lips. The sun felt deliciously warm on her skin, the heat of the day quickly evaporating the wetness of the pool on her body. *Ah, California.* She could definitely get used to this.

"Hey," Jessica said, sitting on the edge of the pool beside her mother. "Taylor had to run to the gallery, she said she'd be back by dinner and that she wanted to take us somewhere cool."

"Sounds good to me. Taylor always did know all the best restaurants in California." Torrey smiled.

The writer looked at her daughter seated next to her and gently brushed her hand across her cheek. "I'm so proud of you, Jess. The way you've taken control of your life. I'm not sorry one little bit that I sent you out here, not after seeing you this way." Tears fell from Torrey's eyes, but she couldn't stop herself. "I always wanted this for you, Jess. Just for you to be happy. I can't tell you enough times how proud I am of you."

"I should tell you the same thing, Mom. I kinda learned a lot of things about you, being out here with Taylor."

"What kind of things?" Torrey asked.

"Stuff we don't talk about. See, Taylor and I have this pact that we can ask each other anything here and we have to tell the truth," Jessica answered.

"And, have you? Told the truth, I mean."

"Oh, yea," Jessica replied, remembering some of the hard truths she and Taylor both learned about one another in the last five months.

"And, you think I don't tell you the truth?" Torrey pondered.

"It's not like you lie, Mom, we just don't talk about stuff like that. You never tell me about when you were a kid and what it was like when you grew up, or what you were like in college. I guess until Taylor started talking about you, I didn't even really know you," Jessica finished softly.

"Then maybe we should do that, be honest with one another," Torrey said.

"You sure you want to do that, Mom? It means that we can ask each other anything and you have to answer and you can't lie. We don't avoid subjects just because they're too *complicated*." Jessica carefully enunciated the last word. Torrey recognized her often used phrase.

"I guess it wouldn't be very fair of me to expect you to go through things I'm not willing to put myself through. All right ask away," Torrey said flinging her arms out at her sides.

Jessica laughed and wasn't sure how to start. She wondered if it was her or her mother, but the older woman next to her seemed very different here in California. This conversation wasn't exactly going as she had planned it. "Okay," Jess said with a grin. "Do you really have a tattoo?"

Torrey groaned. "She didn't." Torrey shook her head, grinned, and then pulled the strap of her bathing suit top down, exposing the area above her breast. The Tazmanian Devil smiled out from her tanned skin.

Jess continued to laugh. "It's so cool. You know I met the guy that did this for you." She explained how Kenny was an animator at one of the larger animation studios now. "I can't believe you never told me you had this."

"God, honey, you must think I'm a total tight ass, don't you?" Torrey looked over at her daughter, the smile disappearing from her face. "Jess, I'm so sorry I didn't encourage you and Taylor to be together after she and I went our separate ways. Seeing you with her now, I think I denied both of you something very special and I never wanted it to be that way."

"Mom, it sounds like you and Taylor had so much fun when you guys were together. Why didn't you ever tell me about the fun you guys had? What happened?"

"I guess life happened, Jess. I never wanted you to have to make all the same mistakes I made, so I tried to protect you from knowing about all the trouble you could get into. I never could have known that by doing that I was having the complete opposite effect on you. I'm so sorry, Jess," Taylor said sadly.

"Mom, you didn't *make* me *any* way. I chose to be this way. Okay, so we could have done some things differently, but now I know that you love me and I know that I love you, too. Taylor says the best thing about second chances is that it's our chance to make things right again. I'd like to do that, Mom. ·I'd like to make it right with you," Jessica said with tears in her eyes.

"Oh, Jess," Torrey said hugging her daughter tightly. "I promise to work at this second chance we've been given. Besides, I wasn't always such a stick in the mud. I did my share of crazy stunts."

"Like what?" Jessica asked.

Torrey proceeded to tell her daughter how she ripped her top off in front of Kenny that night she insisted that she and Taylor get tattooed. They talked about a lot of things that day. When the sun climbed high into the sky they stopped for iced tea and went back into the Japanese garden to continue their conversation.

Torrey told Jessica her version of a lot of the little incidents Taylor already informed the girl of. She described the day she and Taylor first met and the day

Jess was born. For the first time, Torrey told the young woman about the emergency hysterectomy that she had to have and the fact that Jess would always be the only child she would ever give birth to.

Small things added up for Jessica and the more Torrey explained of her young life, the more the young woman realized why her mother acted the way she did about certain things. Finally, Jess thought they needed to cross the big hurdle.

"Mom, I—uhm, there's kind of someone I've been seeing, you know just as friends." She explained Taylor's rules about dating while she was here and how NA felt. "I kind of wanted to, you know, actually have a real date, but I wanted to know how you felt about it," Jessica stammered.

Torrey pondered this bit of information, remembering the kinds of boys she liked at seventeen. Back then, anyone her mother didn't approve of was fair game. She wondered what kind of boy her daughter would be taken with. *He probably wore a leather jacket, he was certain to have a bike, he was—a girl?* "What did you say?" Torrey had to ask her daughter to repeat the last phrase.

"Her name is Valerie." Jessica looked into her mother's eyes and swallowed hard. "Mom, I'm gay."

Torrey's eyes never blinked or left Jessica's face. She was smiling on the inside, but didn't dare allow it to rise to the surface. Her daughter just wouldn't get the joke. "What's she like, is she nice?" Torrey asked.

"Well, yea. She's very nice. It doesn't bother you...about me?" Jessica asked her mother. She was waiting for tears or a little lecture, something. This new aspect to her mother was throwing her off. She and Torrey spent so many years at odds with one another; it felt curiously new, being friends.

"No, Jess, it doesn't bother me at all. As a matter of fact, why don't you see if she wants to come to dinner with us tonight? Check with Taylor first, though. We don't want to mess up any plans she might have. After that I'll have to talk with Taylor and see what she thinks would be best in your first six month of recovery."

"Cool," Jessica responded. "I can't believe I was freaked about telling you this." The young woman was shaking her head.

Torrey listened as her daughter revealed her fears regarding the situation and Torrey knew that holding back the truth about herself now, would be on the same level as lying. She wanted Jess to trust her every bit as much as she seemed to trust Taylor. There would only be one way to do that. She would have to earn it.

"Jess," Torrey began, not really sure what or how she wanted to say this. "That's pretty much the way I am," Torrey said, thinking that statement was about as clear as mud. For a writer she was feeling at a particular loss.

Jessica simply stared at her mother. *She was talking about something else, right? Just because she doesn't date men doesn't mean anything. She doesn't date women either, does she?* Jessica remembered the women who never seemed to be around longer than a couple of weeks at a time. They were always introduced as her mother's *friends.* Just like when she found out about Taylor's feelings for her mother, her world was again being rocked.

"Wow," Jess responded.

"I guess that was the one you didn't expect today, huh?" Torrey asked.

"That's for sure." Jess grinned over at her mother. Why is it that hindsight is so clear? In only a matter of seconds, so many disjointed scenes that involved her mother, suddenly made sense to the young woman. "Are you sure?" Jessica asked her mother.

Torrey laughed at the question that should have been a mother's to ask. "Trust me, Jess. I'm sure," Torrey answered.

"Oh," the girl said. Jessica looked up into her mother's smiling eyes and for probably the first time in her life, she blushed in front of the older woman. "Ohhh," Jess replied, realizing what her mother meant. "You're sure because you, uhm..."

"Yep." Torrey nodded her head. How do you tell your only daughter that sex with a woman was the best thing you've ever experienced?

"I, uhm, I've never, you know," Jess replied. Torrey must have looked surprised. "I know, with as wild as I've been, it's hard to believe, right?" The girl asked. "I guess I thought, I don't know, like it would be more special or something if I waited. Ahh, that's sounds really stupid, doesn't it?"

"It sounds very smart. You're absolutely right. Your first time should be with someone you care about and who cares for you." Torrey was taken back to a night when, held safe in Taylor's arms, the artist whispered the same words to her.

"Was my dad your first?" Jessica couldn't keep

herself from asking.

"Yes, honey, he was," Torrey answered.

"You didn't love him, though, did you?"

"No. I liked him an awful lot, but I didn't care for him that way."

"I guess you didn't know you were into women back then, huh?" Jess observed.

"Honey, I didn't know anything about anything back then. I was one very naive girl at seventeen. If I hadn't met Taylor, I wonder if I would have learned about love and friendship at all," Torrey finished softly.

That's when Jessica saw it. She was surprised at first, but her mother's eyes held the same sad look that Taylor's did, when she confessed to the young girl her feelings for Torrey. It was a sad, bittersweet sort of look. Jessica couldn't help but pursue it. "Who *did* you want your first time to be with?" the young woman pushed.

There it was, Torrey thought. The question that would tell her daughter whether Torrey truly believed in their honesty pact. She expected the truth from her daughter, now would she deliver the same? She took a deep breath and spoke the words, revealing the secret that few people knew. "I wanted it to be with Taylor," Torrey said in a voice that was barely a whisper.

"Do you still? Want to be with her, I mean?"

Torrey smiled slowly at her daughter and Jessica noticed tears forming in the writer's eyes. "I've known Taylor for eighteen years, and I'm more in love with her right this minute than I was the day I fell," Torrey answered honestly. "Actually, I'm surprised she never saw it."

"Yea," Jess answered as if to herself, "I am too. Look, Mom, maybe you and Taylor should talk—"

"No, Jess." A look of panic flickered across Torrey's face. "Jess, please. I could live without a lot of things in my life, but Taylor's friendship isn't one of them. Please, don't do anything to interfere. Promise me you won't," Torrey pleaded.

Jessica's brow furrowed, and her heart was torn in half. The two women she loved most in life and their hearts broke for each other, they just didn't know it. Why couldn't they see it within each other? She promised Taylor she wouldn't tell and now she was about to make the same promise to her mother. "I promise, Mom."

"Hey, I need to get cleaned up if we're going out tonight. We better get a move on," Torrey said to her daughter.

"Hey, Mom?" Jessica said, pulling her mother's eyes back to the seat she'd just risen from. "I love you. You're a great mom, you know that?"

Torrey moved in and hugged her daughter tightly. "Thank you, Jess. That means the world to me. You're a pretty wonderful daughter."

Jessica smirked down at her mother. "Yea, well, you probably could have smacked me around some and it wouldn't have hurt. I don't think you ever hit me, unless we count the time right before I left," Jess teased.

A look of pain flashed through Torrey's eyes and she quickly turned away from her daughter. "We better get going," was all the writer said, as she left Jessica wondering what the big deal with spanking your kid was.

* * * * * * * * * *

"Tay, can I ask you a question?" Jessica caught Taylor in her office. The tall woman just tucked her billfold inside the breast pocket of the Armani linen jacket she wore.

"What's up, squirt?" Taylor asked casually.

The older woman spoke with Jessica earlier, when she got home, and heard the good news about she and her mother's newfound relationship. She couldn't help saying I told you so to the young girl. Jessica left out the parts about her mother's personal life when she talked with Taylor.

"Why would Mom get freaked out about me asking why she never spanked me when I was a kid?" Jessica asked.

Taylor stopped what she was doing and looked over at the girl. "Did you ask your mother that question?" Taylor asked.

"Well, not seriously, but when I teased her about it she kind of put me off," Jessica explained.

"I think it's something for you to ask your mom about, Jess," Taylor answered.

"You're putting me off, too?" Jessica couldn't keep the wounded expression from her eyes.

Taylor took Jessica's hand as she leaned on the edge of her desk. "There are some things that are held in confidence between your mom and me, Jess. It's something that I just wouldn't feel comfortable talking about behind your mom's back. Please, ask her. You know she won't let you down," Taylor said.

Jessica nodded and gave the artist an understanding smile, all the while wondering what her mother would be so afraid to tell her.

After picking up Valerie, the four drove up the Pacific Coast Highway to Newport Beach where Taylor hired a helicopter to fly them out to Catalina Island. Torrey had her eyes screwed shut until about five minutes into the fifteen-minute flight, when Taylor slipped an arm around her shoulders and whispered that she was indeed safe with her. The old habit of feeling safe and secure in Taylor's embrace did the trick and soon, Torrey was enjoying the breathtaking view as they flew in over Avalon Bay.

Taylor explained that they had reservations at The Landing in the town of Avalon. Since that was about a mile from where they landed, Taylor asked the pilot to have a cab waiting for them.

"I picked Avalon just for you, Tor. In honor of a Chicagoan coming to California," Taylor said.

The two older women laughed.

"I must be missing something. I don't get it," Jessica stated.

"That makes two of us," Valerie chimed in.

"Avalon was developed by William Wrigley. In the nineteen twenties the Chicago Cubs used to come here for spring training." Torrey smiled at Taylor as she explained.

Torrey was surprised that a helicopter could be so large and comfortable. She told them about the time, when doing research for one of her books set in Mexico, the military gave them a ride. She said the helicopter had no doors and the engines were so loud you could barely hear yourself think. She remembered it fondly as one of the most harrowing experiences of her life.

Taylor told them that this was pretty much the Rolls Royce of helicopters. It was upholstered in leather and seated six people, not including the pilot. She gave a wry grin at Torrey, when Jessica asked why they didn't just take the ferry. The artist said it took an hour to get to the island by ferry and when the sea was rough flying was the only way to go.

Finally, Taylor revealed the truth behind the helicopter ride whenever she went to Catalina. "I get seasick," she said with surprising candor, raising her voice above the noise of the helicopter's engines.

Torrey liked the sudden and uncharacteristic vulnerability in the dark-haired woman's eyes when she unveiled this fact about herself. The writer remembered times past when the artist tried to appear stoic about it, usually turning green at the first step off of solid ground onto a rolling surface.

By the time they exited the cab, Valerie and Torrey were friends. The writer seemed genuinely interested in Val's experience as a freshman at the University of California. Jessica said a silent thank you, thinking it wouldn't hurt to have her mom hear a few positive comments about the school.

As Torrey and Valerie walked along in front of Taylor and Jessica, the young woman suddenly frowned and turned to the taller woman next to her. "Tay?" Jess sounded worried as she watched the two women in front of her. "You don't think Mom will do anything to...you know...*embarrass* me tonight. Do you?"

Taylor laughed so loud that the two women in

front of them stopped to look. Hugging Jessica by the shoulders she leaned down to whisper in her ear. "She's your mother, Jess. Of course she will." Taylor resumed her laughter as the women walked into the restaurant.

They all enjoyed the Landing's specialty, mesquite-grilled swordfish with mango salsa. Taylor and Torrey indulged in one of the Landing's own microbrewery specialties, a non-alcoholic lager. By the time coffee was being enjoyed, they all felt quite comfortable together.

"I'm still finding it a little hard to believe I'm having dinner with two people as famous as Taylor Kent and Torrey Gray," Valerie said with enthusiasm.

"Hey." Jessica looked at her, feigning a pout.

"Oh, Jess, you know what I mean." She laughed as she nudged Jessica's shoulder. "I mean most girls our age would practically consider it an honor to be raised by two mothers as together as you two." Valerie's compliment indicated that the young woman thought that Taylor and Torrey were indeed a couple.

Jessica saw the understanding half smile on her mother's face and cleared her throat to explain. "Uhm, actually, Val—" Jessica started.

"Taylor, want to enjoy the sunset with me?" Torrey interrupted her daughter. The writer stood and held out her hand to the artist who took it in her own slender grasp and they walked outside onto the deck.

Jessica wanted to explain to Val that the two women in her life didn't have that kind of loving relationship, but as she watched them through the large window, she realized that wasn't exactly true. The young girl saw her mother standing with her arm around the taller woman's waist, Taylor's arm resting lightly across the blonde's shoulders. She realized then, that the two women *were* in that kind of a loving relationship. Granted, there was no sex involved, but that didn't mean that intimacy didn't exist. Of course, they did love each other; they were even very much *in love* with one another. The only problem was that neither of them knew the other person felt exactly the same way. *This could be tricky.*

* * * * * * * * * *

"So, what did you think?" Jessica asked her mother. The three women sat around the living room enjoying the warm evening breeze and listening to the sounds from the surf below the cliffs.

"I think dinner was great, what did you think, Stretch?"

"Oh, yea, I think so too." Taylor played along.

"You guys enjoy being cruel, don't you?"

Torrey's melodic laughter filled up the room. "I like her, Jess. I like her a lot." Torrey beamed.

"Yea, she's nice, huh?"

"Pretty, too," Torrey added with a wink.

"Which is what makes me wonder why she's going out with you, squirt," Taylor chimed in.

"Very funny," Jess responded to the artist's teasing.

"Hush." Torrey tossed a pillow in Taylor direction.

Jessica caught Taylor's eye and motioned for the woman to leave the room. The young girl wanted to finish the conversation with her mother that was bugging her all day.

"Well, if you'll excuse me, I have a couple of calls to make. I'll be in the office if either of you need me," Taylor said as she left the room.

"Since we're alone could I ask you a question, Mom?"

Torrey nodded her assent.

"This afternoon when we were talking, why did you get kind of torqued out when I mentioned smacking me around?"

The same pained look crossed Torrey's features before she answered. "It doesn't have anything to do with you, Jess. It's ancient history, lets just let it go."

Jessica didn't want to play this card, but somehow she felt that this was a conversation they needed to have. She didn't know why, it was simply a feeling. "So, today...our honesty pact. That was just for this afternoon?"

"No, Jess, of course not. You know I'll answer any question you have," Torrey responded.

"Well, then...what's it all about, Mom, this thing you have about hitting me?"

"Ask me something easier," Torrey said hoarsely.

Jessica sat down next to her mother and slipped her hand within her mother's slender fingers. She couldn't quite understand the look of fear and pain that played on her mother's face. "What is it, Mom? Why would you be afraid to hit me?"

The hurt, wounded look in her mother's green eyes brought a sudden realization to Jessica. "Did someone hit you?" Jessica asked in a very soft voice.

The way Torrey looked into Jessica's eyes and the tears that filled the writer's green depths, spilling out onto her cheeks, was the affirmative response that Jessica really didn't want to know. "Who?" Jessica said tightly, her jaw clenched.

Torrey recognized the low growl of her daughter's voice and gave a little smile at how familiar it sounded. She knew right then that she had another protector. Jessica's voice took on exactly the same hard edge that Taylor's did at the thought of someone hurting her friend. "It was a long time ago, Jess, before you were even born. I'm just sorry that it affected the way I raised you."

"It was your mom, wasn't it?"

Torrey nodded and the tears came harder. She thought it odd that you could think of something that happened to you so long ago and the hurt would come back just as fresh as when it first happened. She didn't want to scare Jessica, so she held the worst of the pain in.

"I'm so sorry, Mom." Jessica felt tears fall from her own eyes and realized that she'd never cried for her mother before. Apologizing seemed so inane at this point. She never felt this way about the woman who raised her. Jessica never met Evelyn, even though Torrey's mother lived only an hour away from them, but she had this incredible urge to make the old woman accountable for her mother's pain. As long as she lived, Jessica would never understand how anyone could treat someone as wonderful and loving as her mother, so cruelly.

Taylor quietly entered the living room and found Torrey by herself sitting on the floor, her neck and back resting against the sofa. Taylor dropped down beside the writer and Torrey immediately leaned her head on the artist's shoulder, Taylor moving her arm to pull the smaller woman closer to her. "Where's Jess?" Taylor asked.

"I sent her off to bed. I think finding out her mother had the crap beaten out of her by her own mother was a little more than she could handle in one day. You knew she was going to ask me, didn't you, Stretch?"

"She asked me about it earlier. I told her she'd have to ask you herself. I'm sorry, honey, I didn't really have time to prepare you for what she had in mind."

"It's okay," Torrey said with a gentle squeeze to Taylor's free hand. She absently twirled the band that encircled the artist's left ring finger. The writer couldn't help but notice that they both still wore the wedding bands that Taylor purchased all those years ago.

Taylor watched as Torrey played with the platinum band on her finger. The artist debated over whether to remove the ring before Torrey arrived, but she couldn't do it. The ring was just as much a part of her as her love for the woman she now held tightly against her. She sighed with relief in the airport when Torrey took her hand and Taylor at once caught sight of the familiar ring on Torrey's left hand.

"I wasn't sure what to tell her. I told her the truth. I hope it didn't scare her," Torrey said.

Taylor rested her chin on the top of the soft blonde hair. She smiled to herself, breathing in the familiar scent of the same brand of shampoo Torrey used since she was a teenager. There was a satisfying comfort to the odor that clung to her memory for years after Torrey was gone.

Yes, Taylor knew Torrey would ultimately tell her daughter the truth, as ugly a truth as it was. She was also sure that it did more than simply scare Jessica, remembering how the admission first affected her when Torrey finally relented and confessed her family's secret. Taylor never really felt true, deep down anger until that night.

The artist thought of the nights spent in their Sorority House bedroom before she fell in love with Torrey. The small blonde would wake up to nightmares every night until Taylor told her that maybe she should see a doctor. Her young friend stubbornly refused. The artist attributed the night time behavior to it being the girl's first time away from home, but the first time Torrey went home for the weekend and came back with a split lip, Taylor's heart lurched. Another time it was a bruise on her jaw. When the young woman returned back to the campus with a black eye, Taylor confronted her young friend. Finally, held safely in the arms of someone who cared for her, Torrey confessed that it was her mother who hit her.

She explained that she ran away from home at fourteen to go live with her brother and he told her mother that if she came after Torrey he would make public what she was doing to her only daughter. The woman gave in and Torrey lived with her brother until his death three years later. Torrey cried in Taylor's arms and couldn't understand why her mother always did this to her, more importantly why she seemed powerless to stop it. Taylor cried with the young woman and promised her no one would ever hurt her like that again. Looking at the small, frightened girl in her arms, Taylor couldn't fathom how anyone could hurt such a beautiful, trusting soul.

The next time Torrey went home for spring break, Taylor borrowed a car from a friend and went with her. She told her small friend that she might want to make her separation from her mother more permanent, indicating a place in the car for plenty of boxes. Then Taylor enjoyed herself by sneering at the older woman all week and never letting the small blonde out of her sight. Torrey never went back after that and it would be many years until the young woman was finally able to stand up to the woman who destroyed her childhood.

"Hey, you still with me?" Torrey interrupted the dark-haired woman's reminiscing.

"Sorry, I was just thinking. How are you holding up, Little Bit?"

Torrey looked up as fresh tears slid down her cheeks. "Damn that woman. Almost twenty years and she's still finding ways to fuck with my life."

"Oh, honey, she can't hurt you anymore," Taylor whispered, wiping away the tears with a caress of her fingertips. "She can't hurt you now unless you let her. Don't give her that kind of power."

Torrey nodded in agreement with the dark-haired woman, her tears falling onto the starched white linen of the artist's shirt. "I'm going to ruin your shirt," Torrey warned.

"I don't give a damn," the artist responded, tightening her hold on the woman in her embrace.

Chapter
16

"Tay?" Jessica whispered again, the artist finally showing some signs of life. "I need to ask you something."

"Geez, Jess, what time is it?" The artist responded. She and Torrey again spent the night on the couch. The writer murmured in her sleep, her small form tucked within Taylor's loving embrace. Taylor felt like they just went to sleep, which was pretty close to the truth.

"It's six o'clock. Hey, don't you guys have beds that are more comfortable?" Jessica teased.

"Shut up, squirt and what do you have to ask?" Taylor whispered.

"Can I take the Explorer into Laguna and pick up lox and bagels for breakfast?"

"Mmm hmm." Taylor nodded, already drifting off again.

Jessica smiled at the picture the two women made

on the oversized sofa. The young woman pulled the comforter over them and ran out to pick up breakfast.

Taylor unconsciously snuggled closer to the woman spooned against her, burying her face in the blonde hair. Torrey felt, rather than heard the conversation above her, not wanting to break from sleep's spell quite yet. She pressed her back into the dark-haired woman's chest; hearing a low purr of satisfaction and feeling it vibrate out from the woman behind her. A smile curled at her lips as she listened to the gentle snores that escaped from Taylor, the noises quickly becoming a comfort sound to the petite writer.

****

Jessica walked into the kitchen, depositing her treasures on the counter and noticed that someone already made tea and coffee. That's when she heard it. She couldn't be sure, but the voices definitely belonged to her two moms, and the sounds were definitely not ones she ever heard them make before.

"Oh, God, yesss, right there," Taylor groaned. "Who in the world taught you this?"

"I think it was you," Torrey laughed.

"I am such a smart woman," came Taylor's breathless reply.

"Quit squirming around so much."

"I can't help it...it feels incredible, oh yea, you are really close."

"I can't believe that not one other woman has done this for you in fifteen years."

"I just haven't been...oh, yes...able to find any-one...God, harder...whose hands are as talented as yours."

"Oooh, I definitely think I've got the spot, now," Torrey said.

Taylor merely groaned her reply. "Oh, you are without a doubt in the right spot...there, right there...almost...now, press your hand harder, right there...oh, God!" The artist's voice started at a purr and finished at nearly a yell.

Jessica had no idea what she was going to do, but the only thing that came to mind was to either leave the way she came or make a lot of noise and walk in. She chose the latter, in case the two older women heard her by this time. Clearing her throat and coughing loudly, she entered the living area just as an audible pop resounded through the room.

Taylor sat on the floor against the couch that her mother was sitting on. Torrey rubbed the artist's neck a few more times and another pop was heard from Taylor's neck. Finally, the woman on the floor twisted and turned her neck and shoulders, declaring herself pain free.

"Hi, honey, heard you got breakfast," Torrey greeted her daughter. "You okay, your face is all red?"

"Yea." Jessica's hand went to her face, feeling the heat coming from her skin. "Uhm, I'm fine...breakfast is served." Taylor stood and pulled the smaller woman up from the couch. Jessica shook her head as they passed in front of her to the kitchen. *I have got to get a grip.*

Breakfast turned into a leisurely affair with Torrey and Jessica using all the persuasive powers in their arsenal to talk Taylor into tasting a bite of Nova lox. The artist finally relented, stating that the two would never let her hear the end of it if she didn't at least *try* some. Mother and daughter nodded their agreement and Taylor took a small bite of the bagel loaded with cream cheese and tomato, topped with the salmon.

Torrey found the look on Taylor's face to be priceless. The artist seemed to be trying to chew the fish without having it actually touch her tongue. "Oh, honey, spit it out. I can't watch you go through this kind of torture." Torrey laughed.

The food was devoured, Jessica was thanked, and the two older women left the table for their respective morning workouts.

Torrey appeared on the patio to stretch and prepare her muscles for her morning Tai Chi routine. Jessica sat at the kitchen table, sketch pad and pencils in hand, drawing quick sketches of her mother's actions. When Torrey sat back on her heels, Jessica knew that she would be that way for a few minutes, meditating or doing whatever she did that put her into the state of relaxation and concentration.

Taylor touched Jessica's shoulder as she passed by and the young woman smiled up at the artist. Before they had a chance to speak, Taylor was out the patio door and knelt down slightly behind and to the right of Torrey.

It was as if no time at all had passed as Torrey felt the familiar presence behind her without having to turn and look. She took a little longer preparing her mind to begin than she usually did. So many thoughts and feelings were running around her head concerning the woman at her side, that she wasn't sure she would be able to achieve the first level of relaxation necessary.

Finally, the movements began. Jessica was held in awe at the fluidity of the matching motions. The two women exuded a power and a grace that spread outwards like a whirlpool. At first, Taylor had her eyes open, watching the small woman in front of her. Eventually, both women progressed in their routine so that their eyes were closed, each of their actions in perfect balance by its twin.

Jessica sat there, staring through the window out onto the patio, completely transfixed at the sight. All her life she watched her mother's routine and found that it appeared to her unconsciousness as if something were missing. In the last five months she watched the dark-haired artist perform the same ritual, Jessica still feeling that she was watching something incomplete.

Now, gazing at the slow, methodical movements of each woman, Jessica felt the memory. This time it wasn't fleeting, causing her to think it a dream. This was a true, physical recollection of a time past. She remembered the sun shining in through patio doors, the sound of the ocean outside the window, and the two women, moving as they were now, light and dark, two halves of a whole. As she remained hypnotized by the sight before her, Jess finally felt what was missing in the past, why she had such a sense of incompleteness when viewing this scene. There was only one way her brain pictured this ritual, and it was as a duo, not a single.

* * * * * * * * *

"You want to go with us tonight?" Taylor asked, smoothing the lines of a wood sculpture with a rasp.

Torrey sat on a stool in the art studio watching the artist at work. Taylor wore a long sleeve t-shirt with the sleeves pulled up just past her forearms. Torrey's heart kept skipping beats when she stared down at the artist's tanned forearms, muscles and tendons bunching, then flexing under the skin. The blonde writer thought it was about the sexiest thing she'd ever seen.

"I'd love to, that is if it doesn't bother the two of you."

"We can check with JT, but you know how I feel." They didn't have to elaborate; she knew how the artist felt. Torrey went to NA with Taylor for years before the two separated. The writer's presence was always a comforting beacon for the dark-haired woman. "Here put this on, I'm going to use the sander." Taylor held out a paper mask.

The whine of the motor revved up and finally wound down as Taylor ran her hands over the newly smoothed surface.

"That is so amazing," Torrey complimented the artist.

"You want to try?"

"Oh no, Stretch...I might ruin it."

"Bullshit, it's just a hunk of wood, you can't ruin it. Here, you can do it with me."

Taylor seated Torrey on the same stool she sat on, slightly in front of her. The first thing she knew she was going to have trouble with was the feel of the small blonde as she sat between Taylor's outstretched legs. They put their masks in place and Taylor showed Torrey how to grasp the sander in a firm grip, the artist's hands covering Torrey's. Once the sander was turned on and was gliding across the surface of the wood, Torrey couldn't keep from focusing on those muscular forearms as they helped the smaller woman control the piece of equipment.

Taylor was just as focused, but on the strong biceps that stretched as the small woman held on to the sander. Torrey had on a tight tank top and her arms and shoulders were quickly covered in a fine wood dust. Taylor had a grin on her face underneath her mask, watching the writer. Torrey attempted everything with the unbridled enthusiasm of a child and this was no exception. The writer's sea-green eyes sparkled with excitement and when Taylor shut the sander off, and Torrey turned her head, the innocent glance turned into a white-hot bolt of desire to the artist.

****

Torrey finally met everyone that Taylor and Jessica knew in their NA group. The small writer immediately liked Natalie, the woman's no-nonsense attitude and sense of humor was refreshing. As always after their meeting, people stood about talking and sharing. Torrey couldn't keep track of how many people came up to her and explained how great a girl they thought Jessica was. The petite blonde knew what a struggle fighting an addiction could be. She lived with Taylor's first year and it made her even more proud of her daughter.

Taylor stood off to one side talking to an auburn-haired woman just a few inches taller than Torrey. When she met the artist's eyes, Taylor motioned for her to join them.

"Tor, I want you to meet someone. This is Emily, Corey's mom," Taylor said, turning to Emily she continued. "Em, this is Jessica's mother, Torrey."

Torrey didn't have words for the woman before her. All at once, she was heartbroken and guilty. She ached for the woman's loss, but she felt full of remorse that she should still have her daughter, healthy and recovering. Torrey did what she would want someone to do for her. Instead of coldly shaking the hand that the woman offered, she wrapped her arms around the woman's shoulders and whispered in her ear.

Taylor never found out what Torrey said to Corey's mother. It seemed a private moment between mothers, so she never asked. The whispered words were enough to somewhat shatter the woman's thin veneer of self-control. She began to cry and Torrey led her to a couple of chairs that were out of everyone's line of sight. The two stayed seated there long after everyone else left for the evening.

Natalie stood by Taylor as they glanced over at the two women. "She's pretty incredible," Natalie said, indicating Torrey.

Taylor watched as Torrey sat with Emily. The writer acted, much like she did everyday, with everyone she met. Her sparkling smile shone brightly and she held Emily's hand as she spoke to her. Gently brushing tears away from the other woman's cheek, Torrey was the picture of compassion and Taylor loved her for it. "Yes, she certainly is," Taylor responded after long minutes of watching the petite blonde and her loving manner.

****

"I was kind of thinking of a trip to San Diego, Stretch. Can you get away?" Torrey inquired.

The Japanese garden became Torrey's favorite spot in this house, as Taylor always knew it would be. They sat enjoying the quiet as Taylor took a break from the dirty task of polishing and grinding.

"Absolutely," the artist answered without hesitation, mentally calculating the time she had left before her show and what she had yet to do. Samantha took care of all the little details, but there were always old friends and colleagues Taylor liked to personally invite to her shows.

Taylor knew that a trip to San Diego meant Torrey wanted to visit the artist's mother and that fact would make Jean Kent a very happy woman. The two women became very close in a short amount of time; the writer looking at the older woman as the mother she always wanted. Taylor wondered what kind of contact the two kept up in the last fifteen years. She could have simply asked either Torrey or her mother, but it seemed like it was none of her business, as if their relationship were private since Taylor and Torrey separated.

"Am I presuming too much to say it's to see Mom?" Taylor questioned.

"Not presuming at all." The blonde smiled over at the artist seated next to her. "I sent your mom a

Mother's Day gift that's going to require Jessica's expertise to set up," she finished cryptically.

Taylor raised an eyebrow, but never asked. "What kind of time are we talking?"

"I was thinking just the weekend. I don't want to take you away from your work too long."

Taylor laughed at the comment. "Now, do you think if I came down with you and Jess, Mom would let us get away with a weekend? What do you say to leaving tomorrow and coming back Sunday?"

"I'd say that would be great."

Jessica's face peeked out the door. "I'm making avocado salad for lunch. Anyone interested?"

Torrey raised her hand, nodding, Taylor just raised an eyebrow at the young woman.

"It's Mom's recipe," Jessica said to the artist with exasperation.

"Oh, okay. Count me in then...as long as you use your mom's recipe...and your mom makes it."

"You think you're so funny," Jess returned.

Torrey laughed at the playful banter between the two.

"Mom, please don't laugh, it only encourages her juvenile behavior," Jessica deadpanned, but couldn't keep from grinning.

"Okay, I promise," Torrey responded, holding up her right hand. "Jess, how would you like to take a trip to San Diego for the rest of the week? Think you can pull yourself away for a while?"

"It sounds like fun. To see Grandma?"

Torrey nodded without looking over at Taylor. She could only imagine the look the artist had on her face.

"Yea, that sounds great, Mom. Okay, I'm going to fix lunch, it'll be ready in about a half hour," she said, reentering the house.

Torrey finally looked over at the artist, looking back at her, and she would have laughed out loud at the look on the woman's face, had it not been so serious. Taylor had the appearance of someone who'd just been told they were the long lost parent of a seventeen-year-old.

"I'm sorry, Stretch, I should have told you. You know how your mom is, she insisted that Jess call her that, and you know how persuasive your mom can be. I should have checked with you first."

"No, honey, it's all right," Taylor laughed at herself a little. "I guess it's just one of those things that threw me. I didn't really know how much contact you and Jess had with Mom. I know she loves you, though and it doesn't appear that a child will be coming from me in the future so it makes me happy that Mom has at least one grandchild to spoil."

"Are you sure?"

"Absolutely." The artist turned a sparkling white smile on the small blonde. "Do you...talk to Mom a lot?" Taylor could have kicked herself for asking. She never sounded more like a snoop to her own ears than right now.

Torrey couldn't suppress the smile that graced her features. She knew it was killing her friend to ask about her personal life. "We talk a lot, yea. Jess has never met her, though. It's nice, having a mom sometimes, I just hope you don't mind me borrowing her?" Torrey looked up, concern in her eyes.

"You deserve a mom who can make you feel spe-

cial, Tor. And, no, it doesn't bother me in the least."
Taylor understood how much Torrey, of all people,
needed a positive matriarchal figure in her life after
the one the luck of the draw saddled her with. "Come
on, let's go see how much trouble Jess has gotten herself into. By the way, Tor. Do you mind me asking
what you got Mom for Mother's Day? It's driving me
crazy."

Torrey chuckled and slipped her arm around the
artist's waist as they made their way inside. "A computer."

"My mother and a computer? Why does that scare
the hell out of me?" Taylor asked.

"It should...I gave her *your* e-mail address," Torrey said, quickly ducking through the doorway in time
to avoid the hand that came swinging at her backside.

Chapter
17

Taylor finished putting the bags in the Explorer as the three women prepared to leave. Jean Kent was overjoyed when Taylor called to tell her they would be coming down for a visit. Being Jean, she refused to take no for an answer to having them stay with her instead of a motel and Taylor said a silent thank you. The artist enjoyed staying in the house she grew up in and was anxious for Jess to see it. She also wanted some time with Torrey alone and this way she wouldn't feel too guilty if Jess had Jean around for just one evening.

Torrey walked out of the front door, windbreaker in hand. The day would turn warmer later, but right now, there was a chill in the air and the famous Southern California sun was hiding behind rain clouds. The small blonde stretched and yawned, making a delicious sort of whimpering noise to Taylor's ears. The sound hit the dark-haired artist right between the legs and she had to drag her eyes from the sight or she would certainly find herself doing something that would be embarrassing.

Point Loma was a beautiful small town on the oceanfront of San Diego. Taylor grew up healthy and happy in the small neighborhood that overlooked the Pacific Ocean. She was a Navy brat, but her mother insisted they needed a home base of sorts. So, the year after Taylor was born, her parents built this home practically within sight of the closest Naval Air Station.

"It's as beautiful as ever, Stretch," Torrey said in a broken voice as they pulled into the driveway.

Jean Kent was waiting and she wasn't disappointed with the sight of the three women exiting the vehicle. Her daughter visited at Christmas time, but seeing Torrey and her grown daughter was a tonic for the old woman's soul. She watched and waited as fifteen years went by, neither Torrey nor Taylor ever expressing their passion for the other. With every year that went by, she forced herself not to step in and intervene. She too, believed as the small blonde did, that everything happens for a reason and in its own time. She had an uncanny feeling, however, that if these two didn't verbalize their thoughts and emotions to each other now, they might never have another chance.

Jean was out the door as fast as her legs could move her sixty-five year old body. She hugged Taylor first, the tall woman having to lean down to place a kiss on the woman's cheek. She and Torrey both had tears in their eyes by the time their embrace was complete.

"Absolutely beautiful," Jean said as she took a good look at the woman before her. Torrey sent pictures as the years passed, but it was never the same. She always knew this girl would grow into a beautiful woman and from the adoration that still sparkled in her daughter's eyes it seemed the artist still felt the same way, too.

"Mom, this is your granddaughter, Jessica," Taylor said standing behind the young woman, her hands on Jessica's shoulders.

Torrey smiled as the young woman shyly approached the older woman, but within two minutes, Jean had the girl laughing and smiling. The writer especially enjoyed the way Taylor introduced Jess and the pride in the artist's voice. It was a moment that Torrey waited on for quite some time. It was as close to a family moment as they came to in fifteen years, and her heart felt like pounding right out of her chest. She couldn't remember feeling this happy in a good long time.

****

"Way to go, Grandma...I knew you had it in you." Jessica's voice could be heard from the upstairs study.

Jessica and Jean were sequestered in the study, the girl giving computer instruction to the older woman. Jessica was trying to teach years worth of computer knowledge in the few days they had to spend there. Tomorrow they were supposed to leave and Jessica was feeling a little down. She actually loved being around the older woman, her take no prisoners approach to learning the computer making Jessica smile.

Taylor and Torrey were enjoying the time to do absolutely nothing as they sat in the family room. It had been entirely too long since the women sat in this room talking about everything under the sun.

Jessica came to the top of the stairs and shouted to the two women below. "Grandma sent her first e-mail," she said proudly.

"To who?" Taylor asked with a worried frown as Torrey slapped her in the arm.

"To me," Jessica answered, returning to the study.

"I can just see it now," Taylor said to Torrey as the blonde walked into the kitchen and returned with more iced tea. "My Mom will be e-mailing me like mad. I'll have to listen to that damned *'you've got mail'* message fifty times a day," she hissed.

Torrey laughed and stood over the dark-haired woman.

"Think that's funny, do ya, Little Bit? I'll get you for this, you know."

Torrey put on her Taylor stare, complete with menacing eyebrow arch and slowly took the two steps to the sofa where the artist sat. "Oh, really?" Torrey growled, placing one knee on the couch between the artist's legs and kneeling to within inches of the woman's body. "And, just what makes you think you're woman enough to *get* me, as you put it?"

There was complete silence for what seemed like an eternity. Torrey quickly realized whom she was talking to and just how that comment came out sounding. She also recognized that while she was used to flirting and playing with sexual innuendo, Taylor was definitely *not* used to hearing it come from her.

In the meantime, Taylor's spine simply turned to hot melted butter. The heat that she felt arise from her own body couldn't compare to the rapidly pounding pulse in her ears. The mischievous glint in the writer's eyes was so teasingly erotic that Taylor swallowed hard before speaking. "Torrey...would you go out with me tonight?"

Torrey was enjoying the feeling of sexual power over her dark-haired friend. The artist may have not been interested in her that way, but to Torrey's eyes, she was definitely human. Taylor's eyes turned slightly glassy and her tanned skin flushed slightly.

"What?" Torrey asked in surprise.

Damn Kent! What the hell are you thinking about? This is Torrey, remember? "I, uhm...well, remember you were my date when we came here together the first time. I thought maybe we could...you know, do it again."

Oh, yes, love...doing it with you is exactly what I dream about, Torrey thought to herself. *Okay, snap out of it woman.* "That sounds like fun, Stretch," Torrey responded pulling herself away and looking the picture of innocence, while Taylor looked a bit more uncomfortable than she usually did around her old friend.

* * * * * * * * * *

"You sure you don't mind, honey?" Torrey asked leaning over her daughter's shoulder, watching the young woman sketch quick images on a graphics tablet that materialized on the computer screen.

"Huh?" Jessica asked in a distracted tone.

"I guess that answers my question."

"Oh, I'm sorry, Mom." Jessica turned around, giving her mother a quick smile.

"I just wanted to know if you mind if Taylor and I go out tonight."

"God no, go," the young woman blurted out, realizing by the look on her mother's face that she sounded a little too enthusiastic. "I just mean that you two could use a little down time. I'll be all right. Besides it's our last night here and Grandma and I are gonna play on the computer and eat junk food all night. She promised."

Torrey chuckled at her daughter's idea of a fun night.

* * * * * * * * *

Taylor looked at her watch again. She leaned against the back of the sofa and yawned. *Why is it the older Torrey gets the longer it takes her to get ready?* The artist fidgeted in her seat. She dressed with a bit more style than in her college days, but nothing ever felt as good to her as jeans and a T-shirt. She stood up and smoothed her black leather slacks out, pulling at the cuffs of a blue silk blouse. She leaned her head back to let out another yawn, but she made the mistake of trying to gasp at the same time and suddenly felt she was without enough air to breathe.

Torrey came down the stairs still putting her earrings in looking like she just stepped from the set of some movie. The petite blonde wore a royal blue, one-piece pantsuit that plunged at the neckline. She

had a white jacket over it, with her sleeves as she
always wore them, pulled up to the elbows. Truth be
known, she wasn't trying to make a fashion statement
with the jacket, but when your arms were two inches
shorter than the rest of humanity, that's what you did.
She had on high heels that Taylor thought looked
uncomfortable, but the writer seemed unaffected. It
was a little disconcerting for the artist, however. She
was used to looking down at Torrey and the heels put
the smaller woman quite a bit closer to Taylor's level
than usual.

Taylor was certain she could feel her heart missing about every other beat, watching her friend cross
the room and give Jessica a quick hug.

"Ready when you are, Stretch," Torrey said with a
smile.

Taylor thought she opened her mouth to say something intelligent, but the only sounds she seemed
capable of making at the moment were small whim-
pers. She gave Torrey a weak smile and held the front
door open, silently chanting a mantra in her head. *I
can control myself...I can control myself...I can control myself...I can control myself...*

****

"Can I ask you a personal question, Tor?" Taylor
asked as they strolled along a deserted pier, watching
the nighttime surf roll in.

"You know you don't have to preface a question
to me like that, Stretch."

Taylor looked a little uncomfortable, but still she
wanted to know. "I noticed you brought your laptop

with you, but I haven't seen you use it since you've been here. Is there a problem?"

"I'm on vacation." Torrey tried to sound flip, but she forgot that she couldn't hide much from this woman.

"Uh, huh...well, it's funny because I used to watch you write nearly every idle minute of the day. What's going on, Tor?"

"Did you read my last book?" Torrey asked.

"Of course. It was great."

"You didn't see anything...different about it?"

"I don't know. Maybe like you were holding back a little, but I figured with the problems you were having with Jess and all..." Taylor trailed off.

Now that Torrey brought it up, Taylor *had* noticed something odd about her friend's latest literary effort. The story was entertaining and enlightening, as usual, but it seemed a little...flat, was the only word she could think of.

"You don't have to say anymore," Torrey said softly. "I can see it in your face. You noticed it, too. It's just not there anymore and I don't know how to go about getting it back."

"Maybe now that you don't have to worry so much about Jess, now that some of the headaches are taken care of, maybe things will settle down for you."

"I'm not sure it ever really had anything to do with Jess. Oh sure, running after the girl and worrying about her took up some of my time and energy, but I think it's something more, something buried deep inside of me. Something that I can't seem to bring close enough to the surface to touch anymore." Torrey slipped an arm around the artist's waist and Taylor pulled the smaller woman's body closer against her.

The dark-haired woman wondered how she would feel if the ideas, the emotions that helped her create her art, didn't come anymore. It would be like losing a hand or her arm. A piece of her would be gone. Taylor stopped and leaned against the worn railing of the pier, able to feel tiny drops of moisture against her skin as the surf hit the pylons below, the waves exploding up into the air. Torrey paused also, not releasing her hold on the taller woman.

"Can I do anything to help?" Taylor's deep blue eyes held Torrey's in a tight gaze.

"I don't think a kiss and a hug will make it all better anymore, but it sure couldn't hurt." The blonde smiled up at her friend with sparkling eyes the color of the sea below.

Taylor gave a lopsided grin and pulled the small woman in for a hug that the artist didn't want to end. Torrey allowed herself be held for a few moments and savored the feel of Taylor's body pressed against hers. When she pulled back from the embrace, she hardly recognized the woman who looked back at her. Taylor's smile was replaced by a look of intense concentration, as the artist seemed to struggle with something inside. She obviously made a decision, because suddenly her face took on a soft glow as she brushed the backs of her fingers against the skin of Torrey's cheek.

Taylor couldn't keep it inside, not standing here, so close to the woman she desired for so long. She touched the softness of Torrey's cheek, then ran her thumb lightly across the silkiness of the smaller woman's bottom lip. When Taylor leaned in to kiss the woman in her arms, she actually intended for it to be a kiss between friends.

The artist held Torrey's face in her hands as their lips touched. Neither woman expected the rush of adrenaline or the surge of ardor that flowed through their bodies. It was a simple kiss at first, warm, and inviting, but as it lengthened, passions quickly ignited. Each woman lost cognizance of who they were kissing, as they allowed their emotions free rein.

Taylor's mouth pressed harder, becoming more insistent, more demanding in its eagerness to quench the fire that raged within. Torrey lost all reason as her need struck her with a passionate fury. Taylor's tongue slipped forward almost gently, coaxing Torrey's lips to part without hesitation. Suddenly the artist's senses were on overload as the sweet taste of the woman she loved, filled her mouth.

It was like a jolt of electricity sparked each woman into the here and now, realizing what she was doing and whom she was doing it with. At the same exact moment, they pushed away from one another; terror and fear mixed with a lustful desire, mirrored in their eyes.

"Taylor, I—I—"

"I'm so sorry, Tor...I didn't mean to do that."

Torrey finally raised her eyes to her friend's, catching the look of confusion and fear in the intense gaze. She never intended to let Taylor see this side of her, but everything happened so fast, and she was swept away with the sensations. Taylor's remark brought her back quickly and she could barely contain the tears that threatened to spill from her eyes. The look of pain on the taller woman's face told Torrey that the artist got caught up in the moonlight, the ocean, and the way Torrey looked, but that she didn't feel what Torrey felt. *You knew it; you knew she didn't want you that way. Damn, woman, what were you thinking?*

Taylor closed her eyes tightly before opening them as Torrey looked up at her. Tears were filling the writer's green eyes and the sight broke the artist's heart. Taylor committed the one act of selfishness, when she leaned down for that kiss, which she had hoped to conceal from her friend. Torrey seemed unable to speak, but her silence said more to Taylor than words. The dark-haired artist knew that her best friend loved her and Taylor knew in her heart that Torrey was sorry for not being able to be the woman the artist wanted. *She's probably the first straight woman in history to apologize for not being gay. Damn, Kent, what were you thinking?*

"We better get back," Torrey said, turning back in the direction of the car.

Taylor silently followed, thinking that their beautiful night together was ruined. She wondered, in painful silence, if her long-standing friendship was, too.

They drove along in silence for most of the ride home until Torrey commented about something inconsequential. The artist took that as a good sign and kept up her end of the discussion, but the conversation seemed strained, and that was something new for the two of them.

They both felt responsible for the kiss; neither realizing it was exactly what the other wanted. Taylor pulled the car into the driveway and was quick to

come around the vehicle and open Torrey's side, as
the smaller woman headed for the front door, Taylor
put out a hand and gently stopped her. "Let's go
around back and sit on the patio for a few minutes,
huh? Just so we can talk?"

Torrey followed her friend's lead through the
fenced in yard and around the back of the house. Taylor couldn't help but notice that Torrey chose to sit in
the chair, rather than next to her on the loveseat.

"I thought maybe we could talk about tonight,"
Taylor started slowly.

"I'm sorry, Taylor...I don't know what to say,"
Torrey apologized. The writer knew what she did was
wrong and she couldn't offer an excuse for her behavior. She understood that Taylor was trying to let her
down gently.

"Oh, God, Tor, it's not your fault." Taylor's heart
mirrored the petite blonde's seated across from her.
She could see the pain in Torrey's eyes at not being
able to be the woman the artist wanted. "I'm the one
to blame. I guess I was just, caught up in the moment,
you know? Hey, you're a beautiful woman and I'm
not made of stone," Taylor finished with a sheepish
grin that she hoped would make her small friend
smile.

"You don't have to take the blame for everything
all the time, Stretch," Torrey said with a sigh as she
stood up. She moved to the house and silently slid
open the patio door. Looking back, she knew she
owed her friend at least some sort of explanation.
"I'm sorry about what happened, it's not something I
planned, it just happened. You were there and I was
there, and suddenly...well, I may not be a young girl

anymore, but I'm certainly not made of stone either. Don't worry, Stretch," Torrey said with a chuckle, "it wasn't the first time I've kissed a woman and I guess it won't be the last, so quit looking so guilty."

Taylor may have had a guilty look on her face, but it was utter confusion she was feeling. *Is she saying she kissed me? What does that mean, not made of stone and what the hell does she mean I'm not the first woman she's kissed?*

Taylor was in absolute shock. Any sense of reason she previously possessed simply vanished. Even her power of speech failed her. She wanted to call out to make Torrey stop and turn around, to make her explain what she meant, but the best the artist could do was to sit there and ask in disbelief, "Torrey...have you...*been* with women?"

"Yes."

Taylor heard the small assent as if it was a whisper in the night, and then she watched her friend's back disappear into the house. Taylor knew she should run after her, make her repeat it, clarify it, but she could only sit in the darkness as a multitude of emotions, past and present, whirled around her.

****

Jessica watched through the same patio doors as when she was a child, while her mother stretched and warmed up before her morning Tai Chi. It seemed as if the small woman sat back on her heels twice as long as she ever did before. Jessica didn't know how to tell her mother that it didn't matter how long she waited, Taylor wouldn't be joining her this morning.

The young woman listened as Taylor awoke just before the sun rose and watched out the bedroom window as the artist left the house, walking down to the beach. She hadn't been back, that Jess could tell, and she wondered if the two older women had a fight last night. Her mom seemed a little more subdued than usual and Taylor didn't seem to want to be around her. That was a definite first and the girl worried that the two women had a confrontation of sorts.

She continued to watch as her mother's shoulders slumped a little in an odd gesture of defeat before she went into the slow, deliberate movements of her routine.

* * * * * * * * * *

Jean Kent found her daughter exactly where she thought she might. The dark-haired artist sat on a break wall, her long legs dangling over the side as she tossed rocks into the water below. Jean took a seat on the grassy sand behind the tall woman. "Some things never change. This is still the spot you come to when you're running away from the world. Only this time you're running away from Torrey," Jean said.

Taylor knew it was her mother behind her. She saw the woman from a distance and realized she was in for a lecture. "I'm not running from Torrey."

"Oh, did you tell her where you were going before you left?"

"It was early. I didn't want to wake her," Taylor lied.

"I think she was up all night. I could hear her pacing the floor."

Taylor was aware of that fact. Torrey did pace the floor all night. Taylor knew this to be true because she sat in the chair in the room next door listening to her friend pace and cry all night. It broke the artist's heart to not only realize that she couldn't comfort her friend, but that she was the cause of Torrey's anguish.

"I kissed Torrey last night," Taylor admitted.

Jean sighed. She had a feeling it was something of that nature. *I'd like to shake both of you. You couldn't just tell her you love her, could you?* "So, what happened?"

"What happened?" Taylor turned and looked at her mother. "She jumped away from me like I had the plague, that's what happened."

"Before or after the kiss?" Jean asked.

"Huh?"

"Did she push you away after the kiss or as soon as you tried?"

"Well, I guess...I don't know. Not as soon as I kissed her, though."

"Hmmm. What kind of kiss was it?"

"It was, I don't know, just a regular kiss." Taylor didn't talk about these feelings under normal conditions and discussing her sex life with her mother was even less appealing.

"If that's the way you describe a woman's kiss it's no wonder you don't get kissed very often," Jean said in exasperation.

"I could get kissed plenty if I wanted to," Taylor responded hotly. She shook her head, noticing the grin on her mother's face. Taylor laughed at herself. "I can't believe I'm sitting on the beach with my mother trying to justify why I don't kiss more women."

"Well, was it a quick kiss or a, uhm, romantic...intense sort of kiss?" Jean questioned delicately.

Taylor couldn't stop the smile that played at the
corners of her mouth or the sudden tingling sensation
on her lips, remembering last night's kiss. "It was
definitely an intense kiss...*very* romantic. Mom, do
you think Torrey could be gay?"

"Why don't you ask her?" Jean responded.

"I did. She said she *had* been with women."

"I suppose that's your answer then, dear."

"I kind of expected something a little more pro-
found or at least revealing coming from you, Mom,"
Taylor said with a smirk.

"I'm sorry, dear, but I have two daughters in this
scenario, remember?" Jean laid a hand on her daughter's shoulder and gave it a comforting squeeze.
"Torrey is as much my daughter as Jessica is yours. I
have to consider her trust in me, too. Isn't that the
pact you made with Jess, that she could tell you anything and you wouldn't repeat it?"

"It's just that I'm confused. If Torrey is attracted
to women, then maybe it's just me that she's not
attracted to. I don't want to do the wrong thing and
scare her away. God, I feel like our friendship has
changed just from that one kiss," Taylor said in a worried tone.

"Honey, you take yourself too damn seriously.
Just kiss the girl and tell her you love her. End of
story."

"You know it's not that simple with Torrey and I.
I can't just kiss her and then carry her off. This is my
best friend we're talking about. I risk too much if she

doesn't feel the same way," Taylor responded with a sad look, turning back to face the water.

Jean stood and brushed her hands through her daughter's raven locks, Taylor leaning her head against her mother's leg. "My dear, sweet daughter," Jean began, "you still haven't learned the most important lesson your father tried so hard to teach you."

Taylor looked up at the woman with a quizzical expression.

"There are some things in life," Jean continued, "that are worth risking *everything* for."

The older woman turned and made her way up the beach hopeful that she said enough, but not too much. Taylor simply stared out onto the churning surface of the ocean, reminded of a pair of sea-green eyes.

****

"Remind me to travel with you two again when you haven't had enough sleep. This is fun," Jessica said sarcastically from the back seat of the car.

Taylor wore a pensive frown for most of the ride back home and Torrey looked out the window, lost in her own thoughts. Every time Jessica tried to get the conversation rolling, one of the older women effectively let it die. Eventually they all sat back and continued the silent ride home.

Jessica said she was going to her room to call Valerie, leaving Taylor and Torrey, both standing in the middle of the kitchen.

"Do you want some coffee?" Torrey asked.

"I think if you just threw it in my face it would work better, but yea, that sounds great," Taylor answered.

Torrey ground a small amount of beans and began the automatic pot. Taylor sat at the table watching the small blonde's movement, mesmerized by the strength and grace in the woman's compact form. Suddenly she realized that Torrey had stopped moving, leaning her hands against the kitchen counter, her shoulders shaking slightly. Taylor rose in alarm and went to the woman seeing tears streak her face. "Torrey, honey."

"I don't want to lose your friendship," Torrey sobbed.

"Never," Taylor whispered forcefully. She wrapped strong arms around her friend and held her tightly. "Torrey, nothing we could say or do could ever change that." Taylor placed two fingers under the smaller woman's chin, tilting her face so their eyes met. "You are my best friend, don't you know that? For the rest of our lives, Little Bit, no matter what, you will *always* be my best friend," Taylor finished as tears filled her own eyes. "Come on, let's go sit down in the family room," Taylor said, coaxing her friend into the other room.

Torrey started to seat herself in the oversized chair, but Taylor stopped her. "Sit next to me, won't you?" Taylor asked.

Torrey smiled at the request and it lightened the artist's heart to see that small grin. Both women were tired from lack of sleep the night before, and as was their habit, Torrey's head fell upon the artist's broad shoulders, and it took only minutes before they were both sound asleep.

Jessica shook her head once she saw the pair on the sofa. She quietly turned the coffeepot off in the kitchen and pulled a comforter over the two women on her way into the studio to work.

Chapter
18

Taylor let the hot water from the shower run for a long time over her head and face. She felt her muscles loosening and eventually she started to wake up. It was noon when she and Torrey woke up from their impromptu nap. The writer said she wanted to soak in a hot tub, Taylor headed in the other direction for a shower.

Still running her fingers through her damp hair, Taylor tossed the towel covering her body into the laundry hamper and paused to look at the painting that hung on the wall. She gazed up at the sole reason that she kept her bedroom door locked while Jess and Torrey lived there.

The painting was merely a figment of her imagination, a secret desire that she translated onto the canvas. It was an oil painting of the erotic piece of work that she and Torrey had gotten into so much trouble over at the Sorority House. It started out as a black

and white drawing they placed in the Sorority newsletter. There was one difference now, however, and
that was that the two women in the picture had been
painted in Taylor and Torrey's images. Now the two
women in the clutches of the amorous embrace were
the two best friends.

After putting on a pair of faded blue jeans, the
artist walked to the closet and pulled a lightly
starched white shirt from its hanger. She couldn't
keep the light smile from her face as she looked at a
dozen of the same white cotton shirts hanging in front
of her. Torrey was probably one of the few people in
the world that knew the artist had so many of the
man's style shirts in her closet. Taylor realized that
she was predictable, if nothing else. She enjoyed the
feel of a crisp, brand new shirt; consequently, she sent
her shirts out to be cleaned and pressed every week,
always requesting the light amount of starch.

"Hey, that smells good," Taylor said, leaning over
the small blonde's shoulder and breathing deeply.
Torrey was in the kitchen in her relaxed mode also.
She wore a faded MU T-shirt and a pair of jeans that
Taylor would have sworn belonged to the woman in
college, they were so frayed and discolored.

"Well, you said my bouillabaisse sounded good
the other day, so I sent JT down to the harbor market
while we were cleaning up. She did a good job. The
shellfish look great," Torrey answered.

"You are a treasure," Taylor said punctuating her
statement with a kiss to the top of Torrey's wet head.
"Want a cup of reheated four hour old coffee?" Taylor
offered.

"Sure, as long as you put some cream in it," Torrey added.

Five minutes later found the two women in the family room, relaxing with their coffee. Jessica appeared in the doorway a worried look on her face.

"What's up, squirt?" Taylor asked.

The young woman sat on the sofa next to her mother. Taylor, with her bare feet tucked under her legs, sat on the other side of Torrey. "You like Val pretty well, huh?" Jess asked.

Torrey saw this as a chat up for something and exchanged a knowing grin with Taylor. "I like her very much, hon. She seems like a great girl."

"Enough to let me go out with her?"

"I had a feeling we were headed here." Torrey frowned. The writer knew that NA discouraged new-comers from starting up new relationships within the first year of recovery. "I don't know...Stretch, what do you think?"

"Well, six months was our agreement, and Jess you know what the NA literature says..." Taylor trailed off.

Jessica's face fell. "But, it's not like a date even. It's dinner at her parent's house. Val says none of them drink, so nothing will be available," Jessica explained, with a little bit of pleading thrown in for good measure.

"Jess, give Taylor and I a few minutes to talk this over, okay?"

The young woman walked into the other room and Taylor and Torrey just stared at one another for a moment.

"What do you think?" Torrey asked.

"Well, she's your daughter, Tor—"

"Don't even go there, Stretch...not after everything that's gone on in the last six months. Why don't we just say that from here on in that she has two moms," Torrey finished, a small hand laid across Taylor's forearm.

Taylor felt a lot like crying right about now. She never even knew that she missed Jessica in her life until she was back in it again. Every night she went to bed thinking about the ways in which she could have shared in Jessica's life. She let her own pain and hurt get in the way of a young girl's happiness, and she knew that she was just as responsible as anyone for the affect it had on Jessica. Having the girl here now and hearing Torrey say those words, was like a balm to her soul.

"I know what NA encourages, Tor, but I have to tell you that it's not written in stone. I just happen to be one of those people that don't subscribe to it completely," Taylor explained her position.

Torrey smiled.

"What's that smile for?" Taylor asked about the impish grin.

"Do you realize we just made our first joint-decision as to the welfare of *our* daughter?" Torrey responded.

Taylor grinned back at the small blonde. "Jess!" she shouted from the couch.

"Yes, honey, you can go out. I expect you to be in at a reasonable hour, though," Torrey said as soon as Jessica walked into the room.

"How reasonable?" Jess asked.

Torrey looked at Taylor and raised her eyebrows in question. "Eleven-thirty," Taylor said.

"Hey, I can work with that," Jessica replied with a grin. "Uhm, a couple more things."

"Geez, she's pushy." Taylor looked at Torrey.

"I—I'm a little broke...and I need to borrow a car."

Torrey chuckled at her daughter's dilemma. "I can handle the money," she answered rising to find her wallet. "But, you'll have to talk to her about the car." She jerked her thumb in Taylor's direction.

"What do ya say, Tay?" Jessica asked with a weak grin.

Taylor reached into her pocket and pulled out a set of keys, tossing them at the young woman. "The Explorer, not the Mercedes."

"You're great," Jess said, jumping off the sofa and placing a quick kiss on the artist's cheek.

"Here," Torrey said holding out her hand as she walked back into the family room.

"Oh wow, thanks, Mom. I'll go call Val right now."

"Hey, what about my bouillabaisse?" Torrey yelled after the retreating figure.

"You two enjoy it." Were the last words they heard from the young girl.

* * * * * * * * *

"You missed your calling, Little Bit. You should have been a chef," Taylor commented as the two women sat in their familiar spots on the sofa.

"I've thought about it plenty, lately," Torrey answered sardonically.

Taylor knew the writer referred to her current difficulty expressing her thoughts and putting them down on paper. Both women were in the middle of the large cream-colored couch, sitting facing one another. Torrey had her head resting on her arm on the back of the sofa, while Taylor's head was held in the palm of her hand.

"I'm kind of surprised you let Jess have the car," Torrey said, changing the subject.

"Well, she's been pretty good in cleaning up her act. I just thought showing a little trust in her was the way to go."

"And, she did call you Tay. Admit it, Stretch, it really gets to you when she does that," Torrey teased.

A sheepish grin crossed the artist's face and she nodded. "Yea, it does."

"I'm sorry, Taylor."

"For what?" Taylor's gaze narrowed in concern.

"For not keeping you in Jessica's life more. You would have been so good for her. I made so many mistakes where Jess is concerned. I think the biggest one was not doing anything to encourage you to spend time with her while she was growing up."

"Hey, I wasn't exactly beating a path to your door, either. It was just as much my responsibility to come to her and yet I didn't," the artist responded.

Taylor gave a small, lazy smile to the woman seated across from her, reaching over and brushing light wisps of golden hair from her eyes. Torrey closed her eyelids slightly at the dark-haired woman's touch.

A thousand questions rose in Taylor's mind on account of that gesture. Her mind thought of little else since Torrey's admission that she knew what it was like to kiss a woman other than Taylor. Their past floated across her mind's eye and she wondered what other things the writer kept from her. *What other secrets do you have, Little Bit?*

She caught the way Torrey looked at her sometimes and didn't it seem like she had more in her eyes than friendship? When they touched, didn't her reaction appear to be more intense? *Am I building this up in my mind, or does more exist? Is it possible that I kept my feelings for you hidden so well, that you never thought you had a chance?*

"Why did you leave me, Torrey?" Taylor suddenly found herself asking, like a jilted lover.

"What?" Torrey's green eyes seemed to go wide at the question. It was so unexpected. "I—"

Taylor quickly brought her fingertips up and covered Torrey's lips. "Please, don't say it was because you met someone, because I don't think that was the truth. Was it?"

Torrey looked as if she were going to bolt from the room. Taylor recognized the frightened expression and moved her fingertips to gently caress the blonde's cheek, then rested her hand on top of Torrey's, which lay in the writer's lap.

Torrey looked down at the hand that covered her own, the wedding band that matched her own shining back at her, and she was suddenly so tired, more like exhausted, from hiding her feelings and covering up the truth. It took so much of her energy to keep up the pretense and she wondered why she did it at all. Taylor already promised that they would always be friends, no matter what. *I bet you never thought this would come up when you said that, Stretch.*

After long moments, Torrey raised tear filled eyes and was nearly caught speechless by the deep Prussian blue color staring back at her. Those eyes held so much love and concern that Torrey knew she had to tell the truth. She owed nothing less to this woman who stood beside her through every possible circumstance. She shook her head back and forth, in answer to the artist's question. "No, it wasn't the truth," Torrey said.

Taylor's hand rose and cupped Torrey's jaw in the palm of her hand. "Then why, Tor? Was it something I did?"

"No," the writer answered quickly, her tears spilling down her cheeks and across the artist's hand. "It wasn't something you did, it was something you would have done."

The confused expression on Taylor's face caused Torrey to try to explain. "You gave up everything for us. You would have spent the rest of your life taking care of Jess and I. You never dated, you never tried to start your own life—"

"Honey, you and Jess were my life. I thought we were a family," Taylor interjected, brushing away tears with her thumb.

"You deserved to have your own family, a relationship with a woman who could be your partner. I knew you didn't want me that way, but you would have stayed, just to take care of us. I couldn't let you give up that part of your life. It wouldn't have been fair. I was just being selfish trying to keep you."

Taylor was taken back at her friend's honest admission. "*I didn't want you that way?*" she whispered, as if to herself. What settled into the forefront of Taylor's brain was her mother's admonition from this morning. *There are some things in life that are worth risking everything for.*

As she silently repeated the words, she could see why her father would have wanted her to learn that maxim. He lived by those very words. Robert Kent knew that every time he went up in a jet, he took the very real chance that he wouldn't come back. Even knowing that risk, he still flew. He loved flying. Not more than his wife and child, but it was as much a part of him, as Taylor's art was to her. Her father thought it important enough that he risked everything for it. For him to do less wouldn't have been in him.

Taylor wondered what she had in herself. What else did her mother tell her? *Just kiss the girl and tell her you love her.* Taylor brushed away the smaller woman's remaining tears. The pained look on her friend's face simply decimated any thought she had of holding back the truth any longer. It took eighteen years, but Taylor Kent finally decided to listen to her mother.

"Torrey," Taylor said softly, waiting until the writer's beautiful green eyes locked onto her own. "I love you." Taylor's face was inches away from the writer's. Leaning down slightly, she pressed her mouth to Torrey's. The kiss was as gentle as the artist could make it at first; finally, feeling that her friend had no intention of breaking the sweet contact, Taylor deepened the kiss.

As hunger and passion took control of both women, Taylor learned that the kiss they shared the previous evening was innocent in comparison. Little moans came from the back of Torrey's throat as she pressed her lips more firmly against Taylor's. The artist let herself float on the intensity of the sensations her friend's lips were producing in her body, she could no longer suppress the low, rumbling growl that was drawn from deep in her throat.

Torrey wrapped both her hands in Taylor's dark hair, pulling their mouths together more tightly. Moving her hands to take hold of Taylor's shoulders, she used the strength of her whole body to push the taller woman down, flat against the sofa. The move surprised the artist, but the feel of Torrey's full weight on top of her caused her to involuntarily part her legs wider, pulling the woman more tightly against herself.

Taylor's hands couldn't be contained and they were everywhere at once. They finally slipped underneath the T-shirt Torrey was wearing and settled against the smooth skin at the small of the writer's back.

"Oh, God," Taylor moaned, arching her head back just as Torrey released her lips to kiss and bite the skin along Taylor's neck.

"I love you, Taylor," Torrey breathed into the woman's ear, before moving in to take the artist's mouth in another breath stealing kiss.

"Again..." Taylor pleaded, between kisses. "Tell me again."

"I love you," Torrey repeated, breathlessly.

"Oh...yes..." Taylor sighed, feeling completely helpless as she felt the buttons to her shirt being undone by practiced fingers.

Torrey shifted her body so one knee pushed firmly between Taylor's legs, the artist groaned at the contact, her eyes closed in ecstasy as the writer followed the shirt's open path with her lips. Suddenly Taylor felt her friend's chuckle against the skin of her chest.

"What?" Taylor opened her eyes, running into the mischievous sparkle in the green ones that looked up at her.

"You never used to wear a bra," Torrey stated with a grin, placing a kiss where the tan cloth started.

Taylor dropped her head back against the sofa and laughed. "Gravity gets to all of us sooner or later, love."

It was Torrey's turn to be surprised as the artist took that moment to flip the smaller woman onto her back. Taylor held most of her weight up on one elbow, letting the rest fall upon the woman below her. Taylor's denim covered thighs straddled Torrey's, her free hand slipping up under the T-shirt against the writer's smooth skin. Taylor moved in and took the writer's mouth in a passionate frenzy, her fingertips caressing every bit of bare flesh she could get her hands on.

Again, she whispered the words that started it all. "I love you, Torrey. I've always loved you."

Torrey paused and looked up with her own glassy gaze into eyes that burned blue fire at her. She lifted up her fingers to caress the lips that just issued the powerful proclamation of love. "I'm still not sure what just happened, but I'm afraid to question it. I'm afraid this will all end," Torrey murmured quietly.

"Oh, baby," Taylor began, her free hand moving up to lay light caresses on the face she cherished, "now that I know you want me too, I'm not *ever* going to let it end. Torrey," Taylor said in a voice hoarse with desire, "come to bed with me."

"Oh God, yes..." Torrey moaned.

Chapter
19

They stood in the middle of the large bedroom, the French doors slightly ajar, and the sounds of the crashing surf on the rocks below filtering up to them. Taylor took the small blonde's face in her hands and kissed her again and again. Torrey found her hands brushing the unbuttoned shirt from Taylor's shoulders, wanting to feel as much of the artist's skin as possible. Taylor let her head tilt back, exposing her neck to the caresses that Torrey's lips provided.

The artist's eyes opened and she found herself looking straight into the painting on her wall. "Torrey...honey..." Taylor tried to start.

Torrey slipped her hands up the artist's muscled back, expertly unclasping the hook that held her bra together. She let her fingers glide up and over the dark haired woman's shoulders, pulling down the bra straps and removing the garment in one easy motion.

"Beautiful," Torrey whispered reverently, kissing

the tanned skin of the woman's chest just above the swell of her breasts.

"Torrey...baby," Taylor was breathless by now, "we need to talk."

"Sweetheart, it's been eighteen years...couldn't we talk later?" Torrey reasoned, pulling open the top two buttons of Taylor's jeans.

"It's just that—" Taylor paused, trying to get her breathing under control. "There's something in the room that could be a little embarrassing when you see it, and I wanted to warn—"

"If it's an inflatable doll, I swear I'll never tell anyone." Torrey paused in her activity to look up with a charming glint in her eye.

Taylor let loose a throaty laugh. "You have turned into such a wicked woman."

Torrey smiled back, but watched as the taller woman's grin turned into a frown. "Honey, what is it?"

Taylor gently turned the oblivious woman around, facing Torrey in the direction of the painting. She rested her hands on the smaller woman's shoulders, anticipating a negative reaction. *Okay, Kent, this is where you get shown up for the pervert that you are.*

"Oh Taylor. How did you know that's the way I always envisioned that picture?" Torrey asked in awe.

Taylor breathed an audible sigh of relief, wrapping her arms around the smaller woman and nuzzling her face into the soft skin of her neck, blazing a trail of kisses up to the woman's ear. She caressed the sensitive flesh with the tip of her tongue, using her teeth to send electric tingling sensations down the blonde's spine and all the way down the back of her legs.

"What did I ever do right in my life to deserve you?" Taylor whispered.

Torrey turned in the taller woman's embrace, her body pressing firmly against Taylor's until the artist felt the back of her knees touch against the bed. With a slight push, Torrey had the woman seated on the bed, reaching down to continue the contact between their lips.

Taylor parted her legs and pulled Torrey's hips toward her so the woman was standing between her legs. The artist opened the button to her jeans and slid the zipper down, pulling up the T-shirt to expose a flat abdomen. Taylor let her lips and tongue explore the exposed flesh, tugging at the jeans to pull them down further. Torrey's moans of pleasure, combined with the feel of her skin under the artist's fingertips caused Taylor to nearly explode in orgasm right then. She lifted the T-shirt higher.

"Taylor," Torrey looked down at the woman below her, "I'm not that eighteen year old girl anymore."

Taylor looked at the concerned expression on her lover's face and broke into a sparkling white smile. She lifted the T-shirt off in one deft motion. "Thank God," the artist murmured against Torrey's skin as she buried her face in the valley between the writer's breasts, moaning her pleasure, licking her way to take a hardened nipple between her lips.

Torrey wrapped her fingers into Taylor's dark hair, pulling her head down tighter against her body. The artist took the hint and sucked harder, causing an immediate groan from deep within the standing woman's chest.

Torrey whimpered slightly at the loss of contact as Taylor moved her caresses lower. She slipped both hands into the waistband of the smaller woman's panties at her back and slipped her hands down lower, pulling the undergarment and jeans down in a single motion. Torrey grabbed onto strong shoulders as she lifted first one leg, then the other from her jeans, leaving them in a heap at her feet.

Torrey moved to straddle Taylor's hips, but stopped and moved her hands to the front of the artist's jeans. She grasped the cloth in each hand and pulled the rest of the buttons apart, then pushed Taylor flat on the bed. "Lift," she commanded.

The artist lifted her hips as Torrey pulled her jeans and panties off as one, just as Taylor did with her. Torrey kneeled between the artist's legs, the sight of Taylor lying on her back with her legs spread invitingly was too much for the writer. She placed one hand on top of each of the dark-haired woman's thighs and, with her fingers splayed, she ran her hands up the muscled limbs, feeling Taylor's legs trembling slightly under her touch. She then let her lips follow the same path that her hands just branded.

Torrey gently coaxed the artist's thighs further apart with her hands, as she drew closer to the dark patch of curls. The scent of Taylor's arousal caused the blonde to pause, closing her eyes and breathing deeply, her fingers reflexively grasped the smooth skin under them as if to ground herself. Her mouth watered at the sight and the smell before her. Without further thought, she dipped her head and ran her tongue the full length of Taylor's swollen sex, moaning against the sensitive flesh.

"Sweet mother of...unhhhh," Taylor cried out, twining slender fingers within the short blonde locks.

The sound of Taylor's voice, trembling and full of desire, set Torrey's blood on fire. The writer's passion spurred her on, her control fading quickly as she wrapped her hands around the artist's already rocking hips, sliding a warm wet tongue inside of her. Even as she thrust her tongue into Taylor's slick opening, her thumb teased the hardened bundle of nerves.

Taylor's chest heaved and her body began the tiny convulsive tremors that indicated her orgasm would quickly be upon her. She tried to fight the feelings back, finally realizing she would have to both admit defeat and give in to the flames that attempted to consume her, or slow this delicious torture down. "Torrey...Oh, god...honey, please wait..." Taylor begged.

Torrey looked up from her pleasure in alarm. "Are you okay...did I hurt you?"

"No, baby...come here," Taylor panted, pulling the smaller woman up to hold her in her embrace. She brushed the damp hair on the writer's forehead aside and kissed her lips passionately. Kissing Torrey, with her taste on the younger woman's lips, was something Taylor never would have thought possible and she practically hummed into the kiss.

"I'm okay. What you're doing feels absolutely incredible...too incredible. I—Torrey I've wanted you for so long," Taylor said, stroking her lover's face, "but I was only going to last for another five seconds and I don't want the first time with you to be over that fast. Can we—can we slow down a little?" Taylor asked, still trying to get her breathing within normal limits.

Torrey smiled and leaned up on one elbow.

"Geez, don't look at me that way." Taylor grinned back. "I already feel like a teenage schoolboy doing it for the first time."

"Honestly, it's the most flattering thing anyone's ever said to me." Torrey grinned back. "And, I think I can accommodate your needs," she purred. "Roll over."

Taylor looked at the smaller woman leaning over her. She never thought, in all the times she fantasized about their love making, that it would be Torrey taking the lead and Taylor who couldn't control herself. Somehow, that scenario never entered her thinking, but here she was, utterly quivering and helpless under Torrey's touch. Each moment was pure heaven, so she quickly complied with her lover's request.

Torrey had to focus and breathe deeply to restrain the absolute urge to ravish the perfect woman that lay beneath her. She straddled the artist's hips and shook her own head slightly to will a little self-control into her already shaking hands. It all happened so fast that she barely had time to realize that this was Taylor lying underneath her, moaning her pleasure into the sheets.

Torrey pushed aside the long raven hair and ran her tongue along the nape of a sensitive neck. She started at Taylor's neck and massaged the strong flesh, kneading and swirling her fingers in tight circles out to her shoulders and arms, and down the length of her back. The small woman's strong arms concentrated in the small of the artist's back, knowing that spot and her neck, were the areas that bothered her most. Torrey continued on with the innocent massage across firm buttocks and down the length of her legs. Then the blonde began a more sensual exploration.

Torrey sat astride Taylor's buttocks, feeling the flesh beneath her twitch and flex in anticipation. Taylor let out a soft breath as she felt the writer's wetness spread across the firm globes of flesh, which became a low groan as Torrey slid her aroused sex along the artist's backside. Taylor lifted her own hips in response trying to put more pressure on Torrey's center. The writer's answer was a languid moan of her own followed by her hips, pressing down harder onto Taylor.

Torrey leaned against Taylor's back and kissed and licked her way down the path her massaging fingers had just taken her. Taylor's breathing was again ragged, her moans nearly constant. Finally, the writer breathed in her ear. "Roll over."

Taylor rolled over, Torrey lifting slightly, but not enough so that the woman below her didn't feel her touching every exposed piece of skin on her hips. Torrey pressed herself down against Taylor and the larger woman's hands immediately went to Torrey's hips to guide their mounds together harder.

"Ah ah ah," Torrey teased, wrapping her hands around the confused artist's wrists and guiding them over her head. She moved Taylor's fingers until they were wrapped around the underside of the wooden headboard. "Remember, love. You'll be all right if you look into your partner's eyes. When you're dancing with someone, one of you has to give up a little control. Just lead where my body takes you and don't think so much about where you're going." Torrey used the very words that Taylor had, when they danced together at the little club in San Diego.

Taylor smiled a deliciously carnal smile at her partner and let her trembling body relax back against the bed. She was instantly rewarded with a kiss that made her dizzy in its intensity, and then Torrey performed the same massage therapy on the front of the artist's body. When Torrey reached her lover's breasts, both women knew that heaven had nothing on this spot on earth. The small blonde slid her body between Taylor's legs until she could feel the artist's soaked center pressing against her stomach. She buried her face into Taylor's breasts, first kissing, then licking, and finally sucking on the hard points of flesh. Torrey let her lips surround the hard nipple, pressing it against her front teeth with the tip of her tongue.

Taylor tried to raise her head to watch. It was the sight of the woman above her making love to her breasts and the lustful sounds that escaped from Torrey's throat that turned the artist into six feet of liquid fire. Taylor's breath was coming in short gasps. Arching her back, she pressed her wet mound against the muscles of Torrey's abdomen. "Please, Torrey...now?"

No further explanation was needed. Torrey reached down and slid two strong fingers into the woman's slick entrance, following it quickly by her mouth, wrapping around the swollen nub that pulsed against her tongue. The low guttural moan of satisfaction from the artist's lips caused Torrey to suck harder at the bit of flesh in her mouth. She slipped another finger inside and three fingers drove themselves deep inside Taylor's writhing body, and she lifted her hips to meet each thrust and drive it deeper.

"Oh, Torrey." Were the last strained words the artist could gasp as she held tightly to the headboard, her bucking hips suddenly stilled, letting Torrey's rhythm carry her the rest of the way. She felt her orgasm approaching like the licking flames of a fire, burning hotter and hotter until they reached her core. Then, with a powerful burst, the flames exploded and the artist melted. The cry that was torn from her throat made her own ears ring.

Torrey rested her head against the artist's thigh until she looked up and saw tears escaping from the dark-haired woman's blue eyes. "Honey, are you okay?" Torrey moved to release her fingers from their sanctuary, still buried inside the artist.

Taylor quickly moved to lock her hand around Torrey's wrist. "Please, stay inside. Just move your body up here," Taylor implored.

The two women lay facing one another, one of Taylor's legs draped over the smaller woman's hips. Torrey brushed the tears from her lover's face and fought back her own at the sight. She kissed Taylor's lips, her eyes, and cheeks.

"I'm sorry," Taylor rasped. "It was just a little...overwhelming."

"I know sweetheart, I've got you, now," Torrey said, concluding the sentiment with a tender kiss that sliced through the remaining cords that held the artist's lonely heart together.

Taylor pulled the woman tight against her; the blonde's fingers still trapped inside the artist's sex. Torrey whispered a litany of loving words to the dark-haired woman, delighted at the feeling of being inside her lover, her fingers surrounded by soft, silken flesh. Torrey could feel the quivering and jumping of Taylor's muscles lessen as she moved her kisses to the artist neck and breasts to again, ignite the woman's smoldering passion.

Taylor found the sensation of Torrey's powerful back muscles thoroughly erotic as she slid her hand up and down and across the writer's skin.   She savored the exquisite touch as soft warm lips caressed her neck and shoulders, and closing her eyes, she rocked her hips against the hand that moved in a slow deliberate rhythm. Torrey's lips found her own and as their tongues met, Taylor felt a burning heat sear its way to her center.

Torrey felt the kiss to her very soul, its gentleness infused with an unbelievable passion.   She felt a renewed wetness coat her hand, even as Taylor's sex drew her fingers in deeper. Torrey continued the even motion, the wet friction causing Taylor's inner muscles to betray her, quivering in anticipation. As Torrey gently guided her hand in and out, her thumb reached up to stroke the hard nub of flesh at the top of her cleft. Taylor's inner muscles clutched desperately at the receding fingers, the same muscles spreading to receive them as they penetrated her again and again.

Her climax was just as intense this time, but the feel of Torrey, wrapped so tightly around her, calmed the artist. "Oh, Torrey...yes!" Taylor groaned, her head thrown back, her body convulsing and shuddering in rapturous release.

Torrey finally slipped her fingers from her lover's haven, only to bring them to her own lips, savoring the wetness that coated them.

Once Taylor found her voice she smiled at her lover. "Dear, God, woman. If you were eighteen you'd kill me!"

****

"I want you so much, Torrey. I want to make you mine," Taylor breathed in a sultry voice

"Oh love, I've always been yours for the taking," Torrey replied breathlessly.

Taylor pressed the full length of her body against Torrey, feeling the woman's hips press up urgently against her own. Torrey's moans were captured by the artist's mouth as her lips hungrily devoured the woman beneath her. Taylor's lips found their way around the writer's neck, then to an earlobe that she sucked on, lightly nipping at it with her teeth. Eventually the artist whispered a string of teasingly erotic words into the younger woman's ear, the artist's moist breath combined with the content of her speech causing Torrey to shiver uncontrollably.

Taylor's fingers caressed her lover's firm breasts, thumbs reaching out to lightly brush over the nipples. Torrey gasped and the artist watched in loving fascination as the small areas of flesh hardened in response to her touch.

"Mmmm," Taylor hummed, placing a delicate kiss on each nipple. "I like the way they respond to my touch."

She traced large circles around the erect nipples with her tongue, making the circles smaller and smaller until Torrey ached at the hot breath that

spread across the hard nubs, but hadn't yet touched
them. Taylor reached out with her pink tongue to
flick the tip in a teasing manner. Rolling the nipples
between her thumbs and index fingers, she lightly
pulled them, the squeezing sensation nearly sending
Torrey into the stratosphere.

Taylor's hand took its time as it slid down the
woman's belly to bury itself within the light colored
curls, glistening with moisture. Torrey eagerly spread
her legs wider. The artist's breath caught at the sensation of the velvety softness that lingered there. Torrey moaned loudly when she felt Taylor's strong
fingers glide across the wetness, the artist's fingertips
swirling around the hardened bundle of nerves. Taylor kept her fingers away from the nub of flesh that
begged for attention; instead preparing to suck on the
hardened nipple that Torrey arched her back to
present to her.

"Please..." Torrey begged.

Taylor complied, her lips covering the nipple, her
tongue gently, then more firmly, swirling around the
nub of flesh. Taylor could feel Torrey press herself
up against her face, ultimately crying out her need.

"Please, Taylor...harder."

Taylor sucked at the hard bit of flesh in her mouth
hungrily, while at the same time moving her fingers to
stroke Torrey's clit in small circular motions. The
action nearly caused Torrey's body to spasm off the
bed. Taylor smiled what Torrey thought was an alto-
gether wicked smile, as the artist released the nipple
and let her tongue create a path of burning fire down
the woman's body.

Knowing where Taylor was headed only served to

add fuel to Torrey's already flaming libido. She parted her legs wider, groaning in frustration as Taylor licked the inside of her drenched thigh. "Taylor...I—" Torrey's hips writhed involuntarily, begging for a more intimate contact, but at the same time Torrey's body seemed to be pulling back.

Taylor felt the small blonde's body tense and looked up to catch the look of concern in the woman's face. "Honey, what is it?" Taylor inquired tenderly, moving her body up to cradle Torrey in her arms.

"It's just that...I mean, you going down on me..." Torrey seemed frustrated at her inability to voice her concerns.

"It's okay, baby. If you don't like that, I don't have to." Taylor wanted to reassure her lover, desperately trying to keep the disappointment from her own voice.

"No, it's not that. It's...I've never had anyone...oh, God, I never thought this would be so embarrassing," Torrey stammered.

It took every bit of restraint the artist had to not smile at her lover. "Are you trying to say no one has ever—"

"No," Torrey quickly answered. "It's just that it seemed so special. I could never see sharing it with anyone else. I always wanted it to be you. This sounds very stupid when I say it out loud, you know?"

"No, honey, it doesn't sound stupid at all," Taylor replied in soothing tones. "I can't even begin to tell you how I feel. It's like being honored with a very special gift." Taylor captured Torrey's lips in a kiss filled with desire. "Let me show you how I'd like to thank you for this beautiful gift." The artist once again slide her body down and positioned it between Torrey's legs. Taylor moved her index finger down to her lover's curly triangle and ran her finger along the length of the moist outer lips, capturing the drops of wetness coated there. The artist closed her eyes at the incredible taste that filled her mouth as she slipped her finger between her own lips.

Torrey writhed at the sight. "Oh, Taylor, I want you...I need you, please," she begged in a pleading voice that Taylor fantasized about hearing a thousand times.

Taylor's head bent and it seemed to take an eternity, but her tongue reached out and tenderly lapped at the gift before her. It wasn't fast, or overly gentle, but a firm, slow exploration of the taste and textures that belonged to the woman she was in love with for so very long. That first taste was enough to drive away all sense of reason and control, which Taylor once possessed. The artist gave in to the frantic pleadings of the woman who wrapped tense fingers in her ebony locks, and with an experienced tongue and practiced fingers, she took her lover as hard and fast as the woman dictated.

Torrey cried out Taylor's name as she exploded in orgasm. Her body arched as the waves of release crashed through her body just as the waves hit the rocks below their window. Her muscles went limp, and then her body shuddered and tightened as a series of convulsive movements sped through her. As Taylor continued the penetrating motion of her hand, Torrey screamed, as a second orgasm shook her body.

* * * * * * * * * *

"I love you," Taylor found herself whispering again into the small blonde's ear, as she lay wrapped protectively in the artist's strong embrace.

"I love you, Taylor...with all my heart. Can I ask you something?"

"Anything, love."

"How did you know I didn't move to Chicago to be with someone?"

"One part guess, the other part deductive reasoning. When Jess and I were talking one day, she said she couldn't remember you ever being in a relationship with anyone. That's all she said, but it stuck in the back of my brain. The other day in San Diego when we kissed, and you admitted it wasn't the first time you kissed a woman, I thought that just maybe there was a chance that you felt the same way about me as I did about you." Taylor kissed Torrey's temple, pulling her closer. "I always thought I was an open book around you, boy was I sure wrong. I guess I hid my feelings for you too well. Once I realized that might be the case, I figured leaving, in some selfless act, would be just like you. You were always thinking of me, and never yourself. Did Jess know how you felt about me?"

"Not until we had our talk last week. I was surprised that she guessed so quickly. Did she know about you?"

"Yep. She found...well, you know the painting on the wall? I've got about a million drawings to go along with it. I didn't mean for her to find out at all. She took it surprisingly well, though."

"I'm so sorry, I hurt you by leaving, Stretch," Torrey responded tearfully.

"It's all right, baby. We have each other now and that's all that counts. Besides, it's more my fault anyway. If I was more responsible back then, maybe I would have been able to see what you were going through," Taylor answered, lost in her own regret.

"Your mother always knew. From the very first time we were there. Did you know that?"

"Yea, I did. She told me back then that if I didn't tell you how much I loved you, that you would give up waiting on my heart and find someone else."

"No. There was never anyone else, Taylor. I had lovers, but I never gave my heart away to anyone. It's always belonged to you."

"I feel the same way. Can I admit something embarrassing?" Taylor asked.

"Oh, is this the part about the inflatable doll?"

"You are so bad." Taylor tickled the woman in her arms until Torrey cried uncle.

"So what could you think is that embarrassing?"

"Part of the reason I needed you to slow down tonight was that it's been a good long time since I've been with a woman," Taylor admitted.

"How long?" Torrey asked curiously.

"Six years," Taylor answered hesitantly.

"Wow. Your staying power was mind boggling all things considered."

"Yea, well, it wasn't like celibacy was a conscious choice, I just never wanted to be with anyone else. Even in college, even with other women, all I could ever think about was you."

"And, I slept with Stephen."

"Hey, don't forget what you're always say-ing...everything happens for a reason. If you never spent that night with him, we wouldn't have Jess."

"Your mother told me the same thing this past week. Remember when she and I went out on the beach to walk and were gone so long on Thursday? She said that it was fate that brought us together again here in California and that this was the chance of a lifetime. She actually pointed out that it was meant to be that you and I never got together when we were younger. I think she was just trying to encourage me to say something to you, but what she said did make sense."

Torrey turned around to tenderly kiss Taylor's lips and snuggled into the space against the artist's shoul-der. "Mom said that if you and I would have gotten together when we met it would have been disastrous. She said that I wouldn't have been what you needed; I wasn't strong enough to be your partner. She told me that I would have always been waiting for you to change and you would have grown angry with your-self because you couldn't. She said we would have ended up destroying the love we had for each other, and I think she was right." Torrey turned her face up to the woman who already had tears in her eyes to match those in the writer's.

"She was completely right, Stretch. We were so young. Our love might have ended up being destroyed by all the old baggage we were carrying around with us. But this way, growing up apart from one another, I can honestly say that there hasn't been a day in the last fifteen years that I've been out of love with you. Why did you kiss me and tell me you loved me tonight?" Torrey inquired.

Taylor smiled through the tears that fell from deep blue eyes. "Because my mother told me to."

* * * * * * * * * *

Taylor murmured something unintelligible in her sleep, rolling over to wrap her arm around Torrey's body. The artist's arm fell onto the bed, an empty space where Torrey lay earlier. The loss triggered something in the sleeping woman's unconscious, causing her to pull her mind from the pleasant dream state in which she floated.

A soft, rhythmic clicking noise brought Taylor up on one elbow, her eyes trying to focus in the dim light. In her confusion, she finally made out Torrey's petite frame sitting cross-legged on the end of the King size bed, her fingers flying across the keys of the small computer in her lap. The blonde's tousled hair fell haphazardly, nearly covering the glasses that reflected the computer screen in each lens. She wore Taylor's white shirt and nothing else.

"Tor?"

"It's okay, sweetheart. I just had to get some thoughts down. You don't mind, do you?" Torrey asked, her finger pausing over the keyboard.

Taylor smiled sleepily, glad that the writer's muse returned. "Nope, do you mind if I go back to sleep?" The artist didn't wait for a response before rolling onto her stomach and stretching her long, naked frame under the silk sheets. She threw a couple of pillows against the headboard. "Come sit up here or you're going to have a back ache in the morning."

Torrey took the spot Taylor indicated and leaned down to kiss the already sleeping woman's cheek. Taylor unconsciously snuggled closer to the writer as the keys resumed their soft clicking. The dark-haired woman smiled in her sleep at the sound that would eventually become a comfort sound to her ears in the years to come.

Chapter
20

"Hey." Jessica looked up from the crossword puzzle she sat hunched over at the kitchen table.

"Hey," Taylor mumbled, realizing how much Jess looked like her mother when she wore her new glasses.

"Did you see God last night?" Jessica asked in a serious tone.

"Huh?" Taylor asked, perplexed.

Jessica could hardly keep a straight face. "I just figured the way you were calling to Him last night, you must have got religion or something." The young woman was almost doubled over in laughter now.

Taylor knew her face was turning red, but there wasn't a thing she could do about it. She'd been caught with her hand in the proverbial cookie jar and now she had to own up to it and suffer the barbs that were sure to come her way for a long time to come. Although she and Torrey heard Jessica come in on time last night, and they closed and locked their bedroom door, there was only so much quiet they could keep.

Taylor smirked at the young woman. "Laugh it up, squirt. You can harass me all you want, but I don't want you teasing your mother like that."

"Teasing your mother like what?" Torrey asked in a voice still rough from sleep. The small blonde walked in and made her way to the pot that held the coffee pouring a cup, first for herself, then another for the tall artist leaning against the counter.

She handed the steaming mug to Taylor and just as casually reached up to place a gentle kiss on the taller woman's lips. Taylor smiled into the kiss and returned the affection. "Morning." Torrey grinned.

"Right back at ya," Taylor replied, kissing her forehead.

"Morning to you, too." Torrey walked behind her seated daughter and kissed the top of her head. "What?" Torrey said in her daughter's direction. "You thought I might be walking funny this morning?"

Jessica nearly spit her tea across the table as Taylor broke into an unrestrained, throaty laughter that the young woman never heard her use before.

"I don't think she expected that from me," Torrey said with a wink as she made her way back to the bedroom for a shower.

"Who was that woman?" Jessica asked the artist.

"That's the Torrey Gray that I know. I think you better get used to seeing her, squirt," Taylor said with a grin, leaving her coffee untouched and walking off in the direction the small blonde went.

The door to the guestroom stood open. Torrey was pulling clean clothes from the closet and hanging them on the door. Taylor entered the room and quietly came up behind the woman, slipping her arms around her and kissing her neck lightly. "I love you," Taylor said.

"Mmmm, I like hearing that," Torrey answered, her hand moving up to entwine in the dark-haired woman's locks. "I love you too."

"Will you move your things into the master bedroom?" Taylor asked, holding her breath for the answer.

"Are you sure you want me to?" Torrey returned, giving the woman one last out.

"Absolutely," Taylor answered, punctuating her answer with a kiss. "I'm going to take a shower, care to join me?"

"With JT in the other room? Do you think we should?"

Taylor chuckled against the skin of Torrey's neck. "Do you think she might hear something that she didn't last night?"

"You never know..." the blonde replied with a tilt of an eyebrow. "You just never know."

****

"You sleeping?" Jess whispered.

"Uh Unh." Torrey shook her head, opening her eyes. The older woman sat curled in the oversized chair of the family room, falling asleep to the sounds at the other end of the house, mainly Taylor's sander.

"Can we talk for a little bit?"

"Sure, hon, what's up?"

"I, uhm...I've kind of been thinking." Jess paused and looked into her mother's eyes. She and Taylor were supposedly together now, but what if they went back to Chicago to live?

"You want to stay here in California," her mother answered confidently.

"Do you know how much I hate that you can do that?" Her daughter smiled.

"The minute you give birth, you'll get the power, too." Torrey chuckled.

"I don't think I'm quite prepared to go there," Jessica replied with a dour look. "Well, it works out nice now. I mean, you and Taylor are together, we could all live here, right?"

"Only one problem as I can see, honey, and that is that Taylor hasn't asked me to live here."

"Well, yea, but she probably just thinks that it's a given, right?"

"Still and all, Jess, a girl likes to be asked," Torrey responded.

Jessica thought that the two older women were finally going to live out that happily ever after part, *but damn if these two don't make it harder than it has to be*, she said to herself.

"So, what did you want to do out here that you couldn't do in Chicago, Jess?"

"University of California, the one here at Irvine. I want to go to school to study art. I know being good is something new for me, but I'd be willing to work hard, Mom, even get a job to help pay."

"You know money isn't a consideration, Jess. I'd send you to the moon if that's what you needed to do, but you're still so new in your recovery and I worry about what will happen when Taylor or I aren't around, and you're faced with your first temptation."

"I know. It scares me to think about too, but I can't stay locked in a cocoon until there isn't any alcohol or drugs floating around."

Torrey already knew her answer would be yes. She was simply thrilled that her daughter turned a love of art into a hope for her future. "If I agree, I think I would want you living here for your first year, not on campus, and certainly not in a Sorority house," she said with a wry smile. "Jess, would it bother you if I worked at the University? I mean, I wouldn't be there to keep tabs on you, but...I've been offered a position in the English Department."

"Mom, that's so cool. No, it wouldn't bother me at all. I'd love it," Jessica returned with enthusiasm. She suddenly looked serious, her brows furrowing together. "You're not going to stop writing, are you?"

"I've been having a little trouble with my writing, Jess. It just wasn't there for me. Strange as it may seem, though, I feel like I got it back last night."

"Maybe because you and Taylor..."

"Possibly," Torrey answered her daughter's unasked question.

"I hope you don't give it up, Mom. You're such a good writer, the things you can put down on paper..." Jess trailed off, then looked up into her mother's eyes, "I, uh, read your books while I was here," she added sheepishly. "I guess I'm just sorry I didn't read them sooner."

"Thank you, Jess. Besides, just because I start teaching again, doesn't mean I can't write, too. The position will only be part time, and even if I don't take it and stay here in California, I know Taylor will love having you here."

Even though Jess didn't want to think about that last statement, she reached over and gave a huge bear hug to the smaller woman. "I love you, Mom. I'll make you and Taylor proud of me someday."

Torrey gently brushed a hand across her daughter's cheek. "Oh honey, you've already done that."

* * * * * * * * * *

Torrey leaned against the wooden railing that looked over the patio onto the cliffs below. She heard the patio doors glide open and within seconds felt strong arms wrap around her upper body.

"Mmmm, I love the way your arms feel around me," she murmured to the dark-haired woman behind her.

"Good, because I could get used to this myself." Taylor sighed, standing straighter and feeling Torrey's body lean back against her chest.

"I love being able to see the stars like this. In Chicago you have to compete with the buildings and the lights for a view."

"Well, we aim to please out here on the West Coast," Taylor whispered, pulling Torrey's body closer to her, resting her chin on the smaller woman's shoulder. "I talked to Mom today. I hope you don't mind, but I told her about us."

"What did she say?"

Taylor let out an amused laugh. "You know her. She acted like she knew it would happen all along. I bet she started screaming like a banshee the moment I hung up. She did say something that got me thinking, though. I told her it seems so clear now, our love for each other. I wonder why we couldn't see it all along. She said that it wasn't that we *couldn't* see it; it was that we *wouldn't* see it. You're the philosopher. What do you think she meant?"

"There are none so blind as those who would not see..." Torrey trailed off. "I don't even remember if it's a quote or an adage. Some English professor I am. I think I agree with your mom, though." Torrey turned in Taylor's arms and rested her cheek against the artist's chest, listening to the strong, rhythmic heartbeat.

"I think even if it would have been laid out for me all those years ago. Even if you had professed your undying love for me, I would have run, simply bolted. I never thought you could love me. You know what Evelyn did to me. Hell, I never thought anyone could love me. I just never thought I was worth anything back then, especially worth loving you. It was probably right in front of me, Stretch and I wouldn't let myself see it."

Taylor once again wondered at the one thing she ever did right in her life to deserve the woman in her arms. "You're right," Taylor agreed sadly. "You could have thrown yourself across my bed, Tor, and I would have refused you. I never thought I was good enough for you. I always thought that someday, someone worthy of your love would come along to make you happy. I wouldn't even allow myself to see that it might have been me. You were someone who loved me as a friend and I was just too afraid of losing that, just like I lost my father, to ever realize you that you might want to stay and be something even more."

"Love isn't blind," Torrey said, shaking her head in bewilderment. "She's just plain stupid."

****

"Are you just going to watch me get ready?" Torrey asked, stepping into the black, off the shoulder dress she selected for the artist's showing at the L.A. gallery.

"Uh huh." The artist nodded from her position on the bed. She lay in a blue silk robe, her hands clasped behind her head, watching the sexy blonde dress. "I always wanted to know what took you so long to get ready. But," she added, jumping up behind the writer who indicated the zipper that needed adjustment, "if it makes you feel any better, I *always* thought it was well worth the wait."

"Always, huh?" Torrey asked, tilting her head slightly to allow the taller woman to place gentle kisses on the skin there.

"Absolutely. Mmmm, I love this dress," Taylor responded, pulling the garment further off the shoulder, as her kisses became more passionate. "Take it off," the artist commanded.

"Jess and Val are meeting us at the gallery. We'll be late," Torrey warned.

"Now, ask me if I care."

Torrey's eyes closed and her lips parted in a sensuous sigh as Taylor's lips found the very sensitive spot just below her ear. "Oh, yes. Well, what are you waiting for woman? Unzip me," the writer ordered impatiently.

* * * * * * * * * *

"I'm definitely in the wrong business," Torrey whispered to her daughter's friend as she and Valerie walked through the large gallery, moving in and out of the mingling patrons.

This was the first opportunity Torrey had to actually see price tags on her lover's works, and her mouth went dry at the rates. "I think this one costs as much as the royalties from my last three books," the writer chuckled. "Now we know how she affords the Mercedes."

Valerie laughed at the woman's remarks. She thought back to the beginning of the evening when the artist and the woman that was now at her side came roaring up in the red sports car. Jess teased Taylor regarding the reason for their lateness, but Val didn't get the joke until Jess explained the whole situation in private. Val thought she would never again hear anything quite as romantic as that tale.

Torrey looked up as Taylor introduced Jessica to yet another person that might someday do her career good. It seemed as if Taylor knew everyone in the art world, and tonight everyone wanted to talk with her. The artist shrugged her shoulders apologetically when she caught sight of Torrey from across one room of the gallery. The writer winked and gave one of her *it can't be helped* smiles. Besides Jessica was in seventh heaven, and Torrey really did enjoy Valerie's company. The young woman wasn't the least bit caught up in the hype regarding Torrey Gray, the author, and the writer appreciated that more than words could say.

Finally, Jessica found the two women outside catching some fresh air. "Taylor is looking for you, Mom."

"Well, far be it from me to keep the artist of the decade waiting," Torrey replied and returned to the gallery.

Torrey suffered through the pairs of eyes that watched her as she walked through the rooms of the gallery in search of her artist. Some of the stares were the ones she always dealt with as people wondered if she was really the woman she looked like she was. Tonight many of the stares came from the fact that nearly everyone at the opening saw her and Taylor arrive together and the way the artist held her hand as they walked through the crowds. The final reason was one the writer could live with. She looked good. She may be petite and pushing forty, but she had an air of confidence when it came to her own body.

"Torrey Gray," a female voice purred from somewhere behind the writer.

Torrey stopped, frozen in her steps. She recognized the voice immediately, but never expected to hear it in California, and certainly not at Taylor's show. She turned to face the music, a thousand different escape scenarios rushing through her brain. "Hello, Kat," Torrey said turning to face the woman.

The call girl looked magnificent as always. She held the writer's hand for a second or two and then released it as good taste dictated. She stood a little closer to the writer than she probably should have, but they had a history and that allowed for certain liberties. "I'm here with a client, she's a fanatic for works by a certain California artist and when I heard the name, I have to admit, my curiosity got the better of me. I had to find out if this Taylor was *your* Taylor."

"Well, the truth of the matter is—"

"Honey, I thought you could use this." Taylor held out a fluted glass of champagne for the author in one hand, slipping her arm around Torrey's waist in an unmistakable act of possessiveness, with her other.

"Uhm...thanks," Torrey answered nervously. The writer looked up at the artist, a charming smile situated on the dark-haired woman's face. That's when Torrey saw it; the blue of Taylor's irises was actually a steel gray. There was a gleam that Torrey hadn't seen before. It was the unequivocal glint of jealousy. *Oh, nuts...why me?* Torrey asked herself.

"Who is your friend?" Taylor asked, still the charming smile in place, but Torrey could feel the strain in the taller woman's voice and she would have laughed out loud at the irony of the whole situation, had it not been so damn serious.

"Oh, this is—" Torrey knew her eyes must have been the size of saucers because Kat now had an amused grin on her face. The writer realized she had no idea what Kat's full name was.

"Katherine Berring," Kat said with a smile, offering her hand to the artist. "So, you're Taylor Kent. I feel as if I already know you. From the *Architectural Digest* magazines," she quickly added with a smirk. "Your work is truly amazing."

"Thank you," Taylor replied.

Torrey watched as the two women sized each other up with the small blonde caught uncomfortably in the middle of their imaginary joust.

"So, where do you know Torrey from?" Taylor inquired.

"Well, actually—" Kat began.

"New York," Torrey quickly finished. *Please...please, Kat, you've been a treasure, but could you please just leave!* Torrey took the moment's silence to down the glass of champagne in her hand in one long gulp.

"Thirsty?" Taylor asked, indicating the empty glass with a nod.

"As a matter of fact, yes. Would you mind getting me another? Please?"

Taylor gave a lopsided grin to the small blonde, and then gave a look to the brunette who stared back at her with something like amusement. "Sure, I'll be right back," she said, kissing Torrey's forehead before turning.

"You're right, she's something." Kat grinned once Taylor was out of sight.

"Look, Kat—"

"Torrey, relax. I didn't come here to mess things up for you. It looks like you finally got your artist, huh?"

Torrey smiled in return and nodded in absolute relief.

"Good." Kat leaned down and placed a gentle kiss on Torrey's cheek. "You deserve every bit of happiness this world has to offer, my small friend. I have to admit, I will regret never seeing you again."

"Never say never," Torrey mused.

"Oh, I saw the look in that one's eye. Your number is definitely unlisted from here on in. You take care, Torrey," Kat said, chuckling as she turned to find her client amidst the throng of people.

"Is it okay for me to come back now? You're not going to chug another glass of champagne just to get rid of me, are you?" Taylor asked in amusement.

"Very funny," Torrey said, accepting the glass the artist returned with in her grasp.

"Okay, who is she really?" Taylor asked.

"A...*friend*," Torrey answered as honestly as she could.

"Mmm hmmm," Taylor said taking a sip from her own glass of ice water. "Was your *friend* upset that you won't be sleeping with her anymore?"

Torrey smiled and shook her head. "You knew all along, didn't you?"

"Honey," the taller woman smiled back, "we've lived separate lives for fifteen years. We're bound to run into old lovers occasionally...yours and mine."

Torrey lifted an eyebrow as she canvassed the room.

"Don't worry," Taylor said with a wink. "None of mine are here tonight. I don't think any of them liked me well enough. Where do you know her from, though, seriously?" Taylor asked as an after thought.

Torrey slipped an arm around her lover's waist and gave a gentle squeeze. "I'll tell you the whole sordid story when we get home."

"Fair enough," Taylor said with quickly kissing the top of the smaller woman's head. "Come on."

"Where are we going?"

"I have people I want to show you off to." Taylor

grinned as they moved toward Samantha and her net-
working friends.

****

"So, what do you think?" Taylor asked Jessica, as
they stood quietly outside, taking a break from the
noise of the party atmosphere inside.

"I think I can't wait to charge half a million bucks
for doing something I love to do," she answered with
a grin.

Taylor chuckled at the girl. "Well, the price tag
just lets me keep doing what I love to do."

"Can I change the subject, Tay?"

"Sure. What's on your mind?"

"Are you going to ask Mom to move out here?"
Jessica asked as bluntly as possible.

Taylor looked like she'd been knocked in the head
from her blind side. "Well, I...uhm, I guess I just
assumed she might...I mean, she might not want to
and—"

"Oh, I don't even believe you two. I am not doing
this again." Jessica paced in front of the artist and
Taylor's eyes widened slightly at the young woman's
reaction. "Fifteen years...you guys are the record
holders! I can't believe you didn't learn anything
from that. You're both gonna clam up and think you
know what the other one is thinking, well you don't.
Frankly, I think your track record at thinking you
know what each other is thinking sucks."

Taylor was honestly too stunned to say anything
in response to the young girl's outburst.

"Well, this time I'm not gonna stand by and do

nothing. Forget this loyalty and keeping your mouth shut thing. You want to know what Mom wants? Don't guess 'cause like I said you suck at it. I'll tell you what she told me. She wants to be asked, quote unquote, that's it. She just needs you to care enough to ask her. And, if you don't...well, then I don't know what I'll do, but it'll be something drastic. I'll call your Mom!" Jessica finally threatened, pointing a finger in the taller woman's direction.

By this time, Taylor was very near to bursting into laughter at the young woman's zeal. She held up both hands in a gesture of defeat. "Go find her and I'll ask her." Taylor couldn't contain her laughter any longer.

"Oh," Jessica said quietly then grinned up sheepishly at the artist. "Okay!" she said with enthusiasm, once she realized the artist meant this very minute.

* * * * * * * * * *

"Our daughter thinks we should talk...about our future together," Taylor began.

"Oh?" Torrey drawled in question.

"She seems to think that when it comes to us reading each other's minds, well, I'm paraphrasing here, but basically she thinks we suck at it. She told me so in no uncertain terms."

"I can't say as I disagree with her much." Torrey chuckled and wrapped her arms a little tighter around her lover's waist. "We have to admit our track record may speak highly for perseverance and longevity, but we do lack a little something when it comes to revealing our feelings. Taylor?"

"Hhmmm?"

"What do you want to happen with us? And, I don't want to hear what you think I want, or what's best for Jess, or even what you think I want to hear. I want to know, honestly, what do *you* want?"

Taylor's brow pinched into a frown as she stared at the toes of her boots for a few moments. When she looked up into the sea-green eyes of the woman she loved, she felt that familiar tightening in her belly. It was as if she fell in love with the woman all over again, whenever Torrey looked at her that way. She held the small blonde's face in both her hands and lightly brushed her own lips against the softness of Torrey's.

"I want to buy three round trip tickets to Chicago. I want for all three of us to go back there. I want to pack up your old life and everything you want to bring and have a moving van carry it all here. Then I want us to come back here and be together as a family for the rest of our lives."

Taylor kissed Torrey again, with a firmer touch this time. She brushed Torrey's tears away with her thumbs and smiled down nervously at the smaller woman. "That's what I want. What do you want, Tor?"

"I want you to kiss me," Torrey said, her hands pressed against the dark-haired woman's chest to stop her momentarily. "Kiss me like you want me."

Taylor captured the woman's lips in a kiss that left little to the imagination as to what her intent was toward the small blonde in her arms. "And?" Taylor asked.

"I want you to put your arms around me," Torrey requested, as the taller woman wrapped her arms around the smaller body, pulling Torrey closer against her.

"And?" Taylor continued.

"I want you to never, ever let go," Torrey finally said as her voice broke.

"I love you, Little Bit."

"I love you, Stretch."

"I'll never let go...I promise," Taylor said.

"I'll never run again...I promise," Torrey returned.

Taylor leaned down and Torrey met her lover halfway, for the kiss the two women waited nearly eighteen years to share, their kiss of commitment.

Epilogue

Jessica and Val held hands as they watched the scene from the balcony above. Unbeknownst to the two lovers on the sidewalk below, the second floor of the gallery's balcony opened up above where they stood. Their whispered words of love couldn't be heard by anyone else, but the smoldering kiss they shared as a climax to their promise of forever, was viewed by more than a few.

"Why, that's Torrey Gray, the author, with her." A husband nudged his wife. "I saw her on Oprah."

"Well," the woman standing next to him sniffed, "what kind of example is that?"

"The best!" Jessica and Valerie said in unison.

Coming next from
Yellow Rose Books

Encounters
By Anne Azel

Encounters is a series of five stories: Amazon Encounter, Turkish Encounter, P.N.G. Encounter, Egyptian Encounter, and Peruvian Encounter. The stories are interrelated by the characters who all share a common ancestor. A loop in the space/time continium allows the couples of today to help their ancestors find their own troubled path to happiness.

Available Winter 2000

Available soon from
Yellow Rose Books

Safe Harbor
By Radclyffe

A mysterious Deputy Sheriff, the town's reclusive doctor, and a troubled gay teenager learn about love,
friendship and trust during one tumultous summer in
Provincetown. Reese Conlon, LtCol USMC (Ret), is
the new sheriff who has heads turning amidst specula-
tion as to who will be the first to claim her heart. Victo-
ria King, MD, has tried love once, and found the price
too high to pay again. Brianna Parker, the teenaged
daughter of Reese's boss, wants only the chance to live,
and love, in freedom. These three lives become inextri-
cably bound as these women must risk their hearts, and
their souls, for each other.

Lost Paradise
By Francine Quesnel

Kristina Von Deering is a young, wealthy Austrian
stuntwoman working on an Austrian/Canadian film
project in Montreal. On location, she meets and eventually falls in love with a young gopher and aspiring
camerawoman named Nicole McGrail. Their friendship
and love is threatened by Nicole's father who sees their
relationship as deviant and unnatural. He does everything in his power to put an end to it.

Meridio's Daughter
By LJ Maas

Tessa (Nikki) Nikolaidis is cold and ruthless, the perfect person to be Karê, the right-hand, to Greek magnate Andreas Meridio. Cassandra (Casey) Meridio has come home after a six-year absence to find that her father's new Karê is a very desirable, but highly dangerous woman.

Set in modern day Greece on the beautiful island of Mýkonos, this novel weaves a tale of emotional intrigue as two women from different worlds struggle with forbidden desires. As the two come closer to the point of no return, Casey begins to wonder if she can really trust the beautiful Karê. Does Nikki's dark past, hide secrets that will eventually bring down the brutal Meridio Empire, or are her actions simply those of a vindictive woman? Will she stop at nothing for vengeance...even seduction?

Hope's Path
By Carrie Carr

In this next look into the lives of Lexington Walters and Amanda Cauble, someone is determined to ruin Lex. Attempts to destroy her ranch lead to attempts on her life. Lex and Amanda desperately try to find out who hates Lex so much that they are willing to ruin the lives of everyone in their path. Can they survive long enough to find out who's responsible? And will their love survive when they find out who it is?

Other titles to look for in the
coming months from
Yellow Rose Books

Daredevil Hearts By Francine Quesnel
(Winter 2001)

Storm Front By Belle Reilly
(Spring 2001)

Take Time Out By R. L. Johnson
(Spring 2001)

Prairie Fire By LJ Maas
(Spring 2001)

Turning the Page By Georgia Beers
(Spring 2001)

Heartbroken Love By Georgio Sicily
(Summer 2001)

Many Roads To Travel By Karen King and Nann Dunne
(Summer 2001)